I0716192

A Good Day For Crows

The 7th and Final Volume of
the Forgotten Gods Tales

Christian Warren Freed

Cover design by BroseDesignz
Author Photograph by Anicie Freed

Warfighter Books
Holly Springs, North Carolina 27540
https://www.christianwfreed.com

First Edition: August 2024

Library of Congress Cataloging-in-Publication Data
Name: Freed, Christian Warren, 1973- author.
Title: A Good Day For Crows/ Christian Warren Freed
Description: First Edition | Holly Springs, NC: Warfighter Books, 2021. Identifiers: LCCN 2023909981| ISBN 9781957326351 (trade paperback) | ISBN 8781957326368 (Hardcover) | ISBN 9781957326375 (eBook)
Subjects: Military Science Fiction | Space Opera |Space Fantasy

Printed in the United States of America

10 9 8 7 6 5 4 3 2 1

DREAMS OF WINTER
A FORGOTTEN GODS TALE #1

'Dreams of Winter is a strong introduction to a new fantasy series that follows slightly in the footsteps of George R.R. Martin in scope.' Entrada Publishing

"Steven Erickson meets George R.R. Martin!"

"THIS IS IT. If you like fantasy and sci-fi, you must read this series."

Law of the Heretic
Immortality Shattered Book I

'If you're looking for a fun and exciting fantasy adventure, spend a few hours in the Free Lands with the Law of the Heretic.'

Where Have All the Elves Gone?

'Sometimes funny and other times a little dark, Where Have The Elves Gone? brings something fresh and new to fantasy mysteries. Whether you want to curl up with a mystery or read more about elves this book has something for everyone. Spend a few hours solving a mystery with a human and a couple of dwarves - you'll be glad you did.'

<u>The Northern Crusade</u>

Hammers in the Wind

Tides of Blood and Steel

A Whisper After Midnight

Empire of Bones

The Madness of Gods and Kings

Even Gods Must Fall

<u>The Histories of Malweir</u>

Armies of the Silver Mage

The Dragon Hunters

Beyond the Edge of Dawn

<u>Forgotten Gods</u>

Dreams of Winter

The Madman on the Rocks

Anguish Once Possessed

Through Darkness Besieged

Under Tattered Banners

A Time for Tyrants

A Good Day For Crows

Where Have All the Elves Gone?

One of Our Elves is Missing

From Whence It Came*

Of Elves and Men

Save the Queen!*

Tomorrow's Demise: The Extinction Campaign

Tomorrow's Demise: Salvation

Coward's Truth

The Lazarus Men
Repercussions: A Lazarus Men Agenda
Daedalus Unbound: A Lazarus Men Agenda*

A Long Way From Home+

Immortality Shattered
Law of the Heretic
The Bitter War of Always
Land of Wicked Shadows
Storm Upon the Dawn

War Priests of Andrak Saga
The Children of Never

SO, You Want to Write a Book? +
SO, You Wrote a Book. Now What? +

*Forthcoming   + Nonfiction

PROLOGUE

01 A.G. (After Gods), planet Vau Prime.

They came from across the stars. Humanity's great diaspora struggling to find purchase in a universe previously hidden from them. Generations of hardship, toil, and servitude to cruel masters followed like dragging chains across barren rock. Faced with the threat of extinction, a handful stepped forth with the promise of a better tomorrow, a brighter future. It was a dream. One born through the weight of shackles and insignificance. For the first time in as long as any remembered humanity stood a chance at surviving.

One hundred years had passed since the final battle. With their tormentors fallen, humanity struggled with learning how to survive on its own. A plan sparked, grew into a movement, and took root on the dozens of settled planets. Fueled by whispers and subtle urgings of those choosing to remain in the shadows, humanity's leaders at last decided the time had come to take control.

They gathered in a quiet valley of windswept grasses greener than any they'd witnessed. The brightest minds were determined to preserve their freedom, vowing to never return to shackles. But how? Debate raged for days, often turning into furious dissent. Members stormed off, returning later with cooler heads. When most reached the end of their ropes, pushed to tedium as conversations circling round and round, the first inklings of how to move forward sparked.

Unseen by the delegates, an unlikely pair stood under the boughs of a stand of golden leafed trees on a small rise overlooking the proceedings. Ruma Zzein floated inches above the grass. Gone were her tattered rags and peasant attire from her time spent as the Oracle. She now wore an iridescent robe never settling on a single pattern. At her side stood the resolute Tannus, favored son of the king and catalyst for all that had happened in the last century.

"This will not end well."

Ruma did not turn, choosing to focus on the momentous occasion below. "Lord Tannus, has this not been the goal? To convince humanity to assume control of themselves?"

"It has, though my expectations are tempered with caution. There is too much anger among them."

"I would expect nothing less. They languished under the yoke of slavery for countless years before discovering freedom."

"The gift of freedom does not allow them to choose poorly."

"Yet it does," she countered. "The ultimate freedom of self-governance drives them."

Tannus shifted, facing the woman he respected more than any other. "Oracle, you know what I mean. They border upon heresy with their proclamations of turning my kind being deities."

"They need something to look to," she replied. "Humans are a fragile species. One struggling to break free from the captivity mindset. This is new to them, Tannus. We must show patience if they are to have any chance."

"We are not gods. Nor have we claimed to be. We cannot allow these people to slip into viewing us so." His muscles rippled under the thin fabric of his tunic; a caged animal ready to attack. "We should go down there."

"We agreed to let them do as they must," Ruma warned. "Interference now will only serve to undermine all they are trying to achieve. The future is clear, Tannus. Forever Night will come. Humanity must be prepared to stand against the tide if they are to survive eternal darkness."

He looked at her, piercing the shadows of her hood. This one human contained more strength than the whole of his people. It was through her urgings and subtle warnings that he learned the truth of his family lineage and discovered the courage to stand up and do what was right. His respect for her proved boundless though he questioned her decision now.

Tannus refused to accept the future was set in stone. He viewed it as an unsteady construct capable of manipulation and diversion. Her premonition of the end of all life frightened him more than he was willing to admit. That the universe might end was profoundly unsettling. Panic threatened to undermine his resolve, weakening him when strength was needed most.

"You have doubts." Not a question, but statement of fact.

"I do."

She laid a hand on his forearm. "This is how it must be. Those men and women are the heralds of a better tomorrow. The orders they are forming today will become the bedrock upon which salvation rests. Give them space. Allow them to make mistakes."

He sighed. "You ask much of me."

"No more than you are capable of," she replied. "Tannus, I understand your hesitation at being proclaimed a god but think of this: Without something to ground beliefs on humans will wither away, wasting all you and those few others fought so hard for. This new Conclave will be well protected but the others. Plus, they have the staunchest defender watching from the stars."

He scoffed. "Inquisition and Prekhauten. They seek to deify my people while imposing regulations under the watchful eyes of heretical persecutors."

"A failsafe, nothing more." Ruma returned her attention to the gathering below. "Much yet needs to happen and they will need shepherds in the event your brothers return."

"I will deal with them should the need arise."

"It will."

"Oracle, how much time before this Forever Night of yours falls?" he asked, uncomfortable.

"That remains unclear," she admitted. "Centuries, perhaps more. Regardless of when, we shall never have enough time."

"In that we agree."

ONE

3215 A.G. (After gods), Great Library, planet Wexanos.

Elisa reeled from the backhand blow across her chest. The air fled her lungs in a whuff as pain sparkled through her field of vision. Sweat plastered her red hair to her neck. Every muscle in her body ached from constant strain. Her vison blurred. Mind unraveled. The raw power in her hand meant little if she could not master it in time. Growling, the former bounty hunter regrouped and prepared to launch another assault on the automaton confronting her. Bleeding from a dozen small cuts, she struggled with her rising anger.

"Release your anger and let your instincts control you," Tannus instructed at the beginning of her training.

Months passed and she was no closer to mastering anything, *Grimfurvor* included.

She paused, forcing a deep, slow breath. Her opponent remained stoic. An unreadable monstrosity of regenerating metals. Any damage she'd caused resulted in little more than scrapes and knicks, frustrating her to no end. Elisa was more than competent in a fight, but she had done little to achieve her goals. Sorrow promised the weapon was meant for her, bonded to the Paladin. While she failed to understand the specifics, Elisa knew it was the one weapon in the universe capable of killing Amongeratix. Yet none of that meant anything until she learned how to control herself and wield it effectively.

"Focus, damn it," she muttered to herself. "You can do this. It's just a little robot. Slice him up and move on."

Rather than charging at her opponent as she'd done far too many times, Elisa stalked with deliberate intent. The click and whirl of gears adjusting to her approach echoed across the training pit. Body sized boulders littered the sunken arena, interspersed with open pits and gouts of endless flame sprouting from the sand. It had been Elisa's home for weeks. One she came to loathe and could not escape until she bested *Grimfurvor*.

Recalculating all she'd previously attempted, Elisa walked up to the eight-foot monstrosity and braced for the inevitable blow. The automaton drew back, fingers extended in a knife edge, and swung for the side of her head. Elisa ducked, rolling to her right before popping up to her knees and plunging the blade deep into the automaton's thigh. Circuitry sparked as the living metal sliced apart. The automaton reshaped its hand into a fist and hammered down. She anticipated the blow and ducked. Still the blow clipped her shoulder and sent her into the sand.

"Enough," she wheezed.

The automaton powered down, leaving her alone with her failure. Elisa summoned the remnants of her pride and picked herself up. Whatever aches she felt now promised to be worse in the morning. She sheathed *Grimfurvor*, wiped her face with the back of a sleeve, and gave the robot a scowl before heading back to her quarters.

As usual, Ah'muf had a hot bath waiting and a platter of fresh cheeses with meats. She flashed a smile and stripped down. The heat caused her to flush as she sank into the water. Elisa submerged her head until she couldn't hold her breath any longer. Sputtering, she sat up, tilting her head back and closing her eyes.

"Why do you torment yourself so, *farisi*?"

She grinned despite herself. Ah'muf remained the most curious man she'd encountered. Despite their inherent differences, her being from a forested planet and him the deserts of An'kuruku, she felt a strong connection with him. Elisa refused to admit it was love, The desert dweller, for his part, ignored her protests and professed an endless stream of pleasantries to win her affections. They'd been through more than any two people in the universe had a right to and remained as strong today as they had during their first meeting years prior. For that, she was grateful.

"We've been over this, Ah'muf. I must learn how to use this damned weapon if we have any chance of winning the war."

"We can always return to my planet."

She lacked the heart to remind him his beloved desert had been mired with civil war for the better part of three years with no end in sight. Since the fateful battle of the Deeves where Amongeratix first clashed with Paradise Tear and Mollock Bolle died, the universe insisted on tearing itself apart. Knowing she had the power to end it threatened to bury her under impossible expectations. Elisa felt guilty passing others in the hall or during their frequent councils with Tannus.

Each stare carried intonations she was ill prepared to handle. But for all that, none stung harder than knowing Ah'muf might never go home again. With or without her.

"Home is a lovely idea, but one we cannot think about until after I accomplish my task."

It was an old argument. One neither won nor lost.

She opened her eyes to see Ah'muf settling back in his cushioned chair with a loud exhale.

"There must be another way to use the weapon, vile creation that it is."

"I wish I knew," she admitted. "Tannus and Sorrow both insist I must discover it for myself. Thousands of years of knowledge and experience I can't rely on."

He bobbed his head, the scruff of his beard scrapping against his woolen tunic. "Cruel circumstances. Woe that we have fallen to such." He paused, offering a smile. "I can have a shuttle waiting should you feel the need to escape for a time."

Elisa grinned at the twinkle in his eye. "No, Ah'muf. I will see this task through. Besides, I never step down from a challenge. You'll see, I'm going to destroy that damned robot and prove I am the Paladin after all."

"I know you will."

Ah'muf excused himself, leaving her to the comforts of the bath in peace.

She watched him go, the ache in her heart deepening. Placing him in this situation was beyond cruel, but he chose to stay at her side, even when she repeatedly sought to drive him away. Maybe it was love … She didn't know, and that frightened her. Elisa closed her eyes again and slipped beneath the water.

Fistel served as Chief Librarian on Wexanos for so long he failed to remember when Tannus first approached him. They'd met during one of the many crusades the Three waged against one another. Fistel was found worthy after a violent battle and taken back to the library planet to recover from his wounds. Wexanos was everything he ever dreamed of. He soon lost himself among the sweeping halls, endless libraries, and unique flora and fauna.

With time, his natural propensity for violence dissipated and Fistel embraced a peaceful life. A blissful retreat from the brink of certain demise. His internal constitution altered on fundamental levels as he worked his way through the ranks to become Tannus' right hand. The path of righteousness he'd set upon had grown dire of late and he feared it was all crashing down around him and he was powerless to stop it.

Fistel stared off into the sunset, marveling at the kaleidoscope of colors washing the skies as much today as he had that first day so long ago. His thoughts were troubled. The great enemy was merciless, unrelenting in his quest to destroy all who opposed him. While Fistel understood the need to vanquish Amongeratix, he found trouble reconciling his personal desires with the cost. Knowing Tannus accepted his fate long ago did little to assuage the guilt Fistel bore just from knowing.

The coming of the current crop of selected was the breaking of a storm upon the shore. He bore no animosity toward the Blood Witches or the Inquisitors. Nor did he take issue with the soldiers who often frequented the planet at Tannus' behest. Yet combined, they represented the end to everything. He wished there were other ways to bring about the coming struggle, but his strengths as a librarian were limited at best. His greatest asset lay in the developed intelligence network scattered across the seven hundred worlds. Though figuring how to best utilize it caused him far too many sleepless nights.

"Chief Librarian, it is time."

Fistel turned. The blue skinned warrior stood a respectful distance away, feet spread shoulder width apart and hands clasped before him. Fistel appreciated the man for his discretions. Banak Laminel was one of the best librarians in service. A dedicated force equally capable of enhancing knowledge and cracking skulls. Tannus used the man for covert operations.

"Thank you, Banak. If you would begin collecting the others, I shall inform Inquisitor Breed."

"Senior Inquisitor Breed is already in audience with Lord Tannus."

Is he? That's odd. I wasn't informed of such. Fistel smoothed down the front of his yellow robes. "Very well. Thank you."

"The matter of your brother's murder is resolved?"

Tolde let a breath slip from his clamped lips. "It is, though my mind remains troubled by it. Leganas and I were never close, but he was the only family I had left."

"You question if his slaying was in retaliation to your actions?" Tannus asked with his hands clasped behind him, turning away from the endless rows of books stretching into the soft light of the main halls. Despite their obvious differences, the giant found himself enjoying Tolde's company more as the war stretched on. Perhaps it was from guilt, perhaps a sense of camaraderie he longed for. Regardless, he viewed Tolde as far more than the valuable human ally he presented.

"It is possible, though I fail to see how. Officially I died on Kharsis. The Inquisition has no reason to suspect I've been resurrected and continue opposing them," Tolde replied. His frown accentuated the lines gathered in the corners of his eyes. His new body aged badly, as if it knew a secret he had yet to discover. "I believe my brother happened to be on the wrong planet at the wrong time."

"Such events are beyond our control," Tannus agreed. "I fear many more lives are enduring similar circumstances as we speak. This war is a travesty that should never have begun."

"It is a continuation of your war."

Tannus stiffened. "It is, and I lament each life lost. My grievances do little to stem the tide of violence, however. All that has occurred is but a precursor to the hell my brother will unleash if we are defeated. Even during the height of my people's reign Amongeratix was uncontrollable. His rage has burned a hundred stars."

"Yet you can stop this. You always could have."

"How?" Tannus demanded. "My brother and I are evenly matched in open combat. We have clashed far more than I care to recall. There has never been a clear victor."

Emboldened, Tolde pressed, "You have seven hundred of your kind scattered across the universe. Why not wake them up and unite to stop Amongeratix?"

"That is not as easy as you suppose."

"If they can end the war, they are a wasted asset," Tolde said. "You must have had a reason for placing them in stasis."

"They were never meant to end the war. They are scientists. Scholars. Engineers. The best and brightest of my kind who had not fallen to the depravity of violence. Men and women dedicated to advancing society through knowledge, not martial prowess."

"Not warriors," Tolde echoed. His shoulders sagged.

Tannus shook his head. He felt the impossible wave crash

through his mind. Millenia of keeping only his counsel dissolved in a moment of humanity he did not know he contained. "Not a single one. I personally selected each for what they represented to the future. Imagine being tasked with setting off into the stars to establish a new planet. You would take the best in numerous fields. Perfect specimens capable of colonizing that world and building a new society, one without violence. Without war. A change to start over."

While his explanation made sense, from a singular point of view, Tolde found fault. "A noble concept that fails to account for the potential conflict with unanticipated species."

"A risk all willingly accepted," Tannus said. "It was never supposed to be this long. Amongeratix fouled my plans time and again, until any hope of taking my people to a better life evaporated. We have been reduced to a base existence riddled with conflict and empty hatred. Waking my people up now, while my brother and I continue to war, would cause irreparable harm, as you have witnessed."

"What do you mean?" Tolde asked, tensing.

"Did you ever stop to question why the entire planet of Kharsis died when Presha Von used the key on the stasis pod?"

Tolde cleared his throat. "There didn't seem to be time for that. You'll recall I died as well and woke up in another body far from Kharsis."

Tannus offered a sad smile. "It is easy to lose track of all that has occurred since this war began. My apologies." He paused, struggling with how much to say. "The key Presha Von used was designed to wake my people up. It was never a weapon, despite what your Inquisitor General insists. Somewhere during the last three thousand years the pods evolved. A change began, one I did become aware of until after the demise of Kharsis. The pods became engrained in the fabric of their planets. To my horror, I watched an entire planet die when my kind was awakened. While you were gone, I spoke with Sorrow. Together we came to the inescapable conclusion that every planet will suffer similar fates should any of my people wake up. Simply put, for me to complete my goal and leave this universe I would have to slaughter every man, woman, and child. Enough guilt weighs upon my shoulders. I will not have the annihilation of your species joining it."

"You risk all life in this universe for selfish desires?" Tolde questioned. A dark look swarmed across his face.

"Ware your next words, Tolde. I am not as forgiving as I appear," Tannus warned. "Awakening my kind will only result in humanity's slaughter. Enough blood is on my hands. I do not need more."

"What do you think is coming?" Tolde snapped. "We are barreling toward the final battle where, if we lose, your pious attitudes will provide our condemnation."

Tannus rose. Swift. Authoritative. "You don't believe my brother would die on any of these planets should we attempt to activate one of the pods, do you, because he won't. Neither would I. We are immune to such devastation."

Rage welled within the favored son of the gods. The audacity of Tolde, intentional or not, threatened to reduce the universe to a slew of lifeless planets waiting for their suns to burn out; to driving all life to the brink of extinction. He had given everything to humanity and still it wanted more, at his expense.

Tolde's expression softened upon noticing the agonized look paining Tannus' face. "Does Amongeratix know this?"

"I have my suspicions, but they are unconfirmed. He wanted Paradise. Needed her genetic coding to open the pods because he lacked the key. I thought he merely wished to eliminate the rest of our people on his quest for vengeance. But now I believe the other option is possible. He has always been off kilter. A victim of himself. Amongeratix wants to rule the universe, not burn it down."

"Why Paradise? What makes her so special?"

"It was her DNA coded into the key. She is, in theory, the only living being capable of awakening those in stasis."

"Yet she was in stasis herself until she crashed on An'kuruku," Tolde said with a frown.

"I had my ways to awaken her when the time was right," Tannus admitted, troubled by the memories of the past. "How she was removed from her hiding spot remains unclear. The pod did not survive impact. By all regards, she should have perished upon impact."

"And I led her into the heart of Amongeratix's domain," Tolde muttered after a moment.

"You did not lead her anywhere," Tannus countered. "My cousin has a mind of her own and is seldom prone to following orders, especially from humans. If Paradise accompanied you to *Behemoth*, she had her reasons. Ones I don't disagree with. Of all my kind, she alone possessed the gifts to withstand extended stasis and offer us a chance at redemption."

"But she didn't know Presha Von lacked the key!" Tolde protested. "She could have given him every tool he needs to succeed."

"We are all victims of destiny, Tolde," Tannus said. "Paradise has her role to play, just as you have yours. Do not fault her impudence in this matter. She did what she felt was best, for herself and for the rest of us. She alone is the one person in this universe who has always had my back. I will not forsake her for a lapse of judgment."

Tolde scowled. "It was my mission. I should have known."

"What would you have done different? Can you protect her from Amongeratix? You may have been reborn, but you are no match for him. Or her. We cannot predict what will happen or how. All we can do is trust in ourselves to do our best."

"How can you place so much faith in mere mortals?"

Exhaustion played out behind his eyes. Tannus, ever the stalwart champion of freedom and justice, suddenly felt the weight of his long fight. The strain of generations threatened to rob him of what little strength he had remaining when he needed it most.

Tannus slipped into the oversized chair beside the Inquisitor. "Faith is an interesting concept, is it not? Do you know I argued against your kind deifying mine? I claimed it served no purpose other than to base an entire civilization on lies. Though that knowledge is a closely guarded secret, it cannot remain hidden for long. Sooner or later the entire universe will know the truth. What then does it mean to have faith?"

"It puts my former profession into question," Tolde agreed. "We rooted out heresy against the Conclave wherever it popped up. The worst in the past few years has been the cult of Rengu. Everything we've done has failed. The cult continues spreading, furthering the confusion of the war and lending momentum to our foes."

"A distraction of Amongeratix's fancy," Tannus scoffed. "My brother always idolized our uncle. He saw strength where others knew it was naught but madness. Rengu was a killer, perhaps the most brutal of our kind. It took great effort to capture him. He was one of the changed."

Tolde cocked his head. "Changed?"

"The first of our kind were lone survivors of previous civilizations. Far from paragons of virtue, they exhibited natural tenacity and the willingness to slaughter their own people for the opportunity to be the chosen. How or why, none know. That tale is lost to time. All I know is the old magics are gone, removed from the universe once their purpose was fulfilled. My brothers and I were part of the new generation, born rather than created. Amongeratix's worship of Rengu has ebbed and flowed throughout the years. He uses the cult to fan the flames of his revolt. Useful tools but little more."

"They cause enough damage," Tolde said. "We have been tracking a woman, a human agent, with flaming red hair moving from world to world. Wherever she goes new cult cells sprout up. She has been missing since the campaign on Mannus Prime. I fear until she is caught this cult will continue to strengthen."

"You wish to go after her?" Tannus asked.

"I…I'm not sure," Tolde said then paused. "It would solve one aspect of this war but, as you say, a small one at best. Still, we are entering the final phase of the war, at least I hope so. The less loose ends we have in the aftermath the better."

Tolde's heart skipped. "Can you defeat Amongeratix?"

"I will say no more. Some plans are yet to be announced and I would have secrecy for as long as possible."

Very well, keep your secrets.

"Should I draw contingencies to hunt down the red-haired woman?" Tolde wanted to ask more, but the flighty aspect to Tannus' tone inspired a fresh wave of doubt confronted by finality.

The end of the war. He hadn't bothered thinking ahead. There seemed little point. The universe was determined to tear itself apart, consequences be damned. With losses mounting on both sides and rumors of Vau Prime capitulating, Tolde and his companions were the tip of the spear. Any retaliatory mission needed to be more than symbolic. It needed to stab a dagger into the enemy's heart.

Tannus' brow furrowed. "I can't see how it would hurt. Do you think you can wrap this up within the next few weeks?"

"Time is almost up, isn't it?" Tolde asked.

The giant's silence proved answer enough. Whatever dark times humanity already endured promised to be child's play compared to what came next.

Captain Sharlyn August once prided herself on doing everything by the book. She worked her way through the ranks with a combination of guile, natural tenacity, and perseverance. Never in her wildest dreams did she believe she would stand on the bridge of a massive ship of war born before the foundation of the Conclave. The raw power built into this engineering marvel left her weak in the knees. *Brightstar* was the ship she longed for when first slipping into a Prekhauten uniform. What she could do with a fleet of such beasts. The enemy threat on Vau Prime would be obliterated in short order, the insurrection defeated, and life given a chance to return to normal. Alas, Sharlyn feared normal was lost to them all.

"Captain, everything all right?" Commander Odir, her first officer asked.

He handed her a cup of steaming caf and joined her as she stood at the viewport. *Brightstar* was docked in Wexanos' high atmosphere, concealed by clouds capable of scrambling radar signatures. The brightness of the sun reflected off the clouds, forcing her to activate dimming shields. Her crew, having transferred from the *Solstice*, continued familiarizing themselves with the ancient technology. Since returning from Occanum, Sharlyn directed her people to move everything from their original ship to *Brightstar*.

"Have you bothered to wonder how we wound up in this mess?" she asked after thanking him for the caf.

Odir took a long swallow, burning the roof of his mouth. "Not really. We're at war. Every day we see is a gift. Besides, you know the unofficial rule on thinking about tomorrow."

"Don't," she supplied aloud.

"Don't." After another swallow, he asked, "Has there been any word from Mannus?"

"Nothing. Admiral Falchi knows we've returned."

"Perhaps we've been overlooked," Odir suggested.

"Perhaps." With military preparations ramping up across all friendly strongholds there was the real possibility *Solstice* and her crew were forgotten.

"The admiral tends to be a busy man, especially now he has been made part of the Confederation Council."

Sharlyn set her empty mug down on a rail separating the command chair with the front bridge stations. "What if it stays that way? I don't want our last mission to be a babysitting expedition. Not with the final campaign nearing launch. We've done everything he's asked since the betrayal at Hawker's Gate. Everything. For Falchi to forget us on the eve of the largest military operation in human history is insulting."

The *Solstice* was battered and proven. She was the pride of the fleet. If Falchi hadn't reached out there was good reason. Or so she hoped. "Maybe you're right. I'm tired. The hunt for Von and the escort mission took a lot out of me. I could use a vacation."

"You and me both, Captain," he said.

"Wouldn't that be nice?" She smiled, catching the messenger standing behind them at the edge of her field of vision. "That doesn't seem to be our lot. What is it?"

Snapping to attention and throwing a crisp salute, the messenger said, "Ma'am, you have been requested to attend a conference with Lord Tannus."

Calling him lord now, are we? When did that happen? By all rights we shouldn't have ever crossed paths. That vacation is sounding better by the moment. Schooling her features, Sharlyn replied, "Very well, inform him I am on the way. Commander Odir, the ship is yours."

"Aye, Ma'am."

Sharlyn left the bridge in his hands and went to her wardroom. Meetings with Tannus seldom failed to produce surprises. Mind focused on what Falchi had in store for her, she hurried to the shuttle. One thing she'd learned over the past few years was it not in her best interests to keep her benefactor waiting, even if he wasn't a god.

Tannus looked over those assembled. With Elisa and her desert lover off in the training arena, he found the others reduced, as if the sum of their adventures brought them down. He empathized with them, for he had often felt such during his centuries of solitude. It took a special being to withstand the relentless onslaught of opposition. Nerves ground down. Thoughts degraded until fatigue settled in. Tannus knew if he pushed too hard, they would break. His heart ached with lament, for that was the one thing he needed to do if they had any hope of victory.

Heads turned as Sharlyn August entered the chamber. Several bobbed their heads in greeting. No one spoke directly. The relationship between naval and ground forces being naturally strained, there was a lack of camaraderie among the assembled.

Tannus glanced up as she entered. "Ah, Captain August, thank you for coming on such short notice."

The others took their seats, focus back on him. Born to the pageantry of the royal court, Tannus slipped back into his alternate persona. One of grandiose speeches and philosophical debate. He seldom found cause to use this application, but today was a special moment for all involved. The farce of royalty shined through.

"First, I want to thank you for pausing your schedules to assemble today. It is no easy feat we seek to accomplish and, with as many irons in the fire as we have, the small things are often overlooked, indeed forgotten."

Eyebrows raised. Curious looks passed his way. This version of Tannus proved so unlike the dour giant none but the Blood Witch, Sister Alessandra, understood. He had matured somewhere over the course of this current iteration of his war with Amongeratix. Humans came and went from his life like echoes of wind, but those assembled reminded him of better times, before the darkness of his father's taint soured his people. Once vowing to remain apart from humanity, Tannus suddenly found himself in need of the companionship.

Tannus gestured to Fistel.

The Chief Librarian strode to the computer terminal and activated the viewscreen dominating one of the room's walls. A moment later Admiral Falchi's image blurred to life. He wore a faded set of combat fatigues, his appearance haggard. Upon seeing them a brightness entered his eyes. August's face brightened.

"Ah, Lord Tannus. The timing is impeccable," he greeted with a smile. "Is she there?"

"Right beside me, though a touch confused."

Falchi, pausing to adjust his uniform blouse, cast his gaze on Sharlyn. "Captain August, present yourself."

Confusion deepening, August looked to Tannus who, to her surprise, nodded to the screen. Exhaling to calm her nerves, she did as commanded. The click of her heels as she snapped to the position of attention echoed in the silence.

"Captain Sharlyn August, it is the decision of the newly formed Confederation Naval Command that you have acquitted yourself above and beyond expectations of your rank and authority. Time and again you have demonstrated an uncanny ability to see both yourself and your crew through trying situations you were not trained to handle. As such, it has fallen to me to promote you to the rank of rear admiral, effective immediately."

Tolde stepped forward and removed her old rank badges before August processed what was happening. Pinning the new rank on her shoulders, he grasped both of her shoulders. "Well done, Admiral."

A round of applause spread, reflected by Falchi and a handful of others she hadn't seen standing behind him on Mannus Prime. She returned Falchi's salute, her face flushed. A slight tremble in her hand suggested her frazzled nerves were close to getting the best of her.

"Indeed, August, well done," Falchi echoed.

"Thank you, sir," she managed.

An expectant look on his face, Falchi said, "I believe it is customary for the promoted to give a speech. Simply because we are at war does not mean we abandon our civility, Admiral."

Her mouth opened and closed several times. She looked at each of her companions, saving Tannus for last. Sharlyn cleared her throat. "I, ah, this is most unexpected. Thank you for your trust and confidence in me, Admiral. I won't let you down. Being an officer in the Prekhauten Navy is the realization of a childhood dream. I would spend hours gazing into the depths of space, imaging myself on the bridge of a battlecruiser powering off to regions unknown. While I can truly say it has been an honor and a privilege to have worn this uniform for as long as I have, my dreams have come at a price. I may wear this rank, but it is because of the men and women I served with, many of whom are no longer with us today, that any of this is possible.

"Commanding a naval vessel is more than shouting orders. It is accepting your decisions might cause others to die. It is the constant threat of worrying you didn't do enough, that your ideas or plans aren't good enough. We live with unusual threats, in trying times none of us were prepared for. That changes nothing. Today, like every day before, is filled with opportunity to prove our worth to those who look to us for guidance. It is in their eyes we must all pause to discover the leader we are and the one we wish to become. Thank you."

"A rousing speech," Tannus announced over the applause. "Humility is a powerful asset. I commend you."

"Thank you, Lord Tannus," she replied, caught up in the moment. *So, the old man hasn't forgotten me after all.*

Tannus gestured for Falchi to continue.

"Unfortunately, Admiral August, it is not fitting for one of your rank to serve aboard a single ship, massive as it may be. Effective immediately, you will remain on *Brightstar* and transfer command of

Solstice to Captain Odir."

"Sir? You're taking my ship?" Sharlyn felt like she'd been gut punched.

"Reassigning is more like it," Falchi admitted. "You will transfer your colors to *Brightstar*. It is now the flagship of your fleet."

"Ah, fleet, sir?" August asked. She braced, unsure what to expect next.

"Ships being in short supply, I have it on good authority there is a fleet of dreadnaughts laying at anchor in an undisclosed location requiring a qualified fleet admiral. What do you say? Are you feeling up to the task?"

Shock clashed with unbridled joy as it dawned on August what was being asked of her. Fleet admiral! Of a squadron of *Brightstars*? It took little imagination to see her ending the war in spectacular fashion. "I, yes Admiral, I believe I am."

"Very good. I'll leave the details to Tannus. Crews and supplies are enroute to Wexanos as we speak. Congratulations again, Sharlyn. I can't think of a more deserving person." Falchi's image faded.

Tolde and the others filed by to shake her hand and offer their good will. A career of promotions failed to prepare her for the immensity of weight suddenly thrust upon her. August glanced at the silver rank decorating her shoulder. Whatever feelings of inadequacy or dread with having so many lives under her command she had to push aside. There'd be enough time to worry about that in the days and weeks to come. Today she should be celebrating.

"I envy you at times, Sharlyn," Tannus told her as he handed her old rank back. "You have proven yourself worthy, not only to your command but to me. I am in your debt for all you have done to ensure we have a decent shot at defeating my brother and ending this nightmare war."

"I'm just doing my job," she replied. Her mind swirled with the possibilities of having an entire fleet of planet killing ships under her thumb as she took the war to the enemy thrilled her.

"One well done, as has been said," Tannus tilted his head, studying the sudden hollow look in her eye. "Whenever you are ready, I will take you to see your new ships."

"I should see to my crew first. There is much I need to solidify before the other crews transfer in."

He nodded. "Best make it fast. The fresh crews will be here

before the end of the week. Our timeline is advancing based on new intelligence from Vau Prime."

She thanked him again and departed.

The war could wait until tomorrow.

Today belonged to her.

TWO

3215 A.G. (After gods), Krenz, planet Vau Prime.

Hell unleashed across the Conclave's capital planet without mercy. Thousands of suspected dissidents were rounded up and slaughtered. More went missing, rumored to have been escorted to work camps in the least habitable parts of Vau Prime. Terror reigned, sparked by the coming of Amongeratix. Holovid feeds replayed the moment weeks after his arrival. Images of the giant snapping the Inquisitor General's neck haunted the citizenry and struck fear deep into the hearts and minds of those garbed in the black of the Inquisition. Everywhere Amongeratix went brought unparalleled mayhem. Despite years of civil war, the local population had no way of being prepared for the nightmare among them.

Tensions rose until the city locked into a perpetual state of panic. Neighbor turned on neighbor. People saw the opportunity to eliminate those they held grudges against. No one was safe. Armored patrols dragged children from their parents. Wives from husbands. Executions became commonplace, the victims left to rot in the streets without the benefit of jury or trial. What little remained of civility crumbled beneath the onslaught of depravity devouring the planet. Those who died were spared from the worst yet to come.

Smoke from a thousand fires drifted over the once majestic skyline. Riots broke out in poorer neighborhoods as supply shortages began. Theft and crime rose to unprecedented levels. Civility faded daily. Those unable to flee remained trapped in a world they didn't understand, and one that was determined to break them. The once pristine city, pride of the Conclave and symbol of humanity, bordered on total collapse.

Nestled deep in the heart of the city he loved, Edam Boone slammed a palm on the stack of files littering his metal desk. Bags sunk his red lined eyes. Fresh lines crowded the corners of his eyes. Sleep and nutrition were fleeting of late. The heir to Zoraq Darc's criminal empire felt his world growing smaller daily since the recent changes swept across Vau Prime. With his realm on the brink of collapse, Edam struggled. The report on the holovid continued to play.

Free press was the first institution to die, well, second after Alain Nye was brutally executed for all to witness. State run media outlets churned out propaganda, mocking all the Conclave once stood for. Edam watched as a thin man with gaunt features, a decided grey tone to his flesh and thinning hair stepped before a podium—Ezekiel Goethe. Amongeratix's newest henchman recently elevated to Inquisitor General. His pronounced Adam's apple bobbed as he prepared to address the assembly.

"Effective immediately, the Conclave has been disbanded. All cardinals and clergy who have failed to swear allegiance to Lord Amongeratix are now considered fugitives from justice. Under the complacent watch of numerous Cardinal Seniorus', we have witnessed the once austere order collapse into corruption and incompetence. This cannot stand. We are a society built upon laws. Justice. The Inquisition, in conjunction with Lord Amongeratix, will handle all state matters from this point forward. Anyone with information on the whereabouts of these criminals is required to report to the nearest Inquisition office. Failure to do so will result in extreme punishment and further degrade of our civilization."

Edam watched the man leave without fielding questions. "So, that's it. We've become a dictatorship."

"We should have taken Aliz's offer," Thopos said from his corner seat. "Now we're doomed."

"It would appear so." Edam refused to look the cross-eyed man straight on. Years of rising through the organization together and he still found it disconcerting.

Thopos wiped his lower lip of the beads of sweat threatening to spill down his chin. "What do we do now? There are other cities beyond the immediate madness of Krenz. We could go there. Hide out until the storm passes."

"This storm will never pass. Not while the monsters are in charge." Edam shook his head. "Nor can we fight. We've lost our best and brightest. Those fool enough to stay behind with us are more detriment than aid, perhaps myself most of all."

Thopos winced. "Right. So, we're fucked."

Any reply was cut off by a young woman bursting into the office. Out of breath and covered in grime, she gestured back the way she'd came. "Prekhautens! The hide out is compromised."

Edam's chin sank to his chest. They'd been hunted for years but without the current level of zeal. Never before had the Inquisition tracked down his headquarters. Doing so now left a nasty feeling in the pit of his stomach. He snatched the stack of datapads from the desk and reached for his rifle.

"I had hoped we had more time. Spread the word. Evacuate everyone. Rendezvous by the river in three days. Go!" he ordered. After stuffing the datapads in a satchel, he checked the charge on his confiscated and battered ion rifle. "We need to give them time to flee."

Thopos already had his weapons of choice, a pair of decommissioned power blasters, in hand. "Doesn't sound like there's time. We need to get you out of here."

"I'm not abandoning my people, Thopos," he protested.

Muffled gunfire echoed through the complex. Nestled in a series of confusing tunnels leading to Krenz's sewers, it was one of the established auxiliary command posts dating back to Zoraq's time. Less than three months in their current position, Edam never thought they'd be discovered so quickly. He moved to slip past his second in command but was stopped by a vice grip on his upper arm.

"You know I'm not going to let you do that," Thopos warned. Before Edam could protest, he leaned into the hall and shouted, "Xian, Artus. Gather a squad and hold them back for as long as you can."

The pair of thieves turned freedom fighters looked up from their rifles and gave Edam Boone a look that froze his heart before hurrying off to collect their people. No complaints. No questioning. They obeyed without hesitation. Edam realized Thopos was right. He was the heart of the operation. Men and women from across Krenz willingly placed their lives on the line for him. No, he corrected. *Not me. For the cause and for this city.*

Thopos released him after Edam stopped struggling. Together, the pair scurried down to the escape tunnels and prayed the exits weren't being watched. They fled with the knowledge they'd never see the men assigned to hold the door again. It was, in Edam's estimation, the most humbling moment in his young life.

They ran.

Inquisition Headquarters, Office of the Inquisitor General.

Ezekiel Goethe tapped his foot with impatience as work crews hurried to complete the redesign of his new office. All furniture and comfort trappings his predecessor accumulated over a lifetime of service were scrapped. The less reminding him of Alain Nye the better. Ezekiel knew establishing his power immediately would carry him far. The old regime was fouled from decades of internal debates and power-hungry individuals seeking self-gain instead of doing what was best for the seven hundred worlds.

A relative newcomer to Vau Prime, Ezekiel established himself on a score of smaller assignments before working his way into the fabric of capital life. He'd spent the past three years eliminating all competition and threats to Nye's vision for the future, cementing his place among the top tier of Inquisitors. Now that Nye was disposed of, Ezekiel strode into Amongeratix's adopted throne room and demanded the job. To his shock, the giant awarded it to him on the spot. Like all good things, it came with the promise of an unpleasant demise should he fail. Used to the pressure, he dove into his new role with ruthless abandon.

He began with deploying thousands of lower grade Inquisitors across the universe. Those who hadn't earned his trust or had been marked already for potential seditious sentiments. Each was assigned to a Guard unit with standing orders to eliminate all threats. Ezekiel's zeal proved limitless. Inquisition prisons on Vau Prime overflowed with pronounced heretics, forcing him to ramp up public executions not only as a show of force, but as an example for all. He saw a unique opportunity to further his career while serving Amongeratix.

That meant dealing with monsters like Mobus Kale and Geres Auk. Both of whom stood in the antechamber awaiting an audience—Ezekiel kept them waiting. He'd seen their type countless times before. None of the others survived long enough to influence affairs. He doubted either of these men would as well. The new order did not need men with limited skillsets. To be fair, they served a purpose. One Amongeratix insisted he required, for the time being. The civil war raged unabated. Men of violence, of action, were the prescribed tools to bring the enemy to its knees. Ezekiel envisioned the day when both could be executed and disposed of. Plans to eliminate them were already in place.

Ezekiel turned his attention to his office. Gone was the pristine alabaster on the walls. He replaced them with a flat crimson, soft enough so as not to be offensive, with navy blue accents. The grim coloring suited him and served as a reminder of strength to all who entered. In his mind, the Inquisition had never been stronger.

A commotion in the antechamber drew his attention, sparking his ire. Ezekiel closed his eyes and blew out an exaggerated sigh. "Show them in!"

Stalking to his desk, Ezekiel forced his most menacing glare on the door and waited. Geres Auk stormed into the office ahead of General Kale, their ingrained animosity toward each other growing with each encounter. The Inquisitor General wondered who would win in a fair fight. Their mutual distaste was tempered only by their desire to prove the full measure of their worth to Amongeratix.

Regardless, Ezekiel remained unimpressed. "Make this fast," he snapped. "I have more pressing business needing my attention."

Geres mocked a bow, the movement stuttered and awkward.

Ezekiel rolled his eyes, finding it difficult to believe one so inept at social graces had wormed his way into these halls.

A step behind and to the left, Mobus Kale struck the very image of terror made flesh. The Inquisitor General noted how the man no longer wore a glove to conceal the cold metal of his robotic hand.

"We have located the command post for the criminal element who assisted with the insurrection. As we speak, my forces are eradicating their nest once and for all," Mobus Kale stated.

Ezekiel flexed his fingers before clasping his hands together. "I trust there is media presence documenting this major victory?"

A flush of color traveled up Kale's throat. "No."

No explanation. No excuses for failing to follow protocol. While Ezekiel frowned upon the gross incompetence of General Kale's failings, he admired the man's stalwart attitude and willingness to accept responsibility. "I see. Amongeratix will be most displeased by this lack of foresight, General."

"I will answer to him directly if I must," Kale snarled. "The important fact is I am removing one enemy faction from the board. With them out of the way we can finally secure Vau Prime and direct our attention where it belongs."

Wouldn't you like that? No more mention of your failure to crush the remnants of Strannan's army on the low continent. No more mockery for yet again coming up short. "Our priority has been ensuring the good people of Vau Prime are safe from the predations of misinformation and insurrection. We have been given no orders to take our war elsewhere. Unless you are privileged to intelligence I am not."

Rebuked, Kale jabbed a finger at Goethe. "I have free reign to execute my campaign as I see fit. Do not cross that line, Inquisitor General. We are all replaceable should Amongeratix decide it in his best interests."

"Indeed," Ezekiel replied, pressing his thin lips together. They stared at each other, testing in silent resolve before the Inquisitor General focused on Geres. "Why are you here, Auk? I don't recall having an audience with you today." *Or any other day for that matter.*

"The Crimson Mistress requests your presence."

Ezekiel forced himself to sit still. "You may tell her I will come at my convenience. I do not work for the witch, nor am I at her beck and call."

Clenching his jaw, Geres abruptly turned and left without a word. Ezekiel spied the man's clenched fists. There was a potential problem needing addressing.

"That man needs to disappear," Kale ground through clenched teeth.

"That task does not fall to either you or me, General," Ezekiel replied without taking his gaze off Geres until the man was gone. "Amongeratix has a use for him, and we are not ones to question his authority."

"That changes nothing," Kale pressed. "With the insurrection vanquished I will be taking my command to the low continent where my engineers are building a staging area for the new armies as directed. I find this city unpleasant."

"It is a city of your creating," Ezekiel commented with raised eyebrow. "Prekhauten command is here."

"I am moving it," Kale retorted. "Do not stand in my way, Goethe. I command the Guard now and I have an army to build if we are to put down our enemies. Consider this a courtesy, nothing more."

Kale ground the city beneath his heel for the better part of three years. The rise of the insurrectionists could be directly attributed to his incompetence, yet for reasons Ezekiel failed to understand, the man was promoted and given command of the entire army structure. He didn't deny the time for military leaders was fast approaching. The unexpected naval incursion two months ago rattled the entire command of both orders. Should the enemy launch another assault while planetary defenses were amid repairs the effects could prove devastating.

"I don't suppose you are requesting my permission?" Ezekiel questioned, suddenly unsure why Kale stood before him.

The General snorted. "Hardly. Amongeratix requires us to work in concert."

Shoulders squaring, Ezekiel said, "You might consider sticking around long enough for public affairs to hail you as the hero of Krenz."

"You might consider fucking yourself."

Former Conclave residences.

Magic unleashed upon the walls with fury. Materials melted under the onslaught. At the center of the maelstrom stood the Crimson Mistress. Her rage obliterated all within reach. Flames sprouted around her. The very floor roiled and buckled. Endless decades of languishing under the constraints emplaced by Ruma Zzein twisted her soul into a caricature of what had once been just and holy. Algiss never bought into the Grand Mistress' lies. She failed to see humanity as more than oppressors, incapable of self-governance. Betraying her offered Algiss the opportunity to achieve her true power.

Power she now unleashed on the apartments formerly belonging to the Cardinal Seniorus. The symbol of freedom and justice the entirety of the universe looked to for guidance during dark times. There was no way Algiss Her could feel comfortable sharing these austere chambers, not with so much left unaccomplished. Destroying them proved the next best thing. She broke out in maniacal laughter as the world burned around her.

Each magic strike became her nemesis. The targets shattered in the blink of an eye. Algiss felt strength in acknowledging her hatred for her former mentor. That Ruma had the chance to kill her and fell short suggested the Blood Witches were the weaker sect. A cancer requiring purge. Returning to the abbey proved problematic. She had no ship and no crew. Furthering her impotence was her order was fledgling at best with far too few capable sisters to take the fight to the Blood Witches. Any assault now would be ground down and destroyed with little effort. She needed to change that.

But how?

Rage fizzled as she became consumed with a barrage of conflicting thoughts. Letting the power fade, Algiss drifted off to find

Sister Ibrest. Unlike the others who rebelled with her, Algiss prided herself on showing her face. Scars carried weight and she wanted hers to be seen. Prominent reminders of the dangers of pride and underestimating her foe. Her witches shied away, refusing to look her in the eyes. Algiss scoffed at them all.

She found Ibrest training the newest crop of initiates. Sixteen young women determined to have been born with latent talent stood in two neat ranks. Garbed in white gowns, they shared nervous looks as Algiss swept into the hall. None of those assembled volunteered for their induction to the Crimson Sisterhood. They were abducted, torn from the arms of loved ones, and broken from their human constraints. Those who failed to master the necessary skills of each training level were disposed of. There could be no desertions or defections. Not with the fate of the universe at stake.

"Sister Ibrest, a word."

Ibrest, perpetual scowl twisting what had once been attractive features, dismissed her initiates and followed Algiss into the hallway. "These delays do not serve to inspire confidence among the others."

Algiss ignored the barb. Where once Ibrest was competition for the splinter order, she had successfully been cowed by Algiss aboard *Behemoth*. Animosity remained, if subdued. "Find me a way to infiltrate the comet and bring Ruma Zzein's precious order down around her."

"How am I supposed to accomplish this? We have no idea where the comet is or what her plans entail. This pitiful group of initiates will be fortunate if they survive the week. We lack the forces necessary to assault Ruma Zzein."

"Find a way," Algiss pressed. "Begin with securing transport. I'm sure we can commandeer one of the Prekhauten vessels. Amongeratix has other concerns. We can ill afford to allow the Blood Witches to interfere with our plans."

"Forever Night is predetermined."

"Is it? We spent our lives following Zzein's course. Without question. Perhaps the time to usurp our former grand mistress is at hand," Algiss theorized. "Turn over training to another. I want that ship. We are going to strike the head from our foe and turn the rest of the order to our cause."

Ibrest stiffened. "If they refuse to comply?"

"We kill them."

Tenemenah, planet An'kuruku.

The desert winds blew harsh off the plains, drowning the city in arid heat, drying skin, and parching throats. Fine dust particles coated clothes, turning building facades into grim stained mockeries of fallen glory. Life was seldom kind on the desert planet. The weak perished. Water barons rose with claims affecting entire cities. In their hands was the power of life and death. Their control tightened after the uprisings of a few years ago when the Bone Father led his rebellion against the Prefecture.

Anarchy settled in. So many perished, leaving the planet in disarray. Prekhauten recruiters arrived, conscripting thousands of survivors in the name of the Conclave and Alain Nye and leaving An'kuruku a shadow of its former self. Broken families struggled to put food on their table while the rich grew fatter off the embargoed trade emplaced by Vau Prime. No succor for rebels, the desert slowly began reclaiming its due.

Kaline cared little for the plight of the civilians. She ignored the current ruling elites, choosing to bury her face in the bottom of a bottle. The sting of losing so much during her last effort to spread the word of Rengu left her shaken. Hollow when she needed strength. Seeing all her plans ruined inspired raw terror she hadn't felt since the first night she was approached to spread the word. Once considering herself the definition of strength, Kaline suffered from endless nightmares. She watched the captain, a man she'd grown to respect and care for, gunned down night after night. Sacrificing his life in *her* name.

No matter how hard she tried, Kaline failed to understand how it had all gone so wrong. How each of her crew died in that jungle and she survived. The travesty insulted her to no end. The captain's final glance, the kindness in his eyes, remained a constant threat to drive her mad. None of it was right. How did she alone survive?

She lacked military prowess or tactical intuition. Had little to no experience surviving off the land or dealing with true hardships. The men who laid down their lives were among the best in the business. Men she considered family, to an extent. Alone and heartbroken as they fell one by one, Kaline fled back across the stars to the one place she felt she might blend in and be forgotten. An'kuruku.

There was a unique sense of forgiveness to be found in the

cleansing sands. A chance to scrub clean her failures and find a way forward again. Fearing a repeat of the last disaster, Kaline lacked the drive to continue her project. Instead of clarity or succor, she found the numbing comforts of alcohol. She cut her pilots free, dyed her hair a faded black to match the locals, and crawled through open air pubs and drinking spots for months.

Streaks of her red hair began showing, forcing her to take to wearing a linen scarf. She didn't know why she felt the pull to return to the desert. Perhaps it stemmed from a false sense of vanity. Perhaps from knowing this was the beginning of where so much went wrong. Stumbling upon Mollock Bolle, she thought, had been a godsend. The passion with which he preached against the gods inspired her. She found him intriguing from the moment she first heard his voice. Little did she know he would not only fail, but his actions would haunt her steps across the stars.

One of the first acts she performed upon landing in Tenemenah was to travel to the shores of the Bo and visit the cairn raised in his name in search of answers. The location of his corpse remained unknown. The only certainty lay in knowing the truth of his demise. Yet three years later, the people of the Deeves continued pilgrimages through the desert to see the place where the voice of the people fell. For them. In their name.

She suppressed the urge to spread his truth. Zealots seldom bothered considering differing points of view. Besides, it was too late. The legend of Mollock Bolle swept across the desert in an unstoppable tidal wave. Effigies were erected in a hundred villages. His name was praised by low and high born alike. Slowly, he became more than a legend. He became a hero to a world desperate for salvation. She didn't doubt a crop of children were born with his name.

"Damned fools. All of them," Kaline snorted as she kicked back the last swallow of the clear anduzi. Distilled from a small cactus, the local alcohol burned from the lips to the stomach. She found the taste revolting, a mixture of sweat and hatred. Kaline slammed the glass on the table and gestured for another.

The proprietor ambled over with a bottle in hand. His jowls quivered. "Please, I warn you, this is a dangerous drink. It will creep up on you without warning. Do not indulge."

Suppressing a burp, Kaline pointed at her empty glass with a glare.

He bobbed his large head several times and filled her glass. "Do not say you weren't warned. I ask you leave before becoming too inebriated."

"I ask that you mind your own business."

Muttering, the man stormed back to his bar and the handful of patrons began whispering. She knew they were talking about her. How could they not? An offworlder with no sense. No one in their right mind consumed as much of the anduzi as she was without consequences. Their talk gradually turned to the past. One man with a hawkish nose and deep desert tan stared at her.

"Shit," she murmured. Too drunk to fight back or flee should it come to it, Kaline suspected the man recognized her despite her paltry disguise.

"It is unwise to provoke the locals when they are in their cups, offworlder."

She jerked, hearing footsteps from behind her. Frowning, Kaline kept her gaze on the man across the bar. "It is also unwise to interrupt a woman out for a good time."

The man rounded the table, standing between her and her quarry. A pencil thin moustache decorated his upper lip, accenting the sunken cheeks and multicolored eye patch. His head was shaved down to stubble. Gesturing to the empty chair he said, "Ah, but you are far from having a good time. I have been watching you for days. May I sit?"

He did so without awaiting her response. Kaline sat straight, back against the stiff wooden chair. "I don't recall seeing you before."

"Because I am very good at what I do." His voice brimmed with confidence—she disliked him for that alone.

"Right," she replied. "Well, thank you for your time. I have everything under control."

"It is a wonder you have any control." He made a face and nodded at her drink. "Vile stuff. I hear the desert tribes use it to fuel their fires."

Kaline felt the familiar sickening warmth spreading through her stomach; they used it for much worse. She made a show of taking another drink. "I didn't catch your name."

"I did not offer." He smiled. "I know who you are. There are many who have not forgotten the poison of the redhaired woman. You are not safe in Tenemenah."

Part of her recognized the danger she'd placed herself in by returning here. Part of her longed for it, praying anyone might step forth and end her misery. "What do you want?"

Running his tongue over the center of his lower lip, the man said, "That is rather complicated. Certainly not a topic meant for the open air." He slid a piece of torn parchment across the table. "Go to the address on the paper. There you will find the answers to all you seek, and many you didn't know you needed. But do so quickly. The city is about to turn on you."

He excused himself, tan robes flowing in his wake.

Kaline blinked rapidly, mind locked in conspiracies and theories—the hawknosed man was also missing.

Wrapped in a dark robe with the hood drawn, Kaline stalked through the side streets of Tenemenah. Each step came with a cursory glance over her shoulder. She harbored no illusions about her situation. She was in trouble, had been for years. It came with her higher purpose. A constant companion nestled between certainty and doubt. Wind rustled the metal shutters of one of the poor tenement buildings and Kaline picked up her pace.

The address provided held no special relevance. As far as she could tell the building was all but forgotten by the citizenry. Curious how anything so large could be lost in plain sight. She drew a calming breath before striding up the door. Her knocks echoed down the street. Kaline stepped back, expecting the stranger to show himself. The echoes faded to nothing, and the door remained closed. Frustration mounting, she stepped up and repeated the act, only to meet similar results. She spun and started towards the street.

A creak from behind stopped her in midstride. Kaline's heart raced. The door cracked open, darkness beckoning. She couldn't remember the last time she felt true apprehension that battled against the thrill of the unknown. It took little imagination to envision being tortured or murdered once she stepped inside. For all she knew a tribunal awaited, eager to pronounce judgment and hang her for her crimes. Not that she minded. She'd committed more crimes than any one person had a right to get away with. *How many countless thousands lay dead in my wake? How many more were yet to come if I continued my purpose?*

Gathering her courage, Kaline strode through the door.

Absolute darkness met her, but that old taint of arrogance kept her moving deeper into the building. Closer to her destiny. She only halted when the door ground to a close. Kaline closed her eyes and steadied her breathing. She listened, desperate to pick up any nuance of her hosts.

The sharp clap of hands forced her eyes open. Soft orange lights flickered to life in a circle around the otherwise empty room. Kaline spread her feet a little wider and braced for the doom she knew she'd earned long ago. Ten figures in dark robes surrounded her, prompting her left leg to twitch. Even with the blaster at her hip, Kaline wouldn't be able to fight her way free before one or more took her down.

"I was starting to think you wouldn't show," a familiar voice boomed.

Face concealed by shadows, Kaline failed to spot which robbed figure spoke. "I do not have time for cheap theatrics. State your reason for summoning me or I walk. Now."

She caught the faint snicker of laughter.

"Most impressive speech for a woman surrounded, friendless, and wanted by the Prefecture."

Wanted… That was new. She seldom found adoring fans during her travels, but she had never been reduced to a wanted woman. The concept sparked a niggling of amusement despite the severity of the charge. Kaline once thought herself pragmatic. Recent events altered that perspective. Abandoned and estranged from all she once held dear, Kaline was backed into a corner. That alone made her more dangerous than any of the people surrounding her likely anticipated.

"If the Prefecture wanted me, they had ample opportunity to take me. I've made no secrets about my return to An'kuruku."

"She lacks subtlety," a female voice commented from the shadows. "And humility."

"Attributes of weakness in our profession," another man replied. "What say you, Kaline? Is it possible to set aside your personal failings and hear us out? Or have I made a grave miscalculation of your truths? Speak now and speak true, for any wrong answer will prevent you from seeing the sun."

"Petty threats?" Kaline mused aloud. "What makes you think I am afraid to die? Do you think I would have come back to this pit if I feared being caught or killed? I walk the righteous path; set upon by none other than Amongeratix himself. I spread the word of Rengu, converting all to his universal truth. Whatever this cabal pretends to be, I shall do as I must."

Murmurs rippled through them. One by one the candles extinguished, until only the man who contacted her remained illuminated. He took a step forward. Then another. Kaline held her ground. One man she could beat, providing the others shuffled off as their footsteps suggested.

"Congratulations," he told her. "You've passed our test."

"Wonderful," she spat. "Do I get a prize?"

"You get to keep your life. Seems prize enough, all things considered," he replied. "Do you still plan on shooting me?"

She wanted to. The urge to remove a potential threat made her fingers itch. "I doubt that would solve my problems."

She saw his smile, predatory and hot, from beneath his hood.

"No, it wouldn't. We will be in touch. You are the exact person we've been waiting for. Perhaps you can atone for your previous sins and make old wrongs right."

His candle flickered out and she shrank back despite herself. Kaline railed inside, a rush of questions, concerns, and fears swirling through her mind. "I don't know your name. How am I supposed to stay in touch?"

Reverberations danced throughout the empty room.

THREE

3215 A.G. (After gods), Sorrow's Keep, planet Inselcor.

Globs of lava splashed across the protective shields surrounding the automatons collecting the resource from one of the planet's smaller flowing streams. Ash clouds mingled with dust, permanently twisting Inselcor's atmosphere into a mixture of death and toxicity. Despite this, several species called the planet home, though Sorrow seldom caught sight of any. They preferred the opposite side of the planet, the more temperate zone containing the few patches of greenery that adapted to the brutal environment. Just as well, he preferred solitude.

Automatons delivered the raw ores to his processing facility built upon the river's shore. Once broken down to rare elements and ores it was cooled and sent to the production factories where machines produced an endless tide of new battle automatons for Sorrow's army. The robotic soldiers didn't need sleep, food, or water. They were tireless in their pursuit of the enemy and the perfect weapon for zero gravity and limited atmosphere worlds of operation. Sorrow detested turning his mechanical talents to enhancing the war machine between his brothers but saw little choice.

His run in with the last god hunter left him rattled. The belief they'd all been killed gave him and his brothers a false sense of impunity as they played their eternal game. Akin Brohl was once considered the best. And now he was working hand in hand with Tannus and the Blood Witches. Turning a threat into an ally was almost laughable, even if for a short period of time. Yet he knew none of them were escaping the coming battle unscathed. Determining the best demise occupied his quiet hours. Watching the ranks of automatons swell daily filled the rest of his time.

Each artificial being entered the army only after his personal inspection. Sorrow had always been meticulous when it came to detail and coaxing the best from any situation. It wasn't until madness took him and he flensed the flesh from his muscles that he began exhibiting disturbing traits. A fractured mind kept him moving without purpose until he became aware of the last unique pair born on a quiet world far from interests of universal concern.

Sorrow boarded his shuttle and headed to Crimeat to set the Paladin and the Prophet on their way. He instinctively knew they would be the last. The harbingers of the final war between the Three. While he vaguely recalled arriving in that peaceful village, now decades ago, his madness prevented him from anguishing over the memories of slaughtering every man, woman, and child save for the precious child that would one day grow into his Paladin.

She hated him. Even after their time on the Forsaken Path and his professed apologies before sending them deeper on their quest, Elisa might very well use *Grimfurvor* on him once her purpose was fulfilled. The thought both frightened and exhilarated him. Millennia of pointless years dulled his wit, rendering his lust for life down to a middling miasma without direction. Perhaps death might offer a new adventure. He contemplated asking her to avenge her family should he survive the final battle, even while knowing the former bounty hunter might simply turn her back on him and repay his deeds in kind.

Brooding, Sorrow clasped his hands behind his back and left his observation chamber. A fresh battalion of automatons awaited his inspection. Dressed only in uncomfortable loose robes made from advanced microfilament preventing him from dripping blood, the giant had worn his Bloody Man persona so long he no longer gave his weeping body second thought. Instead, he focused on his failures.

There had been numerous Paladins and Prophets throughout his three-thousand-year exile. All perished well before their time, through no small failings of his own. None were prepared to tackle the unique challenges of the Forsaken Path. Haunted by memories of those who had gone before, enduring the transformation from last of their kin to the first of a new race, those stalwart men and women chosen as Paladin were slaughtered. Forbidden to interfere, Sorrow watched each perish. That impotence rattled his psyche for many generations before he grew inured to pointless waste.

Now his Paladin had succeeded. She trained with the god-killing weapon daily on Tannus' secret world. While Sorrow debated whether she could kill Amongeratix, she at least had the best, and last, chance to do so. He had since stopped questioning what called him to his chosen. The selection became secondhand, a pruning of humanity struggling to meet their destiny. Sorrow had lived long enough to know destiny meant nothing. The fragility of survival depended on vagaries and nothing more. Death stalked them all, striking at random.

Despite this knowledge, Sorrow knew Elisa was special. Tempered and proven over the course of a hard life, she rose to each new challenge. Perhaps she could kill his brother and end their eternal nightmare once and for all. This amused him, not once in his long years had he contemplated what life would be like in the aftermath. He supposed it didn't matter. Nowhere in the universe did he fit in. Remaining on Inselcor ill-suited his temperament. He longed for open waters under a pristine blanket of endless stars. A virgin planet far from humanity's triviality.

Ranks of automatons, faceless and glistening in their resplendent armor, lined the hall into the inspection floor. Sorrow ignored them, his face darkening as his thoughts turned to the debacle of the Prophet. Mollock Bolle was a rare specimen. He assigned himself the position through his stumbling upon the stasis pod Tannus emplaced on Crimeat. It was this single act that sparked the opening salvos of the war. With Mollock spreading his newfound word across the planet it was inevitable Amongeratix would learn of it. Plans set in motion long ago awakened. The wheel began turning.

Mollock Bolle had been nothing before and his name remained mostly forgotten throughout much of the universe. A vagabond and petty adventurer, Mollock roamed his planet trying to make a few quick credits. He seldom remained in one village long, less after the wards Tannus emplaced on the pod activated and hounded him all the way to the Great Barrier Forest and his eventual imprisonment with the Ugri. Stealing him away after the battle on the frozen plateau and depositing him on the desert planet An'kuruku hadn't been part of the plan, leastwise not at the time. Sorrow had no way of knowing Paradise Tear would show up almost simultaneously.

The confluence of events suggested to him he had made the correct choices while confirming the prophecy of the Grand Mistress was at last approaching. Sorrow felt a great weight slip from his shoulders with the knowledge. For years he labored under the burden of having to facilitate the universe's advancement to total and final war. Mollock Bolle served his purpose, exposing truths few willingly accepted. Now it was up to Sorrow and Elisa to finish the task and do what they had been created for. He sighed; his heart unexpectedly heavy with the knowledge it was all coming to an inevitable conclusion.

Stepping into the inspection room, he went through the motions before sending the battalion commander his acceptance. As one, the automatons executed a right face and began marching toward the airfields were massive troop carriers awaited to ferry them to the sight of the final battle.

Forever Night beckoned.

Krenz, planet Vau Prime.

Using stolen registration identifiers, Akin Brohl piloted his shuttle down to the planet's surface. Word had come to him of Amongeratix's arrival. The prospect of confronting his ancient nemesis inspired him. While he dreamed of killing the murderous giant, Akin had a task to perform. He was here to lure the giant out, to unnerve and rattle him and, if all went according to plan, seduce Amongeratix to follow him to the trap prepared in the ruins of Occanum.

As far as Akin was concerned, he'd made a deal with the devil. Tannus may present as the honorable one, determined to see justice done for both species, but he had equal amounts of blood on his hands. He too needed execution and, as Akin was the last of his kind, he was the only one capable of doing so. Thrilled at the prospect of testing his mettle against the greatest killer the universe had ever known, he plunged down through the lower atmosphere to the small landing field on the outskirts of the capital.

Landing crews swarmed his ship, instantly refilling the fuel pods and inspecting for inflight damage. Akin strode down the boarding ramp to present his identification to local customs officials. He saw the jet-black uniform of the Inquisition lurking in the background. The telltale, blue-tinged red rose lapel the only spot of color in an otherwise oppressive presentation. Curious. He wondered when the Inquisition began monitoring spaceports. Akin felt his skin warm. It was an old sign. A warning. Evil was at work on Vau Prime. Evil perpetrated by one of the Three. He decided that if matters developed in his favor, he was going to slay Amongeratix and end the tyrant once and for all. Plan be damned.

Aching to release his pent-up aggression, Akin took the datapad back from the customs agent, slipped into his jacket, and strode deliberately past the Inquisitor. He met the man's glare, refusing to back down. The Inquisitor moved to intercept him before but instead, settled back and let him pass. Akin heard the crackle of a radio from behind him and smiled.

Trouble awaited him a block later. He rounded the last corner to exit the terminal and found a squad of Prekhautens barring the door. Several had truncheons in hand, others their blasters. Akin was delighted. He'd come expecting a fight—they would give him one Setting his shoulder bag against the wall, Akin rolled his shoulders and cracked his knuckles one at a time.

"Come with us and there won't be any trouble," the sergeant ordered. His voice carried the slightest echo of a tremble.

Akin narrowed his eyes, focusing on the small bead of sweat forming on the man's brow. His grin widened.

The Prekhautens tensed, unsure of their advantage.

Akin launched his assault. He came up with a hand to the sergeant's throat. The crunch of bone and cartilage was drowned out by repeated blows to the chest, groin, and face. Akin dropped his first opponent to the floor in an unconscious heap. He immediately ducked under a wild swing from the woman behind the sergeant, punching her in the kidney with enough force to shatter her lower rib. She screamed and released her truncheon.

Akin caught the weapon as it dropped and was soon in their midst. Men and women trained for warfare fell. A blow shattered a kneecap. Blood spilled from the ears of another after a smack across the back of his head. When the skirmish ended, Akin was barely out of breath. Dropping the blood smeared truncheon, he reclaimed his bag and slipped into the open streets of Krenz. A circle of moaning battered soldiers lay behind. A warning for all.

Akin Brohl had come to collect his blood price and none of Amongeratix's defenders were a match for the visceral nature of his fury.

Great Library, planet Wexanos.

"Fleet integration is continuing at the expected pace. I anticipate running the ships on their first training exercise within the next few weeks," Admiral August reported.

Falchi's image remained stoic. "Very good, though I must caution we have no idea when the next phase will kick off. I need your fleet at full capacity as soon as possible."

She spread her hands, palms up. "We're getting there, Admiral, but you must understand these dreadnaughts are unlike anything we've ever seen. The engineering that went into their construction is beyond our capacity. It takes time to properly train a full crew, much less ten."

"I understand, and I'm not criticizing your actions." His voice softened. "Tensions are rising here. The new leadership is clamoring for action. No one wants this war to continue any longer than necessary. Tannus' ships can break the stalemate and bring Vau Prime to its knees for negotiations."

"Surely the Inquisitor General will have planetary defenses emplaced and ready for any such assault."

Falchi cleared his throat. "Sharlyn, this stays between us, leastwise until the new council is ready to broadcast it across the universe. Alain Nye is dead. Killed by Amongeratix's hand the moment the monster landed in Krenz. With Khe-Zhehan's rescue efforts we exposed a serious flaw in their defensive scheme. They will not fall for it a second time."

Sharlyn failed to understand why Amongeratix would slaughter his right hand and the heir to power. "Admiral, who commands on Vau Prime now?"

"We are still working on that. Our intelligence network is practically nonexistent with Aliz and her teams pulling out." He paused. "The one certainty is Amongeratix has settled in the old Conclave headquarters and began a campaign to eliminate all potential threats on Vau. The body count is said to be in the tens of thousands."

The unspoken implication brought a lump to her throat. "Understood. I'll have Captain Odir and the others ramp up training. We'll be ready when you need us."

"That won't be necessary for the moment. Continue at your current pace. We don't want any unnecessary accidents reducing potential combat power," Falchi replied. "When your fleet passes their final trials, we will discuss how to get our divisions aboard."

"That brings me to a second point, Admiral." She cursed herself for the constant use of his rank, reminding herself she was now and admiral as well. "I'm going to need more crew who think outside of Prekhauten doctrine."

"Go on."

"I have a few people in mind," she said, noting his neutral tone. "I'd like permission to find Vicente Blackheart. He's the perfect fit for the coming fight."

"Can he be trusted?"

The notorious pirate lord was far removed from the heyday of the pirate base over planet Spindl. Drespai once commanded fear and respect throughout the entire sector. Until Nye betrayed the pirates in a master stroke and destroyed their haven. Her interactions with Blackheart took her far from the rigid policies enforced by Vau Prime. She found herself, much to her chagrin, liking the man and his foppish behaviors.

Good question. "That remains to be seen, but he is competent and a capable fighter. He has no love for the Guard or Nye's minions. I believe I can coax him to our side one final time."

"Can you afford to leave your new command at this juncture?" he pressed.

She paused. Under normal circumstances she'd never think of it, but this felt different, final. "Sir, I can leave behind a select team capable of handling the transition of our crews. They know *Brightstar* as much as I."

"Very well," Falchi said after a pause. "Take who you need and find him, but do not dally. My old bones tell me we are about to launch the largest counteroffensive in the history of the modern universe. I'm going to need you at the tip of the spear when the call comes."

She beamed. "Aye, Admiral. I won't let you down."

"You never have, my friend. You never have."

The image flickered and faded, leaving her alone in her cabin with far too many thoughts. First up was telling her crew they had to get back on *Solstice*. After that it was a matter of tracking down a man who was adept at disappearing.

One step at a time. Falchi's words sat like ill omens on her conscience, making it difficult to focus on her self-appointed task. She knew she needed to be on Mannus to help with planning the coming campaign but knew in equal measure how much she needed Blackheart and his people.

Reaching into her desk, Sharlyn withdrew a small datapad. It contained one item. A personal identification tracker for one Vicente Blackheart. The clever bastard knew better than to include any voice capability, forcing her hand. Deciding whether to use it or not became the problem. She didn't know how he'd react to her reaching out so soon after their last adventure, or if he'd be receptive to her proposal. Repeating what would become her mantra in the coming days, Sharlyn slipped the datapad back into the drawn and went to find Odir.

One step at a time.

The Prekhauten Naval Vessel *Solstice* had been among the last commissioned before the civil war. Boasting the fastest engines, most advanced weaponry, and state-of-the-art armor, she was the first step into the future. No one could have predicted the nightmare unfolding after she first received her commission or that she would be the only one of from her class still in active service today. Sharlyn August showed her pride in the ship. She drove her crew to be the best. Her Marines were the pride of the fleet. *Solstice* sported scars, they all did, but she remained a staunch defender of the just. She remained Sharlyn's first true love.

The ship lost some of its luster during her time away and Sharlyn struggled to find a way to bring it back. Most ship captains were fickle. They needed routine, craved it. She was no different. *Solstice* would forever be hers, dreadnaughts aside. A scattering of crew and maintenance teams deployed from Mannus scurried about. She passed them with indifference and entered the bridge. No surprise, Captain Odir was already there.

"Admiral on the bridge!" a new ensign barked.

"As you were," she ordered before they disrupted their tasks.

Odir beamed at her. "Admiral, I hadn't thought to be back on her so soon."

"Feels like coming home," Sharlyn replied. "How soon before we can depart?"

"A day, perhaps two. The ship is ready. We ensured it would be when we transferred to *Brightstar*. Integrating new crewers is taking a bit. They come from different classes. Few were ever assigned to ours."

"We can drill them enroute. The sooner we get this finished the better," she said. "I have a feeling we have little time to spare."

Odir slid a step closer and lowered his voice. "Are you sure this is a good idea?"

"This might go down as one of my dumbest ideas. But it is one I feel we need to attempt. Like him or not, Blackheart has proven himself repeatedly."

"The man is a pirate, Admiral," Odir reminded. "He'd just as soon cut our throats. Sure, he helped track down Presha Von, but it wasn't from the kindness of his heart. Villains never change."

She wished she had a defense for that comment, but deep down she knew Blackheart abandoned his humanity long ago in favor of fast plunder and a life of excess. Sharlyn was one of the few people in the universe who knew his truth and that skewed her feelings. Knew he was the disenchanted son of a successful merchant. Deciphering how to use it to her advantage remained just out of reach, however.

"At this point I don't think it matters much. The only way we are going to win is by stretching our moral code," she admitted.

"We ha—"

Sharlyn held up a hand. "I don't like it any more than you, but we've tried fighting it our way and look where that's landed us. Half the universe is devolving into pointless civil war. No matter what we do, we remain a step behind Amongeratix. The only way to beat him is by fighting by his rules."

"What does Admiral Falchi say about that?" Concern twisted his face.

"He's given me the green light, though I don't think he understands precisely what I have in mind," she said. "This is a dangerous game, Odir. One I will not command you to play. If you choose, you can return to *Brightstar* and continue readying the fleet. I won't look down or hold it against you."

A stunned look bloomed. "Admiral, how dare you insinuate any of your crew would abandon you when you need them most? Myself most of all. We've been with you since the start of this godsdamned war and I'll be damned if you finish it without us."

She grinned despite herself. Loyalty proved a hard trait to come by these days. Sharlyn felt ashamed for doubting him. Odir was the best first officer she'd ever served with and a better voice of reason, and she'd just insulted the man.

Placing a hand on his shoulder and squeezing, she said, "Captain Odir, it would be my honor to sail with you again. You bring out the best in me and, when times demand, provide a whisper of caution through my blind spots."

"I'm just trying to keep us all alive," he said, failing to keep the pride from his voice.

"You've done a remarkable job thus far. One I expect you to continue," she confirmed. Sharlyn stared into her second-in-command's eyes, searching for any lack of resolve or hidden weaknesses. "Have you addressed the crew?"

"Only the bridge officers. I figured it best to wait until we are underway."

Good point. We don't know how they'll react to working with the pirates again.

"Understandable," she said. "Keep preparations on schedule, here and with the fleet. I'm placing Commander Erith from tactical in charge of training the new crews on the dreadnaughts. I anticipate returning in time to lead the coming campaign. I owe us that much at least."

He nodded, calling the bridge to attention as she turned and departed; of which she quickly waved off. The doors slid closed behind her, leaving him to return to barking orders. Much needed doing if they were to sail on time.

"Fighting alongside pirates," Odir muttered. "I never thought I'd see the day."

Abandoned. Alone. Betrayed.

For the first time in her life, Presha Von, former Lady and one of the twelve lords of Lethendweil, found herself mired in an inescapable situation no amount of guile or cunning could solve. Since surrendering to Paradise Tear on *Behemoth* and arriving on Tannus' secret world, she had barely spoken to a soul. Yellow robed librarians delivered her meals, pausing only to inquire if her needs were being met. She expected prison bars but was sequestered in a suite filled with hot baths, open windows overlooking verdant fields rolling across soft hills, and books and flowering plants to occupy her mind. Songbirds flit in and out of her rooms through the wide opening to the deck, dropping feathers of every conceivable color where they went. She stopped being annoyed days ago. It was, in a word, paradise. Leastwise it should be.

The simplistic beauty of it meant to calm her shattered nerves and repair the damage to her soul. As much as she wanted the release, Presha found part of her resisting. The hardened woman she had been on Crimeat refused to fade away. Wicked talons dug deep each time she attempted to break free. Presha once prided herself on being strong in a world of men. To a degree, she still was. A secret member of the Black Council and catalyst for sparking the opening salvos of Amongeratix's war on humanity, she played no small part in helping him escape from his chains at the Inquisition prison on Prophet Isle.

Where does this leave me? Regrets crowded her conscience. Pain devoured her waking moments. She longed for a return to simpler times, before the Black Council first approached her and she decided to follow in her father's footsteps.

Killing him proved the catalyst to the fundamental change sweeping through her. Presha no longer desired power. No longer dreamed of commanding entire planets. Her previous efforts ended in ruin. Atonement became an adopted mantra. One she devoted her waking moments to. Locked away from every other living soul on the planet, she had no outlet, no opportunity to prove her worth. Why then was she still alive? Her crimes alone demanded execution, lifelong imprisonment at worst.

Sighing, Presha rose from the plush bed and slipped into a pale blue robe before heading to the balcony. Her suite was several stories up, enough she could see for kilometers. She'd never seen such majesty in a planet. Flocks of strange birds danced over the tops of distant forests. Endless open skies beckoned. Herds of animals she'd never seen roamed. If any place offered the opportunity for redemption, it was here. Why then wasn't she content?

Knocking on her outer chamber door reverberated through the walls, startling her. Presha turned, pausing to ensure her robes were tightened, and said, "Enter."

Instead of one of the librarians, a giant swept in. Presha's heart fluttered. Cold dread spread through her body at the sight of Tannus. Dressed in simple robes, the giant halted a respectful distance away. His deep eyes stared down on her, taking measure. Presha was frozen, unsure how to approach him. She had been expecting, and dreading, this moment.

"You are surprised to see me."

She nodded, not trusting her words.

Tannus held up a hand. "Please, be at peace. I have not come to chastise you. Perhaps a time will come for intense interrogation, but I must make up my mind about you first."

She offered a false smile, thin, deceiving. "How kind of you, Lord Tannus."

"Why must your kind insist on titling my brothers and I?" he questioned. "If you truly understood what we are you would not be so fast with accolades."

"I have witnessed what your kind offers, Tannus and I am terrified of it," she replied.

"My brother is not a man of patience. Rather, he is a creature born to violence. I regret you spent time with him."

"As do I."

Gesturing for her to sit, Tannus continued, "It is my understanding you have been in his service for many years."

"A choice I would take back if I could," she admitted. Inwardly, she wondered whether she regretted her bid for power or the act of being caught. Presha settled into the dark blue divan, folding her hands atop each other.

His piercing gaze struck deep into her soul. "Yet you remained even after the death of Kharsis. Surely you knew his true nature by then. The singular purpose he has staked the entirety of his existence on."

Presha licked her lips, wilting under his scrutiny. "Change is seldom swift, if ever. I felt trapped. Locked into the misery of service to him. Make no mistake, I once sought to gain much from our alliance. He whispered promises of grandeur, first with Crimeat and then Hawker's Gate. I was to be an empress. One of the new order. Have you any idea how difficult that is to sweep aside and return to a life of quiet obscurity?"

"I have wandered alone far longer than you might imagine, Presha Von," he said. "And I do know the guile with which my brother speaks. He seduces through false promises, grinding all who fall under his sway until there is nothing left. The same would have happened to you if you had not been brought here."

"It was not an easy decision."

Tannus cocked his head. "You continue having doubts."

She nodded. What else was there to say? Honeyed words seduced her wholly, prompting her to abandon the principles of her foundation and betray her species. Shame burned her cheeks. Presha yearned for the special oils she once wallowed in. Through them she could forget and lose herself forever.

"Tell me, what changed your mind? What revelation sparked to convince you to abandon him?" he pressed.

Self-preservation? The arrival of the rogue witches? Geres Auk turning his back on me to prostrate himself before Amongeratix? The list was endless. In truth, Presha could use any number of excuses, but they were more lies. Her crisis of conscience was born through her actions on doomed Kharsis and the cunning ministrations of Paradise Tear during their shared captivity. The bond she felt with the woman proved strong enough to do what Presha lacked the strength for on her own.

"Your cousin. It was her words that inspired me to see Amongeratix for what he truly is. Had I remained, I would be dead. Or worse. It became clear there was no place for me in the universe he created. My kind turned its back on me after I… murdered a planet. Where else could I go?"

She studied his face, searching for any betrayal of emotion as to what was to be her fate.

"What do you hope to accomplish here?" he asked. "I am not in the habit of providing forgiveness upon many. You are a unique situation. One I am unsure of how best to deal with."

"To be fair, I expected a cell. Never to see the sun again," Presha said.

"A fate many would condemn you to without pause. Alas, there are no cells on this world. In the aftermath of my kind's final war, I had much time for contemplation. I struggled with the weight of grief and the knowledge of my actions. No doubt I deserved a cell as well. Instead, I set out on a quest for peace. One capable of alleviating my guilt. What you see is the product of self-forgiveness. This planet has never known violence. Nor does it have an army, but do not think it lacks necessary defenses. Pristine in every conceivable concept, it is how the entire universe should be.

"No, Presha Von. You will not find a cell waiting you. I encourage you to look inward, rediscover your truth and learn to live free again. Redemption comes in many forms. What will yours take?"

She lacked answers, having given up on the future long ago. Presha softened, running nervous hands over the front of her robes. "I do not know what future awaits me, Tannus, but I believe I can help atone for my sins. Allow me to provide you with what I know of your brother's designs. Let me prove myself to you and the others. It is all I can offer."

Tannus nodded. "You shall have your one chance, Presha Von. Do not waste time with thoughts of apology or promises of change. It will or will not happen according to its own merit. I look forward to seeing if you can change after so much." He paused, noting the first tear slipping from her eye. Perhaps salvation awaited her after all. "Oh, there is one to whom you could apologize if your conscience demands it. There is a man here you once murdered. I have a feeling he would be most interested in reacquainting himself with you."

She blinked. "I-I don't understand. Who did I kill? How is he still alive?"

"That is a fact I think it best for you to discover on your own. You are now free to move about the entirety of the library. As usual, should you require anything at all let one of my librarians know. You are my guest here, Presha Von. Do not abuse the privilege." He bowed and excused himself before she could respond.

Presha stared at the door long after it closed behind him. For the life of her, she couldn't figure out who she might have killed or how they had come back to life.

Tannus was a man of private struggles. He'd endured centuries of loneliness in his quest to stop his brother's aggressions. Every effort collapsed into failure, furthering the wedge between them and dragging the human empire into chaos. Sedition became a game each played, for the brothers were nothing if not petty. Many considered allying with Tannus a benefit. He knew better. While attempting to right his past, he only served to drag the rest of the universe into his squabble. Fresh regrets opened. He wondered if he had chosen poorly in allowing this batch of allies into his confidence.

Tannus swept through the empty halls. He hadn't had a quality conversation with his cousin since her escape from *Behemoth*. Though the two were close, there was little love lost between them thanks to his persecution of the war. Tannus braced himself for the storm he was sure to find awaiting him.

He wasn't disappointed.

Paradise Tear stood, arms folded across her chest, jaw set, just inside the door to her suite. Her face locked in a mass of unreadable emotions, putting him on guard. They stared at one another for a moment, neither willing to unleash the opening salvo. While he felt he had the moral high ground, Paradise remained a scorned woman. He took a steadying breath and began, "Paradise, I—"

"I shouldn't have gone," she interrupted.

Her admission caught him unexpectedly. Neither were prone to apologizing or admitting mistakes. He'd come prepared for a fight, leaving him unsure how to proceed.

"We, ah, we suffer under blankets of pressure none of us are ready for, Cousin. I do not place blame upon you for your decisions. Rather, I had come to apologize for mine. I should have been more persuasive in keeping you here. Amongeratix is cunning, apparently more so now he has had time to subvert the ruling orders."

Some of the stiffness left her. "I couldn't defeat him. I thought I could. I was certainly mentally prepared for the confrontation. He has evolved, Tannus. He is not the same man you once knew."

His face hardened. "How do you mean?"

A dark look came over her. "He has become more cunning. I was certain he meant to kill me, but he settled for mild interrogation after I was captured. I didn't know what he was after at the time. He skirted important questions. Seemed content with toying with my mind."

Tannus rubbed his chin. "He was testing you. Trying to see how much you knew about our plans. This is new for him. Amongeratix's strength has always been through blunt force."

"And now he controls Vau Prime, with all three human orders under his thumb."

"I had not expected him to move so quickly," Tannus admitted. "His removal of the Inquisitor General is but the first step in consolidating control. Our window for victory begins to close."

"I can't believe he executed the man that way."

"It is an old tactic. Pretend to become a powerful ally and cut off the head at the right moment. My brother seeks to establish his dominance. I leave you now. There is much I need to consider."

Paradise watched him go, a curious look in her eye. Much yet remained she did not understand of the universe, but one thing was certain. Tannus had changed during the three millennia she had been in stasis.

FOUR

3215 A.G. (After gods), Eger City, planet Mannus Prime.

"Tell me again why I signed on for this?"

Adris Moscasco collapsed on the small navy-blue divan under a bank of windows overlooking the city proper. A half empty bottle of Fallorian brandy sat on the desk. Endless days of back-to-back meetings demanded her attention in too many directions. She wasn't sure what to expect when the idea of abandoning her position as governor of Dalafar to join the rebellion first sparked. She brought value to the fledgling organization, but at what cost? Newsvids branded her an arch traitor with orders to execute on sight. Her home and savings, the little she hadn't transferred to secure accounts outside of Conclave reach, were confiscated. There was no going back. No other way than forward through the political hurdles blocking her way.

Flowing in behind her, Cardinal Virom went straight for the brandy. "They will come around. They must, else this will all have been for naught."

"I thought running a single planet challenging. This is damned near impossible," she groused, accepting a glass with the flash of a smile. "How did you do it before I arrived?"

He hefted the bottle. "This and no small amount of military coercion. Adris, I was here throughout the campaign to secure this planet. I provided a moral conscience to the soldiers while placating the population's fears. Tomorrow was never promised. Not until I contacted Admiral Falchi and his unique confederation of forces."

"Unique is an understatement. I still have doubts about working with any of the Three, though Tannus seems the easiest to handle," she replied. "My greatest concern is, once we establish this new rule of whatever it is going to be, not repeating the mistakes of our predecessors. Vau Prime has fallen due, in part, to their greed and recycling individuals who should never have been placed in any leadership position to begin with. We must avoid this mistake at all costs."

Virom fought back a grin, having endured more than his share of similar conversations with Torgast and the others before her arrival. Virom chose to remain on the side rather than lead the rebellion. He was moral support at best, far from prepared to rule. When word of Adris' defection reached him, his heart pounded. The fledgling rebellion had a proper chance.

"We are not so bad off as you believe," he said. He went on to explain the private political aspirations of those under consideration for the new ruling council. Rather than stick to three unique factions, the delegates from nearly one hundred worlds decided a council might prove more effective and, in doing so, allow more voices to be heard. He failed to find any major issues with the notion and had no trouble saying it.

Adris held out her empty glass for a refill. "I have no doubts about the strengths of this proposal, Virom. But there is a war on and until we can figure out a way to gain the final advantage and bring down the nightmare on Vau Prime this is all mere political grandstanding."

"I'll let General Torgast speak to the readiness of the military," Virom commented, unconcerned. "From what I can tell, we seem to be on even terms with our enemies."

"Subterfuge is the first lesson of war, Virom." Adris closed her eyes and gulped down her brandy. "I won't feel comfortable until we can infiltrate our spies on Vau Prime. With the unexpected retreat and dismantling of the remnants of Davith Strannan's armies we are effectively blind."

"I didn't know this was to be a strategy meeting," he said with a wry grin.

Her pause said enough. "My apologies. My mind tends to race when it comes to important matters. How much longer do we have before returning to that nest of vipers?"

"While I would hardly call our new allies venomous snakes, there is some time still. The loudest voices will seek to delay, hoping the others file in before them, thus allowing for a grand spectacle and unspoken promise of authority." Virom finished his brandy. "These are the games we chose to play when we accepted our roles. You already hold the nomination for First Counselor. I suggest using the time to secure additional votes, though I find this brandy to be particularly distracting. Perhaps a recess is in order."

"As much as I would enjoy drinking my concerns away, you

and I both know we must force the issue." She laughed. A brief note of contentment lingering between them. "Speaking of issues, where are on we on that secondary matter?"

Virom cleared his throat. He expected the subject to come up far sooner. "Progressing. I have it on good authority it should be executed before the close of business."

"Good. The sooner that thorn is removed the better. I'm tired of looking over my shoulder for an assassin's blade."

The prospect of Vaumagians planetside without sanction or knowledge plagued them. Curiously, the assassin order hadn't been heard from since a string of failed contracts on Vau Prime. Perhaps Nye had succeeded in eliminating them or perhaps fear had driven them underground. If not, they would no doubt pop up again and when they did…

Footsteps echoed down the grime-stained, stone floor. Tinnus Har cringed as they neared. Though no physical abuse was doled upon him, he suffered from limited food and water and the decided lack of human contact. The only time he saw anyone other than his captors was when the odd pair of soldiers made a lackluster attempt at making him divulge his true designs on Mannus Prime. A foolish attempt at best, but one he felt certain was the only one he was going to get before matters turned dark.

His meals were already reduced to military ration bars, tasteless protein bars designed to keep line infantry on their feet long enough to push through to their objective. Tinnus Har had come to hate his life and the brash decision bringing him here in the first place. What started with dreams of harnessing control in this splinter faction of government quickly devolved into an unending nightmare threatening to steal his soul.

The footsteps halted outside his door. Tinnus backed against the wall, unwilling to give his jailor any additional power.

The door slid open and in stepped a tall, dour man with a fresh facial scar. Presence notwithstanding, it was the jet-black Inquisitor uniform which drew Tinnus' attention. His executioner had come at last. The red rose emblem sewn into his jacket sparked raw terror in the former Cardinal Seniorus. Of the myriad conclusions to his story he envisioned, falling prey to the entity he sought to overthrow never entered his mind.

"This is it, eh? No trial for Tinnus Har. No public humiliation for the universe to mock my memory for all time." He hung his head despite the desire to stare death in the eye. "Come then. Make it quick."

"Excuse me?"

Tinnus found a glimmer of confusion in the young man's eyes. Studying him further, Tinnus was surprised to find the Inquisitor was unarmed. "You're not here to kill me?"

"Why would you say that? I've been given another assignment, Cardinal. My mission is to escort you to safety."

A trick. It must be. "What is your name, Inquisitor?"

"Dowan Mun, sir."

"Well, Dowan Mun, surely you must understand my unwillingness to trust one of your kind," Tinnus said. "What assurances can you provide me this isn't some grand ruse to make me trip over my tongue before you stab me in the back?"

"There is no knife here, Cardinal. I must caution, we do not have long. I slipped in during shift change. The guards will notice if I take much longer."

Confident. Assured. Tinnus found the Inquisitor too reassuring. He didn't move.

"Cardinal, we don't have time. Either come with me now or stay here and die," Dowan stated "You have allies here. It is a matter of reaching them in time."

Deciding he was dead either way, Tinnus gestured to the door. "Very well. Lead on, Inquisitor. To whatever end I deserve."

Tinnus Har was not averse to taking risks, yet fate was beyond his control. Together with his rogue Inquisitor, he hurried into Eger City's night and the promise of one final opportunity to show his worth to universe and, if events flowed in his favor, revenge on all who'd done him wrong.

"So that's that," Matthias leaned back in the chair, interlacing his fingers on top of his head. His gaze fixed on the small monitor showing the fallen Cardinal Seniorus' cell.

Streaks of grey tore through what had been a blanket of dark hair. His face was beaten and weathered thanks to a distinguished military career. Any excess fat was burned from his bones, leaving him a hardened man with a dire outlook on life. Matthias was a proven veteran, having endured more than most others over the last three decades. Hitching his destiny to the rebellion after retiring was a gambit, but one he felt the need to undertake. He'd seen the nightmares promised by Amongeratix firsthand and vowed to do everything in his power to prevent them from spreading across the universe.

At his side, his Marine counterpart, Gunnery Sergeant Asom chewed on a breadstick. Trapped in a cycle of shipboard duties and assisting Matthias with his assignment for the fledgling council, Asom stopped bringing up his current situation. Matthias empathized with the man. It took him far too long to learn how to serve two masters.

"Why are we doing this, again?"

As much as Matthias wanted to ignore the obvious, he slipped back into his former leadership roles too easily for his own good. "The big bosses want to give him enough rope to hang himself."

"We could save everyone the effort and take care of it ourselves." Asom stifled a burp. "Men like that are part of the problem, not the solution."

"You're not getting an argument out of me. The question is, can we trust the Inquisitor? He was in a jail cell before this, after all," Matthias shifted in his seat. "I don't trust him any further than I can spit."

The comment produced a shrug.

Matthias learned early in his career not to question the motivations of his superiors. Men and women riding desks and answering to the Conclave instead of being in the field with the line troops. From what he could tell, Torgast was a strong leader, but he was already being sucked into the power vacuum, losing bits of his command authority amongst the soldiery along the way. Lose too much and morale would plummet.

"I don't like these games, Matthias," Asom muttered. "Cut out the cancer and let's be on with the war."

Matthias didn't disagree but was helpless to alter their assignment. He recalled what they'd been told. The enemy had hidden agents loose in Eger City. It was paramount to discover their network and either coerce the spies to transmit false information back to Krenz or eliminate as many as possible to disrupt the information flow.

"Let's do it," Asom pressed. "Just you and me. Give them the knife and that's it."

Matthias rolled his eyes. He'd had the same thought. "You know we can't."

"A guy can dream. What's our next move?"

"Wait for Mun to make contact, gather intel, and bring their world crashing down."

Asom's eyes lit up before he turned to watch the monitor placed in front of them. "When do we report to the council?"

"As soon as we have something actionable. Right now, Har isn't convinced of the. He'll be wary until Mun gains his trust."

"Which is where I begin to worry," Asom countered. "Putting them together is bad business, Matthias. You and I both know it."

"That's out of our control. If you think about it, they make perfect sense. Mun isn't an ally any more than Har. He played the power game and came up short," Matthias explained. "All that anger has been welling in him since he surrendered to custody."

"Anger makes a man dangerous, not the other way around. Our talents are wasted here, Matthias. I should be back on my ship training the new recruits."

Matthias understood his plight, having struggled with similar feelings since initially retiring. "Maybe, but the council lacks the proper units with our skillset. We uncover the conspiracy and deliver the whole damned thing to Virom and Torgast. Then we can go about our business." *Too bad I don't know what my business is these days. I've spent so long working for others I can't remember the last real idea I had.*

"When do you suppose the next campaign begins?"

The digital representations of Mun and Har turned right and headed for the middle-class district comprising shops, markets, and eateries. They weren't concerned with losing them since each was secretly implanted with tracking chips. Staying ahead of the fugitives almost felt like a crime.

"Not soon enough. I'm ready for it all to end," he said, resigned and exhausted.

Asom took another bite of his bread stick, brushing the crumbs from his uniform. "How did you get roped into this, Matthias? You're a veteran, and a respected one at that. I didn't figure you for one who jumped on a cause."

Matthias grinned despite himself. "I was there you know. At the beginning."

"Crimeat? I heard that was a hairy campaign."

"No, long before Crimeat. Amongeratix escaped from a

Conclave prison decades before he was sent to Prophet Isle. I was just a buck sergeant at the time and assigned to a squad to help bring him down. I had an Inquisitor and a Blood Witch with me."

Asom's eyes widened. "Shit. I never heard about that."

"You wouldn't have. Guard headquarters kept it quiet. They didn't want the universe worrying about the worst of the Three free and loose." Matthias' eyes glazed over as old memories produced the ghost of a smile.

After a low whistle, Asom asked, "How did you survive that?"

"I almost didn't. We tracked him down to a derelict freighter. I lost most of my squad in those corridors. Lost the Blood Witch as well. But we got him. Got the bastard good and shoved him into another Conclave prison. We thought for good … I guess not."

Matthias felt the Marine stare a little harder at him, seeing the scars he didn't bother to hide. He knew he shouldn't have survived a quarter of what he had.

Silence settled between them as they settled in to watch the monitor.

"I don't deserve this," Aliz said to her reflection.

The full-length mirror showed who she once was, dressed in regal finery befitting her former station, not the bitter, hardened woman she had become. Years of fighting against the brutality spreading across Vau Prime hollowed her until naught but a fragile shell remained. She'd seen enough death, having caused more than her share along the way, for a hundred lifetimes. Each precious soul had a family. Loved ones. People who missed them when they did not come home. Once she would have poured her heart out to them. Today…

"Ma'am?"

Aliz closed her eyes and forced herself to remember what life had been like before the war. Before the end of civility. Her robes were a callback to better days. White with gold embroidery, she looked every bit the proper lady who had been born into politics. Face settling into a mask, she turned to the attendant. "I would have preferred more appropriate clothing."

"The First Counselor Elect thought it would be best if you went before the new council according to who you are."

Oh child, you have no idea who I am. "Please inform her I am no longer the woman I was. Surely, she has bigger concerns than doting on an old woman.”

The attendant remained silent beneath the thin fabric of her grey hood. Aliz felt guilt for snapping at the woman. She'd done nothing wrong and wasn't responsible for the current disaster. Sure, she might have found a better dress that didn't cinch at the waist, but the woman was simply following instructions—bureaucracy already hard at work in the new world order. Were it not for the smoldering desire for revenge, Aliz would have snuck off in the night, never to be heard from again.

“When does this First Counselor expect an audience?” Aliz asked, changing the subject.

“I am to escort you to her at once, ma'am.”

She flashed a false smile. “Of course. Well, if I can't get out of it. Lead on, child.”

Aliz found nothing remarkable about the new seat of government on Mannus Prime, nor with the woman elected to organize the rabble into an effective form of leadership capable of sustaining all seven hundred planets once under the former Conclave. Word had reached her of the Conclave's dissolution. Amongeratix moved swiftly, clearing out the defective parts standing in his way and reshaping humanity in his image. The people she passed here in Eger City were supposed to represent the best of those unwilling to bend the knee. In her estimation, that remained to be seen.

“Ah, Aliz, please come in,” Adris Moscasco greeted with open arms and a warm smile. “I have been looking forward to this for some time. It does my heart good to see you escaped Krenz before the fall.”

She shifted, uncomfortable. “I would have stayed behind if it were up to me. Too many good people were left behind.”

“I understand. I do. Leaving Dalafar under Inquisition control continues weighing on my conscience, but I know I did the right thing.” Moscasco's expression softened. “My people would have suffered had I remained or allowed myself to be captured. The Inquisition wanted my head. Coming here, with my wealth of knowledge and experience was my only true option. I can contribute so much to the cause, Aliz. Just as you can.”

Aliz ran her tongue across the roof of her mouth as she decided what to say. “I am tired of causes. I've seen what happens when they fail. For the past three years I have carried on while the world burned down around me. At first, I was enraged, distraught. Lorenu and I had been together for most of our lives. Seeing her slain by those claiming to be her allies shattered my heart. So, I fought back. I helped Davith Strannan in his campaign to win back Krenz. We both know how that ended."

"Through no fault of yours," Adris countered and motioned for them to take a seat in side by side chairs. "Aliz, few of us get the luxury of choosing what we become. You have been a quiet hand behind the true power in the universe for as long as I have been alive. Those decades of peering over the shoulder, of watching, of listening, make you more valuable than anyone else on this new council. We need you. I need you."

"You don't know what you're asking of me." Aliz fought back the tears threating to fall as realization dawned.

A comforting hand landed on her knee. "But I do, only too well. I need to know everything about Krenz, the Conclave, and the rest. Your knowledge may be what brings our enemies down for good."

"What about all those who died pretending to do just that?"

"What about the countless trillions you can save?" Adris replied just as fast. "I'm not expecting an answer now. Take some time. Integrate back into proper society and think on it. I will send my valet, Tempest, to you in a few days. Whatever you need is at your disposal. Think about it, that's all I ask."

Aliz left without another word. She came to Mannus Prime thinking to leave the past behind. Yet here she stood. Once more in the eye of the storm. Perhaps this time it would be different.

Revenge was a powerful motivator the strongest struggled against. The First Counselor Elect resumed her seat at her desk and had motioned for Tempest to enter as the woman hovered in the doorway. The younger woman appeared energized like never before. Her adventures during the escape from Dalafar awakened something raw, hungry, deep within.

"Governess," Tempest said.

"What did I tell you about that?" Adris scolded.

Cheeks flushing, Tempest stood a little straighter. "Old habits. My apologies."

Adris waved off her apology. "Never mind. I need you to keep your eyes on that one. She wants to help. I can see it, but she teeters on the verge of breakdown. Give her a gentle nudge when needed. We can't afford to lose her. Not now."

"I'll do my best," Tempest affirmed.

Adris smiled. "You always do. Is there anything else to report?"

"The former Cardinal Seniorus is now free. He and the Inquisitor are searching Eger City for rumors of those loyal to the insurrection. If all goes well, we can spring the trap by the end of the week."

"At least one item is going according to plan." Adris sighed. "Go ahead. I have a feeling I won't be needing you for the rest of the day. No doubt our esteemed new counselors will feel the need to orate and lock us in debate for the rest of the night. Damned politicians."

"Something tells me neither of us are going to have a fun day," Tempest commented. "I'll be here when you need me."

Adris watched her go and prepared herself for the madness yet to come.

Tempest headed through the winding corridors of the new administratum's housing floor, almost making it back to Aliz's door before being seeing the woman was talking to a man in a Guard uniform. Pausing, she watched Aliz slip into her quarters after a brief conversation. His gaze immediately fell on Tempest. She halted in midstride. She recognized him from when Aliz arrived but knew nothing else other than he appeared dangerous.

"She doesn't want to be bothered."

"None of us do," Tempest said, giving him a warm smile.

She found him rugged, attractive in his own way. His eyes bore a haunted look. The scars, the slight hunch of his shoulders suggesting weariness she'd never endured. His stance whispered lethality. The sidearm on his hip reinforced her theory. Men like this were most often found at the tip of the spear, where the worst happened.

"You can go back to whoever you work for and tell them," he insisted, unimpressed.

Pushing down her thoughts, Tempest extended her hand. "My name is Tempest. I am the First Counselor's assistant. You are?"

"Captain Julian."

That was it. Nothing more. The perfect soldier's reply. She knew the name. Knew the hells he'd gone through during the final days before fleeing Vau Prime. Her respect rose.

"Captain Julian, it is my pleasure," she wiggled her fingers for emphasis before he reluctantly shook her still outstretched hand. "Perhaps we've gotten off on the wrong foot."

"Doesn't seem like we've gotten off at all. Whatever you're pushing, I'm not interested. Neither is Aliz. We've been through enough and don't need your political games. Hells, the lady needs a year alone on a vacation."

"I'm sure we all could use such, Captain." Tempest replied. "But these are dark times for us all. I wish we could allow her to slip away to quiet retirement. I do." She sighed. "The First Counselor holds her in high esteem and would see her regain a measure of that old confidence she wore when Lorenu Phos was still alive."

Julian folded his arms across his chest. "Just leave her alone."

"These are desperate times. None of us can afford to sit idle while the enemy grows stronger," she insisted. Frustration seeped into her words. "If it were up to me, none would ever call upon her again. The First Counselor is insistent, however. We need her, Julian. She has decades of experience navigating the halls of power. Without an asset like that, Adris will be hard pressed to hold this new council together long enough for it to cement and take hold."

At his silence, she stepped closer, looking up into pained, green eyes. "We can do this, Julian, but only by working together. The first council meeting is later this afternoon. It would go far to have Aliz there, even if she does not speak. She is a symbol, whether she acknowledges it or not. In this age, we need all the symbols we can get."

Julian softened. "I'll see what I can do but know this. Anyone seeking to turn her to their political advantage will have me to answer to."

"That is all I can ask. Thank you."

Eger City celebrated the dawn of a new era. Premature, in the eyes of many. Thousands took to the street as the foundation of the new council began. It was a momentous occasion, spurred on by criers and well-wishers fueling propaganda. The old ways, complete with corruption and greed, were done. Today was a new dawn. A better chance for the common man to rise above his station and fulfill his dreams. For some, it remained an illusion born from the deepest regrets.

Music drifted between the streets. The smells of meats and other delicious treats followed. Wine and beer flowed. Mannus Prime languished beneath the blanket of despair for so long few were willing to let an opportunity go to waste. For those locked inside the council chambers, it proved far tougher.

Adris found the notion of a round table amusing, if somewhat concerning. She wondered how long before others thought themselves equal to chief triumvirate and caused problems among them. She saw the careful representations of the old regimes, minus the Inquisition. There was no room for their prejudices in this dream. Careful not to abandon the old ways entirely, the new members were a mix of military and politician. Statesmen and reluctant opportunists. She wondered if any, herself included, were up to the task before them.

With a crisp glance to the attendant, Adris signaled the commencement. The chime ran through the room. She felt the first glimmer of true hope, even as she refused to believe it herself. Her gaze swept over the eight others. Standou of Orlei sat to her immediate right. His elevation to Second Counselor proved one of the more difficult tasks. To her left sat Virom in his position as Third Counselor. The others were Torgast, Matthias, Falchi, Phaesl, and Yazie of Storbor. Completing the new council was Aliz who looked like she didn't belong, despite her years of working behind the scenes at the Conclave's highest levels.

Arrayed against the far wall was a host of reporters and photographers waiting to spread word of the official start to a new human empire. The momentous occasion would be documented and spread across the stars. Adris argued against it, knowing the declaration would only spark outrage among those planets loyal to the Inquisition and incite increased violence on her allies—she'd been outvoted. The fledgling council wanted the publicity. Without knowing how the wind might turn, Adris gave in. There'd be more than enough opportunity for infighting in the coming months. No need to ruffle feathers right from the start.

A slender balcony ran the length of the room, just wide enough for the ring of armed men and women in the new navy-blue uniforms of the Council Guard. Taken from the best Guard units on Mannus, each was a distinguished veteran with incomparable service records. They were all volunteers, selected from thousands. At their head was Captain Julian, resolute and determined to prevent the disaster of Vau Prime from repeating. His command group were survivors of Krenz.

Drawing a steadying breath, Adris Moscasco called the meeting to order; the click and whirl of a hundred cameras and video recordings began. "Ladies and gentlemen, today marks the beginning of a new life. The dawn of the Confederation is one long in coming. Overdue. Each of us has taken up the call to become the first defenders of the scope of humanity. We are pledged to serving the countless lives of former Conclave jurisdiction, even those on planets under the twisted regime of Alain Nye's Inquisition. Humanity deserves more than the base corruption of the former ruling orders."

Murmurs rippled through the assembly. Adris strengthened her tone, raising her voice.

"I make no false promises. The way forward will not be easy. We must first defeat a sizeable and capable enemy before peace can return and society can advance the way we were always meant to. My friends, we embark upon a journey that has only occurred once in our storied history."

She paused to look those closest in the eye. "Three thousand years ago we escaped the shackles of the gods. Forced into lives burdened by torment and unspeakable cruelty, our ancestors struggled to live. They cut and clawed their way across the stars to forge better lives, all while promising to never return to the cruelty once inflicted upon them. Now, one of those very monsters we fought so hard to escape from sits on a throne of broken bones in the very heart of all we once held dear! Amongeratix, the destroyer of worlds, seeks to ensnare us under his will. Should that happen, our way of life will shatter, and we will find ourselves locked in shackles once more."

Heads nodded. Tears welled. She had them.

"We shall fight Amongeratix with every available resource. We shall not stop until he is defeated, once and for all. Many of us will not survive the coming storm, but humanity will go on. We will grow stronger, better. We will finally discover our full potential and spread a shining light across the universe for all species."

Adris envisioned the rising wave of cheers and hope spreading through all who listened to her words. They would spread her message across the stars, to every planet, city, and village. Perhaps a fresh wave of support would pour into Mannus Prime. Perhaps not. She was under no false pretense of the population's total support. Some would adhere to the Inquisition until the last shot was fired, possibly longer. It didn't matter. The war would end.

Finished, she nestled back in her chair and waited. She'd felt

Standou stir. The Second Counselor proved a most difficult man and, while she had no reservations to his loyalties to the new order, found his sly manners deceiving. He'd been the unanimous choice for second. She doubted he would have accepted anything less. Adris had seen too many like him during her time in government. Dalafar was littered with petty politicians hungry for advancement. While she knew little of Orlei, it took little imagination to envision Standou exerting his dominance. True to form, he didn't disappoint when he began to speak.

"Thank you for those words of encouragement, First Counselor. It is evident we voted wisely. The immediate future may be troubled with storms, but together we will see our people through and begin a new empire the likes of which have been relegated to dreams."

She winced at the term empire. The great human diaspora of three thousand years ago ensured the unsustainability of one massive government. Talk already had begun of breaking the universe into regional confederations akin to neighboring kingdoms. In concept, it would strengthen individual planets and encourage increased commerce and diplomatic relations. However, it took little imagination to envision a host of problems. That was inevitable. Cautious, she'd warned Standou to hold back on such a declaration.

"Thank you, Second Counselor. I'm sure we will have plenty of opportunity to bring our new vision for the future to life in the aftermath of this war. Are there any other points of order?"

One by one, the others on the fledgling council announced themselves and their initial concerns. Adris listened to each with placid interest. The meeting felt like it dragged on, but then didn't they all? After the last finished she rose.

"If no one has anything further to add, this inaugural session is ended. Thank you all for attending and being here at the start of something far greater than each of us."

FIVE

3215 A.G. (After gods), Great Library, planet Wexanos.

Haggle grunted as the boot struck his forehead. He popped up from his bunk, an angry scowl of confusion gracing his features. Laughter sounded. The rest of the platoon was already dressing and preparing for the day.

Haggle found little to gripe about in his current state but failed to appreciate adhering to military discipline and rising before the sun. In his estimation, they'd more than earned some time off and the opportunity to forget, just for a while, the severity of their situation. Clearly command felt otherwise. Pausing to rub the sore spot on his forehead, he slipped from the bed.

"I'm keeping this!" he shouted, brandishing the boot overhead to another round of laughter.

Jelin Quint, squad leader who had replaced Haggle, entered at the declaration. A wet towel hung over one bare shoulder. The veteran tossed his shower kit on his bed and glanced at Haggle. "What in the hells happened to you?"

Haggle feigned confusion. "With what?"

Jelin pointed. "For starters, you have the impression of a boot print on your forehead. Did I miss something?"

More laughter. Haggle's face darkened.

"Nothing special."

"Uh huh. Let's not make a habit of it. How am I going to explain why my assistant squad leader is starting to look like a rotting fruit?"

Unable to contain themselves, the squad broke out in uproar. Even Haggle laughed. He'd learned long ago not to take himself too seriously. Their lives were hard enough without a sense of humor. Morale being everything to a line unit, Haggle was the first one to laugh at himself. Anything less was a disservice to the others.

"Roger that, Sergeant."

Jerlin sighed. "You've got thirty, people. El-Tee wants to see everyone in the main hangar in one hour. You know the drill. Shit, shower, and shave, and head to the mess hall. I have a feeling this is going to be a long day."

"We live charmed lives, people," Hollis sniped from across the bay. Her comment inspired a round of groans.

The heavy gunner, Beve, yawned and stretched. His bones snapped in a way they all felt. "Charmed. Funny."

"Careful, Beve. Wouldn't want you hurting those vocal cords," Doc Little jumped in as he slid his uniform top on. "Although, it's been a while since I had to practice any battlefield medicine. Maybe you could sing us a song?"

"I like songs," Palco added. "My granny used sing us classics about a drunken old man stumbling home and, well, guess it wasn't a happy song after all."

Several of them paused to give the big man a wary glance. Haggled headed towards the showers as Jelin closed his eyes, stating, "I'm thinking we push back the muster and do some old-fashioned squad drills for the rest of the day. You people have too much free time on your hands."

"I'm getting tired of you being promoted," Annalilly muttered. She stepped out of the shower and reached for a towel.

Fies did his best to remain calm. It was the old argument and, for reasons he failed to understand, she enjoyed waking up ready for a fight. "What are you bitching about? I didn't make you a lieutenant this time."

The newly promoted captain brushed imaginary dust from his rank pip on his shoulder. A playful twinkle in his eyes.

"Yeah, thanks."

Fies refused to back down. "Look, you're still an NCO. The brains behind the platoon and all that."

"I'm a fucking master sergeant!" she ranted, running a hand towel over her scalp. "You do remember what they do? Paperwork! Admin! I'm reduced to a babysitter."

"You still have your platoon. I can't afford you bumping up. Not without a suitable replacement. And it doesn't look like that's going to happen anytime soon. Falchi can't send anyone in time for the next assignment," Fies soothed. "It's not like my job is any easier. I didn't ask to make captain. Couldn't even refuse. You know the drill. I get promoted. You get promoted. That's just the way of things."

"Will you shut the fuck up already," she grumbled. "Maybe I

should have taken that looey promotion. To keep you from bitching if nothing else." She glared at him over her shoulder. "When are we expecting orders?"

"I don't know. Rumor has it Mannus is ramping up everything from weapons and ammunition production to combat units. Shouldn't be too much longer now that word has gotten out about the Inquisitor General's assassination."

"I wouldn't call Amongeratix murdering him in front of everyone an assassination," Annalilly snapped. "We're heading for a shitstorm, Fies. Mark my words."

"You know all the right things to say to a guy, don't you."

"Ha! You're lucky you called muster, or I'd do more than speak to you."

He held up a hand. "Tonight. I'm already worn out."

She snapped her towel, catching him in the upper thigh. "Pansy. You're getting soft."

"Small price to pay for staying alive. Come on. We have work to do."

A wicked gleam entered her eyes. "Are you sure we don't have a little time?"

"Maybe," he replied, and pulled her closer.

They stood in formation for the first time in longer than any remembered. One hundred and twenty men and women in combat fatigues standing at attention as their platoon sergeants inspected them. They'd come from across the stars, from eighty different planets, to serve the ideals of the Conclave. Before the dark times. Before the war. Most were veterans, having proved themselves in places like Hawker's Gate, Crimeat, Kharsis, and Mannus Prime. Those who hadn't been on the front lines had the benefit of integrating into the company through their exemplary service records.

The weak and the slackers had been weeded out long ago. All that remained were the dedicated. The survivors. One hundred and twenty souls.

And they belonged to Fies.

He stood before them; hands locked behind his back. The immensity of the moment wasn't lost on him. Company inspections were a time-honored tradition dating back to the foundations of the Guard. Though his unit was far removed from the front-line divisions, permanently assigned to the whims of Tannus, Fies was determined to maintain a semblance of standards, if for no other sake than his own sanity.

They'd been behind the lines too often, left to small unit tactics in dire situations they weren't properly trained for. The invasion of Mannus Prime was the closest they came to a traditional battle in years. A return to normalcy came at cost, however. Ranks depleted. The promise of casualties rose. Integrating replacements was part of the military condition but he wished more of his people had chosen to leave the uniform, like Jers. Far too many of his Guards had been placed in body bags over the years, others sent home missing limbs or so stricken with posttraumatic stress they were shells of their former selves.

He wondered how many of those before him were going to meet similar fates. Haggle? Desril? Beve? Himself? He ran through the names, squad by squad, until the inspection ended. They looked good. Damned good. Platoon leaders resumed their positions before their units, snapping to attention.

Clearing his throat, Fies focused on the task at hand. "Master Sergeant!"

Annalilly snapped to and marched from a step behind him to standing before him. Her salute was crisp. "Sir!"

"The company is yours. I want all squad leaders and above in my office in ten. Dismissed." Fies returned the salute, executed an about face, and headed towards the closest building.

From behind him he heard Annalilly shout, "You heard the man. Put your people to work and report at the double. Fall out!"

Power vibrated through her, causing her teeth to rattle. Grimacing, Elisa loosened her grip on *Grimfurvor*. The vibrations slowed but failed to stop. Satisfied she focused on the automaton. As usual, the robot showed no emotion, betrayed no inherent flaw. It lumbered toward her with clear intent. In place of hands, it bore a small axe and round ball designed for crushing bones.

A handful of slashes scrapped across the silver body, accompanied by countless dents. Sparks danced from a small hole under the left arm—the only victory Elisa managed to date. It was enough. She felt emboldened for the first time since escaping the Forsaken Path. Victory, small as it was, meant she was improving. It also meant the machine could be destroyed. Blood stained her teeth from an earlier slap across her face, lending her the look of a feral creature fighting for its life. She sensed weakness in the automaton and confidence bloomed.

They clashed in a whirlwind of violence. Sparks rained down after each strike. Flesh bruised. Metal dented. The last Elisa recalled was scoring a strike in the automaton's chest, but when she tried to dislodge *Grimfurvor* she felt the impact against the side of her head and then darkness.

She awoke with a groan, stars dancing behind her eyes. A rag was pressed against her head and the pain subsided beneath a wave of cold. "I'm beginning to fucking hate this machine."

"Ah, *farisi*. Give me the cursed weapon and I shall vanquish your foe!" Ah'muf boasted.

She laughed at his false bravado. Another wave of pain washed through her. "Ah'muf, please, stop making me laugh. My head is going to burst open."

He made a show of bowing before holding the cloth back against her head. "Of course. Of course. My sincerest apologies. Were it within my power, I would fight your battles for you, but alas, I am a mere desert dweller with little knowledge of combat."

"We each have our place in this life, Ah'muf. I was never given a choice. Yours is yet before you," she replied and gestured for a glass of water from the pitcher on the table beside the bed. "One day I'm going to beat that damned machine. Mark my words."

"What will you do then?"

"Shove that blade straight up the Bloody Man's ass for getting me involved in this disaster."

Ah'muf shook his head. "We have been through this. The giant did as he must, so that you may fulfill your destiny. He is not the evil your mind contrives."

"He killed everyone I ever knew," she spat, but the argument felt stale. She already accepted the past, having come to terms somewhere along the Forsaken Path.

"I'm sorry," she said after seeing the hurt in his eyes. "I'm never myself after getting the shit beaten out of me by a robot. Can you help me to the bath?"

"I was hoping you'd say that," he said with a wink.

"You dirty desert dog."

*

The next fight proved more of the same. Elisa got closer to taking her foe down, but close seldom won battles.

Elisa went to find Tannus. He had the answers she needed. Getting him to talk was another matter. Determination marking every step, she refused to back down this time. Her measured gait concealed most of the aches and pains, but a slight limp prevented her from moving with full fluidity. She passed a handful of librarians, ever their faces averted, though whether out of respect or shame remained uncertain.

She found Tannus flipping through the pages of a manuscript. His brow furrowed. Elisa spied the ornately designed pages, accented by images of creatures she'd never heard of. She caught the image of a mother and daughter and paused. Her mind drifted, going down roads she'd long forgotten. An image of her mother holding her hands and dancing with her in a circle spread warmth through her, until she realized she could no longer remember her mother's face. The golden tint in her voice had faded. Only the smile remained. Beautiful. Loving. It was all she had left of her mother.

Tannus' booming voice broke her thoughts. "My apologies, Paladin. You should have said something. I did not realize you were waiting."

She flushed. "I don't like being interrupted. I figure you'd be the same way."

"Normally I would agree with you, but these are unique times."

Elisa cocked her head. "Are they? Surely you've been through this a hundred times."

An unreadable emotion flickered in his eyes. "In a manner of speaking, yes. My brother and I have waged war across a hundred worlds over the course of our feud. None have carried the finality of this conflict though."

"What makes this time so special?"

"You."

The answer caught her off guard. Elisa swallowed the lump growing in her throat. Weight settled onto her shoulders, threatening to steal what little strength she clung to.

"I'll be the first one to tell you there's nothing special about me."

The mask concealing his true emotions slipped. "What is on your mind, Elisa?"

"I'm not getting the hang of it," she admitted, sliding down into an empty chair. The softness produced a groan. She needed to make it quick, or he'd be in for a fight getting her out of the chair. "What am I missing? Why can't I get *Grimfurvor* to work for me?"

"You ask questions I lack answers for," he replied.

"I highly doubt—"

Tannus held up a hand. "Hear me out. Paladin and Prophet were never in my arena. They are creations of my brother and, as such, so is *Grimfurvor*. He forged it through arcane arts long lost to time and memory. Sorrow has always been a tinkerer. He thought the weapon would be deterrent enough to keep Amongeratix in check, negating his abilities to an extent at the proper moment in time. That none have succeeded in obtaining the weapon until now suggest he may be right."

Uninterested in the specifics of the weapon's creation, Elisa asked, "Where did he find the magic for it? I don't recall seeing any of you use magic."

"You would have to ask him." The blunt reply amplified her rage. "I know you are worried. The task handed down to you is one I do not envy anyone. No answer I provide will enlighten you to mystic secrets. Nor will they provide a blueprint from which to alleviate all your problems. What I can tell you, encourage even, is for you look within. Find your inner spark and quiet your mind. It will come to you. It must."

"I know, I know. I have a destiny to fulfill," she groused. "I'm getting a little tired of being told what I must do. My entire life has been dancing at the end of strings to unseen masters. Just once I'd like to be free."

He said nothing.

The silence grew to the point Elisa knew little else would come from their discussion. She needed clarity and, if that was the only way she was going to access the true strength of the dagger, she knew now what to do. "Tannus, I need to leave the library."

"I know," he replied. "Summon Fistel. He will guide you to a place untouched by any human life in centuries. The answers you seek are there."

PGN *Solstice*, high orbit over planet Wexanos.

Sharlyn settled into the familiar chair, reflecting on how the seat perfectly molded to her figure. Alone for the first time in recent memory, Sharlyn took in the banks of terminals and computer screens. Soon they would be filled with incoming data streams. Thirty sailors would bring her ship back to life as they set sail across the cosmos in search of an elusive prize. But for now, she enjoyed the solitude.

She inserted the disk given to her by Vicente Blackheart, one only she knew about, keyed in her command code, and waited. Sharlyn began drumming her fingers on the armrest as the seconds dragged by. She began to wonder if Blackheart conned her. If he never had any intention of being contacted by her or one of the Guard again. He'd been adamant about maintaining his neutrality in the aftermath of the hunt for Presha Von and she couldn't fault him. They'd been pushed to the edge too often.

The screen hummed to life, revealing his face. She smiled despite herself. Men like Blackheart were a pox on the Conclave. They took what they wanted, ignoring the rule of law for base desires and personal greed. Blackheart was no different. He'd raided and plundered countless ships and space stations throughout the course of his pirate career, making a name as one of the most notorious villains in recent history.

"That too less time than I imagined," he greeted. "You just couldn't stay away."

Sharlyn refused to rise to the bait. "I have a business proposition for you."

"The last time I worked with the Guard almost got me killed." Blackheart shook his head. "You specifically nearly caused my demise, Captain Sharlyn August."

"That would be Admiral," she corrected.

He hummed. "Regardless, I am not in the position to come to your beck and call whenever the wind blows wrong. I gave you this device for use in the direst of circumstances, not for social calls." He smirked. "Congratulations, by the way."

"Thank you—that's not the reason I reached out. I've been given an assignment and I need you and your crew," she said. She fought to keep the smile from her reaching her face.

"Sorry, hon. The *Shrike* is holed up for repairs. She's not going anywhere."

She wanted to curse at the easy way he deflected. "I didn't say anything about that rust bucket you call a ship. She's too old, too outdated, and no match for what's fallen into my lap."

Darkness flashed in his eyes. "Careful, *Admiral*. I don't take kindly to insults."

"Truths, not insults. We know each other too well for bandied words." Sharlyn noticed she had him off guard with that. Now was the time to swoop in for the kill. "You've seen the news from Vau Prime I assume?"

"Who hasn't? That monster seems to have settled in nicely. I wish you the best of luck going up against him and that beast of a ship."

She caught the sincerity in his words mingled among the brutal honesty. Not that she blamed him. The prospect of facing *Behemoth* frightened her until a few days ago. Now, she believed she had a fighting chance.

"What if I told you I was in command of a fleet of ships just like his?"

He turned his head and rubbed his jaw. When he spoke it was measured, deliberate. "I'd say you needed some shore leave. There are no other ships like that, and good riddance. Nothing good could come from it."

"What reason would I have to lie, Vicente?" she asked. "We both know you've been officially pardoned by the new Confederation."

"They're not in power yet," he countered. "Whatever their aspirations on Mannus Prime are, they haven't reached across the stars yet." A thoughtful look stared back at her. "Still, supposing I did believe you. What would you need me for?"

Got you, you snide bastard. "Admiral Falchi and the new council are sending me trained crews, but I need people who break the rules. People like you. We're going up against the worst threat the modern universe has ever seen, and I want to handpick the people who I believe will give me the best chance at surviving." She paused, giving him the opportunity for doubt. "Unless I called the wrong man. I know you're covering those grey hairs up. Past your prime. Out of touch and waiting to be forgotten."

Silence settled between them.

She knew, whether he admitted it or not, how much he longed for a true place in this new universe. Sharlyn was giving that to him, if he accepted.

"I need an answer, Vicente. I'm shipping out soon, with or without you."

"How long do I have to give you an answer?"

Just like that. No delay. No hesitation.

"Sounds like you've already made your mind up."

"Whether I have or not is irrelevant. You're asking me to put my people's lives on the line for your cause, again, not ours. I need to show the courtesy of presenting this to them before you get my answer."

"I can give you one day."

"Not big on leeway, eh?" His familiar smirk returned. "Fine. One day it is. You'll have my answer."

Her finger hovered over the termination button as he calls out, "Hey, August?"

"Yes?"

"Good to hear from you."

He cut the transmission before she had the chance to retort, leaving Sharlyn grinning like a child.

This is stupid. What was I thinking? Tannus manipulates as easily as his brother. Presha Von swept down the immaculate halls, past statues of historical figures, tapestries dating back to the foundations of Conclave, and paintings worth more than some planets. Shadowing her was the blue-skinned warrior turned librarian, Banak Laminel. No doubt to ensure she caused no mischief with her new freedom. Her old self would have spun and confronted him. Humility suggested otherwise. She had no choice but to go forward, to forge a modicum of humanity back from the debacle she'd placed herself in.

Her thoughts swirled as she headed towards the suite she'd been told to visit, desperate to figure out who she might have killed and how they could possibly be alive today. Plenty of faces taunted her, but none stuck out enough for concern.

She arrived at the doors before she knew it. Her resolve weakened. Hand shaking as she raised to knock, Presha felt the rug pulled from under her when the door opened, and a young man stood before her.

"I don't know you."

His jaw clenched. Presha wanted to flee. To run back to her chambers and let the world forget she existed. She forced herself to stand fast. To look him in the eye. Doing so only reinforced her initial assessment. She'd never seen this man.

"Perhaps you should come inside," the man suggested, before looking over her shoulder. "There is no chance of violence, Banak Laminel."

The librarian grunted before departing.

"He means well, and I certainly wouldn't cross him," the man explained when Presha hesitated. "Come in, please. We have much to discuss."

Presha cleared her throat. "I would like to know your name first, if you please."

"Ah, that." He studied her a moment before replying, "I am Senior Inquisitor Tolde Breed and you stabbed me on Kharsis." His tone remained neutral, lacking emotion or animosity.

Presha flinched. He was dead. "You can't be. I remember his face. He hunted me long enough."

"As I said, there is much to discuss." Tolde gestured for her to enter.

They settled across from one another in uncomfortable silence. Presha waited for the barrage of accusations and spewed hatred. Yet his face remained an unreadable mask as Tolde explained his story after their fateful encounter on the now dead planet. Reborn for purposes still unknown, she marveled at the confluence of universal energies going in to return him to the land of the living. With such powerful allies, how could evil possibly win?

"That is a difficult tale to accept, even after all I've seen and experienced," she replied.

"I don't profess to understand the intricacies, only the results," he said. "The Blood Witches are most effective, as I'm sure you are aware."

"I may have had a run in or two with them, yes," she agreed. "Tolde, I am a proud woman. Arrogant one might say. But I have fallen far since you last saw me. It appears neither of us are the people we once were. None of that changes the fact I am sorry for my actions. I … I lost myself somewhere in the delusions of power and fabricated glory."

Tolde waved a hand. "There is nothing to apologize for. This is war. As you can see, I made it through that little trial."

She shook her head. "That doesn't make it right."

"No, but I accept your apology."

And like that, the weight slid from her heart, taking with it the ice wall suffocating her emotions. Presha buried her face in her hands and wept.

"You must think me a monster," she said between sobs.

His silence caused Presha to laugh. She, for good or bad, remained the same polarizing figure she'd always been.

"I'm not that woman anymore, Tolde. I swear it," she offered.

"Tannus wouldn't have allowed you on his planet if you were," Tolde replied. "For reasons he refuses to explain, he finds value in your presence."

She shook her head, still uncertain how far she trusted her host. "I bring no value. The only act of justice I performed was in rescuing his cousin."

She watched various emotions flitter across his face before he responded, "I've learned much from them since my rebirth. Tannus is headstrong and proud, but there is a softness he hides well. I believe he longs for a return to the time when the brothers were unified."

Her eyes widened. "Before he dared question his father openly."

He nodded. "We are approaching the end of whatever this is. I suggest you provide Tannus with whatever intelligence or information he requires. If you are truly who you claim to be, you will save lives and take the next steps on your road to redemption."

"Will you help me?" She surprised herself. Presha had never asked for assistance, especially not from a man she once held as a foe and killed.

Tolde's gaze softened. "I cannot. My focus is on another cancer loose in the universe. She is a creature far worse than any aspiration you might have held."

"She?"

"The only name we have is Kaline. She is an agent of the cult of Rengu, moving from planet to planet to subvert the population and bring chaos. Stopping her is my top priority."

She gasped. Presha hadn't heard that name in a long time. Long enough to almost have forgotten.

"You know her," Tolde stated.

"I did. She is a creature of habit and a servant of darkness."

"Tannus agrees." He paused. "How would you like a purpose? A means to redemption?"

Presha opened her mouth but closed it quickly lest she betray her true thoughts. "What do you have in mind?"

"Join me. Together we can hunt her down and end the threat and, I could use the help."

"But Tannus—"

"Let me worry about Tannus. This might prove beneficial for both of us."

His matter of fact tone awakened a measure of confidence she hadn't felt since stepping onto Hawker's Gate. Her mouth went dry as she contemplated her next words. "What do I have to do?"

SIX

3215 A.G. (After gods) Zevistya Spaceport, low continent, planet Vau Prime.

The last stand. Seven hundred loyal Guards under the command of Colonel Freyote stayed behind to stall the advancing enemy long enough for the rest of the army to escape. Seven hundred men and women dead and left to the elements, for Mobus Kale refused to honor the old codes and bury his foes with respect. Bodies littered the abandoned spaceport, ignored as engineer battalions ferried in to begin reconstruction. Thousands of pressganged civilians tore down all buildings but the old command and control center. Debris flowed out on a steady stream of haulers to reprocessing facilities built along the coast. With the threat of enemy interdiction, resources became high commodity.

Mobus Kale cared little for the hardships of the Navy. The faults among the admiralty in being unprepared for the intensity behind the recent incursion lay squarely on their shoulders and had little impact on his efforts. With Krenz under new leadership, Mobus solidified his hold on the Army. Fresh divisions were being trained on Tatarast Island then being shipped to the staging areas on the low continent for pending deployment. Thirty thousand Guards were settling in as they awaited orders.

Change in leadership held those orders in limbo. Kale was infuriated, having finally vanquished the last stains of his nemesis, he longed to take the fight across the stars. Amongeratix promised him his due, but on a different schedule. The end approached, but it would be through Amongeratix's direction. He assured Kale much still needed solidifying before unleashing their full fury upon those foolish enough to stand against them. Mired under the bureaucracy, Mobus Kale kept his head down and focused on his primary task.

A task made more difficult thanks to the Navy's incompetence. The enemy fleet had been beaten back, but not without great cost to the planetary defenses. Dozens of capital ships destroyed. Several more crippled and towed to drydock. Thousands dead due to sheer incompetence. Soldiers were expendable, but only to a degree and then only through victory. Death by defeat was insulting.

Mired beneath his perceived impotence, Mobus stood on the control tower balcony staring at the pit of burning bodies. Much against his will, his surgeons insisted on burning the corpses lest disease spread through the camp. Either way, the stench permeated all. Flames reflecting in his eyes, his thoughts turned toward the inevitable campaign to crush the upstart armies growing on Mannus Prime.

Latest reports suggested their foes had established an impenetrable ring of orbital defense platforms while amassing a substantial fleet. Squadrons of Prekhauten ships defected almost daily. Those who weren't stopped made their way to Mannus. Soon, he knew, the enemy would have enough strength to move. Regardless of the propaganda spewed nightly, Vau Prime had never been weaker. A single strong push and it would topple—if he failed to act.

A flight of troop transports emerged from the western haze. Nose twisted from the stench of burning flesh, Mobus headed inside to brood.

Inquisition Headquarters, Krenz.

Ezekiel Goethe set the datapad on his desk and closed his eyes. It was the third similar report received in the last week, suggesting their consolidation efforts were falling behind schedule. No one expected the enemy to move as fast as they were. With matters on Mannus Prime advancing rapidly, Ezekiel started to feel the pressure. No doubt Amongeratix's wrath would be fierce once he learned this information. The Inquisitor General expected a summons shortly.

"You are certain this is accurate?" he asked, the question directed to the woman standing before him.

"As near as we can tell. The enemy has established a ruling council and is calling itself the Confederation. They are building fresh armies, collecting fleets of ships, and manufacturing munitions, equipment, and arms at a rapid pace."

"All on one world," he mused. "Imagine what it must be like having so many independent agencies working toward the same goal."

"Inquisitor General?"

Realizing he'd spoken aloud, Ezekiel cleared his throat. "Is there anything else to add? I don't want to be caught with my trousers around my ankles when I am called to answer."

"No, sir. Our intelligence is restricted due to distance and their impressive internal security mechanisms. We estimate a minimum of twenty-three spies have gone silent."

Killed, or worse. His agents were trained to commit suicide in the event of compromise, but humans were notoriously weak of will. When pressed, he wasn't sure how many would willingly bite down on the poison capsule, or even have time to ingest it before being apprehended. *Could I?* A cold chill trickled down his spine. Ezekiel built his career on the backs of those less suspecting among the Order, sacrificing any standing in his way. A ruthless man in every regard, he was what the Inquisition should have been from the beginning.

Until standing before Amongeratix, he had never felt true competition. The Three terrified him, and for good reason. The man's raw power, fueled by hate and aggression impressed Ezekiel in ways he'd never experienced. It also opened his eyes to a new wave of threats no one on Vau Prime was prepared for.

Threats he now answered to. Calling Amongeratix unstable fell short. Ezekiel found the man irrational, driven by old hurts long forgotten by the rest of the universe. He'd also surrounded himself with psychopaths. The rogue Blood Witches and that ape Geres Auk proved equally daunting for any seeking to establish their claim on the new universe.

"Sir?"

He waved the Inquisitor away, having forgotten she remained. "Dismissed. I want all actionable intelligence brought directly to me the moment we receive it. Is that understood?"

"Yes, sir."

Once the door closed behind her, Ezekiel slammed a fist into his desk, cursing under his breath at how his bid for control continued being stymied by the interference of what he deemed lesser beings.

The end had come. She'd been on the run for days, desperately trying to remain one step ahead of her hunters. Rumors reached her, whispers of friends and colleagues already caught and executed on sight. Images of red robes swinging from ropes on random light poles plagued the nightly newsvids. Every monk, priest, and Cardinal was to be executed on sight. Everyone except for those few surviving members of the defunct Forum. The ruling one hundred Cardinals responsible for allowing this nightmare to unfold. So intent on playing internal power games, none foresaw the arrival of Amongeratix and the end of a three thousand year old dream.

Porii Daam wasted no time regarding her fallen companions. Each fled in separate directions, determined to escape, and reap vengeance upon those who'd betrayed them. She knew it was but a dream. Far too many of the Forum were dead to mount any effective counteroffensive. Strannan's insurgent cells hadn't been heard from since the surprise assault on the Vau System. Porii imagined those with enough sense took to whatever shuttles they could find and left the capital far behind.

A flare popped in the street adjacent to the one she crept down, bathing the surroundings in a red light. Whistles blared. Vehicles roared to life. Patrollers on foot hurried in her direction. Caught in a trap, Porii Daam saw what little remaining of her life dwindle to a few short breaths. Tired of hiding, she moved to the center of the street to await her fate.

"Hey shithead, you're going to get yourself killed standing there like that," a man's voice called.

Porii turned, surprised to find an odd pair lingering in the shadows of a nearby building. Neither looked like they belonged with each other. The shorter waved her over; a quiet desperation twisting his face. He bore the look of a man who had witnessed enough death, even if he was crosseyed.

"Come on! Are you daft, lady?" he called.

Porii hesitated. Another flare popped. Time was up. Shedding her robes of state, stripping down to the form clinging bodysuit most Cardinals wore under their official attire, she hurried across the street. The taller man slipped into the shadows, accessing a concealed tunnel leading down.

"Smart move dumping those robes," the shorter man said as he gestured for her to go before him. "I'm Thopos. The dour man ahead of us is Edam Boone."

"Porii." She saw no harm in the truth of her name. Not now. Her face was plastered across the city, making her instantly recognizable. If either of these men had the inclination to turn her in and claim the reward, there wasn't much she could do about it. It was either face instant death in the streets or be led to it on a leash—she followed.

They pushed forward, leaving her soaked in sweat and gasping for breath. A luxurious lifestyle left her sore and out of shape. Porii stared at the back of the man before her, wondering when the trap might spring. Cloistered in half-darkness, she envisioned the ease in which he could stop, turn, and slice her throat. Or worse. The fallen Cardinal felt her steps falter.

"Keep moving. There's no time," Thopos said from behind.

"Where are we going?"

"To a safe house. At least for now. The Inquisition is choking the city, forcing us deeper into hiding," Edam replied without looking back. "We must adapt or we die."

Choked by the rush of disparate thoughts, Porii picked up the pace.

They wormed through old service tunnels, stepping through muck and piles of refuse. She stared into the eyes of more dispossessed than she could easily count. The people of Krenz, once proud and elitist, forced to cower in the shadows and pray the gods would save them. Fools. If only they knew the gods were a lie.

"Come, we are almost there," Edam announced.

They rounded a corner, stepped over a sewage runoff, and stopped. Edam pushed a stone in the wall and a secret panel slid open. He waved them in. Once the door closed, he confronted Porii, blaster in hand. "Why are you here?"

Confused, she held out her empty hands. "I thought that was evident."

"Maybe. Maybe not. You wouldn't be the first Cardinal seeking to get into the Inquisition's good graces by turning traitor," he replied. "You have one more try."

"I am fleeing for my life," she said after calculating the odds of survival. "I've been on the run since the Conclave was dissolved. I've seen too many friends slaughtered and have no desire to share their fate."

Thopos leaned against the nearest wall and folded his arms, silent in his judgment.

Edam cocked his head. "Yet you were willing to meet the Guards in the street. Alone and unarmed. That tells me you wanted to die."

She shrugged. "I'm tired of running."

"What of your oaths to the people?"

"Broken. The Conclave is no more. Any oaths or bonds lie shattered now that that monster has assumed authority." Porii fought back tears. "It's gone. All of it. The dreams of the future. The promise of a bright tomorrow. We squandered it through petty struggles and brought ourselves to our knees."

Edam holstered his sidearm. "Do you know who I am?"

"No. Should I?"

He broke into a feral grin. "No. That's my point. Recognizable people are targets in this new regime. What if I told you I am the leader of the largest criminal organization in Krenz? Well, I was until Goethe assumed command."

"Of course you are," she replied flatly.

Edam scowled, clenching a fist. "I don't need to justify myself to you."

Rumors of the underground had circulated the Conclave for years, but for reasons unknown to most, Lorenu Phos forced investigators to look in the opposite direction. She protected them… but why?

Porii's eyes brightened. "You knew Aliz."

"We worked together right up until she fled the planet."

"She's still alive? That's impossible. She was killed the night Lorenu was assassinated!"

Edam's grin deepened. "I doubt she'd enjoy hearing that. She spent the last few years working with Strannan's splinter cells and my organization."

The tenacity of the resistance suddenly became apparent. Only one with insight into the inner workings of the three Orders could have orchestrated such a dogged campaign against the combined powers of Kale and Nye. She never envisioned it was Aliz. The least likely of them all, Lorenu's lover made her career by slinking through shadows and operating behind the scenes. Porii's respect for the woman rose in tandem with her guilt in how Phos fell.

"Cardinal, I need to know how far you are willing to go to follow in her footsteps," Edam said. "That or I cut you loose here and wish you luck."

"What good can I possibly be? I'm just a tired woman struggling to figure out where I belong."

Thopos chimed in, "One doesn't need robes and fancy titles to help people. All you need is compassion."

A warning light flickered to life.

"Time's up. We need to move. Now," Edam ordered.

Without waiting for her to react, he snatched her hand and dragged her into a smaller tunnel leading deeper into the forgotten world of the Krenz underground. Surviving came first. Porii fell in line behind him, whether she wanted to or not. Thoughts of an early demise vanished as she found herself caught up in the mad dash to escape.

Conclave Headquarters, Krenz.

The Crimson Mistress stared at her counterparts with casual disregard. Humans were beneath her and she made every opportunity to remind them. Nearby stood Geres Auk. His usefulness failed to materialize, despite his claims otherwise. His journey became a tale of failures, from serving under Baron Scura on the Plateau to betraying Presha Von and losing the artifact on Prophet Isle. Little better than a blunt instrument, she grew bored listening to his whines for attention and a last chance to prove himself. Human or not, no one being should ever abase themselves before another. Like far too many in her experience, Geres Auk lacked dignity.

She turned her attention to the diminutive new Inquisitor General. She knew little about Ezekiel Goethe and believed even less of his reputation. Men like him tended to embellish their resume, giving the false appearance of ruthlessness or strength. In her eyes, Goethe was weak, a servant to the greater evil, and a puppet to be manipulated on whim. There was no place for him in the new order.

Her musings cut short when Amongeratix swept into the room. Behind him marched half a dozen abused men and women, stripped down to stained tunics. Former Cardinals of the Forum, they were reduced to little more than shells of themselves. Broken and forced into servitude in exchange for their lives. Algiss sneered at their lack of resolve. True leaders would have never been taken alive. The human population was little more than a blight in need of excising.

Amongeratix swept his gaze across his allies. "Where is General Kale?"

"The low continent. He is finishing preparations for the new Guard base at Zevistya," Ezekiel Goethe answered.

"He should be here."

"His defiance is a stain on your authority," Algiss supplied when no one else spoke. "A lesson needs to be made."

"I will deal with the General at my convenience. We have other concerns." Amongeratix's voice came out an angry drawl. "The matter of the rebels on Mannus Prime demands my attention. No doubt they plan on bringing the battle to me. I want to know where and when they intend on striking."

"We have agents deployed to discover these answers as we speak, my lord," Ezekiel said with a bow.

Amongeratix ignored him. "There is another matter requiring immediate address. Reports of squads of Prekhauten Guards and Inquisitors being eliminated suggest a greater threat is among us. It is a terror from old times, one I wonder if you can defeat alone. Geres Auk, you and one of the witches will devote your efforts to finding and stopping the killer. Use whatever tactical strength you deem necessary. Bring me his head. Am I clear?"

Geres broke into a leering grin short of drooling at the command. Muscles bulged under his sleeveless tunic, the veins popping. Algiss grimaced. "I shall bring you the head and his heart ripped from his chest, my lord!"

Algiss shifted considering her options. "Evangeline, go with him."

"Yes, Crimson Mistress," the lesser witch agreed then bowed.

"Report to me as soon as your task is complete, and someone send for General Kale. His focus must shift to the coming war." He turned to Goethe. "Give me the intelligence I require, Inquisitor General, or your reign will prove far shorter than your predecessor."

Algiss Her watched Amongeratix then the others depart, choosing to remain behind until she was alone.

The hold Amongeratix maintained was growing tenuous. If she pulled the correct thread, exploitation might be possible. And if she could topple the monster when he was most vulnerable…the opportunity for domination opened for her.

Outskirts of capital district, Krenz.

He moved swift as death. Each step measured. Every blow calculated to produce the appropriate amount of force and fluidity. Graceful. Deadly. He was nightmare made life.

Akin Brohl plunged his short blade into the Inquisitor's unprotected stomach three quick times, pausing to twist the blade and rip half the woman's side out as he pulled it free. She died with a confused look, falling on top of her comrades. The god hunter knelt to wipe her blood off his sword before sheathing the weapon.

He'd left a trail of bodies even a junior investigator could follow and still no sign of Amongeratix. The giant refused to play his game, infuriating Akin. Deciding the old ways needed reintroduction to modern society, he began a campaign of terror, killing everyone in uniform he came across and leaving the bodies where they'd fallen. Increased presence patrols and hunter teams scoured the city. They fell one by one. Newsvids labeled him the covert killer. Akin wanted the attention. He wanted to infuriate Amongeratix, draw him out, and slay the monster who had eluded him for far too long.

Akin stalked down the street, passing burned out wrecks of former Conclave official's homes. Ornate gardens, statues of long dead heroes, and fountains lined the streets leading up to the now darkened pillars of light once considered the shining example of the future. All he spied was the ruination of humanity. There was no splendor left on Vau Prime. Depravity became the currency of the day. It was an old ploy following in Amongeratix's wake. Whether the giant went doom nipped at his heels.

In his view, there was little left to help the people of this planet. Salvation dissolved before their eyes. So, he ignored the rising tides of filth and violence. His sole focus was on his prey and his mission. Kill Amongeratix. Complete his purpose.

A quartet of armored Guards rounded the corner half a block ahead of him. Akin drew his blades. The faintest clip of boots behind suggested another quartet had come up behind him. Expecting the simplistic tactic, he burst forward, sprinting the distance and slashing into the Guards with reckless abandon. Ion rounds struck the street, buildings, and one blasted the head off a fountain statue.

Akin moved too fast for the shooters. Dropping below a stream of fire, he hacked through the legs of the nearest Guards, amputating both at the knees. The first man dropped screaming. His backswing caught a third Guard in the thigh, severing the artery. One of the Guards slammed his rifle butt into Akin's shoulder. Pain sparked, igniting madness in the god hunter. He plunged both blades into the Guard's chest, penetrating the armor and both lungs. Akin snatched the falling ion rifle and unleashed his full fury on the remaining Guard before turning it on the quartet stalking him from behind.

He despised energy weapons, preferring the cold familiarity of a blade. Yet the four Guards fell dead, riddled with superheated energy wounds. Unwilling to take unnecessary risk, Akin stalked toward the corpses and put a round in each of their heads. Limbs twitched. Satisfied, Akin hurried back to the body containing both of his blades. He planted a boot on the Guard's chest and yanked both free.

He needed to get Amongeratix to come and play.

"This is recent."

The iron smell of fresh spilt blood lingered. The Crimson Sister searched for additional clues as Geres Auk plodded around like the angry brute he was. Her enhanced vision detected multi-spectrum imaging. The faintest traces of residual body heat clung to the deepest core of the dead.

"This happened fast. Impossibly fast for a mortal," she continued. "Look at these blade marks. No one on this miserable planet should have this skill."

Geres sniffed with indifference. "It's just knife work. What's the big deal? You never killed anyone with a sword?"

A slight breeze ruffled her robes. "Look. There."

Geres knelt to where she pointed, wiping two fingers through the drying blood. "Still wet."

Sister Evangaline stared at the partial bloody boot print. Their sole clue and the barbarian all but ruined it. Distain growing, the witch did her best to ignore Geres. They'd spent too long in each other's presence already. Completing this assignment offered her the ability to sidle closer to the Crimson Mistress, if she made the correct moves, and after that…

"Big boot," Geres mumbled. "Bigger than a human."

Sister Evangaline sighed and leaned forward to look closer. Geres was correct. The print was extraordinarily large. She'd seen similar, but only among the Three and their wayward cousin. The implication caused her heart to clutch. Could it be another of their race had awoken and now was operating on Vau Prime right under their noses? She needed to report back to Algiss immediately.

"This changes matters," she replied, trying to stay calm.

"It's still a man, and all men can be killed."

*

Tenemenah, planet An'kuruku.

Weeks had passed. Endless days of looking over her shoulder, fearing the inevitable. Fresh worry lines crowded her face. Spots appeared on her hands and arms. Kaline felt old. She'd lost weight. Grey invaded the once solid blanket of red hair.

"When will it end?" she muttered as she crept down the street.

Music came down the street, bouncing from one sand colored building to the next. Kaline turned, surprised to see a wave of women concealed behind bright robes of every color. They wailed in tune to the music, waving the fronds of a soft white flower. A rank of tall men in black robes marched behind the women. Their conical hoods towering over the procession and the gathering crowds.

"A funeral procession," a man said from behind her. "It is a rare sight these days, but for some the old ways yet hold sway."

"I have no words for it."

The casket was borne by small armor backed desert creatures she'd never seen before. Kaline was startled to find the entire casket was made of clear glass. The body within was wrapped in plain linen, decorated by trinkets and baubles likely to help ease the soul's passing to the next life. Garlands of blue and white flowers were heaped upon it from the crowd as men and women alike joined the ritualistic wailing.

Kaline shook her head. "What are they saying?"

"It is a death chant. The family seeks the hand of a god to assist the transition. The people voice their support."

"It is beautiful," she whispered.

"To some. There are many of the new mindset who have no tolerance for outdated ceremonies." The sneer in his voice stained his words. "A new way of life emerged after the war in the Deeves when the Great Enemy threatened to destroy us. The new generation abandons the old ways, claiming we cannot continue as such. I long for the old ways to return."

"The curse of modernity," Kaline replied turning to face him. "Ever does the wheel of progress grind the past into ash and dust. We seem doomed to an endless cycle of advance and forget."

"Where do you come from?" the man asked, viewing her with caution. "I am not accustomed to hearing my people speak like so."

She huffed, having forgotten her birth world long ago. "Does it matter? This is the moment in which we find ourselves."

"You are a strange woman, offworlder."

Kaline ignored the man as he left abruptly. The men of Tenemenah were arrogant by nature, believing to be the direct descendants of the gods themselves. She found the trait annoying. Ignorance often burned deep within, spreading through an innate ability to accept fault in personal belief. She'd seen it far too often during her travels. A current of darkness flowed among humanity, camouflaged and seductive. The time of reckoning approached. Kaline began to believe perhaps none deserved to survive.

The promise of Rengu once inspired her. A herald of the great change, she assisted the necessary purge humanity required before evolving. Alas, resistance increased the more she tried. The cleansing fires spread across the universe, stalling in the face of the ignorant. Kaline began losing hope, knowing time grew more finite with each passing day. Soon the mythos of Rengu would either flame out or rage in an unstoppable conflagration forever altering the course of the future. Personal sense of faith flagging, Kaline prayed for the strength to keep pushing.

She felt, more than heard, a presence sidle behind her. Her eyes widened, hand slipping into the folds of her robes while knowing it wouldn't matter. "I am surprised to see you again so soon. Has my fate been decided?"

A familiar voice replied, "Who are we to determine the fate of others? The gods write such upon the winds for us to read, little else. Take that man in the casket. He had dreams, a family. Was it fate perpetuated by other men to claim his life? Or had the gods decided his moment of demise before his birth? Any attempt to answer is foolish."

"What do you want from me?" Kaline turned to him, a minor sense of relief on him. "I am not the woman I once was. I've told you this."

His grin showed stained teeth. "Redemption is possible for us all, Kaline. I have come to escort you to a holy place where you will learn what the gods have in store for you."

"I've seen enough holy places to know they are little more than fabrications of our imagination," she retorted. "The gods do not listen to the likes of you or me."

"Only when we refuse to accept their truth. The desert has bled for too long. You inspired the great change. You alone can heal it."

Her mind danced back to the violence of the campaign in the Deeves where she tangled with the Bone Father, wielding Mollock Bolle in one hand and an army of fanatics in the other. Thousands were slain, though she admitted most were killed from Amongeratix's arrival to capture his cousin. Disaster befell them. Kaline didn't consider any the victor. Both sides suffered. The word of Rengu lost amidst the nightmare. She considered An'kuruku her greatest failure and her most important lesson to date.

"I am in no position to heal anything," she replied, head hanging. "Whatever happened here is beyond redemption, as am I."

"That is not for you to decide."

She wanted to laugh. To cry. To show any other emotion than defeat. She dared look the desert man in the eyes, flinching at his predatory gaze. "Look at me. What you see is a shell of the woman I once was. I have nothing left to give. You have the wrong person."

"Why did you return to An'kuruku if not for the chance at redemption?"

I came here to die. Gods, grant me strength. "I, I don't know."

His nod soothed her, as if he heard her unspoken words. "Come with me. Allow me to open your soul to a new tomorrow. One where you will not remain trapped to the torments you have caused. The future is a many faceted entity, one we can take inspiration from."

"You just said fate is not for us to decide," Kaline instantly grew suspicious.

His smile brightened. "And so, it is. That does not mean fate is static. We may influence our futures, to an extent, but only if you open your heart and mind. Will you join me?"

Curiosity awakened, aroused by the promise of salvation from the ghosts of her soul. To be free, truly freed from all the wrongs of her life and breathe the open air once again, lured her into a decision she knew she was in no mental state to make. "I don't even know your name."

"You many call me Dejak."

SEVEN

3215 A.G. (After gods), Eger City, planet Mannus Prime.

"Are you certain this is the place?" Tinnus Har demanded for the fifth time upon arriving.

Dowan Mun ignored him, again.

The Inquisitor had taken him to an old café in the heart of the city center. Closed thanks to a substantial bribe, the owners had immediately slunk off to count their new fortunes while turning a blind eye to the subversive meeting taking place. Tinnus had been told many on Mannus remained defiant in the face of the new Confederation. Adherents to the old ways wanted a return to the true rule of law. To the Conclave. A miniscule portion of society began gathering in clandestine groups, like they were now, seeking ways to overthrow the new regime.

The former Cardinal Seniorus and resumed pacing. Answers were few and far between since his release. Tinnus found the convenience of the escape far too readymade to be believable. He had been set free, though for what reason remained hidden. He determined to bide his time, find necessary allies, and strike out at his foes.

"I am not a patient man, Inquisitor," he hissed.

He saw the newsvids of the total collapse of the Conclave. Allies and enemies slaughtered in the name of a monster born from myth. The dream of Vau Prime died ingloriously at the hands of madmen. He watched the holovid of the pompous Alain Nye dying a hundred times with rapt amusement. The arrogance of the man sat ill with Tinnus from the moment they first met. Nye deserved his fate, for hubris ever led to the downfall of those presumed untouchable.

"You insist on asking questions of little importance," Dowan said through gritted teeth. "I suggest you sit and recover your strength while we wait."

Tinnus trembled with restrained fury. He failed to recall the last time he'd been spoken to like this. "Do you have any idea who am I?"

The Inquisitor squared on him. "I know what you were, for a brief moment. Do not consider me impressed. Your regime faded in a span of heartbeats. You are a minor footnote to a forgotten chapter in our history. Perhaps if you understood this you would find your mood improved, *Cardinal Seniorus*."

"I've had men killed for less," Tinnus snapped.

"Of course, you have." Unimpressed, Dowan remained seated by the door, one hand on his sidearm and an eye on the street.

He still hadn't figured out why he bothered helping the men chosen to be his enemies. A bereft loyalty to the deceased Inquisitor General provided little solace to his broken conscience. Dowan's betrayal against Bela Cass solidified his ostracization. Accepting the assignment of Tinnus Har from his captors was little more than a ploy to escape his shackles and open paths to a better life.

Now that he was here, mired beneath constant complaints from a man disillusioned by his current situation, Dowan longed for nothing more than to slip away, book travel offworld, and find a new planet to start over. *Could I?* He'd served in the Inquisition long enough to know no other way of life. His indoctrination ran deep, as it did in all bearing the red rose. Yet with Alain Nye dead, Dowan felt his old allegiances strained, ready to break given the proper situation. Dealing with the almost child-like Tinnus Har aroused his psyche for the first time since first being detained by Torgast during the war.

Dowan ever sought to improve his station in life. Tying to the departed Bela Cass in defiance of Torgast and the rebellion set him back, pushing him to the edge. Rotting in a cell took little imagination to what came next. Yet instead of the executioner's noose he was presented the unique opportunity to turn heel again and serve a new master. The unspoken promise of violence should he fail accompanied him. Dowan, being an Inquisitor, was no stranger to animosity. Unafraid of death, he accepted the task.

He began drumming his fingers on the windowsill. With most of the celebrations moved on to different parts of the city, few civilians were on the streets. Dowan had no idea who to look for, or how many. He tensed when a Guard patrol entered his field of vision. Only a handful knew he now worked for the new First Counselor. To everyone else he was a fugitive. His hand curled around the blaster grip. The Guards moved past, ignoring the closed café.

"Something the matter?" Tinnus asked from the far side of the seating area.

Dowan forced out a breath. "Nothing I can't handle."

He saw three men crossing the street. They fidgeted, bobbing back and forth for signs of being watched. Dowan sighed. Fools. They invited their own demise by their actions. Waiting, Dowan scanned the surroundings for any sign of pursuit. He watched them crowd around the door as if deciding which one would go first. Little men with no leadership capability.

The door opened and three men slipped in. One flinched at the click of the door latching closed. Dowan rolled his eyes, deciding to let Tinnus do his part in fomenting the rebellion.

"It's about time. I am unaccustomed to waiting on laymen," Tinnus snapped in greeting. "What kept you?"

"This is a bad idea," the smallest of the trio muttered. "We should go."

"Too late for that," Tinnus said. "You are the supposed leaders of the resistance. I am the exiled Cardinal Seniorus. Let us dispense with the foolishness. You have the ears of a great many influential citizens and I have much to say." He paused and gave a leering grin. "Take me to your leaders."

Dowan's eyes widened at the force with which Tinnus issued his statement. *Fuck me. These idiots are going to get me killed.*

Confederation Military Headquarters.

Matthias replied to curt greetings from soldiers and sailors as well as administratum staff. The retired Sergeant Major knew the game and, despite spending most of his career in line units, built a strong reputation as a strategist and tactician. As such, he was railroaded into a seat on the new council. He'd refused, at first, but Adris Moscasco and others proved persuasive.

In the span of a few short days, he'd already been mired with logistics, troop requests, and deployment schedules for a campaign that, as of now, didn't exist. Sleeping less than five hours a night, Matthias pushed beyond anywhere his career previously took him. Armed with a newfound appreciation for the desk riders, he began the transition from soldier to bureaucrat.

He wanted no part in inter-faction rivalries, choosing instead to walk a tight line basing his decisions on right over emotion. He made it to his office and collapsed into the far too soft leather chair. Tipping his head back, Matthias closed his eyes and pushed away thoughts of the day. A string of endless meetings with little actionable moments left him drained. The respite did not last long.

"What?" he groaned without opening his eyes at the sound of the door chime.

"Counselor."

Matthias groaned again at the familiar voice. First Fies insisted on calling him by his old rank, now this. *Can't I just be me for one day?* "Tempest, what can I do for you?"

"Adris would like an update on the Har project."

"That's what we're calling it?" he asked. Blinking, Matthias sat up. "Well, from what we have been told, he and the Inquisitor have contacted the dissidents. You can tell Adris matters are proceeding according to plan. With a little luck we should have this wrapped up shortly and can move on to more important matters."

Tempest cocked her head. "You still don't approve."

Statement, not question.

A vocal opponent to letting one of the most dangerous men in the universe loose in their midst, Matthias wanted nothing more than to ship Tinnus Har off to a penal colony and be done with it. "My answer hasn't changed, if that's what you mean," he replied. "Any number of factors can work against us. If just one goes wrong all this is in jeopardy."

"I'm sure you have contingencies in pace to ensure that doesn't happen."

Clever woman. "We are playing a dangerous game none of us are willing to invest fully in."

"I think you underestimate what we're trying to achieve," Tempest insisted. "Politics can be delicate."

"Perhaps you're right," he conceded. "I've spent my career looking down a barrel. This," he gestured to the office, "is foreign to me."

"We all must begin somewhere."

"Isn't that the truth," he muttered. "Please tell Adris we should have the names and locations of our enemies in short order. I don't anticipate any delays. Tinnus seems in a rush to achieve his goals."

She hesitated before leaving.

"Is there something else?" Matthias thought he spotted her neck above the collar of her flat green tunic shading crimson. A minion of the halls of power, Tempest held her cards close to the chest, seldom offering more than the minimum necessary to convey a message or perform assigned tasks. He recognized her as one of the more efficient people in the new government.

"Has there been any word from the squad responsible for bringing us here?"

He hid a grin at her question.

"They have returned to their homebase and are refitting and preparing for their next assignment," he replied.

She nodded.

"I will keep you updated with what information I am allowed to share, but make no promises," he continued, watching her closely. "We are entering the final stage of this war, for good or bad. They've been at the front end of the advance since the first shots were fired. I doubt they'll be anywhere else than present when the last are."

"Why do you do it?" she asked abruptly.

"Do what?"

"Fight. I admit I haven't spent much time with Guards and do not profess to understand your ways, but I know enough to see the torment hiding behind your eyes," Tempest said. "I've never understood the desire to march into harm's way and take another life."

"How can I answer so it makes sense?" he mused. *How many times have I asked myself the same question*? "I don't think anyone wants to go to war. Getting shot at is certainly not the sort of thing a normal person aspires to. I would argue most of the Guards do what they do to prevent war. Sure, there are exceptions, but the goal is to stop a conflict before it escalates. Most of us are unmarried, yet there are ones who are leave their families behind so others won't have to."

Tempest cocked her head, leaning back against the doorframe. "You do it out of a sense of glory?"

"Anonymity at best," he countered. "Who remembers our names other than the historian or grieving widow? There is no glory to be found in violence. Only broken hearts. No heroes. No saints. With the exception of a small percentage, none of us thinks we are more than regular people doing an irregular job. You perform your job. We perform ours. That's really all there is to it."

She seemed to consider the answer before offering a nod and slipping away.

*

Orbital Shipyards, planet Mannus Prime.

Repairs from the ill-fated raid on Vau Prime's principal defenses continued at a rapid pace. Crews worked around the clock to fix what could be fixed and turned those ships too badly damaged into spare parts. Far too many smaller ships drifted through the core system, aimless until touching upon a gravity well and plunging to a fiery demise on the unfortunate planet below. Thousands of lives were lost on both sides, reducing combat power substantially. For a rogue fleet struggling to grow, the effects proved detrimental.

The Confederation Council concealed disappointment over the near totality with which the Prekhauten Navy chose to stand with Vau Prime's authoritarian regime. For Khe-Zhehan and her immediate staff, it forced the expansion of recruitment efforts. The call went out across the universe for all true patriots to rise up and add their fires to the fleets. Tens of thousands of ships, ranging from a handful of major capital ships to smaller fighters and frigates, choked the airspace around a dozen worlds. The shipyards of Mannus Prime were crammed to capacity. It wasn't enough.

Khe-Zhehan, the highest-ranking Naval officer in the Confederation, stood watching her battered fleet being repaired. Hands clasped behind her back and dressed in her field uniform, she had never felt more impotent. Nor more responsible. The disaster in the Vau System stemmed from the overestimation of her abilities. Others argued against it, despite the agreed necessity of saving as many of Davith Strannan's divisions as possible, but she'd been insistent. Roll calls were still being conducted but many of the smaller ships lacked proper manifests. Some of the dead would never be counted for. The reality was a dagger to her heart.

She suspected, without being able to prove, her maneuver resulted in her exclusion from the Council. Not that she minded, but seeing Falchi and Matthias appointed as Counselors rankled her ego. She belonged on the bridge, not mired behind stacks of paperwork and pointless investigations. That notwithstanding, Khe-Zhehan had done her time on the line and earned the opportunity to at least decline the appointment. Instead, she was shunned. Confined to the fleet and monitored by those who had never been on the wrong end of a cannon. A quiet anger simmered deep within. One she refused to acknowledge. For now.

Losing interest in the activity filling the viewports, Khe-Zhehan went in search of the one man on Mannus capable of empathizing with her plight. She'd learned long ago sympathy served no purpose in the military. Feeling sorry for someone did nothing to improve the situation. She could, however, empathize. That shared suffering inspired camaraderie on unspoken levels and bore the ability to improve the aggrieved.

Perhaps Falchi felt similar. Reaching his modest office suite, the Admiral calmed her roiling emotions and entered.

"Ah, Admiral, I wasn't aware we had a meeting today," Falchi said as he looked up from the datapad in his hands. His eyes were red, deep lines circling them.

"You do not look well," she told him. Despite him holding a seat on the council, he remained her subordinate. "When is the last time you got a full night's sleep?"

"I could ask the same," he replied. "Perhaps we can rest once this is finished."

An old soldier's adage. The promise of enough sleep when you're dead. She concealed her amusement, noting how easy it was to fall back on instilled euphemisms and overused catch phrases.

"Perhaps." Khe-Zhehan slid into the empty chair opposite Falchi. "I am tired. A far cry from the woman I was but a few short months ago."

"None of us are the same," he admitted. "We do what we must. The war goes on and our subordinates look to us for guidance."

"Do they still after this disaster?"

"You brought back thousands of valuable soldiers," he countered. "Do not doubt yourself, Admiral. To do so now is an insult to the men and women who died."

Her tone hardened. "I've lost battles. We both have. This war grinds upon the soul, gnawing away at our defenses while rendering us caricatures of what we might have been. You were there at Hawker's Gate when the deception was exposed. How many friends were you forced to kill? How many betrayals ate away at your resolve?"

Falchi licked his lips, growing pale. "Too many. We are far from the Gate, Admiral. Our future is in our hands for the first time. Together, we can break Kale's back, but only if we cast aside our doubts."

"Sometimes doubt is all we have," she said. "Falchi, I haven't always been kind. Nor have I been the attentive leader I should have been. The results of Vau Prime lie solely upon my shoulders. For that, I accept blame and responsibility. However, I do not appreciate being kept on the outside while the rest of you prosper. Perhaps I can best serve this new Confederation by resigning."

His eyes shot wide. "What are you saying? We need you now more than ever. This is the most critical stage of our efforts. We need our most experienced fighters in the proper positions."

"I am in no state of mind to lead more sailors to their deaths."

"Admiral Khe-Zhehan, you know, as do I, we have no control over who lives or dies," he started, anger in his voice. "Each and every person in uniform accepts death as part of the price. While none expects to meet their demise, none cast blame on their leadership for their fates. You decided based on experience, gut instinct, and the tactical situation. You've taken us this far. Don't fall aside when you are needed most."

"Is this the counselor speaking or the admiral?" she spat. "I, strike that. I should not have said that. Forgive me. It was poor of me." She hadn't meant for her resentment to be so blatantly throw it out in the open. She wasn't sure what to do.

"Admiral, we can deal with whatever you think there is between us when the war ends, but for now please remember I hold you in the highest regard," Falchi said in a calculated tone. "You are just as important to this as I am."

She sighed, fighting back the urge to cry. "I know. I know. I don't know what came over me."

"Guilt," he said.

As much as she wanted it to be otherwise, Khe-Zhehan knew he was right. Mountains of guilt threatened to render her inoperable, more a liability than asset. She'd once been counted among the most powerful naval officers in the fleet. A rising star without ceiling. The war destroyed that.

"Of course. You are correct. It was a momentary weakness and ill of my position," she sat up straighter, adjusting her uniform. "Let us turn to more important matters. Are you able to continue in your current position considering your new responsibilities?"

Falchi cleared his throat. "I don't see why not. The council is not slated for daily meetings. My priority remains building our combat power for the coming campaign."

She nodded, accepting his response for what it was and not wanting to rile him further. "I notice there are several crews missing. Have they defected?"

"That is, ah, classified, Admiral."

"Wha—" Eyes filled with fury, Khe-Zhehan bristled at being closed out once again.

He held up his hand. "All I am at liberty to say is they have been transferred to Admiral August's command. They will be there when we need them most. I assure you."

"You can understand my reluctance to accept this," she countered. "Has the council determined I am not to be trusted with military matters?"

"Not all," he replied, too fast for her liking. "These orders came from Tannus himself."

A dark mask settled over her face. "I don't understand why we continue acquiescing to one of *them*. The Three have proven nothing but detrimental since their return. We bleed for their crimes and are expected to fall in like good little sheep!"

"History shows us it has ever been so."

Animosity among the rank and file grew stronger the more involvement the Three had in human affairs. And rightfully so. There would be no war if not for the subversions of Amongeratix. She'd already gotten the answers she sought and, though they kept her trapped in a prison of her own design, she yet had purpose.

"Perhaps it is time to break the cycle and discover true freedom," she said.

"I have a feeling such is within our grasp, but only if we win. Amongeratix must be destroyed for that to happen and the only way to achieve it is by working in hand with his brother. There is no other way, Admiral."

"Doesn't mean we have to like it." At his look, she swallowed a sigh. "At any rate, I look forward to your reports on refit status. Continue pushing the work crews. We must be prepared for whatever that monster on Vau Prime has in store for us."

"I'll have them on your desk before the end of day," he confirmed.

Unsatisfied, Khe-Zhehan rose and dismissed herself.

Capital District, Eger City.

Guard in tow, dressed in finery far too formal for her liking even while understanding the function and symbology, Adris Moscasco moved through the back corridors where only the council were permitted. Her stomach growled. She didn't recall her last meal. She entered the counselor's private cafeteria and did a quick scan. Mostly empty, she found three tables with senior level ambassadors and the one person she had no stomach for, Minister Standou of Orlei.

Making her way through the food line, Adris avoided eye contact and went to an empty table on the far side of the room. She had just unfolded her napkin across her lap and put fork to plate when a shadow fell over her.

"Adris, do you mind if I join you?"

"If you must," she replied before shoveling in a mouthful of steamed vegetables t. "I do not have much time for pleasantries, as I am sure you do not either."

"Is it ever different for professional politicians?" Standou asked with an exaggerated wave. He slipped into the chair opposite her. "Difficult times and such. I have been inundated with material requests resulting in a chain of logistics nightmares. I fear I shan't sleep for days."

Adris set her fork down with a clank. "Is there a point to this, Standou? We are both busy people and I do so detest cold food."

If he was shocked at her behavior, he concealed it well. "Ah, my apologies. You must understand how difficult it is to slip away from our societal responsibilities. Have you given any further thought to my proposal?"

Not this again. Does this man ever rest? "I have not, but rest assured, the alliance treaty with Orlei and surrounding sector is important. We need as many allies as we can get in these trying times. Developing both the army and navy takes priority above all else."

"Think how much my proposed alliance will deliver to the Confederation. Manpower, equipment, weapons. An entire sector locked down from our enemies. Thirty-seven planets working alongside us to defeat the usurpers."

"Counselor, I hear you. Every effort is being made to ensure your treaty happens," she reiterated. Adris grew tired of having to repeat herself. "Unfortunately, there are far more important immediate matters demanding my attention. Now, if there is nothing else, I would like to enjoy whatever this is while it is still hot."

He cleared his throat. "There is one more matter, perhaps even worthy of your focus."

"That being?"

"Word has reached me of the former Cardinal Seniorus loose on Mannus. What do you know of this?"

"Where did you hear this?"

He gave a sly smile. "Come now, Adris. We all have our resources. My people have spotted Tinnus Har slinking through the city accompanied by an Inquisitor. What games are you playing at?"

"Standou, even if your assertations were true, I would not be in a position to tell you or anyone else," she replied. Fears of Inquisition spies among their ranks undermined all they strove to achieve. "There are some matters only a select few are entitled to know."

He flinched. "I am your second."

"You are first in line to replace me should the Council deem it," she corrected. "Hear me, Standou. I consider you my most important ally in what we are attempting to build. You bring value to every endeavor. Our little council would not be where it is today without your assistance, but I must do what I deem best for the Confederation."

"You confuse me with a twisted tongue."

Adris leaned closer. "Standou, there are subversive elements among us. I am using our fallen Cardinal to root them out and eliminate them before they can strike. The sooner this affair is concluded the sooner we can shift our full attention on defeating Amongeratix and turning this Confederation into the beacon of hope and justice the Conclave forgot how to be."

"That is an interesting approach. Not one I would consider," Standou replied, appearing pleased. "Still, there is merit in your words. Thank you for confiding in me. Truly. It goes far in cementing our relationship. I trust you have adequate forces on standby for when Har makes his play."

"I do, as well as contingencies should he evade them," Adris confirmed. "With a little fortune his sad tale will come to a forgotten conclusion in short order."

"I will keep your confidence," Standou said. "You have given me much to consider."

She watched him slink away, knowing whatever he'd come proposing took a severe hit. She snorted. Fools often underestimated their prey, thinking themselves superior. If he'd done his research, Standou would have learned she was no stranger to the game of politics. She curated her skills for decades, honing her instincts to the razor edge she wielded with implacable precision. Now warned, Standou would delay any power move and, if he didn't, she had a plan in place for that as well.

Appetite ruined, Adris pushed her tray back and left.

She wandered for a time, no clear destination and no immediate meetings on her schedule. Having never felt so far out of her element, she eventually wound up on a fifth story garden balcony overlooking the city center. Surrounded by flowers, Adris found a measure of comfort.

"Adris, you look unwell."

Startled, she turned to find Cardinal Virom seated upon one of the stone benches in front of a fountain. "Cardinal, I hadn't expected to find anyone here at this time."

"It is one of the few luxuries I allow myself," he said. "The trappings of power are cruel, making this special regardless of the moment. Please, join an old man."

"I fear these moments are going to become few and far between the closer we get to the end."

"Nothing ends, Adris. We are mere passing moments in an endless story," Virom said, motioning for her to sit. "What troubles you?"

Straight to the point. Her head pounding, she answered, "We face too many unresolved threads. Each holds importance on varying magnitudes but all are necessary to complete before we can be free of the growing nightmare of Vau Prime."

"We all feel the pressure, Adris. What is at the core of this moment of weakness? I may not have known you for long, but I am considered a good judge of character among the clergy."

"Am I that obvious?"

"You do tend to wear your emotions for all to see."

Exhaling, Adris detailed her sudden issue with the Minister of Orlei and the complexities of keeping secrets in an impossible scenario. A weight came off her heart despite the wave of guilt she felt for bringing another of the council into her problems.

"Standou is not the threat you imagine, Adris. He is confident and always working an angle, from what I have seen but is on our side,"

Virom explained. "There are others I would place more caution on."

"Yazie," she said, voicing her suspicions.

He nodded. "There's good starting point. Like most politicians, Yazie is an opportunist more concerned with his bottom line than the greater good of the universe." He shifted in his seat. "Every den has snakes, Adris. Leave Standou to his ministrations and keep your eye on Tinnus Har. You never know what might get uncovered."

EIGHT

3215 A.G. (After gods), Great Library, planet Wexanos.

Somewhere over the course of the last four years the universe stopped making sense. Friend turned against friend, families torn asunder by conflicting ideologies once considered sound and unifying. Fractured societies crumbled under the empty weight they been built upon. Once stalwart institutions sworn to protect the weak and innocent became oppressive tyrants slaughtering whole civilizations. For those planets outside the conflict, it was the clarion call to action. Armies popped up, no longer under the Conclave's banners. Riots and protests grew, pressure mounting on every ruling body in the universe.

Luma Kai read the daily reports with a measure of sorrow. She'd once considered her charge holy and the ultimate service to humanity. She'd grown up in a strict family, taught to believe in the righteousness of the gods and the guiding hand of the Conclave. Meeting Tannus cast her carefully constructed world into an unending spiral of chaos.

Discarding her Inquisition uniform took little thought. How could she support an order determined to undermine the sovereignty all humans should enjoy? Luma Kai abandoned the Inquisition in the same manner it cast her aside. She saw evil for what it was and devoted herself to the overthrow of Krenz.

She needed clarity but had nowhere to turn. Each of her companions were obsessed with their own priorities, barring herself and young Ragan Sandinsol. The boy from Rastarok was her only link to innocence and that grew more fleeting as the days sped by. Far from a boon companion, Ragan brought youthful enthusiasm to each new quest. She almost admired the boy. Almost.

Frustrated, she stormed through the library in search of a stiff drink. The best place for that was in the soldier's barracks. A fragile alliance lingered between the Prekhauten Guard and the Inquisition and, despite her having worked with the units on Wexanos on and off for the past few years, Luma knew acceptance remained elusive at best. Knowing the librarians offered no companionship and her own group was busy with individual endeavors, the Guard was her best chance at forgetting her troubles if just for a night.

She heard them long before finding them. One hundred and twenty Prekhauten Guards under the nominal command of the freshly promoted Captain Fies filled an empty wing of the Great Library. Tannus ordered the long halls furnished with everything they needed, from bunks to showers, and tactical planning rooms. What he couldn't have planned on was the totality in which the Guards, having slipped the leash from a traditional command structure, occupied their new quarters.

Conversation died down to murmurs as they spied her. It was a familiar scenario. One Luma grew accustomed to over the course of her career. While each of the three orders were equal, in theory, the hierarchy demanded unwritten respect and more than a dose of fear. Faces hardened; some looked away. Not that she blamed them. Corruption in the Inquisition bore sole responsibility for the civil war killing many of their friends. To them, she was more than an outsider. She was unwanted.

"Don't mind them, Inquisitor. They're a little morose now. Care for a drink?"

Luma took an empty seat at the table and accepted the canteen cup. "You're new."

The sergeant shrugged. "I signed up with these miscreants during the Mannus campaign. Been regretting it ever since—Jelin Quint."

"Luma Kai."

Her first sip of whisky burned the instant it touched her lips and kept going down to the pit of her stomach. Snickers and laughter followed when she choked on a cough. "Good gods, how do you people drink this without going blind?"

"You've had our field rations, Inquisitor. This isn't half as bad," a familiar voice answered.

At least she recognized Haggle, as well as several others lingering in the bay. Forcing down a second swallow in the hopes of deadening her senses, Luma said, "Please, it's just Luma. I'm not in a uniform."

Haggle blushed. "Sorry, old habits."

"Understandable, but I'm not the one you need to worry about," she replied. Before she knew what she was doing, added, "I've been thinking about turning in my rose."

"It does look good on the uniform though," Haggle teased and took a drink.

Luma drained the last swallow of possibly the worst thing she had ever tasted. "I know why I'm feeling low, what's the deal with the rest of you? Why is everyone so morose?"

"We got our deployment orders," Jelin said. "Heading out to some secret moon base as advance party for the coming campaign. What about you?"

She had found out earlier about a new quest to find the mysterious Kaline. It was so soon after their excursion on Romalle and felt wrong. Rushed. "Heading off to hunt down a woman responsible for burning a dozen worlds."

"Doesn't sound like too many will be coming back," Jelin said. "From either task."

She snorted. "If not us, who else?"

Jelin, noting her unease, changed the subject. "How long have you served?"

"Less than a decade. I had just been promoted to the Office of Heretical Persecution when the war started," she said, gesturing for a refill.

"Been anywhere exciting?"

"Define exciting."

He raised his cup. "Spoken like a true veteran. Here's to exciting and the hopes we never find it again."

Luma barked a laugh. She clanked cups, holding it in place long enough for the others at the table to join in. Any trepidation she'd brought in evaporated in the shared suffering of the homemade whisky line units were subversively famous for.

Luma drank deep. She'd willingly suffer the consequences in the morning. Tonight was for forgetting what came next. "Whose got the cards?"

Cheers went up from several Guards amidst a choir of bragging and friendly threats.

Cirsen Station, orbit of planet Solecca.

"Are you certain this is a good idea, Cap'n?"

Vicente Blackheart glared at his First Mate. "Sedge, I doubt none of my decisions have been good since we took our dearly departed Inquisitor General's contract at the start of the war. Each situation gets worse. The *Shrike* is held together by good will and tape at this point."

Ignoring his dire outlook, Sedge plucked the knife point from his teeth and slapped Blackheart on the shoulder. "But we're still here, aren't we?"

"Sedge, what have I told you about touching me?" Blackheart let out an exaggerated sigh. "I have a reputation to maintain."

"Reputations are good for whorehouses and wanted posters. Neither of which have been visited for far too long," Sedge countered. "The men need a good time, Cap'n."

"Why did I promote you?"

Sedge shrugged. "Therill was an asshole."

The former First Mate's traitorous moves endangered them all. Knowing he'd been killed was reward enough, Blackheart's only regret stemming from not having done it himself. The betrayal had also showed him he had much to learn about leadership. Working for his father while growing up gave him logistical experience but no practical examples of being in charge. Time tempered all wounds, however. Years later, Vicente Blackheart grew as hard as his namesake suggested.

"He was, wasn't he," he finally replied.

Sedge nodded. "Just like the two you're considering bringing aboard."

"One might argue I fit in that category myself," Blackheart mused. When Sedge opened his mouth, he continued. "Before you speak, remember I am the one of the most feared captains in the universe. The two on the station are some of the best at what they do. Whether or not they decide to join us again is another matter."

"Well, I suppose we could always knock a few heads together if we have to."

"My sentiments exactly, though I doubt it will do any good." He looked at the approaching space station. "Prepare the shuttle. There's no point in delaying any further."

"Aye, Cap'n."

Cirsen Station loomed and with it the unwritten promise of a new adventure. *What have I gotten us into this time?*

Solecca was a jungle planet nestled against one of the major trade lanes. Thousands of ships flowed past annually, making Cirsen Station a highly lucrative proposition for the right sort of entrepreneur. Blackheart once had a strong network in place but, with the pirate fleets all but decimated and his name dragged through the dirt thanks to a vindictive Inquisition, he struggled to find any old contacts willing to work with him. Frustration set in the longer he stomped across the cold decks. With no one to unleash his anger upon, Blackheart decided for the next best thing.

The cantinas were situated near the station's center. A robust district filled with restaurants, bars, and casinos. A tourist trap by any other name. Blackheart spent his share of long nights gambling away the spoils of his labors. Knowing the quality of his quarry, he aimed for one of the smaller cantinas. *There they are.*

"Gentlemen, mind if we join you?" he asked, coming up behind them.

Krimpen Mass cringed upon hearing Blackheart's voice. At his side, Time stiffened. "I had hoped our business was concluded after that most unpleasant affair on Crimeat."

"We liked where we were," Time added. "We were going to retire there."

"Retire from what?" Blackheart sat without being offered a seat. Sedge and the other three remained standing. "You know, I've never been able to figure out precisely what your occupation is." Reaching between them, he plucked a piece of skewered meat from their tray.

"We are businessmen," Krimpen boasted. "Opportunists, if you will. You see, Vicente Blackheart, there are numerous people in this universe with problems they can't solve. That's where we come in. We're problem solvers."

Time cracked his knuckles, leveling his gaze on Blackheart's accompanying pirate gang. "You're not hunting that big son of a bitch again, are you?"

"Geres Auk? Haven't thought about him since we captured the woman," Blackheart said, waving a hand. "Why, you're not still afraid of him are you?"

"Ain't afraid of nobody, especially not your goons over there," Time threatened. He relaxed, slightly, when Krimpen placed a hand on his forearm.

"Now, now, Time. We aren't here to start a fight," Krimpen

said. "Besides, our esteemed pirate lord here doesn't look to good to me. What do you want with us this time? We're busy men."

Blackheart swept his gaze over the plates of meats, cheeses, and raw vegetables. Half empty glasses of golden beer sat before each man. The only business they seemed about was filling their stomachs. His own stomach growled in response.

"I've been called back to help our dear friend once more."

"Give Captain August our regards," Time said and reached for his beer. "We're retired."

"It's Admiral August now and you were retired the last time we met," Blackheart countered. "I wouldn't be here if it wasn't important."

"Vicente, I'm not sure you've caught on but we're not responsible for the salvation of the universe. We've done our part. On Kharsis and then Crimeat. How much more can you ask from us? We're just two men. Granted, many consider us the best at what we do, but that doesn't change the fact we're tired, Vicente. We need a break, and this is the beginning of a new life for Time and me."

"We're trying to enjoy our cheese platter," Time reinforced.

Blackheart rolled his eyes. "What if I told you this is the opportunity of a lifetime. A chance for you to prove your worth and become heroes to the entirety of the universe."

Krimpen snorted. "Everyone knows heroes never survive. I've grown attached to this ole life of mine."

"I could tell you, or I could show you."

"Tell him to fuck off and be done with it, Krimpen. We have better things to do," Time growled. He finished his beer and wiped the froth from his lips with the back of a sleeve. The accompanying burp rattled the empty glass.

Blackheart waited for their show to end. He learned long ago not to give in to their antics.

"There's nothing you can show we haven't seen before," Krimpen muttered. "Best you go about your way, Vicente. We're not interested."

Snatching a piece of light brown cheese, Blackheart said, "You've heard the stories about Amongeratix's ship I assume."

"You want us to go after it? You're madder than I thought," Time said.

"We want nothing to do with the Three, Vicente," Krimpen threw in.

"Just answer the question."

Exasperated, Krimpen shared a look with Time before he answered, "Yes. Who hasn't heard of that monstrosity? It's the most powerful ship in the universe."

"What if I told you it wasn't the only one?" Blackheart teased. "What if there was a whole fleet of them just waiting to be unleashed and what if I said they were on our side?"

"I'd say you're mad."

He winked. "Comes with the job. I've been given the chance to get my hands on one of those dreadnaughts and I want men of quality at my side."

"We got all the quality you can handle, and then some," Krimpen said. "You're going after Amongeratix?"

Time muttered and reached for his beer.

"That's the part I don't know yet," Blackheart said. "What I can tell you is I'm going to need all the help I can get. That means you two, loathe as I am to admit it."

"Fuck off," Time reiterated.

Krimpen beamed. "Nonsense, Time. Our esteemed pirate here finally recognizes us for the assets we are. A little humility goes a long way." He leaned forward, elbows on the table. "Say we're interested. What are the details?"

"Link up at the Shirke later today. Docking Bay 7. We leave first thing in the morning."

Krimpen spread his hands. "That sounds nice and all, but I'm referring to our cut."

Got you. "You'll be paid enough to buy your own planets and live like kings for the rest of your days."

Time's eyes narrowed. "You don't have that kind of money."

"No, but the new Confederation does. Sign on with me and I'll ensure your set. You have my word."

The mercenaries exchanged looks. Whatever passed unspoken between them set Blackheart on edge the longer he waited.

"Docking Bay 7," Krimpen confirmed.

Satisfied, Blackheart motioned for his crew, and they headed off into the station to requesition supplies.

"No, Krimpen. We don't need his problems again." Time shook his head, drinking the rest of his beer and slamming the empty glass on the table. Nearby patrons jumped at the sound of shattering glass.

Krimpen leaned closer to his longtime friend. "Relax. We're still here, aren't we? If he's honest, which I have my doubts, we're about to become the richest men in the universe."

"You're forgetting one thing."

Krimpen's eyebrow rose. "What's that?"

"He never guaranteed we survive," Time glowered.

Great Library, planet Wexanos.

"Everything is proceeding on schedule. I have twenty thousand automatons developed and awaiting pickup," Sorrow explained. "More will take time."

Tannus studied his brother's flickering image. "We'll need more than that to stop Amongeratix. You forget the strength of his skulldaerth. We have no idea how many survived."

He kept the events from Braewynd private. The less his brothers knew the better. Tolde's encounter with the mystical warrior creations on the forgotten planet of Rastarok reopened old wounds. Amongeratix retained his army and, by all accounts, collected them thanks to a rogue wizard.

"My creations are a match for his," Sorrow insisted. "Tannus, you push too hard. There are limitations to what we may achieve. Our brother does not follow our timeline, rather we dance to his strings."

"That must change if we stand any chance at victory," Tannus replied, frustration in his tone. "The pieces are in place. Our allies gather. This is the moment we have long awaited, my brother."

"One that might easily swing back in his favor and perpetuate this pointless war for generations."

Tannus frowned. "We don't have generations. Your Paladin progresses with her training. Soon she shall be ready to execute her purpose."

"And the god hunter?"

"Loose on Vau Prime as far as I know. There is the chance he might succeed, reducing our role in the coming battle."

"Amongeratix has ever been the wiliest of us. He will not fall to Akin Brohl," Sorrow admonished.

The god hunters were useful tools created by the Grand Mistress of the Order of Blood Witches, but they had their limitations.

None had so much as left a scratch on any of the Three. For the last one to succeed required powers far beyond theirs. Still Tannus said, "Perhaps, but he does not need to kill our brother. All he needs to do is draw the bastard out. We can lure him to Occanum on our own."

"Along with his new human army," Sorrow added.

"Countered by ours." Growing weary of the conversation he ordered, Prepare your automatons, brother. I will send ships to collect them soon."

"They will be ready. You have my word." Sorrow's image flickered. "Brother, have you given thought to what happens after this ends?"

A curt laugh escaped him. "Is there a point? We have been at war for so long I no longer remember a time of peace. I do not think we are made for a lifetime of joy or happiness. Though, it would be nice to slip away, off to unexplored regions of space where our kind was never falsely revered. Planets with no wars or violence. It is, I am afraid, just a dream. What of you, brother? What does your eternity look like?"

Tannus paused. The one question he had been seeking answers for and now, here at last, he found himself confronted by it. "No more pain."

"The sad truth is I do not envision any of us surviving the end. The Oracle's promise of Forever Night has at long last fallen upon us," Tannus replied, his heart constricting at Sorrow's admission. "We are not out of this yet."

Sorrow caught the hitch in his tone and asked, "What are you planning?"

Tannus stiffened. "I believe it is time to take my plea to the humans directly. I am heading to Mannus Prime to speak with this new Confederation. I have relied on humanity for far too long, using them like a crutch when I doubted myself. No longer. That ends now. Today, brother, we set forth upon the great crusade to cleanse the universe of the old wrong. A new dawn arrives. One altering the course of his history forever. I shall see you on Occanum."

Sorrow's image faded.

Unable to cope with the finality of his designs, Tannus stalked off in search of the sole being capable of offering solace. He found Fistel perusing a pile of ancient texts for reasons the Chief Librarian seldom explained. Wexanos remained a world shrouded in secrecy; Tannus' minions included.

"My lord," Fistel said upon hearing Tannus' soft cough. "What may I do for you?"

"The time has come," Tannus began. "I will soon be departing to confront my brother one last time. I leave the library and this planet in your care."

"My lord, I… I've known this day was coming but suddenly find myself ill-prepared to accept my responsibilities."

Tannus' smile felt stiff. "As do I. Wexanos was meant to inspire. To show the universe peace could be achieved with a little effort. What we have built here far exceeds my expectations. Most of that success stems from your commitment. For that, I cannot express my gratitude enough."

Sitting straighter, Fistel declared, "I shall endeavor to maintain your lofty standard for the duration of your absence. You can count on me."

"I'm afraid you don't understand. While I knowingly go to war one final time, I am unsure if I will return," Tannus admitted. "None of us can predict the future, not even the Oracle for all her assurances. Should I fail, or fall, the library belongs to you. I have taken measures to ensure the transfer of power goes smoothly. You have been a boon companion for far longer than I deserve. Knowing you has been one of the great privileges of my life."

"You leave me at a loss for words," Fistel managed.

"It is no easy decision, marching back to war after so long," Tannus said, noticing the man's tears. "The time is right. The pieces are in play. One way or another, the long war between brothers will at last reach a conclusion."

He fell silent. The words spoken felt inadequate for the moment.

He turned to leave, pausing in the doorway. "Fistel, take care of my planet. Spread our message to the stars. Make this the example the fallen Conclave should have been. I have complete faith in you and your cadre."

"Wexanos will stand," Fistel vowed.

Sister Alessandra found Ragan Sandinsol in a forgotten sitting area overlooking the western plains. Blankets of wildflowers wove an intricate tapestry of colors marred only by tufts of grass poking through. She found inspiration among the soft rolling hills. A tranquility experienced far too little. Ragan, she saw, failed to notice it at all.

"Why are you so glum, Ragan?" she asked. They'd forged a tentative bond during the ordeal on Romalle. She felt she could speak to him about the mundane, providing both the opportunity to relieve stress and remember what it meant to feel again.

"Sister Alessandra. My mind is unwell. It has been since we left Romalle."

"I have no experience with love," she told him, remembering his plight. "You must train your heart to obey your mind. Do not let emotions dictate who you are."

"Aren't emotions the core of what we are though?"

"Humans perhaps," she conceded. "Did you truly fall in love with that girl?"

"Riles …I thought so, but not really," he said. "I think it was more the thought of escaping this unending nightmare and starting over that attracted me. Don't get me wrong, she was nice and easy on the eyes. She just happened to love someone else. Who am I to get in the way of that?"

"True. She had no reason to accept your advances when a viable alternative, one she'd known since birth, stood before her. You made the correct decision, Ragan. Remaining on Romalle presented additional problems you would not have been prepared to handle in your current state."

"Still hurts." He did his best to ignore the almost inhuman harshness of her words.

"There is one way to get over premature infatuation," she said, noting when he winced.

"Find someone else?" he asked in a glib tone.

Alessandra cocked her head. She failed to see how rushing into another lustful situation would help. "Occupy your mind with greater tasks. Come, I am on my way to speak with the Inquisitors. We have been idle for too long."

Grumbling under his breath, Ragan shook his head but followed.

Tolde stared at the monitor along the wall of the antechamber. Arms folded across his chest and face pinched in concentration, he questioned his recent decisions. Vanquishing the cult of Rengu felt important, even if fell to a secondary matter when compared to stopping

Amongeratix and reclaiming Vau Prime. He glanced up at the sound of swishing robes. Any thoughts he had fled.

"Has there been any word?" Sister Alessandra asked, coming into the room without knocking. Ragan came up behind her and offered a small smile.

"Nothing yet. I have every resource on this planet searching for Kaline. We've hacked into Inquisition and Conclave databases with no active results. It seems she has disappeared. The last known location was Mannus Prime. Reports of a tribal uprising on the far side of the planet suggest she was actively attempting to subvert the locals."

"I presume she failed."

Tolde nodded. "Seems that way. The Confederation has recovered a few bodies of men clearly ex-Guard. Survivors say a redhaired woman fled in her shuttle before they could capture her. After that, nothing."

"A ghost," Ragan muttered.

"Not quite," a female voice uttered from the doorway.

Tolde turned as she froze upon seeing the Blood Witch. He decided to take control of the situation before it worsened when seeing Sister Alessandra's expression. "Presha, what news?"

Casting a lingering glare at the witch, Presha cleared her throat. "I think I found her."

"Where?" Tolde asked. He unfolded his arms and began cracking his knuckles. It was an old habit he failed to break.

"An'kuruku."

He shook his head. "That doesn't make sense. She's already tried to turn the population to Rengu and failed. Why would she return to a planet that had already rejected her?"

"We cannot pretend to understand the minds of villains," Alessandra interjected.

Presha stiffened and said nothing.

"None of the official channels mention her on An'kuruku," Tolde said, breaking the silence. "Are you certain?"

"As much as I can be," Presha replied. "I still have a network outside of legitimate channels. They confirmed she's been seen in several of the local drinking establishments in Tenemenah. And before you ask, tall redhaired women aren't common in the desert."

"How recent is this data?" he asked.

"Days."

Tolde looked at each of his team. Proven veterans, even Ragan now, they'd been through life and death together. This was the reassurance he was looking for in having made the right decision with Tannus. "How soon can you all be ready to depart?"

"Say the word," Luma said coming to stand in the doorway.

Tolde's heart swelled at the support. He'd come to rely on them more than any knew. In the span of a few short years, they'd become family. "Very well, make your final preparations. I'll inform Tannus. Let's go get this bitch and move on."

The tides of war ebbed and flowed with no regard to mortal concerns. Planets were consumed with unprecedented violence even as others entered a period of undeniable peace. Lives were lost. Others born. Time proceeded its eternal march. Heedless. Uncaring. And there, lurking in the quiet forgotten area between time and space, was the time of confluence. Threads once cast against the ocean of stars wove together. The time of the Three drew closer to its zenith. From it would be born a period of human history no living being could comprehend. One no one would forget for generations yet to come.

Tannus listened from the hallway as his chosen humans finalized their plans. They reminded him of another such council held long ago. Sighing, Tannus turned back the way he had come and left them to their devices.

All hail the gods of war.

NINE

3215 A.G. (After gods), Prekhauten Guard Training Facility, Tatarast Island, planet Vau Prime.

Sergeant Icarn checked his squad, again. They were spread out in a standard tactical wedge, advancing through the thick underbrush in the heart of the Tatarast field training area. Weapons dampened by inhibitors to prevent fatalities, the infantry squad was part of a full company deployed on a movement to contact drill. In theory, his people would make contact with the enemy and deploy on line. His squad was to lay down a base of fire while the second squad would come up on his right and attempt to flank the enemy. This was well established Guard doctrine executed on a hundred planets. Easy enough for those units already operating in the field. For Icarn, it was his first ride with the green troopers under his command.

He glanced at his time counter on his helmet's visor. A professional with over a decade of experience, Icarn hated relying on the helmet computers linking every Guard in his unit. He remained a visceral man in a technological society. He needed to smell the battlefield. See the terrain with his unenhanced sight. There was no substitute for the body's natural senses.

The point man crouched, grabbing his attention, throwing up a gloved fist over his left shoulder. The rest of the squad froze instead of spreading out like they'd trained a hundred times. Icarn fumed, though he supposed practical exercise was a far cry from the theoretical classroom blocks of instruction. He'd taken this squad out in dry runs a handful of times, each producing the expected amount of chaos and disappointment. This was their first run with live ammo. Icarn considered no one getting shot accidentally a mission success.

Much to his surprise, the junior team leader was already snapping at the others to remember their training and get in line to lay down the suppressive fire for the assault team. *Good man. Now if they can get their shit together before the Opfor makes contact we might be working with something here.*

Movement to contact was one of the simplest drills standard

infantry units executed. The main squad patrolled through an assigned sector or route of march in search of the enemy. Once contact was made, they performed assault operations to destroy the enemy and secure the objective. Easy enough, unless you were a green recruit still in training. Icarn held his breath, reserving judgment until they completed the assignment, and he conducted an after-action review.

The squad stumbled through the underbrush, breaking branches and announcing their presence. Icarn, a few steps behind, winced, thankful his face remained concealed behind his mask. Still, he gave them credit for making the attempt. With the base squad in position, nestling down behind fallen trees and any natural cover capable of concealing them, the assault element peeled off to the left where, in theory, they'd form a wide L shape and catch the advancing Opfor in a murderous crossfire.

His heart beat faster, as it did when he'd conducted active combat operations. Instincts kicked in, ones he repressed. This wasn't his operation and, as much as he wanted to get behind the trigger, Icarn was relegated to watching. Unarmed, all he could do was silently urge his trainees on step by step.

The first ion rifle snapped, followed by dozens more. The immediate area drowned under a barrage of fire—Icarn flinched, struggling not to take cover as the opposing elements became fully engaged. Flashbacks of the last major battle on Destriu III when he took a round in the thigh taunted him.

Individual icons representing Guards began flickering from blue to red as they were hit and, nominally, killed in action. Cries for medics went up and what should have been a superior action devolved into a nightmare only recruits were capable of creating. It was over in moments. Of the twenty Guards in his squad, only two remained untouched by enemy fire, and they were captured. Total mission failure.

Icarn removed his helmet, ran a hand through his close cropped, sweat soaked hair, and glared. "Fuck me," he muttered, already dreading the eventual report he'd have to send to higher. It was times like this he wished he smoked. Anything to calm his anger enough to think straight.

Icarn wondered if the Guards who'd sided with the rebels were experiencing similar results. He supposed he'd find out soon enough. Scuttlebutt said both sides were gearing up for one major campaign that might decide the fate of the universe. Icarn didn't know about that. Right now, his focus was on teaching his twenty knuckleheads how to survive.

He slammed the helmet back in place and stormed across the engagement area, a roiling storm no recruit in the universe was capable of withstanding.

"This is unacceptable," Mobus Kale snapped at the training command assembled in the war room.

Anxious faces stared back under the low lighting, fearful of his individual ire. Since assuming command of the Prekhauten Guard, General Kale enacted sweeping changes. Hundreds of senior officers and noncommissioned officers were relived and sent to forward operating units as punishment. The old command structure no longer existed. Those few who remained loyal to the Guard were watched with intense scrutiny. Should they fail or betray any part of his Guard, Inquisitors swept in and either executed them on the spot or hauled them away to clandestine Inquisition prisons for interrogation. Fear clashed with discipline under Mobus Kale's blanket of terror. Just the way he wanted it to.

"I expected this division to be trained and ready to fight. Instead, all I see is fodder incapable of surviving first contact," he continued. Raw anger twisted his face.

A junior colonel cleared his throat. "General, we have had this batch for less than four weeks. They have barely had time to learn the basics, much less advanced infantry tactics. We need more time if they are to be of use in the field."

"Time? How long do you think we have, Colonel?" Mobus pressed. "The enemy is building their strength faster and more efficiently than I am. They will soon be ready to launch a major assault, and this is the garbage you provide me. The only good these people will serve is by dying so better trained Guards survive. I expect better."

Uneasy silence settled in. They fidgeted. Shifted under his uncomfortable scrutiny. *Good.* Radiating aggression, several closest to him flinched.

"Correct these issues and get this division ready for combat on time and above expectations. I want them deployed to the staging area on the low continent and ready to deploy. Do not make me regret assigning you to accomplish this task."

The same colonel affirmed, "It will be so, General."

"It had better, or your head will decorate the front gates to this installation, Colonel."

Kale stormed off before they could rise to attention. His thoughts already on the fresh divisions of recruits passing their entry physicals and receiving the multitude of vaccinations and medical clearances necessary to join their basic training units. Thousands of men and women eager to do their part for the war. Though Kale doubted most entered service voluntarily, the conscripts would either fight or they would die. He didn't care which. The machine needed new parts to keep working. One body in uniform with a gun was just as good as the next.

His march took him through the winding corridors of the famed Prekhauten training complex. Orderlies and menials snapped to attention, pressing against the nearest wall as he swept past; Kale ignored them. His mood darkened with each step.

One thought kept circling his head—he needed to end the war. The only viable solution for that was to crush his enemy, obliterate all they stood for and represented to the point no one would seek to pick up the mantle for generations. He could not accomplish this without better quality recruits. Every indication pointed to raw failure. He considered removing the training cadre en masse.

A private, barely old enough to fire a weapon, walked up to him. Her legs trembled, giving her a wobbly presentation. Her cheeks flushed crimson, burning patches down her neck. Halting a respectable distance, she stood at attention.

"What?" he growled.

Swallowing, the private managed, "Sir, you have been ordered to contact Amongeratix immediately. He … he did not say why."

Kale knew his reputation. Whispers followed him. Monster, they called him. Barbarian and murderer. He relished the titles, knowing the value of fear. Snorting, Mobus offered a mock salute and dismissed her. *Of course, he didn't. I don't answer to him anymore than he does to me. Perhaps he has the news I have been waiting for. Perhaps, finally, it is time to unleash the full might of my war machine and crush our enemies once and for all. If only I can get this army trained in time.*

*

Krenz, planet Vau Prime.

The scourges swept through the city with intense frequency. Value was placed on the diminishing number of clergy. Of the original one hundred members of the Forum, thirteen remained on the wanted lists. All aspects of Conclave jurisdiction and mandates were being systematically removed.

Porii Daam watched the nightly newsvids, aghast at the caricature her beloved city became. The concept of such utter desecration infuriated and appalled her in equal measure. Vau Prime had been the jewel of the universe. The shining example all looked to. Now Krenz burned daily. The great beacons of light on Redemption Boulevard were dark. Statues of past leaders were pulled down to riotous crowds chanting Amongeratix's foul name. Sanity declined, replaced by the fervent fanaticism of the growing movement. Crime soared, ignored by the local authorities in favor of hunting down dissidents.

"Save your tears, woman. The time is past for such sentiments," Edam Boone told her as he found her weeping, again. The repeated phrase was becoming a mantra she hated

"How can I not? I am partly to blame for this nightmare," she countered. "We all are."

"I've been working against the Conclave for years. You professed to care for every citizen while lining your coffers and ignoring the plights of those unfortunates who did not serve your vision. I do not blame you personally, Porii Daam, but your robes and your inherent greed allowed that monster to subvert all we know."

She had no answer. Amongeratix brought his war to Vau Prime with such assurity no one, not even the wayward Inquisitor General, anticipated. Violence brought the planet to its knees.

"How do we make amends?"

"Can we?" Edam countered. "Every day sees our enemy grow stronger while we weaken. My network is being reduced faster than I can rebuild. The soul has been torn from Krenz. I fear there can be no return. Like it or not, this city will never recover. Those of us who remain will wither and fade."

"There is one last act of redemption we might enact," she said. The thoughts stewed over the past few days, prompting her careful introspection of who she was while limiting the conflict with who she wanted to become.

Edam cocked his head. "Go on."

"A handful of Cardinals have not yet been captured. There is a small chance we might reclaim the good will of the people and find restoration of purpose. We were not all bad, regardless of what you believe."

Edam had been around long enough to know a rat when he saw one and she fit every category. Working with Aliz and Julian opened his eyes to the corruption of the Conclave's inner circles. They'd been infiltrated and degraded from the inside. Aliz warned him of the bad actors playing both sides in the hopes of growing individual status in the new order. Edam knew Porii was part of the problem, not the solution. Yet for as tempting as the thought of turning her in for the reward money was, he couldn't abandon anyone fleeing for their life.

"I'm not in the refugee business, Porii Daam," he said.

"You took me in," she fired back.

"We happened to be in the right place at the right time," he countered. "Do not mistake humanity for kindness. The Conclave has choked and strangled this city for generations. You sat in your lofty towers, your richly appointed apartments without a thought for those you stepped on to reach your positions. When was the last time you went into the streets in your fancy red robes and met with those who look to you for succor? When was the last time you handed out bread or served soup in the homeless shelters? When has any of the Conclave done so?"

"I... I was part of the Forum. My duties prevented such interactions," Porii protested.

The words tasted flat between them. Edam looked away.

"No, that's a lie. The higher I rose, the easier it was to ignore the needs of the people. Everything became about status. Clout. I was working toward the top, where I would stand in consideration for Cardinal Seniorus should the position change again."

"And where did that get you?"

She bared her teeth at him. "Cast no judgments on me, Edam Boone. You and your band of criminals were once the most wanted people in this city. We all have demons struggling to break free. I looked after myself. If that is a crime, so be it."

"How dare you compare your ignorance with what my organization did for the citizens *you* left behind! Do you have any idea the stranglehold the Conclave put on ordinary people while you enjoyed your privileged lives? I've spent my life working through the slums, the forgotten bulk of society the Conclave shunned and turned a blind eye to."

Edam paused, the unwanted visions of a mother and child he had been unable to save teasing his psyche. "You were supposed to protect us. You were supposed to put the needs of the people ahead of your own. We looked to you for guidance, trusting in your closeness to the gods to ensure our lives were fruitful. Instead, you abandoned us when we needed you the most. That is a sin I can never forget."

From the corner of the room, huddled on a stool that had seen better days, Thopos chewed on the inside of his lip. He'd never seen Edam worked up like this and it disturbed him. Thopos feared any freed animosity threatened their already fragile plans. Frowning, he knew he had to do something.

"Edam is a passionate man," he began, startling Porii. "We were not always prone to violence. Our organization thrived under the Phos administration. You might not know this, but we had her ear and her quiet support. Aliz often came to us, when Zoraq Darc ran the crew. She took our grievances and concerns back to the Conclave and through her we finally had a voice. So much has changed in the last few years. We are shells of the men we once were. Do not think less of him for voicing his passions."

"I don't. I think less of myself for it," she admitted, surprising him. "How did you get involved in whatever this is?"

Thopos grinned. "That's a story for another time. What matters is we find a way to mend this bridge and work together. Time is running out. Sooner or later we're going to need to evacuate the planet, perhaps for good."

Porii allowed her head to drop. A show of humility she'd long forgotten. Consumed by personal quests for so long, she had abandoned all that made her the driving force she'd once been—a humble woman from a small planet. "I know my words feel little more than empty assurances. I do, but there is a way we may all benefit from our plight," she began, resolving settling in. "I propose we work together to get as many of our people away from the growing nightmare Krenz has become while there is still time."

"That's what we've been doing," Thopos said, though not

unkindly. "Edam and I stuck around after Aliz left to help as many as we could. The noose is getting tighter though. Amongeratix has turned the Inquisition into his personal shock troops. It might be time to cut and run."

She considered his words, knowing her heart warred with her mind on the issue. She still had contacts in the halls of power. Good men and women who went along with the enemy for fear of their lives, not base human hunger. "Let us do a little good in a world gone mad. Together, I believe we can make a difference."

"We've tried that and it didn't work. Kale tightened the screws on us," Edam snarled re-entering the room. "If you truly want to help, we need food, medicine, basic supplies for the countless families affected. Resources are dwindling the more trade is cut off from Vau Prime. What little remains is being horded by the new Guard. You help us and I'll see what I can do about getting some of your colleagues offworld."

Porii slumped as the adrenalin began to fade. "Thank you."

"Don't thank me yet. There's an army out there ready to stop us."

Thopos beamed at them. "See? I told you he could be reasonable."

Conclave District, Krenz.

He was patient from years of practice. Slowing his breathing, focusing on his mind, he sat in the shadows of a burned out building and watched the empty streets. Ironic that he was now the one being stalked but Akin Brohl was a man used to irony. His path of destruction across the city finally elicited the desired response. Garnering Amongeratix's attention proved more difficult than anticipated. The monster had grown cunning during Akin's slumber, forcing the god hunter to adjust tactics.

His foes were out there, scouring the city for the killer slaughtering entire squads of Guards and Inquisitors. Not a single civilian had been targeted, nor did he have any inclination to involve them. The innocent always suffered under the rule of the gods. Pawns and playthings, they toiled and died without notice from their cruel masters. Akin kept his targets to those in uniform, choosing to cut away the myriad weapons at Amongeratix's disposal. By his count, Akin left more than one hundred bodies across the cityscape, more than enough to build fear and demand attention.

Current conditions on Vau Prime proved as difficult as those on Occanum during the final days before the gods slaughtered each other. Remaining ahead of his pursuit and unpredictable allowed him to further infiltrate the degradations of Krenz unseen.

He decided on the fallen Conclave district for his battleground. The clergy were all but extinct. Those who remained went into hiding, desperate to escape from the planet. He made his lair on the second floor of an office suite overlooking the main boulevard. Clear fields of fire stretched for as far as his enhanced vision could see. Blind spots were covered with a tracking system capable of picking up movement from the smallest insect. Akin laced traps throughout the blind areas and focused on his chosen target areas.

Motion sensors emplaced on the far end of the street alerted him. Akin glanced at the monitor on his wrist. Numerous heat signatures approached, fanned out in standard infantry formation. His face remained impassive. Humans were far too easy to eliminate for his unique skillset.

He watched. Letting them approach with the false impunity advanced weapons and body armor imbued. This was an appetizer designed to steal his attention. Fools. Three thousand years and they failed to look beyond their preconceived notions on how the universe worked. He almost felt sorry for them.

Almost.

Akin punched in a code on his wrist monitor, bringing twin motion activated miniguns to life. Embedded in the rubble on both sides of the street, they were his first line of defense. The barrels spun as the Guard squad entered the kill zone. Blue-white ion rounds lanced from the darkness in steady streams, shredding the unsuspecting Guards in moments. The guns ceased fire, their barrels whirring as they slowed to a stop. Akin watched the heat signatures fade before he reached for his long rifle.

Akin ran the soft of his thumb over front sight and brought it to his lips as he nestled in behind the weapon. The barrel tracked slowly from left to right. Two figures crept into view, just on the edge of his periphery. Akin blinked. On the right was a large man wearing a twisted mask of a face. Fanatic. He'd encountered such before. It was the figure on the left capturing his attention. A Blood Witch, but unlike any he'd seen before.

Crimson robes declared her lethality, summoning visions from a violent past he'd all but forgotten. Magic danced from her robes. The Grand Mistress had not mentioned any divergences in her Order. Was this a new faction or a special unit designed for covert activities? Either way, for one to be working in concert with Amongeratix boded ill for the universe. He'd never killed a witch. Never even considered it. Until now.

The rifle fired. A silent projectile covering the five hundred meter distance in a single heartbeat. Yet instead of watching the blossom of blood on the man's chest before he fell, Akin saw his round dissipate in a splash of blue. Cursing, Akin fired again. And again. The big man stopped moving, head thrown back in laughter. Akin shifted to the Blood Witch and found her staring at him. For the first time, the god hunter felt doubt. He cranked off a pair of shots before collapsing the bipod and displacing to his fallback position. A moment later his hideout exploded in raw energy.

Debris pelted his back as he sprinted down the small hall to the stairs leading down to ground level. Alarms tripped. He would not panic. A god hunter never panicked. Lifting the trap floor, Akin dropped down and crawled the final thirty meters to his position across the street and began searching for new targets. His radar picked up another full squad approaching from the rear with twice that many coming up behind the witch. Perhaps he'd miscalculated …

An explosion rocked the ground, bringing down a pair of abandoned tenements. The rear Guards tripped his largest munitions and paid for it. Satisfied he only needed to contend with a single avenue of approach, he settled behind his rifle and took aim once more. The witch was gone, leaving the big man with his Guard entourage. Deciding numbers proved the greater threat, Akin began eliminating the Guards. They died without a sound. The big man produced a tulwar and strode forth, unconcerned about being hit. Akin was almost impressed.

With the last of the Guards dead or too wounded to continue, and an appropriate measure of fear instilled in any unseen squads, Akin set aside his rifle and drew his sword to meet the man head on. He closed the gap, moving to the center of the street. He needed to work fast to kill the man before the witch popped back up.

The big man reeled from his repeated blows, driving back step by precious step. Sweat beaded on his brow. The wild look in his eyes transformed to mild concern. Akin knew the man hadn't counted on hand-to-hand action. His eyes darted around, clearly searching for his companion. Akin pressed the attack. Steel ranged against steel. Sparks showered with each blow. The god hunter stepped to avoid a mighty swing of the tulwar, darting left to clip his foe above the knee. The blade was sharpened enough it should have sliced through flesh and bone—it did not. Unless he could break through the magical protections the man wore there was a real danger of losing this fight.

Akin stepped into the blow aimed for his head, shifting enough to avoid the impact. Their bodies collided. Muscles strained. They abandoned their steel and began pummeling each other with calloused fists. Akin landed three quick strikes to the ribs, earning a face full of spittle and blood for his efforts. The big man recoiled, lowering his profile and bringing his elbows in to protect his ribs. Akin's blows continued. Dark bruises sprouted on his opponent's face and chest. Sensing victory, Akin went in for the kill.

He was met with a head butt cracking his forehead. Stars filled his vision. Akin stumbled back a step a blow landing on his chest. Then another. The big man launched into a rain of aggression capable of breaking a lesser man. Akin tasted his own blood for the first time in memory then matched rage for rage. Regaining his footing, the blows continued.

Fresh squads of Guards swarmed in, careful to keep their distance. Akin ignored them, so intent on defeating the closest thing to a god he'd ever faced.

The world erupted in fury and magic. The witch's full power unleashed, turning the area into a melting hellscape. Hair caught aflame. Clothes singed.

"Enough!"

Akin took advantage of the witch's return by landing a crushing blow to the big man's chin, felling him as he spat a mouthful of teeth. Knowing he was in no condition to face her, he gestured with one hand and hurried down one of his escape routes, leaving that single word hanging in the air between them.

"You are certain?" Algiss Her asked, face twisted with consternation.

"Yes, Mistress. It was the only word he uttered before fleeing."

Fleeing? "We must tell Amongeratix at once. He will not like the news that one of Ruma Zzein's pets has resurfaced and is hunting him."

"But what of Occanum?"

"That is not for us to decide," Algiss replied. "He can deal with Occanum. Our focus must be on stopping the god hunter. I had not believed any yet lived. It would be a shame if he succeeded."

Evangaline remained silent. Like many of the sisters, Algiss knew they had no knowledge of the Grand Mistress's prized creations. God hunters were shunned creatures of myth. Forgotten relics of a time none remembered. Evangaline's introduction came at the cost of forty-seven Guards and Geres Auk being placed in the medical center.

"Mistress, the god hunter proved most formidable. It will take more than one sister to defeat him."

"Magic cannot kill them," Algiss replied. "Ruma created them to withstand the worst the Three had to throw at them. What they lacked in numbers they made up for in skill and tenacity. They slaughtered hundreds of Amongeratix's race. Now it appears they have returned to finish the job. You are certain it was just the one?"

The Crimson Mistress concealed her true emotions, all while wheels began to turn. This might prove beneficial to her desires. If she played it right. Her sole hope stemmed from understanding the god hunter's goal: Kill Amongeratix. The god hunter would not rest until either he was dead, or his target eliminated. Algiss saw a way to use that to her advantage. To shift the balance of power and alter the pieces on the board.

"He operated solo, with no backup or support," Evangaline confirmed.

Algiss nodded. She'd underestimated Ruma Zzein one too many times. None of the god hunters were rumored to have survived the last war, making the presence of one here unsettling. Her thoughts raced. The god hunters were the perfect killing instruments, blunt tools with singular purpose. They had no master. No morality. Stopping one proved all but impossible under the best circumstances, as the numerous Guards and Inquisitors already fallen could attest.

"Perhaps there is a way to wrest back control of this nightmare," she mused aloud. "Is that Assassin Guild still operating on Vau Prime?"

"I have no knowledge of such, Mistress," Evangaline said after a pause.

"Find out. If so, I want a contract secured. Send them after the god hunter. No price is too high. I will inform Amongeratix at the proper moment."

"Crimson Mistress, you just told me the god hunters cannot be killed by mortal hands."

Algiss glared at the junior Sister, eyes glowing orange beneath her hood. "They cannot. This is our one opportunity to eliminate a potential threat and bring our opponent into the open. Take away his hiding places and he with be forced to confront Amongeratix before he is ready or flee. Regardless, the damage done will be enough to spark our noble lord into action beyond his myopic fascination with this dying city."

And give us renewed authority. Algiss pursed her lips. It was thought so dark it inspired delight she hadn't felt since declaring her freedom from the oppressive Blood Witch regime.

"The Vaumagians might not take the contract," Evangaline said.

"Convince them."

Evangaline bowed. "It will be done, Mistress."

Algiss moved to dismiss then stopped to ask, "Updates on the barbarian?"

"He lives, though it may be some time before the medics heal his wounds. The god hunter proved most formidable. Geres Auk suffers from a punctured lung, internal bleeding, and numerous broken bones."

"Perhaps it would have been best to let the man die in the field," Algiss said. *Why did you not seize the opportunity while you have the chance, I wonder.*

"The surviving Guards were swift to recover from their shock. Their medics are most efficient in the field."

"Too efficient is appears," Algiss huffed. "Better they had let that monster die and rid of his incompetence for good. We have enough complications facing us."

"I did my best. The blast struck them both, making it appear an accident. Geres Auk has an uncanny knack for surviving," Evangaline explained.

"The worst of us often do. Go now. Find the assassins and set them on the hunt. I shall report to Amongeratix."

Evangaline bowed again and flowed from the room.

*

Occanum. The name bore little significance for her. That fateful battle on the now dead world had been long before her time. Her knowledge stemmed from ancient texts all but forgotten by most of the Order. Algiss never assumed the planet might resurface, but fate is ever fickle. *Would Amongeratix make more of this news than necessary?* Part of her wished for it. The prospect of death forces hands in desperate directions… She hurried off to meet with Amongeratix, plotting how best to twist the information to her advantage.

Abbey of the Order of Blood Witches, Acumensiis Comet.

Ruma Zzein's head snapped up. Pain lanced between her eyes, burrowing into the folds of her mind. The intense range of emotions assaulting her drove her to her knees. Her ancient body trembled. Eyes rolling to the back of her head, the Grand Mistress struggled to regain control. Moment by agonizing moment she reclaimed her affected systems. The pain lessened, though the ache remained. After long minutes she managed to get to her feet. Ruma extended an arm to the nearest wall to steady herself as the alarms began

Sisters hurried about, some aimless. Others lay collapsed in the halls. Ruma surveyed her kingdom with distress.

Forever Night had begun.

TEN

3215 A.G. (After gods), Eger City, planet Mannus Prime.

The grounds vibrated from the thousands of pairs of boots marching. Divisions of Prekhauten Guards, under the watchful eye of General Torgast moved into formation. Thirty thousand men and women, many of whom he'd fought against less than a year ago, forming proud ranks in their crispest uniforms, shined boots, and rifles slung over their shoulder. Guidons waved in the morning wind, declaring newly constituted unit colors. They represented the core of the Confederation's military strength. Formidable against any foe.

Still, too many whole divisions remained loyal to Vau Prime to be overcome by traditional warfare. Fortunately, Torgast had entire groups of special forces under his thumb. Non-kinetic warfare was the path to victory. He'd seen it with the opening of a second front unburdened by doctrine. Matthias' mercenaries ran rampant over the enemy supply lines while the Guards mysteriously detached to Tannus' command operated with impunity, reaping heavy casualties while incurring nominal losses.

Torgast quickly grasped the significance of creating a new doctrine. He and Matthias spent hours in discussion on proven special warfare tactics over the standard military doctrine. Regardless of the level of confidence he felt, Torgast knew he needed more of everything if he was going to best Vau Prime to the point they back downed and surrendered.

Shoving those thoughts aside, he watched the last battalion move into position under the band's drumroll. Horns blared over the parade field. He went to his hoverjeep and climbed abroad before giving the driver a nod. The smell of exhaust wrinkled his nose as the engine cranked over. Soon they were on their way to the far end of the division.

As much as Torgast would have liked to have avoided the situation entirely, he also recognized the need for unit pride. The Guards arrayed before him needed to know they made him proud and vice versa. The newly minted General of the Army let his mask of office settle into place as the jeep pulled into position and waited for the final bugle call. He caught furtive side glances from those Guards nearest, eager to see him for possibly the first time. A smile crossed his face in fond remembrance of those times when he stood in their boots.

The strangled bugle call dominated the field. Battalion commanders snapped to attention and executed an about face. Their orders barked at the top of their lungs as each commander called their unit to attention.

Torgast raised his arm to return their salutes. It was a time-honored tradition dating back to the formal founding of the Prekhauten Guard. A sign that the commanding general was paying his respects to those who were willing to fight and die by his word.

With another nod to his driver, he was taken back to the review stand where a gaggle of politicians and junior commanders awaited. He gave his adjutant a crisp salute, prompting the woman to spin around and bark the order every person in formation waited to hear.

"Pass, and review!"

The mighty war engine ground to life under the dominating sounds of the division field band. Torgast watched, duty and obligation clashing with his desire to be among them, as each unit marched closer, rendering honors to him in passing before they marched out of sight and back to their barracks to be released for the day. This moment signified the finality of their training.

They were ready to return to war. He could already see the crows beginning to circle.

Virom poured himself a glass of wine and collapsed into his favorite chair. He was in the official council lounge, a large room filled with bookshelves, antique furniture, and walls of tapestries and star charts. It was the one room unaffected by the war. The Cardinal relished in the sip of luxury as it touched his tongue before asking, "My back hurts from all that standing. How do you people do it?"

General Torgast grinned as he joined him, taking a seat nearby. He took a moment to fill his own glass. "Give it twenty years or so and it's all you think about every time you crawl out of bed. Your back hurts. Knees are shot. There are aches and pains far beyond what normal old age inspires. Some days it just isn't worth it to get out of bed."

"Nonsense. If we all felt that way nothing would ever get done,"

Virom countered and took another sip.

"Nothing getting done means there's no war, which doesn't sound like a bad thing to me."

"True," Virom conceded. "How many more of those insufferable parades do you have?"

"An endless stream from what I can tell. The army is coming together. I have almost ten divisions ready to deploy. Another ten in various stages of training. Six hundred thousand combat troops. By all accounts, a formidable combat force. The Conclave operated with less for much of its tenure."

"But?" He knew Torgast well enough by now to know the man held his concerns close, careful not to burden his friends with them. An admirable trait in most circumstances, but one serving little purpose in their current setting. He took in the lines forming on Torgast's face. The dark bags circling under his eyes. The sag of his shoulders when he once sat firm and dominant. Virom recognized the strain threatening to overwhelm him, for he felt it himself.

"Amongeratix's arrival on Vau Prime changes everything. We don't have the strength to face him and Mobus Kale simultaneously."

Virom drained the last few swallows his wine. "You are forgetting Kale's forces are spread across the universe. All activity suggests he hasn't been able to mobilize his full strength. We have a slim window to launch our offensive."

"And risk being hammered from behind by a counteroffensive," Torgast countered. "As much as I have confidence in our forces, we cannot withstand a two-front war."

Virom smiled. "All war is risk, at least that's what a close friend in the army is fond of reminding me."

"Don't throw my words back at me," Torgast scolded. "I know what I said, and I meant it, but this is different. We throw our shot in one blow and then what? Kale runs rampant over the universe and hope dies."

"Torgast, a lifetime in the Conclave has left me with one indelible conclusion. Humanity is more resourceful than you give them credit for. Evil may rise, but it seldom remains. Balance is the key to all life. The trick is discovering it before the hours grows late."

"You might want to lay off the wine. It's making you speak in riddles."

Virom laughed. "Perhaps. Perhaps. Of course that does nothing to alleviate the fact we must discover the path to balance. Amongeratix brings millennia of ill will and hatred. But he is not the end all. There are forces for good in the universe. Forces allying themselves with us even if we don't yet know it."

Torgast swirled the wine around in his glass. "Tannus."

"Tannus and the forces we have aligned with him," Virom said with a nod. "I know the basic facts, but not everything. He has a fleet of ships capable of destroying Amongeratix's command ship, thus giving us dominance over Kale's fleets as well. Also, Tannus has been working with a select group of Guards, Blood Witches, and Inquisitors for years now. From what I've been able to piece together from Falchi, they have been working in concert to destroy Nye's infrastructure. Our side has scored great victories in the field, paving the way for our next move. A move that must come now or we lose all momentum."

"I hear what you're saying, but the warning in my heart prevents me from committing our resources without actionable intelligence." Torgast set his glass down and gestured to city lurking outside his windows. "Show me concrete evidence this Tannus is on our side and not just using us to propagate his feud with his brothers and I might change my mind."

Virom reached into the folds of his robes and slid a piece of parchment across the table. "Balance, my friend."

Torgast took the parchment and read it. His eyes widened. "Is this true?"

"As far as we have been able to confirm."

"You realize this changes everything."

"Yes, but there is much work to be done before we begin scheduling the victory parade," Virom said watching his friend fight the hope wanting to break across his features. "Come, Adris has called a meeting. It appears Lord Tannus is requesting a virtual conference while he prepares his battlefront."

"Something tells me there is a lot more to this than a simple meeting."

"We shall see. A new era is beginning. Imagine the stories our grandchildren will have!"

"If we survive."

Brightstar, transit to Mannus Prime.

Admiral August stood in the center of the bridge staring into the vastness of space. Gone was the stress and intense sensation of always being behind. Thanks to the professionalism of her crew, August felt comfortable on Tannus' flagship at last. She marveled at the lack of vibrations in the decking. No obvious sense of travel other than the streaking stars flashing on the viewscreen. A quick scan showed her the crew adapted to their new stations with ease. Odir moved across the bridge, addressing issues and ensuring the ship ran at peak performance, making her job easier.

After a handful of rotations, Odir made his way back to her. "Hard to believe, isn't it, Admiral?"

Her eyebrow raised. "What?"

"How the *Solstice* fits in one of the docking bays with room to spare."

Her ship was considered large by Guard standards but appeared little more than a toy compared to the bulk of *Brightstar*. And she had ten of them under her command. Soon, they would be ready to undertake the first phase of Tannus' masterplan.

"The wonders of the universe never cease," she said. "Can you imagine an entire civilization of them? All giants waging a war of total annihilation while humans scrambled to escape before the end?"

"I'd rather not," Odir admitted.

August caught the pain behind his eyes and softened her stance. "I know. Fortunately, we only need to worry about the Three, two of which are on our side. I think."

"What side is that, Admiral?"

Heads turned at the sound of Tannus' voice. The favored son of the king stormed onto the bridge a god in his own right. Dressed in a sleeveless tunic and loose-fitting trousers, he cut a dashing figure. Long dark hair swept over his shoulders in an impressive mane. Sparing a glance at the bridge crew, Tannus settled into position beside the command staff and motioned for her to speak.

"We were discussing whether or not if your brother Sorrow can be counted upon to keep his word," August said after a pause.

Tannus barked a laugh. "Admiral August, Sorrow is many things. Dependable far from them. But I have every reason to suspect he will keep his vow, this time. He has always been the voice of reason among us. The one man desperate to stop the feud between Amongeratix and myself. We often thought him foolish at best. Neither of us believed he had a grasp on the situation. Turns out he was the only one who did. No, Admiral, Sorrow is not a trustworthy man, but he has no love for violence. He will do his part. One way or another, this war will end, and we can all find peace at last."

"Until another of your kind awakens to renew the nightmare," August caught the reluctant stares of the bridge crew, enraptured by the conversation while pretending not to listen as they went about their tasks. "Thousands of years may have passed since humanity served his people as slaves, yet the old resentment remained, and she wasn't ready to give it up.

"Sharlyn, there is no danger of that. I have taken every precaution to ensure I am the only one capable of awakening any of the seven hundred I scattered across the universe." She could see that Tannus was attempting to calm her fears. "Should that fail, I have failsafes in place. The tyranny of Amongeratix will be the last of our kind. You have my solemn vow."

August offered a clipped nod. "As you say. Forgive my questioning."

"Nonsense. We all need to be checked from time to time," Tannus reassured. "How long before we arrive at Mannus Prime?"

Odir cleared his throat. "Seventeen hours."

"Good. Have you already contacted the council?"

"We have," August answered. "They are awaiting you now. I can patch them through to your private study if you like."

He waved her off. "This works fine. I may be a man of many secrets but even I know there are times when history intersects with the present and witnesses are required. Let the crew hear our words. They deserve that much, and more."

August found no argument and allowed Odir to give the command.

As they waited for the council to appear onscreen, Tannus said, "Once we are in orbit over Vau Prime you may take *Solstice* and gather the remaining personnel you require. Take your time, but not too long."

"Of course," August replied.

"Onscreen now," Odir barked.

The images of the new council flickered before them. Tannus moved to the center of the bridge and began speaking. "Ladies and gentlemen of the Confederation, thank you for giving me a little of your time. As you are aware, these are unprecedented times for the human race. I come bearing arms and word of my intention to end the war once and for all."

At some point, August tuned him out. Words turned to promises. Promises to political overtones. She'd had enough of the trappings of power during her limited time in Eger City.

Docking bays, planet Wexanos.

Fies dropped his pack on the first seat of the troop ship behind the pilot's compartment and, rifle strapped to his back, went back to the rest of his company. The banter was gone. Guards finalized their precombat checks. Squad leaders inspected their personnel a final time. They wore combat fatigues and were all business. He appreciated their ability to flip the switch from clowning around to being battle ready.

Standing on the boarding ramp, watching his people conduct their final preparations, his mind drifted back in time to another deployment. Kastor had been his friend and mentor. No finer example of professionalism existed as far as Fies had been concerned. Losing him during the operation on Crimeat, before they knew there was a war, left the squad rattled and forced Fies to step up to fill the void. He did so, dragging the ever-reluctant Annalilly along with him. He wondered what Kastor would have thought seeing him now. His gaze was drawn to the giant woman picking her way through the Guards.

Paradise Tear held both hope and damnation in her hands. Fies felt like the woman had more to prove than any of his people, making her a potential liability on the battlefield. He needed his people sharp, not worrying about having Tannus' cousin among them. She spied him and headed his way.

"Good morning," he said as she approached.

"Good morning, Captain," Paradise replied. "I trust you will be able to depart on time."

"Looks that way. We've already loaded the bulk of the supplies and rations. All that remains is a final check by squad leaders and we can begin boarding. Can't say I don't wish you were coming with us."

She paused, cocking her head to fix him with a queer look. "Captain Fies, I have already given you all I have to ensure mission success. I am needed elsewhere."

"Cranking up three thousand year old machinery can't be that easy," he replied stiffer than intended. No matter how many times he dealt with the Three, and now their cousin, Fies found himself uncomfortable.

Paradise shifted. "You will be fine. I promise. We built our machines to be almost self-sufficient with unique human interfaces from a darker time."

It took him a moment to process the entirety of her words. "You mean from when your kind kept humans as slaves."

"Unfortunately."

Fies swallowed as his face reddened.

"Relax, Fies. Those days are long behind us all. Keep in mind yours is the dominant species in the universe," Paradise's sad laugh haunted him. "I wish I was going with you, but my cousin is most adamant about where I need to be at the end. Good luck, Fies. All shall work out."

I hope so. This isn't a complication I need today. Clearing his throat, Fies excused himself and barked, "Squad leaders! Make it fast. We got a job to do!"

Walking away, he decided her not joining the expedition wasn't a bad thing after all. Pairing Annalilly with Paradise might be the worst of all possible scenarios. He already had a narrow grasp on his sanity. Two of them teaming up on him would shred what little remained.

Jelin Quint adjusted the last strap on his soldier's pack and gave the man a slap on the back, signaling for him to join the rest of the squad. Staring at the squad, his mind raced over a million potential issues. *Do we have enough rations? Enough ammo packs? Medical supplies?* An endless string of questions, threatening to devolve into doubts, nagged him. Despite their crippling nature, these were problems every leader inherently shouldered the moment they agreed to step in front of others.

But he was a line soldier, unaccustomed to the loose operating style the rest of Fies' company felt so comfortable with. He'd grown through the ranks of the main army and brought a more rigid discipline to the field. Learning this new style of warfare thrilled him, even while the pit in his stomach continued growing.

"Everything all right, boss?"

He started, brought from his thoughts, and stared at Haggle. "Fine as can be. I still don't get it, Haggle. How can so many of you be this nonchalant about what we're attempting?"

Flashing his trademark grin, Haggle replied, "Easy. We don't have a clue what we're getting into! All we know is we're supposed to deploy to one of Occanum's moons and help Paradise Tear active the something or other. I figure that planet has been dead for so long there can't be much of a threat waiting for us."

"What if there is?" Jelin countered.

Haggle patted his rifle. "We can handle it. I hope."

Huffing out a stifling breath, Jelin said, "Seems a lot of this plan is based on hope."

"You've been in the Guard long enough to know that's all we need to make it through to the next mission."

"Here's to praying the are no more missions," Jelin added quietly.

Haggle stared at him then shrugged.

"Load up!"

As one, the company moved, lurching toward the boarding ramp and whatever destiny awaited. Jelin Quint hefted his pack and started walking. The ghosts of all those who had fallen followed him.

Annalilly counted heads as they passed. Many of her new company, thanks to Fies' philanthropic nature when it came to promotions, were strangers. Replacements brought in with the ship crews Admiral Falchi sent. What little she knew about their mission didn't suggest they needed the additional combat power, but the universe worked in mysterious ways. She'd endured enough to know not to pass up help when freely offered, even if it came with conditions.

Born for battle, she leapt at the opportunity to leave her homeworld and join the Prekhauten Guard. Coming from a warrior society, she viewed it as her chance to prove her worth in the field and return home to the glory and honor she deserved. She never counted on falling in love or discovering a passion to keep those around her alive. Those she'd served with the longest became family, replacing the empty sensation eating away at her confidence. One of the major recruiting pitches was claiming people found a home in the Guard. Annalilly certainly had and she wondered if these new recruits had as well.

"All packed up and ready to depart," Jelin announced from her side.

"Make sure they rest up. We don't know what we're walking

into on this one, Quint."

"At least it won't be fish," he countered.

She almost laughed. None of the squad who deployed to Dalafar had touched seafood since their return. "Strap in. I'll let the Old Man know we're good to go."

"Roger that."

Each Guard needed to be locked into their seats. Gravitational strain during departure was enough to tear a man in half. Every unit had a legend about that one Guard they saw it happen to. The old boots knew better, choosing to propagate the myth at the expense of the new recruits. One of the more popular cadences told the tale of a fresh-faced Guard meeting a gory demise when his harness failed.

Annalilly gave the bay a last look before heading into the belly of the beast. Wexanos was the closest to home she'd had in many years. A nagging feeling in the back of her head whispered she might not see it again. *Get a grip.* Emotions got in the way of the mission and, right now, she needed clarity.

Sweat streamed down her face. Her muscles ached. Pain throbbed in a dozen places. She watched sparks shower down from the automaton where one arm used to be. Elisa grinned; teeth smeared with blood. The voices in her head stilled. Elisa gave in to the quiet, her heart thundering. She'd wounded the machine for the first time. *Grimfurvor* hummed in her hand; the magic of the god killing weapon poured into her, a tidal wave of power and wisdom. For the first time, she felt unstoppable.

Elisa stalked toward the automaton. If the machine had the capability to understand it had gone from predator to prey it didn't show it—Elisa attacked. Her blade sliced through the fingers on the machine's remaining hand. Fluids shot out, bathing her tunic. She ignored it, pressing her advantage with a whirlwind of strikes driving the machine to its knees. A sad sound rattled around the automaton's chest cavity. The final blow severed its head. Elisa watched with grim satisfaction as the light faded from its eyes.

At last, her hated foe was dead.

Elisa picked herself from the dirt and brushed off what she could. In her hand, *Grimfurvor* stopped vibrating. *I did it...*

Ah'muf's clapping echoed throughout the arena, swelling her heart with pride. She'd lost so many times over the past few months victory felt impossible.

"Wonder of wonders! You have at last bested your hated foe!" Ah'muf shouted as she approached.

Elisa blushed despite herself. No matter how dire their circumstances grew, his support remained as high as it had been upon their first meeting in Tenemenah what felt a lifetime ago. Elisa had come a long way from the simple village girl on Crimeat when she had the misfortune of running into Mollock Bolle the first time. Now, she finally had something to live for. She accepted his embrace as he reached for her.

"This is a glorious day, *farisi*. You have at last proven you are master of that accursed weapon," he said into her shoulder. "Now we can complete your quest and be free at last!"

She clutched him tighter, unwilling to explain she doubted she could ever truly be free. Not after a lifetime spent in Sorrow's shadow. Not after being molded into the woman standing before Ah'muf now. A warrior of forgotten realms. A die cast against forgotten gods. The Paladin.

"But, by the gods, you smell bad!" he added.

Elisa barked a laugh. "I think I need that bath."

"With extra soap."

She stepped back and playfully punched him in the shoulder. "I need to see Tannus first."

Ah'muf brushed locks of his curly, black hair from his face. "But *farisi*, he departed this morning."

"He did what?" she snapped.

Ah'muf held up his hands. "Tannus departed for some planet. I don't recall the name. He and most of the others are all departing on different quests."

Why wasn't I told? Bastards! "Who is left, Ah'muf?"

"I do not know."

Anger aroused, Elisa stabbed *Grimfurvor* into its sheath. "I know who does. Come on."

He trailed after, jogging to match her stride.

She found Fistel in his usual domain, the elder librarian comfortable among his books and histories. His reaction at seeing her told her all she needed to know. Tannus had decided to leave her to her training while he went off to marshal forces for the coming war. Noble, if arrogant; Elisa fumed. Months training to master the weapon and her prized audience was gone. Without a goodbye or word of parting.

"I trust you have completed your task?" Fistel asked, going back to the tome before him.

"Yes. What am I supposed to do now?" she demanded. "Tannus was supposed to lead me to the next steps. How am I supposed to guess his plans like this?"

"You direct your anger at the wrong person, Elisa," Fistel replied with an even tone. "I am not your target, merely the only one here. That being said, I am not one to suffer ignorance."

Rebuked, Elisa stepped back. "My apologies. What am I supposed to do now, Fistel? I can't kill Amongeratix if I don't know what to do."

Fistel looked at her. "Elisa, I have been informed Lord Tannus will be in touch with you as soon as he is ready. He is currently on the way to meet with this ruling council of the new Confederation. The long game draws to conclusion. Your moment approaches. History will remember our deeds, if not our names."

"You're losing me, old man."

He smiled. "Tannus wishes you to be ready to depart on a moment's notice. I do not pretend to know what awaits you, Elisa, but I can tell you one small fact. You will be heading to Occanum next."

She cocked her head. "Occanum? That's a dead world. What could possibly be there?"

His eyes watered. "The final battle between brothers."

ELEVEN

3215 A.G. (After gods), north of Ankrit, planet An'kuruku.

Her skin itched from the relentless sunlight. Kaline cursed herself for not being fully prepared when Dejat hustled her aboard his skiff and south toward the deep desert. Returning to An'kuruku never felt more unbearable. A persistent dryness choked her. She no longer sweat. The desert sun sucked the moisture from her flesh. Despite her lament, Kaline knew it was too late to turn back. Dejat did not feel like the sort of man willing to let others back out of deals once struck.

The light scarf covering her face did little to prevent the sand from stabbing her face in passing. Microparticles lingered in the air, remnants of past sandstorms. Everywhere she looked Kaline saw naught but sand, red-stained rocks, and the promise of distant mountains. Scant clouds peppered the pale, blue sky. There was no hope of rain. No water sources in the open sands. It was, in her estimation, the sort of place hope went to die.

Kaline knew better, even if her mind struggled with maintaining sharpness. The desert was a land of secrets. Life abounded in the hidden, overlooked places outsiders lacked the desire to discover. She spied the tiny bushes lurking in the shadows. Lizards hiding in the lee of standing stones. Water hid beneath the rock, waiting to be used. She'd learned much during her previous stint on the planet. Given the proper education, one could live out in the desert for years.

She lacked that desire. Entirely at Dejat's mercy, she nestled into a corner of the skip and did her best to keep track of their journey south. Kaline knew little about their destination, only that it was the fourth largest city on the planet and the sight of the local religion. She scoffed at the idea of organized faith, knowing it for what it truly was. A lie meant to keep the masses in line and obeying the whims of the overlords on Vau Prime. Part of the allure of Rengu stemmed from her buried need to expose the truth to as many citizens as possible. Or so she lied to herself when no one was looking.

A shadow fell over her. "Dejat," she mumbled.

"Kaline, how are you enjoying your trip into the desert?"

Gone was the impressive stature she first encountered in Tenemenah. Dejat shed his cloak of civility, returning to his desert roots. His flowing robes were tanned and light, protecting from the worst the desert had to throw at them. His skin darkened under the sun's perpetual kiss. Dejat belonged in the desert. His appearance bore a sinister undertone, inspiring the thrill of fear deep within her. Kaline found a match for her ruthlessness in him.

"I have been here before, Dejat. The desert holds no value for me," she replied.

His thick brows pinched, darkening his face. "Ah, of course. I forget you were responsible for the great war along the Bo."

"I was but a pawn in a much larger game," she countered.

"Amongeratix. We have long sustained legends surrounding that monster, as we have his brothers." Dejat nodded. "They hold little sway over the worlds of men. Their glory is too far in the past to have bearing on tomorrow."

"Why are we traveling to Ankrit? I wasn't aware of any conclave seeking the word of Rengu."

"All secrets have layers, Kaline. You of all people should understand that," he reprimanded. "Ankrit is ancient. Revered among the true desert people. Ankrit is the ancestral home of all religions on An'kuruku. Temple complexes draw tens of thousands of pilgrims each year."

"I have no interests in local religions," Kaline repeated the mantra ingrained in her thoughts. "Rengu is the only faith we require."

"Why?"

Stunned, she asked, "What do you mean?"

Dejat extended an arm to the deserts. "Why Rengu? What does that relic offer the other gods do not? You bring purging fires in your wake, destroying families and burning worlds. I have done my research on you, Kaline. You are no paragon of virtue, despite what you would have us believe."

She rose, instantly regretting the decision as the sway of the skiff threatened to deposit her in the sand. "You think you know me? Tell me, Dejat. Tell me who I am. Where I come from. Why I am the way I am. Please, I am all ears."

He pressed closer, looming over her. "You are a shadow of a human being. A lost soul unsure where she is going and afraid to look back on where she has been. You hide behind your purported divine purpose and the false promises of Rengu while absorbing the hatred and pain of generations."

She swallowed, fidgeting under his scrutiny. The others on the skiff ignored them if they heard at all. Kaline had never felt so alone. So fragile. It was, when she finally admitted it, exhilarating in no way she'd ever experienced. The quiet part of her soul begged him to continue. To expose those dangerous thoughts she couldn't face herself.

"How many innocent lives lie in your wake? How many families torn asunder through your greed?" Dejat shook his head. "Ankrit will expunge your crimes, reshaping your sins to ones you will never forget."

"I don't understand." She clung to his presence. She needed more. Warmth spread through her body as she picked out the scent of spice wafting off him.

Dejat reached forth to lightly grab her chin between his thumb and index finger. "Your old persona has become irrelevant. Rengu no longer matters. The universe has moved on. Whatever mandate you once served is little more than a broken dream. The world is changing, Kaline. Word has reached us that the Inquisitor General is dead. The Conclave has officially been disbanded. The monster Amongeratix now rules Vau Prime. What little cohesion remaining in the universe hangs by a thread."

"But what—"

"Now is the time for a new order to arise. A new way of living humanity has not envisioned since the time of the great diaspora." Dejat released her, stepping back in a display of dominance.

Kaline ran through his claims, struggling to realize the full portent in them. If what he said was true, there was no longer a need for Rengu's cleansing fires. She was irrelevant. Just as she had been before Amongeratix came to her. But it was his divine plan setting her on this path. Why would he not have told her of his designs so she might adjust accordingly… A knot formed in her gut as the answer dawned.

She'd been naught but a pawn from the beginning. A damaged plaything with little value other than what he imbued within her.

Instead of rage, Kaline found herself void of emotion. "I shouldn't be here," she mused, avoiding his gaze.

Dejat sat opposite and clasped his hands. "Why did you return to the desert? What solace did you hope to find?"

She had no answer. For so long the only driving factor in her life was through spreading the flames of freedom. Or so she had been deceived into believing. The emptiness inspired by Dejat's words threatened to consume her. She needed an out. A way to prove her worth stemmed from more than the need to serve a higher power.

"What awaits me in Ankrit?"

He broke into a grin, predatory and appraising. "Everything."

Tenemenah Spaceport.

Tolde Breed felt abused by the constant heat bombarding him. His career took him across the universe, placing him in harm's way more than any man had the right to endure, but never in his travels did he encounter such misery. His body wept sweat in endless torrents despite the climate adapting microfabric woven into his attire. Surprisingly, only offworlders shared his misery. A look around showed none of the locals suffered, nor were they enveloped by formfitting clothing. He made a note of finding more appropriate clothing at the first opportunity.

The city was a far cry from what it had been before the start of the war. Amongeratix's campaign in the desert left the planet fractured on numerous levels. Most of an entire generation lay where they died, now little more than skeletons. The desert had a way of reclaiming what it was owed. Streets were half empty now, as were most shops and bazaars. Tolde took comfort in knowing the planet abstained from supporting either side in the war effort, deciding they'd suffered enough. He found no agents of the Inquisition or Guard patrols as he led his team to the nearest administratum offices.

A pair of guards in black robes and turbans stood watch at the base of the small flight of steps. Their curved swords, more for decoration and tradition than practicality, lent them an air of danger. Tolde spied the concealed blasters each wore. He suspected they were more than guards and as comfortable using their bare hands to neutralize threats as weapons. Catching the eye of the bigger one, he nodded and strode past.

The air inside caressed him with the false promise of coolness. Tolde knew better. However long their meeting with the administrator proved to be, they would soon be back on the streets in the unforgiving heat. He consulted with front desk clerk then followed her directions to the third floor where he found an overweight man with pinched glasses dozing. Tolde cleared his throat.

The man started before adjusting his glasses. "Ah, well, excuse me, but you do not have an appointment."

"I wasn't aware we required one," Tolde replied in an even voice. "We are here to see the administrator."

Flustered, the man shook his head. "Administrator Las'drul is a busy man. You need an appointment to see him."

Tolde rested his hand on his blaster and stepped closer. "We have come a long way on a special assignment for the Inquisitor General. You wouldn't want me reporting how uncooperative you were, would you? He is not a man prone to accepting disrespect."

"Er, no. No. That won't be necessary." The man swallowed nervously. "Let me inform the Administrator you have arrived."

Tolde sensed power building behind him. Sister Alessandra harbored no hesitation should matters not go their way. The clerk mumbled and excused himself before getting a response.

Tolde gave Alessandra a stern look to which the Blood Witch remained impassive, commenting, "I should have turned him into a lizard."

"You can do that?" Ragan gulped.

"I am a witch. A user of the ancient magic. I can do whatever I set my mind to."

Ragan slid a step to the side, almost bumping into Luma Kai who shared a look with Tolde. Presha Von snickered.

Their private moment ended as the clerk returned and held the door open for them. "Administrator Las'drul will be happy to see you now," he huffed.

They found the administrator of Tenemenah at his desk, remarkably small given the size of his office. Three walls of windows covered by thin sand colored fabric overlooked the heart of the city, filtering the sun while allowing the sounds and smells in. Young for his position, Las'drul bore all the hallmarks of a man who relished his role. His long fingers steepled in front of his face were thin, borderline arthritic. His gaze was sharp, contrasting with the weathered look on his face. Tolde remained unimpressed.

When he spoke, it was thin, rasping. "I was unaware of any official envoy visit from Vau Prime given the current circumstances."

"We aren't here representing the Inquisition," Tolde replied. "It was a necessary ruse to alleviate any potential issues."

"Under false pretenses, potentially creating more problems than solutions," Las'drul countered. "My people are accustomed to subterfuge, fortunately for you." His gaze settled on Sister Alessandra. "A Blood Witch. Here. What ill portents have brought to my planet?"

"Nothing that wasn't already here, I'm afraid. We come in search of a criminal," Tolde answered.

Las'drul gestured to the windows. "Take your pick. There are plenty of riffraff to choose from. Times have not been kind to An'kuruku in the aftermath of the Great Desert Ordeal."

Seems a bit pretentious. The entire universe is locked in a civil war, and this is your takeaway? Small wonder no one on either side has made an effort to sway the planet to their side. "The woman we are looking for is one of the propagators of your war, Administrator. We have every reason to believe she has returned and may possibly seek to reignite her previous efforts at dragging An'kuruku deeper into conflict."

Las'drul's eyes widened. He dropped his hands, placing them flat on his desk. "We have barely begun recovering from the first conflict. Additional violence might push our society to the brink of collapse."

"It will be far worse," Presha Von offered. "This woman is the sound of insanity. She twists and corrupts minds in an unholy crusade leaving entire planets bathed in revolution. Death follows her on swift wings, eager to feed. She must be found. She must be stopped, or the damage done in your desert will appear as mere child's play."

Tolde made a note to speak with her once they were alone. He appreciated the fervor of her speech, though questioned her eagerness to use this moment to contribute.

"Her name is Kaline. A woman of flaming red hair and silvered tongue," Tolde said, reasserting his control of the situation. "She is a fugitive and a wanted felon. Any assistance you may provide in helping us root her out will be most appreciated."

The administrator licked his lips. Tolde found over time that a true politician seldom offered something for nothing. This man was no different. "If I had knowledge of this woman, I would assuredly turn it over. Tenemenah has enough problems without an offworlder sparking revolution. What assurances can you provide that war will not return?"

"None," Tolde said flatly. "We have nothing to do with your politics. Our mission is capturing Kaline. Nothing more."

"Please, take a moment to understand my position. I am a businessman with a passion for my people. You come to me under false pretense, igniting my suspicions. You say you have no part in the war yet introduce yourself to my frightened clerk as a member of the Inquisition," Las'drul stated. "What other lies might drip from your silver tongue, I wonder."

"While I understand your—"

Magic flashed before Tolde could continue, blinding them. Las'drul squawked in terror, his fingertips charred. Smoke drifted from them, carrying the stench of burned hair and flesh.

"Enough," Sister Alessandra said. "We did not come here to bandy words with a man more intent on lining his pockets than stopping evil from taking root. Where is the woman? My next blast might not prove so accurate."

Blanching, Las'drul swallowed. "Whispers of this woman have reached me, though I have no knowledge of their truth," he told them. "She was last seen with a notable trader several days ago."

"You are certain?" Tolde pressed.

"Look around you, how many redhaired women have you seen upon arriving?"

"Do you know the man who met with her?"

Las'drul nodded, so slight it was almost imperceptible. "Yes. His name is Dejat. He is one of our more notable offworld traders. He has offices in the merchant district. They are not hard to find."

Sensing he wasn't going to get anything more from the man, Tolde said, "Thank you for your time, Administrator. With a little luck we will remove this cancer from your planet once and for all and in short order. We will be in touch if we require additional assistance."

"It would be my pleasure," Las'drul wheezed.

They found Dejat's offices easy enough. People in the city were more than happy to part with information, for a nominal fee. The hardest part of the trip proved to be avoiding the endless string of pickpockets and grifters manning every street corner. Older men and women worked through the crowds offering piping hot glasses of heavily sugared tea, followed by hawkers carrying large sticks of unfamiliar meats. Tolde was amazed anyone willingly drank the hot beverage in the sweltering midday heat.

The noise and bluster of the bazaar faded as they entered the merchant building. The air was dry and cool, temperature likely regulated to prevent goods in the warehouse from spoiling. The staff on duty were as cooperative as Las'drul had been—no one gave information freely in this city. Infuriated, Tolde threatened to have the entire workforce arrested and tried in the name of heresy. Only then did he get his answers.

"We must move quickly, lest we give the villain a chance to gain a foothold," Sister Alessandra said once they were seated in a quiet corner of a near empty café.

Meats, cheeses, freshly made flatbreads and more filled the table. Wine and water were plenty. It was the first true feast they'd enjoyed since leaving Wexanos. Each bite more delicious than the last.

"All we have is a city and a direction. We know nothing about Ankrit or what Dejat is planning on doing with our friend," Tolde said. His nerves were calmer now that he allowed the city to enter his mind.

Luma Kai pursed her lips. "I don't like it. A city that large won't be easy to sweep. They'll disappear before we can get close."

"What choice is there? We let her dig too deep, and she'll have an army surrounding her," Tolde said. "The quicker we wrap this up the quicker we return to Tannus and the war."

Eger City, planet Mannus Prime.

Dowan Mun pulled the curtain aside for the tenth time, scanning both sides of the empty street. Night had fallen on Eger City, cool and crisp as the seasons turned. Scattered clouds broke the moonlight bathing the quietening city. Crowds hurried home. Shops closed. A handful of pedestrians moved at the far end of the street. Nothing drawing additional focus from the former Inquisitor. A glance back into the room showed him Tinnus Har in deep conversation with the handful of locals seeking to restore the rule of the Conclave.

Men like Har seldom troubled him. He knew them for what they were, vipers lurking in the grass. It was the others, the locals working to undermine the legitimacy of the new government, that worried Dowan. If he had his way, they'd all be rotting in cells or corpses already.

Satisfied the street was clear, for the time being at least, Dowan focused on the odd assortment of people reaching far beyond their limits. To see them walk down the road sparked immediate suspicion. No two looked like they belonged together. If Dowan spied this, so too would the local patrols. Their leader was a short man professing to be a shop owner on the far side of town. His nasally voice made Dowan's skin crawl.

"We have several hundred at least," the self-proclaimed leader of the rebels admitted, though to what question Dowan hadn't heard.

Tinnus almost hissed. "Child's play! You come to me with pitiful numbers. How can I be expected to restart my reign as Cardinal Seniorus with mere hundreds?"

Their leader blinked. "I don't understand. We have been working diligently since the first announcement of this abomination."

"Clearly not hard enough." Tinnus sneered. "The numbers you bring me will result in little more than a minor skirmish. Their bloodshed will scarcely be remembered by the end of this generation. We need more."

"Where are we supposed to get the numbers you require?"

Dowan thought the man's name was Clarit, but he wasn't sure. Not that it mattered. Men like that were just as Tinnus said, unremembered.

"Not my problem. I did not come to you, if you recall."

Flustered, Clarit threw his hands up and walked off muttering. Dowan found the scene amusing. He'd been around enough power seekers and do gooders thinking to gain the upper hand in negotiations throughout his career. Few succeeded. The machine had a way of grinding you down, breaking your resolve and leaving you a shell of the man you began as. Dowan's gaze shifted to Har.

The former Cardinal Seniorus began pacing. His face a twisted mass of emotions, none of them pleasant. Whatever he thought was going to happen hadn't materialized.

Raised voices from the far side of the room drew his attention back to the locals. A fiery redhead gestured back toward Tinnus. Anger smoldered in those green eyes, intriguing the Inquisitor. Perhaps there was some resilience among them after all. He hooked an index finger behind the antiquated window shade and checked the street again. Two men stood on the end of the street, watching the building with rapt attention—this wasn't part of the plan.

Dowan made a noise to draw attention. He pointed outside

when he saw Tinnus and the others looking. The civilians became jerky, ready to bolt out the back door. Fools. If they'd been tailed every entry point would be watched. Reaching back through his memories, Dowan failed to discover any point during his operations brief where Matthias promised to apply pressure this early in the game. The inevitable conclusion was another player had entered the game. One determined to remove as many threats as possible.

"We need to move," he said. The command was hard, leaving no room for discussion.

"What is it now?" Tinnus demanded. "I'm in no mood for games, Inquisitor."

"This isn't a game. Armed men are watching the building," Dowan said. "My guess is they followed our friends here."

"Impossible!" the redhead spat. "We took every precaution. You must be mistaken."

Dowan gestured to the door. "See for yourself. I'm not here for you."

She balked. He watched as reality swept in. He'd seen similar situations before. Every attempted coup failed without proper planning. Planning none of the seamstresses, merchants, and businessmen seemed to have given consideration until now. Under different circumstances Dowan might have considered turning them in and being done with the mission. Intuition whispered he shouldn't. Watching their paranoia rise suggested they were about to make a devastating mistake.

"They're coming closer," Dowan observed. "Time is up."

Tinnus sneered. "Let them come."

"I don't think you understand," Dowan said with a frown. "These men are coming to kill you, not talk. I don't have enough firepower to stop them all."

Tinnus slammed a fist into the nearest wall. After a deep breath, he dismissed Dowan with a backhanded wave. "Very well. Get us out of here, Inquisitor. Quickly."

Giving the street a final look, Dowan ushered them toward the back under a chorus of protests. It took the flash of his blaster to silence them. Undeterred and praying it wasn't too late, he led them down a small corridor. The back door was in sight, but he had another idea. Dowan stopped at the second door from the end of the hall and, punching in the access code, revealed a passage leading down. He gestured for the redhead to go first. Perhaps some time in the subterranean realm would temper her fury.

The others followed like sheep, Tinnus Har the last in line. Dowan checked both sides of the hall to ensure their pursuers hadn't entered yet and hurried to join them. The door slid closed and locked, leaving them in near darkness. The fetid stench of sewage assaulted his nose. Dowan was no fan of enclosed spaces, but survival seldom considered personal preference. He pushed his way to the front of the line, taking note of the panicked civilians realizing they were in over their heads, and lead them deeper into the dark.

"Are you certain this is the best path forward?" Adris asked. She tapped a fingernail on the desk, beating a steady drum. Governing came easily to her, though she had no experience with large scale warfare. "We are taking an awful risk with this."

"Risk is necessary to make this diversion stick," Torgast said, his tone gruff.

She looked up, noting the red streaks in his eyes. None of them had slept much since Tannus announced his plans to finish the war. News spread unchecked. Ripples of discomfort gripped the council even as the population celebrated the end to the long war. Victory far from assured, Adris found it all but impossible to maintain focus on the growing list of tasks facing them. She needed more time.

"We have what, three hundred thousand soldiers ready to fight? Throw in Khe-Zhehan's fleet and we might last for a while," she mused a loud, shaking her head. She saw a flash of grey and sighed. The stress of the job threatened to make her an old woman well before her time. "It won't be enough."

"More forces arrive daily," Torgast countered. "We have established training facilities on a dozen planets. I expect our numbers to double well before any engagement with Amongeratix. There is also the promise of Sorrow's army."

Adris frowned. Her faith in the gods lay shattered, and she never developed a trust for any of the Three, despite the assurances of many now in her inner circle. They were relics of a brutal age responsible for nearly wiping humanity out of existence. During what little private time she managed, Adris read the histories. She learned enough to suggest this was but another iteration of an endless cycle of war between the brothers. No generation who'd fought for either side had come away unscathed. And with nothing to pray to, Adris Moscasco found herself confronted by her own mortality.

"Do you trust that creature?" she asked, choosing not to bandy childish insults. The Bloody Man was a nightmare mothers frightened their unruly children with. Knowing he was real, and a viable threat, unnerved her more than she wanted to admit. "The Bloody Man."

"How much can we trust any of them? My understanding is limited but I get the feeling we're little more than pawns."

She nodded in agreement. "We must take every precaution to ensure we don't suffer a similar fate to past generations. Tannus may come with promises of finality, thinking to sway us with his golden tongue but he is not human."

From his now favorite chair by the window overlooking the city center, Virom set down his small cut of caf and said, "I dare suggest they are all more human than us."

"Come again?" Torgast asked.

"Think about it. Three brothers. Each represents a different faction. One is wholly evil. A threat needing to be put down. One is the personification of good. His actions, though somewhat skewed, are done with good intentions and the future in mind. The third brother is the key. He is indecisive, often choosing which side to follow based on whim. He lacks the strength to stop either from their war. Good. Evil. Indifferent. They are not so different from the rest of us."

"They are responsible for countless deaths over the past three thousand years, Cardinal," Adris pressed. "They are anathema to all we hold dear."

"They have done nothing we haven't done to ourselves," Virom countered. "I submit the Three are a reflection of us."

"That's unsettling," Torgast said and slumped into his chair. "Are you sure that's caf?"

Virom smiled. "Best in the city."

He passed the cup to his friend, who took a tentative sip. The Cardinal chuckled as Torgast spat out a mouthful of pure liquor.

"Be that as it may, they hold our destruction in their hands," Adris said, finding no amusement in their antics. "The question remains, can we trust the Bloody Man to uphold his oath?"

"Tannus says he has an army of automatons ready to deploy. I believe him. I have to," Torgast answered. "The machines will prove formidable in the field. Each one used saves a human life, Adris. Lives you have already pointed out are in short supply."

"And if they turn on us?" she asked. "History is littered with past examples, Torgast."

He shrugged. "Doesn't matter. If it gets to that point, we're all dead."

"You still intend on deploying with the army?" she asked.

"Is there a choice?" he countered.

She simmered, knowing he was right. "I don't like it. You are a member of the council and an important voice in our Confederation. We can't afford to lose you."

"Adris, I won't be in the front lines. I am the commanding general of the army, not a battalion commander," he soothed. "I'll be fine and like I said, if I'm not it won't matter."

Adris turned her gaze on the Cardinal who remained a happy bystander in their argument. She wished she had the luxury. "Very well," she said at last. "If there is no swaying you, I trust you will do what is necessary to keep as many of our people alive as possible."

"I wouldn't be good at my job otherwise."

A measure of tension slipped away. Her shoulders relaxed. One problem gone. A million others remained. She reached for the intercom. "Tempest, we're ready to see the Admiral now."

This was a meeting she had no stomach for. Khe-Zhehan was a shadow of her former self, by all accounts. Adris never knew the woman before now, leaving her without a baseline to judge her by. The perceived failure in the Vau System left their most seasoned naval commander rattled with self-doubt. The sooner Adris helped her come to terms with the situation the sooner they could both return to leading others.

TWELVE

3215 A.G. (After gods), entering orbit over Ferom, planet Occanum.

"Entering Ferom's gravity well. Estimated time on target is fifteen mikes," the pilot called.

Fies drew a deep, calming breath. He'd been deployed more times than a Guard deserved over the course of a normal career. Too often to succumb to jitters.

He tromped through the troop carrier, slapping Guards on the shoulder. Joking with others. They weren't expecting a combat drop, but he'd learned long ago not to become complacent. The entire universe was screwy. He chose to leave nothing to chance. A hand gesture later, his company began slipping into their combat gear and cycling through their individual prebattle rituals. He left them to it, knowing the importance of the moment. One factor no one questioned was the superstitions of the Prekhauten Guard.

Reaching his seat, Fies reached down for his body armor. Thoughts of Wexanos comforted him as he geared up. He'd taken to the planet in ways he never thought possible. The serenity stilled the voices in the back of his mind. Whispered it was all going to be fine. He desperately wanted to believe them, even while knowing this might be his final mission. Thus far, his unit escaped the mauling so many others endured. Sure, they'd lost a man here and there. Nothing as devastating as the enemy army on Mannus, however. Fies didn't see that trend continuing. War had a way of devouring souls with ruthless indifference.

"Hey, you sure we're not in for a welcome down there?" Haggle asked over the low hum of the transport.

It would be Haggle to ask this. The portly Guard had been with him from the beginning and never lost his sense of humor. "Not for me to say. Keep your people alert. Intel states nothing of value is on that moon. Doesn't mean Amongeratix hasn't laid a trap for us."

Haggle fell silent, clearly that was not the response he had hoped for.

Fies took the opportunity to address as many of the company as were in hearing distance. "That goes for all of you. We've come this far. I don't want any unnecessary casualties. Do your jobs. Keep your squads in check. Take nothing for granted. Do it right and we all get to go home when this shit show is over. Understood?"

Nods, grunts, and less than enthusiastic cheers came back to him. Typical banter for soldiers about to step into the unknown. An unwritten rule stated never talk about home. Don't even think it. Stash it in the corner of your mind and pick it up again when you boarded that final bird out of the engagement zone. Too many Guards died because their focus was on home and their loved ones instead of the enemy. Fies knew there was no stopping it. Human nature dictated such, but that didn't mean he couldn't try and beat it into submission.

He took another deep breath and pulled his helmet down over his head. With the visor up, he gave his people a final look over, taking time to catch the eye of each squad and platoon leader.

An alarm sounded. The troop transport's interior lights switched to an eerie red. Guards took their seats, strapping in as the craft began the long descent to the surface and whatever fates awaiting.

Ferom was much like its planet, dead. The ruins of an ancient civilization were evident across the surface, most of them destroyed by meteor strikes through the years. A thin layer of sickly grasses and scrub brush dotted the endless plains. With no sustainable atmosphere, the Guards were forced to rely on their equipment to keep them alive. Fies hadn't worked in such a harsh environment before. Not many in his strike force had. That didn't stop them from rushing forward to secure their initial objectives and establish a defensive breach. Hunkered down behind whatever natural cover was available, the Guards scanned the horizon for signs of an enemy.

Only when he became certain they were alone did Fies rise and signal the lead squad to advance. They used thousand-year-old schematics to navigate the ruins. Tannus assured them the facility had been constructed long after the conclusion of the seventh war between brothers with the sole purpose of providing a staging base for subsequent assaults. He mentioned the base had been armed with heavy weaponry capable of targeting planetary surface units on nearby Occanum.

Fies marveled at the simplicity of the ruins, finding it difficult to imagine a thriving colony ever existed. They followed the trail to a pair of fallen columns depicting various alien creatures he hoped were either extinct or figments of imagination. The rest of the company spread out in formation covering the entry point while Annalilly punched in the access code Tannus had given them. The ground began vibrating as a loud humming sound shattered the calm. Fies felt his knees buckle the moment the massive doors parted. A gust of wind pushed out, telling him the facility was intact.

Perfect. Now all we have to do is figure out how to get it online before the army arrives. "Annalilly, send them in," he ordered.

He noticed the yellow lightning bolt painted on the side of her helmet. *That's new. Where did she find the paint?*

"Roger that. Quint, you got point."

His old squad filed inside, instantly taking up both sides of the hall. Motion sensor lights activated in their passing. Fies couldn't imagine the power plant keeping this monstrosity running for so long. Then again, Wexanos ran as efficiently as any Conclave made complex. He supposed the work of the gods was meant to stand the test of time. *Not gods, fool. They're just an older race of assholes determined to get everyone killed. Come to think of it, we never did learn who they really were. Tannus never bothered saying either. Fucker.*

"Secure," Annalilly confirmed.

Fies ordered the rest of the company to follow him in. Gravity became lighter the instant he stepped inside. He felt the difference at once. "Are the air purifiers running?"

"Confirmed," Quint answered. "Oxygen is nominal for humans. We should be able to go without the helmets once the outer doors are sealed."

Good enough for me. Fies opened a channel back to the drop ship. "This is ground commander. We are secure here. Go ahead and move the ship to your coordinates and await further instructions."

"Roger. Transport moving now."

Fiest caught the blue-white flare of engines as the ship lifted off. He watched until it disappeared enroute to a small basin an hour west, just large enough to hide a ship with active cloaking. Occanum loomed in the background. A constant reminder of what awaited should they fail.

"Get these doors closed. Quint, push forward to the operations center. Might as well find out what we're working with," he ordered.

"Everyone else move to your secondary objectives. Report in once clear and secure."

The company splintered, each squad and fire team burrowing deeper into the belly of the beast. Fies had never felt more alone.

CNV *Solstice*, planet Solecca.

Sharlyn August watched the planet get closer, filling the monitors with various shades of green and blue. As much as she loved being onboard her ship, she needed the feel of solid ground to remind her of what she fought for. Orbiting traffic streamed to and from the planet and the handful of satellite stations. Nestled off the main trade route for this sector, Solecca was a hidden gem. And she was bringing war to it. Guilt gnawed on her, inspiring doubts far too late to do anything about. Somewhere in the tangle of ships and personnel was Vicente Blackheart and his crew. Her heart beat faster at the thought of him being on her bridge again. She didn't deny she had feelings for him. He proved charismatic in all the right ways. Alluring in the wrong ones.

"Entering planetary orbit, Admiral," Odir announced.

She admired her former First Officer for his patience and unwillingness to grow agitated at giving up his place on the bridge. August understood the pressures of having senior officers aboard. Fortunately, they'd served together for so long neither minded the other. She nodded. "Very good, Captain. Secure a berth and let's get this over with."

He started to reply, then paused, before saying, "Aye, ma'am."

She knew his thoughts. Many of which were shared by the crew. Working hand in hand with pirates went against every Guard code. Their first combined endeavor left many with rankled feelings. Locked in the conflict, she empathized with her crew. Duty and loyalty altered the deeper into the war they plunged, forcing each individual to look within to determine what they were comfortable with. Thus far, not a sailor aboard had walked away. August hoped the trend continued.

Making a note to speak with Odir when they had a moment alone, August turned her attention to the approaching planet. "Let's hope this works."

"We already know their operating mode, Admiral," Odir

reminded. "A handful of miscreants aboard shouldn't pose much of a threat if we keep them confined to one area without access to important operating systems."

August flinched. "We cannot afford to treat our guests like prisoners. They come willingly to assist us, Odir. Remember that. We went to them."

He bristled. "Aye, ma'am."

"Odir, this is temporary."

They'd gone over the plan several times, ensuring all parties understood their role and the expectations for Blackheart's crew. Khe-Zhehan's failed gambit over Vau Prime provided enough intelligence to suggest the only way the ragtag fleets of the Confederation could find victory was through a vastly different approach. Easier said than done. Enlisting Blackheart threw the manual away and, she hoped, presented a new threat no one in Krenz saw coming.

He stiffened. "I didn't say a word, ma'am."

Oh Odir, how do I tell you I plan on giving Blackheart one of Tannus' ships if he proves worthy?

"Put me through to Blackheart. The sooner we're heading back to the fleet the better," she decided to say.

Moments later, Blackheart's voice filled the bridge speakers. "Took you long enough. My men have already blown all their pay. A bored crew is a dangerous one."

"Blackheart, your men will get all the action they require soon enough. Transmit your coordinates. We will be on station in minutes." She stifled a smile at hearing his voice.

"Copy."

Armed guards lined the docking corridor. August held a modicum of trust in the pirate but wasn't foolish enough to take unnecessary chances. Blackheart's ship was old and falling apart, making the *Solstice* a tempting target. A contingent of Marines led by Sergeant Talore stood ready to handle any threats, perceived or real. With Odir at her side, August awaited the airlock opening.

Krimpen Mass and Time entered her ship with bemused looks. August felt the scream building. Her previous experience with these two left her annoyed, rattled, and disturbed. Their quick banter infuriated her to no ends. If Blackheart brought them along, he must have good reason, even if it wasn't good enough for her.

"Permission to come aboard, Cap'n!" Krimpen announced.

Talore's Marines shifted, rifles raising just a hair.

August tried to conceal her scowl. "If you must. I wasn't aware Blackheart intended on hiring you."

Time shrugged. "Guess he's smarter than he looks."

"That's debatable." August stepped aside. "Please follow my escort. They will show you to your quarters."

Krimpen's head bobbed. "Good. Good. When do we get our weapons and uniforms?"

"What exactly did Blackheart tell you was happening here?" she pressed.

They exchanged a private look, further confusing her. "Why, we're signing up for the big crusade. I think."

"But you're not enlisting," she countered. "There are no uniforms or Prekhauten weapons. What you have is what you get."

"Do we at least get to fight?" Krimpen asked, running a hand over the stubble on his chin.

"More than you could ever wish for," she replied.

He slapped Time on the back. "Good enough for us! Lead on. I'm famished."

"We just ate," Time reminded.

Krimpen winked. "They don't need to know that."

August watched them being led away, her blood pressure already rising.

"I see you've already become smitten with my recent additions," Vicente Blackheart said as he stepped into the *Solstice*. "I couldn't resist a bit of theatrics to brighten the mood."

"You also couldn't be bothered to give us a heads up," August snarled. "I should have them vented."

"They're more valuable than you give them credit for," he soothed. "You know their worth, Sharlyn. Besides, they're not so bad once you get them to shut up."

Taking a moment, she glanced behind him and saw a ragged mob of sailors, convicts, and wanted felons. The Marines remained still. Not a shot was fired. Nor a word spoken in anger. August considered it a minor victory.

"Get aboard before I change my mind."

With a bow, he followed her.

"How many men did you bring?" she asked as they wound their

way through the belly of her ship.

"Seventy-eight. My whole crew minus a few who'd had enough of Prekhauten regulations."

Nowhere near what he needed to bring one of the massive dreadnaughts to life, August would be forced to round out his crew with staff from Mannus. She would have to consider assigning his people to *Brightstar* to alleviate some of the issues bound to pop up.

"Including your two friends from Crimeat?"

"No. They are in their own little world. I learned long ago not to question their motives, you won't get anywhere," Blackheart said. "Krimpen Mass and Time are unique people. For some odd reason they believe they are here for my private security."

She paused midstride. "Private security?"

He shrugged. "Best not to rock the boat too soon. They'll hold their own in a fight. You've seen that. Just let me handle them. It shouldn't be an issue. Though, they do wish to know where we are headed."

"I'm not at liberty to say," she replied, holding up a hand when he frowned. "Not to them or you. Tannus wants to play this op close."

"Tannus? You are working with one of the Three?" he gawked.

"And that's all I'm at liberty to say."

They reached the bridge to find the crew abuzz with activity. Warning alarms glowed red on several screens. Odir stood in the center of the storm directing the response. He glanced over his shoulder as they arrived.

"What in the hells is happening here, Odir?" she demanded as her eyes were pulled the data arrays.

"It started with a squadron of small craft flying dangerously close. That escalated to a demand from their carrier that we turn over the villain Vicente Blackheart," Odir replied. "I told them no."

"Good man. Any idea who they are?"

He shook his head. "Their ship isn't registered in any database we can access. Whoever they are seem fairly determined to get him in their custody. We've come close to opening fire several times."

She studied the tactical situation, desperate to find a way out of the mess without compromising their mission or dragging the Confederation into a fight with an unknown entity. She turned to Blackheart. "Friends of yours?"

"No one I know, but that does not mean they don't know me,"

he answered.

August sighed. "Out with it." Premonitions of the future plagued her, making her question her decision to involve him.

"Well, as I mentioned, my crew have blown through their earnings and, well, empty hands inspire foolish deeds. Some of them decided it was in their best interests to knock off a local bank. I assure you I had nothing to do with such an act and admonished them appropriately once I knew you were coming."

His wince convinced her he wasn't being fully honest. August forced aside her personal misgivings to focus on the threat. "Class of the carrier?"

A nearby tactical officer replied, "Strike class. Crew of one hundred-thirty with a full squadron compliment. Light armament and anti-ship weapons."

"Nothing long range or capable of taking us out?"

"No, ma'am. There is a risk from the fighters however."

Fuming, August ordered, "Activate all anti-ship batteries. I want a firing solution plotted on that carrier. Put us in general quarters, Odir."

The warning activated. She felt her crew hurrying to their battle stations. Satisfied *Solstice* was battle ready, she ordered, "Hail our new friends."

"Attention enemy vessel, this is the Confederation Naval vessel *Solstice*."

A burly man with a patch over his left eye appeared on screen. The scar ran from his temple down to his upper lip. August spied missing teeth under the cast of shadows.

"There's no enemy here, Guard. Not unless you don't plan on handing over that son of bitch you have hiding behind you," the captain replied. He coughed, wet and phlegmy. "Give us Blackheart and we're square."

"Captain Blackheart is a guest of the Confederation Navy. As such, I am responsible for his safety and wellbeing," August replied.

The man blustered, spittle flying from his cracked face. "I said give him to me!"

"Who am I speaking to again?" she asked. "I don't recall catching your name."

He paused, eyes pinching together. "Eh? My name isn't the issue. He's a criminal and I owe him for what he did to me."

Making a note to confront Blackheart later, August offered the captain a cold smile. "Then I'm afraid our conversation is concluded. Order your fighters to stand down and return to their hangars or we will blow you out of orbit."

"On whose authority?" he spat.

"Mine." She rose, ensuring he caught a good look at her admiral epaulettes. "You have sixty seconds to comply."

Odir cut the sound, leaving the man's rants unheard. Blackheart, to his credit, made himself small in her shadow. Unwilling to provoke a battle in innocent airspace, August couldn't attempt to flee either. She was trapped.

"Captain Odir, if this idiot fails to comply plot a course to empty space far away from the shipping lanes," she said. "We'll take care of him there."

"Aye, ma'am. Cripple or kill?"

"Depends on what sort of mood he puts me in," she blustered.

Blackheart began to speak when she cut him off with a glare. She certainly didn't want to kill unless she had to. "Put him back on. Time's up, Captain. What's your response?"

A trio of fighters swooped in across her bow, firing as they went; August nodded. *Fight it is.* "Odir, back us away. We don't have time for this."

Solstice edged away from their foe, luring the carrier away from any help. She hadn't come to Solecca looking for a fight, but Sharlyn August was damned if she was going to run. Her nails dug into the worn cushioning armrests, slipping into familiar grooves. Her gaze steeled, disappointed to find the small carrier giving pursuit.

Inquisition Headquarters, Krenz, planet Vau Prime.

Reports streamed in. Countless casualties mounted across the city as the god hunter attempted to draw out his ancient foe. From his offices overlooking the now darkened Redemption Boulevard, Ezekiel Goethe found it impossible to sit still. Ghosts crowded the night and he grew certain they clamored for his blood. Ascending to the top of the throne proved a far cry from what he imagined during the countless years toiling through the junior ranks. The Inquisition was a mighty dragon, wild and untamable. Ezekiel failed to grasp the nuances of previous Inquisitor Generals.

Not that their leadership mattered much. Only one suffered through Amongeratix's guile. How Alain Nye turned remained a mystery to Ezekiel. He understood the why, if not the how. The Three were cunning beyond human comprehension, capable of twisting the mind to serve their nefarious purposes with little effort. While Ezekiel liked to think he was made of sterner material, he wondered how long his mind could withstand the pressures of daily encounters with the destroyer of worlds.

Compounding his misery was the unanticipated arrival of the god hunter.

Ezekiel studied the recent casualty numbers. A sick feeling built in his stomach. "Three hundred and seven. How in the fuck is that even possible given the levels of security in this damned city?"

From the far side of the office, his assistant, a man he hadn't bothered to learn his name, perked up. "Sir?"

"Nothing. Why can't anyone explain to me how one man is responsible for so much wanton death? No use having those blasted witches around. They can't stop him either. So here I am, forced to send my resources into a hopeless situation when the one being on this planet cowers on his new throne!"

To his credit, the assistant remained silent.

"Is that ape Geres Auk out of the medical center yet?" Ezekiel changed subjects. He couldn't waste the time on a single point.

"We've received no word on his condition," the assistant said after checking his datapad. "I can send a runner to confirm his whereabouts, sir."

Geres served his purpose but lacked basic human social graces. "No, that isn't necessary."

A datapad beeped, drawing his attention.

"There is an envoy awaiting you in the antechamber," the man continued, confusion in his voice. "Odd, I don't recall seeing this on my schedule before."

"I have no meetings on my schedule for the rest of the day. Where did they come from?"

"I don't know. Shall I send them away, sir?"

Ezekiel decided he needed a change of pace for the distraction. "No, send them in, but have my guards on standby."

Bowing, the assistant left.

Ezekiel wasn't alone for more than a moment before a pair of men entered the office. Dressed in traditional Guard attire, they bore little resemblance to fighters. Little hairs on the back of Ezekiel's neck rose. "Who are you and why have you come to me? Quickly else I take both your tongues. I am a busy man."

The shorter man clasped his hands. "Pardon sir, but we come with news from Mannus Prime."

Amongeratix's spies. But in person instead of transmitting secure messages. Ezekiel felt his throat tighten at the prospect of what these men represented. He placed his palms flat on the desk and demanded, "Tell me everything."

Eger City, planet Mannus Prime.

Aliz failed to recall the last time she felt so constricted. Since arriving on Mannus, she had been pampered and catered to like some minor celebrity, all under the guise of protecting her from any retaliation from Amongeratix's allies. She found the notion ridiculous.

Regardless of protests, she continued being pulled into the nightmare of the new Confederation. Mere months since conception, the coalition already showed signs of weakness among the council members. She hoped it wasn't a sign of worse to come, but three years spent in the Krenz underground prepared her for the worst. Frustrated, Aliz struggled to find a way, any way, out of her predicament. She stared out her office window without seeing the near endless cityscape stretching before her.

"You worry too much," Sel told her with a disapproving frown.

The former Guard and insurgent settled into her new role as council guard, brandishing her fancy uniform and ceremonial weapons with unusual gusto. Aliz found it annoying, even if she was a familiar face.

"Why does it feel like you are my mother scolding me?"

Sel shrugged. "Somebody needs to. You've acted like a child since we pulled out of Krenz."

"You mean ran with our tails between our legs," Aliz countered.

"How doesn't matter." Sel's reprimand struck a nerve. "We survived and took a lot of people with us to continue the fight. You're missing the bigger picture, Aliz."

Aliz struggled to hold back tears. "What's that?"

Sel leaned closer, lowering her voice. "People like us, we don't have the luxury of hiding behind our personal wants. That option disappeared the instant we stepped forward to do what was right for the greater good. Once you can forgive yourself and accept this, the rest will fall into place. Who knows, you might find out you've been wrong this whole time."

Rebuked for her growing feelings of self-pity, Aliz searched deep, struggling to find that inner strength others reminded her she had. She knew healing couldn't begin until the enemy was defeated and old wrongs righted. Alain Nye was dead, if the rumors were true, but the stain of his insurrection ran deep. There would be no moving forward until the travesty ended.

"What happens if we can't win?"

A mask slipped over Sel's face as she answered. "Then it won't really matter."

Abbey of the Order of Blood Witches, Acumensiis Comet.

Sister Deius Mlth studied the portents laid out before her. Lingering in the shadows without comment was the Order's navigator, Sogress B'mn. She'd gone to Deius with concerns over their present course of action. At first, the Mistress of Novices found the request uncomfortable, for it was not in her normal duties. These matters typically went to the Grand Mistress. Mlth suspected, without being able to prove, the two were the sole remaining original members of the Order. That relationship went deeper than any other connection Ruma Zzein held. Under normal circumstances this matter would never escape the duo.

With the recent assault by Amongeratix and the foundation threatening quake throwing the comet off course the Order was unsettled. The rebellious coup by Algiss Her did more damage than all that combined. A purge ensued. Ruma Zzein proved a harsh mistress. Those suspected of harboring treasonous sympathies were stripped of their power and stranded on the nearest planet, forever doomed to spend their days in regret and longing. Three more Sisters were executed, their loyalties to Algiss too strong to break. Suspicion and terror rippled through the ranks for the better part of a year as the Grand Mistress reestablished her dominance.

Deius Mlth shoved all that aside and focused on the swirling magics in the pewter cauldron. Wrought at the foundation of the Order, the bowl held more power than most of the Sisters combined. The knowledge within almost as much as the wealth of the Conclave, the cauldron represented the totality of the Order and could only be deciphered by a select few.

Frustration mounting, Mlth stepped away and rubbed the growing ache behind her eyes. She didn't know how long she stared into the kaleidoscope of swirling power. It was easy to lose oneself in the storm.

"Tell me," Sogress bade.

Mlth shook her head. "This makes no sense."

The navigator took a step closer. "What did you see?"

How can I explain the voice of magic? Words flowed, a script only she could read. She staggered beneath the weight of the portents. "It will take me days to translate."

"Say the first words that come. Do not think. Do not resist. Just … speak."

Drawing a calming breath, Mlth closed her eyes and let the magic enter her mind. Thoughts and patterns clashed. Her knees buckled. Pressure built. Her eyes flashed open, rolling back. She felt her mouth drop open—"The moon wept blood the night the achedaetha was born."

Mlth snapped back to her body, trembling as a sheen of smoke wafted off her robes. Sparks of power danced through the fabric. Elated she succeeded, Mlth turned her gaze to Sogress and froze at seeing how pale the navigator had become. "What is it?"

Sogress worked her jaw. "A name that should never be uttered. A prophecy from old times."

"Tell me, Sogress, for I have no memory of what I spoke."

"I cannot. That name shall not be uttered again in this hallowed chamber," the navigator replied. "We must see the Grand Mistress. She will know what to do."

Confused. Frightened. Worse. Mlth pressed. "I must know, Sogress. What have I said?"

The navigator fixed her with a wild look. "You have evoked the end of all creation. We will not survive this."

THIRTEEN

3215 A.G. (After gods), Great Library, planet Wexanos.

Dawn's golden light swathed the land in warmth. Calm settled over all within, oblivious to the turmoil consuming the universe. YetElisa felt no sense of calm. She doubted she would. Now that she had mastered *Grimfurvor* her brief period of tranquility drew closed as the ache grew for her to fulfill her role as Paladin With Tannus being offworld, she had to go through the Chief Librarian for instructions. Instructions he had not yet given her.

Reluctantly pulling her gaze from the rising sun, Elisa returned inside to go find Fistel. Perhaps today he would have something to tell her.

The great library was a sprawling complex of barracks, offices, dining halls entwined in an impossible collection of books collected from the dawn of humanity's reign. She found the concept overwhelming. How could anyone store so much knowledge only to leave the rest of the universe mired in chaos? Tannus may not be the villain many human myths purported him to be, but neither was he the hero he imagined.

She passed a score of yellow clad librarians beginning their day. A few muttered greetings. The mood of the library shifted with Tannus gone. A growing sense of finality spread. Many believed, without voicing, the time of peace was at an end. She had heard Fistel doing his best to ensure them the dream of Wexanos would live on, even with Tannus gone, but many seemed unappeased. Elisa wished him luck. Experience told her the man was going to need all the help he could get.

"Ah, Elisa. Good morning," Fistel called to her as she entered the dining hall. "Enjoying another Wexanos sunrise?"

"How could I not?" she replied with a smile.

He bobbed his head. "Indeed. I have been to a hundred worlds and have yet to find another spectacle like ours. This is a truly special planet."

Elisa had no argument. She enjoyed being here, despite the

unspoken promise of it all crashing down and the knowledge Tannus could call on her at any time. Waiting for Fistel to speak, she thanked one of the hall attendants as he presented her with a small platter of cheeses and fresh fruits. She took her first sip of caf and understood what Fistel found so enticing.

"But you did not come to hear my stories of galactic sunrises," he said after noting her silence. He took a sip of his caf, the steam wafting up his face. "I trust you have come to ask if Lord Tannus has sent for you?"

"I have."

He took another sip. "He has sent a message."

Caught off guard, Elisa set her plate and cup down. "What does it say?"

"Allow an old man his one pleasure of the day," he pleaded, gesturing towards his caf.

Elisa sat, acceding to his request. She nibbled at the food on her plate. Her appetite reduced with the prospect of learning her next steps. Curiously, Fistel had no food. The old man seemed content with his cup of caf. Eager as Elisa was to move forward, she forced herself to acknowledge all their worlds were being upended. She couldn't begin to imagine what that meant for Fistel.

Once finished, Fistel said, "Thank you for that. Now come, the message is encrypted in the main terminal."

They walked together in silence. Elisa struggled with her thoughts; envisioning stabbing *Grimfurvor* into Amongeratix and ending it. Odd, she failed to consider what might happen after. If she survived.

"Shut the door behind you."

Blinking at the request, Elisa found herself awed by the immensity of Tannus' private study no matter how many times she entered. Striding through the grand library was one thing, but the size of this room made her feel small. A quick glance around showed not a speck of dust after she shut the door. Fistel had been busy indeed since the lord of Wexanos departed. She followed him to the human sized screen in the middle of the desk against the far wall. Drawing a deep breath, her hand dropped to the now comforting hilt of *Grimfurvor*.

With the click of a button, Tannus' image flickered to life, cold and emotionless.

"Paladin, I have been told you at last have mastered the weapon.

That is commendable. You are the first in a long string of failed lineage to have reached this point. But you already knew that. As you are aware, I have dispatched the others on various missions in preparation for the final battle with my brother. Now it is your turn. I have one final task in store for you before you are ready to fulfill your destiny."

She shifted balance to her opposite foot. The last time he sent her off nearly cost her life.

"Ishis Gul is prepared to transport you and Ah'muf to the Acumensiis Comet where my cousin will continue your training. Once on the comet you will be granted an audience with the Grand Mistress of the Blood Witches. To face my brother, you will need more than your guile and that dagger. She is expecting you. Go to the witches and join me on the moon Ferom."

The message faded. A tremor of terror awakened deep within the mirrors of her soul. First the Forsaken Path, now this. *Blood witches? Comet?*

Clearing her throat, Elisa said, "Fistel, it appears my time to leave Wexanos has come."

"It does," he agreed.

Krenz, planet Vau Prime.

The noose tightened. Cordons of scared Prekhauten Guards surrounded the central districts of the capital. Inquisitor hunter teams, reinforced with additional Guards and conscripted city militia, scoured the neighborhoods building by building. The bodies stacked up despite the new security measures. Terror gripped the city. No one felt safe, though the killer had only gone after uniformed personnel. Nothing the population endured under the decline of Alain Nye's regime compared to the horrors gripping Krenz.

And then, inexplicably, the bodies stopped showing up. The silent killer seemingly disappeared or so the newsvids had said. Nothing the Inquisitors or Guard did produced results, further spiking the paranoia among the new leadership's upper tiers. Panic danced on the edges, ready to sweep in. The harder the Inquisition looked the less they found.

Akin Brohl sat in the dark comforts of his bolt hole and rubbed the ache in his neck. He'd lost track of the number of targets he'd eliminated since he began his quest to draw Amongeratix out. His foes were soft, unworthy of his efforts. The one outlier being the rogue witch who forced his retreat.

Thanks to Blood Witch magic, his wounds healed in hours. What would otherwise be fatal injuries, it had left him depleted for a period. God hunters were the perfect killing machines. All but unstoppable and, unwittingly, the model upon which the Vaumagian Assassin Guild was born—Akin glanced down at the golden faceplate confiscated from his most recent kill. The assassin was mostly robotic. His knowledge of their guild was limited but was enough to suggest they preferred working solo. Which was to his advantage.

Musing over the circuity laden into the mask, Akin briefly wondered how many more were on his trail. Surely Amongeratix would send an entire contingent, giving the wealth and riches the Conclave horded over the years. The assassins were cunning but far from his caliber of fighters. The first ambushed him spectacularly and died a few moves later.

A warning chime on his wrist guard alerted him to a perimeter breach. Akin activated his monitor to find a half squad of Guards led by an Inquisitor moving stealthily through the area. No doubt searching for signs of him. He yawned. Their patterns were too predictable. It almost felt wrong killing them. But needs must. A creature of habit, Akin Brohl rolled his shoulders, stretched out his arms and reached for his rifle.

He skipped down a flight of stairs and moved into a prepared firing position. Moments later the Guards edged into view.

 The last one died before the first body hit the rubble.

Akin swept his rifle over the engagement area but found no additional targets. A quick glance at his wrist showed no further breaches in the perimeter. He looked at the bodies again, contemplating whether it was worth the effort to conceal them. The Guards evolved their tactics over the course of their hunt. Command surely knew where this squad was, along with its destination. Akin had no choice. He broke down his rifle's bipod and hurried back to his nest to pack and displace before reinforcements arrived.

Sister Evangaline surveyed the damage. Perfect round placements in the Guards told her much about the man, she felt giddiness when thinking of confronting him again. She relished the challenge.

"What use is it hunting this killer? All we do is lose men," the Guard sergeant assigned to her muttered.

"We do this for the thrill of the hunt. He will not stop. Nor give up once cut loose on a target. This is a worthy fight, sergeant," she reprimanded. Evangaline's right hand balled into a fist as the urge to punish the man surfaced. She fought it back, begrudgingly admitting she needed the allies. If for no other reason than to take a bullet from her.

Rebuked, the sergeant remained silent. Evangaline lifted her head, scanning the winds with her enhanced senses.

She could smell his fear. "What is that over there?" She pointed to what looked like a corpse partially concealed beneath a pile of rubble.

A pair of Guards hurried over and began pulling pieces of rubble away. Evangaline floated over, her perpetual scowl deepening upon seeing what remained of a Vaumagian corpse. Headless and twisted, the body showed signs of extreme violence. Both arms and legs were broken and twisted beneath the torso. Fluids, both human and mechanical, pooled around, suggesting the assassin had met its demise here.

The Guild would be furious. It was tempting to spread the myth of the god hunter to further draw the Vaumagians into the hunt. Compassionless killers beholden to their contract, the cyborgs had the potential to shift the dynamics in her favor.

Wheels turning, the witch spun and drifted back to the slaughter. "Summon the mortuary detail," she ordered. "I want these bodies taken care of with the honor due them."

What little she knew of his kind suggested he would not lay low long. An unnatural desire to fulfill his purpose made him equally predictable and not. She needed to find a way to get a step ahead without betraying her position.

On the far side of the city, lost among the endless streets of warehouses and storage facilities, sat a woman mired in frustration. Another string of clergy was publicly executed. Their bodies swung from light poles for the city to see.

Porii Daam had no tears left. Her eyes burned. Her chest ached. Her efforts with the criminal gang resulted in minimal results. So far only a score of junior priests had been funneled out of the city to one of the smaller towns on the far side of the planet in the hopes of securing offworld transport. Too many others were being caught each day.

She scanned the faces on the newsvid and froze. There, swinging by his neck beneath burned robes and blackened flesh, was Porii's friend and colleague, Cardinal Amest Hour. The older man had been a quiet ally during their dark moments when Nye first usurped leadership. Never one to make waves, Hour preferred to create lasting change for the betterment of his constituency. She remembered him as a good man, now nothing more than a charred corpse to be mocked and picked apart by crows.

"A good day for crows," she muttered.

"What's that about crows?" Edam asked entering the room with a tray of food.

Porii cast a baleful gaze upon him. "Harbingers of the dead. Crows sweep in at the final moment to carry off the souls of fallen, or so Conclave doctrine preached as we perpetuated deceit upon our flocks. Gods. What fools we have been."

"It doesn't matter if Amongeratix and his ilk were gods or not. Three thousand years of indoctrination gave humanity something to look forward to. They gave us a reason for being. For discerning the difference between right and wrong." He paused when a pair of black winged birds landed on one of the clergy and began pecking. "They became gods through our worship. Whatever they may have begun as, they are now part of our core identity. Faith is a funny thing."

She snorted a laugh. She'd been part of the lie, even if she hadn't known it until her elevation to the Forum. Discovering the truth about the gods had been a shock. Each new member of the Conclave ruling body struggled through the news in their own style. She chose to accept it for what it was and continue her bid to raise her standing for contention for Cardinal Seniorus. Until recently, she failed to consider what impact her knowledge might have on the general population.

Amongeratix was the great evil, a boogeyman in every regard. His arrival on Vau Prime was proof to many that the gods existed. Countless trillions needed that belief to see them through the night. Perhaps keeping the secret was in the universe's best interests. Porii no longer felt sure of anything, and Edam's speech did little to assuage her angst.

"Being clergy, we were taught how to preach, how to present ourselves to the people," she started slowly, the thoughts still forming.

"There was little point in debating the semantics of our secret knowledge. We performed according to what the Cardinal Seniorus dictated. Few of us paused to consider the impact of faith. Now we cannot escape it."

"People continue praying, for it Amongeratix is real, so too must be his brothers," Edam said with a nod. He settled into the chair beside her, offering Porii a small bowl of hot soup. "Here, you will need to keep up your strength. There is still a long road ahead of us."

She gestured at the screen. "All roads end. Few the way would like. I have no illusions about what comes next."

"No one can predict the future, Porii. All we can do is our best."

Accepting the soup, Porii replied, "To what point? Sooner or later, it will be my neck in that noose. Food for the crows." She paused. "Do you suppose there is an afterlife?"

"That's not for me to say. I know I'm in no hurry to get there," he gave her a strained look. "You need to stop. That grief will consume you if you let it. Focus your energy on helping as many of your people as possible. If you are destined to meet your demise, so be it. Do it with a light heart and a smile."

She cocked her head. "Go down fighting?"

"Is there another way?" He smiled. "Eat your soup before it gets cold. Thopos doesn't like seeing his food go to waste."

She lifted the spoon, staring at the odd lumps of what she hoped were vegetables. Never in her wildest dreams did she consider this was to be her fate. Failing to conceal her grimace, she put the spoon to her mouth and swallowed fast in the hopes of not tasting it.

Eger City, planet Mannus Prime.

For the first time since allying himself with this human faction Gedrick Silk found himself without a purpose. The urgency he'd endured on the low continent was absent, leaving him with too much idle time to sit and think. He replayed the most tragic events from their harrowed flight in the aftermath of Strannan's death. Friends now dead haunted his dreams. They cried, begging to know why he failed them. The prospect left him rattled and with no one to talk to.

His first inkling was to go to Bryn or Mal. The junior lieutenants were his closest friends among the survivors from the low continent withdrawal. Both had been assigned to the new council guard under the command of Captain Julian. He lauded them for their selfless service, while secretly lamenting the wounds each bore. Unlike him, however, they moved on, eager to fill new roles to keep their demons at bay.

Gedrick's true pain stemmed in being the only of his kind among a sea of humanity. His ability to alter his appearance into anyone he chose was little more than a façade. He knew he did not belong, just as much as those claiming to have his best interests at heart did. The duality threatened to fracture his dwindling confidence, rendering him incapable of escaping his past or moving into a brighter future. Any oath of loyalty he once gave the Prekhauten Guard had long since evaporated under the amplified operating pressures. With no people or homeworld to return to, Gedrick needed to find relief before he lost his grasp on sanity.

So lost in thought, he stumbled into someone as he turned the corner of the hallway.

"Excuse me," he mumbled and stepped out of the way.

"You're Gedrick Silk, correct?"

He tensed, not recognizing the woman. "I am."

She extended her hand. A most human gesture. "I am Adris Moscasco. I have wanted to meet with you since you arrived."

His cheeks flushed, recognizing the name. "I wouldn't presume to take up your time. You are perhaps the busiest woman on the planet."

Adris laughed. Gilded and songlike. "I won't dispute that. Probably why I'm wandering the lesser used side corridors. Have you any idea how difficult it is to avoid impromptu meetings and petitions? This is the only moment of solace I have throughout the day. But you are most welcome to my time."

He felt the unspoken "but" coming. People in his line of work were seldom praised on face value. Gedrick offered her a curt bow. "First Counselor—"

"It is my pleasure finally meeting you, Gedrick. Your former colleagues spoke volumes on the quality of your character," Adris went on before he could continue. "They have all moved on to new assignments. Continuing to serve the ideals of what the Conclave forgot it stood for. We are on the cusp of creating a new order for everyone, Gedrick. A home for all races and peoples where all can share in the rewards. I," she paused at his snort. "I would like to see you become part of this order. I know what befell your people and there are no words worthy of assuaging the pain you must feel. Instead, allow me to offer you this sole comfort. You have proven yourself time and again to be a man of the highest quality. A man trustworthy beyond reproach. I can use you."

"It will take much to alleviate the pains suffered on the low continent," he admitted.

She laid a gently hand on his arm. "I understand, trust me, I do. My own final days on Dalafar bore similar wounds. I watched as a man I'd grown to care about deeply was gunned down for protecting me. These are the unfortunate scars we must bear if there is to be a way through this nightmare we find ourselves in."

"I did not know," was all he managed to say.

"I'm sure if you ask enough people, they will all share similar stories," Adris said. She continued walking, pulling him along. "While we may never escape our pasts, we can work to make the future better. That is the sole reason I accepted my position as First Counselor. I know I can make a positive difference, but I cannot do it alone."

He halted, noticing with wry bemusement they were outside of her offices. "I'm not sure how I can be of assistance. Humanity has shown me what lies in store for the universe, and it is a grim place."

"Gedrick, help me make the universe a better place, for all of us. I too have seen the future you predict, and it shakes me to my core. The only way to prevent it from coming to fruition is my throwing everything we have at it, no matter the cost."

"A suicide mission," he guessed.

The look of pain in her eyes rocked him. "Gods no! I'm not a monster, regardless of how some of my compatriots might view me. No, what I need is a man who can work his way into any situation without detection. A man of impeccable character with a keen eye for detail. I'm not asking for violence. Just a pair of eyes to report back to me with information necessary to keep this drudging bureaucracy rolling on schedule."

His face darkened with realization. "You want me to be a spy for you."

"My spymaster, if you will," she said with a nod.

"I would not be expected to kill again?" he asked.

"Gedrick, if I had my way, I would end this war today without another life lost," she revealed. "No killing. You will be free to act accordingly. Draft recruits to your office and operate under my sole jurisdiction. Only a select few on the council will know of you. You have my word."

Her words were soothing. The proposition alluring, if not wholly tempting, but he harbored reservations. Gedrick refused to be dragged into another desperate situation. "If I find the pressures too much and decide to walk away?"

"I'll lend you my personal shuttle to take you wherever you wish to go. No questions asked. You will, naturally, have a substantial budget for what you need to perform the job."

"Can I take time to think on this?" he asked. "As I mentioned, my heart has not yet healed from the wounds of Vau Prime."

"Of course. I won't deny I need you, but neither will I force you into a role you are unprepared for," she answered and reached for her door handle. "Gedrick, for what it's worth, I agree with how you handled the Alain Nye operation."

Adris disappeared into her office, leaving him bewildered and pondering the meaning of his existence.

Bastion Command Platform, Confederation Headquarters, planet Mannus Prime.

"You are certain the enemy has received word we are coming?" Khe-Zhehan asked for the third time as she paced throughout her ready room.

The sting of failure lessened in the aftermath of her conversation with Moscasco and in its wake she discovered the growing desire to prove herself once more. Khe-Zhehan was a professional soldier, having attained the high rank the Navy had to offer for her insight and ability to perform under pressure. She'd allowed meaningless guilt to subsume that personality for too long. Losses in battle were unavoidable. Through Moscasco's guidance she focused on the number of lives her raid saved. Nearly twenty thousand men and women, a mixture of fighters and civilian refugees, were now safe from Amongeratix's foul reach. That was what mattered.

"Aye, Admiral. Our relays we left in the Vau System confirmed personal delivery of the news to the new Inquisitor General. They know we are coming to force a final battle," a dark-skinned Captain replied. "All is on schedule. We have been given orders to deploy the scout squadrons at will."

She considered the man before her. Captain Drukali graduated top of his class from the Naval Academy. He came with a distinguished career before the civil war and continued growing his reputation as a fierce combat leader with a keen eye for tactics and reading scenarios resulting in high numbers of enemy casualties. Drukali represented the future, should they survive. Khe-Zhehan knew she was fortunate the man joined their cause at the onset of hostilities, after having survived the ambush and massacre at Hawker's Gate.

"Is the First Fleet ready?"

"The last supplies are being loaded now. It took more time than anticipated for us to secure the deep space drones the battle plans call for," Drukali confirmed.

She frowned. Despite promises from a dozen manufacturing planets, production continued falling behind schedule as more troops and volunteers filled the ranks. Entire squadrons and divisions needed to outfitted and trained, straining Confederation resources. Khe-Zhehan pushed her needs through the fledgling chain of command, using her influence and importance of her mission to get what she wanted. She feared it still wasn't enough.

"How soon will the reconnaissance ships be ready to deploy?"

"Hours."

She nodded. "Send them. We must establish tactical dominance before the enemy can bring his ships to bear. Provide enough escorts the minelayers won't have to look over their shoulders."

"Yes, Admiral."

She ran through ship numbers. All told, the Confederation had enough space worthy vessels to fill five entire fleets. Khe-Zhehan wasn't willing to risk deploying all of them to the same theater of operations, however. There was no guarantee Amongeratix would fall for it. With the war stretched across half the universe, she needed to keep a sizeable combat force in reserves. The council agreed. Three fleets were scheduled to deploy over the next week, each to different coordinates in the Occanum System.

"Drukali, don't take unnecessary risks. We're going to need every combat ship available to counter the fleets of Vau Prime," she cautioned.

He smiled, snow-colored teeth gleaming against his uniform. "Admiral, we'll have the minefields laid and be moved to our scheduled positions before the enemy will know we've arrived in system. Do I have permission to engage if necessary?"

"Yes, or if you see the proper opportunity," she said after a pause. "I leave that to your discretion. Pave the way, Drukali. The rest of the fleets will be hard on your trail."

He snapped to attention and presented his best salute. She returned the gesture and extended her hand. Some events were too important to rest on tradition. They parted as friends; Khe-Zhehan watched him walk off, purpose in every step. She wished she had a thousand more like Drukali. She was going to need them all to pull of the victory the council envisioned.

Argus Station, Prekhauten Naval Headquarters, planet Vau Prime.

Flanked by a trio of adjutants and junior aides, Grand Admiral Achen Tuth stormed through naval command. Recently promoted with a new rank established on Amongeratix's orders, Tuth was a hard man. His stern gaze wilted those he passed. Having learned early in his career to bury emotions, the Grand Admiral Tuth held little regard for those who'd failed him, or the Guard. The disaster at the system edge proved his suspicions. Channeling his anger, Tuth went to Mobus Kale and demanded his position.

Now he burned through the highest levels of naval command. Those he deemed slacking in their duties were demoted and reassigned to front line vessels. Entire fleets were being restructured to better serve his vision. Tuth was ruthless in his pursuit of unifying the new Navy under his thumb. But it wasn't enough. He needed more. Reports of massing fleets of enemy ships, well beyond the scope of his reach, disturbed him even as they provoked his ire.

He reached the main command room and proceeded inside. Tuth ignored the panicked staff and went straight to his office. Plaques and awards collected over the course of three decades decorated the walls. A pair of ceremonial flags crossed in the far corner. One belonged to the Guard, the other the Conclave. A traditionalist, Tuth believed in exhibiting pride in every aspect of daily life.

He sank into his chair, pausing to look out the wall of windows overlooking the rest of the operations center before opening the channel down to Krenz. Amongeratix's face filled the screen.

"My lord," Tuth acknowledged, the title lingering on his tongue in distaste.

Amongeratix squinted. "Grand Admiral, word has reached me that my brother intends on rallying his armies on the dead world of Occanum. I want all fleet assets to be ready to deploy within the week. General Kale has similar orders. His armies are marshalling on the low continent as we speak."

"It will be done," Tuth confirmed. "I have been in contact with General Kale and have already begun sending transports and troop carriers to the planet surface in support of various operations. It will be no issue altering plans."

Amongeratix jabbed a finger at the screen. "Do not fail me in this, Grand Admiral. I sense this may be the final battle I have been waiting for. We must crush the enemy and bring the rest of the universe to heel in short order. My moment of victory is at last at hand."

The feed cut, leaving Tuth stewing in frustrations. Keen as Amongeratix was at establishing his dominance, the giant had little understanding of logistics, or the amount of personnel required to shift entire plans at a moment's notice. Aside from forcing a final battle, he found little to inspire confidence. There was no accurate count of enemy numbers or weaponry. His fleets would be deploying blind, putting them all at risk. Face grim, he prepared for the moment he'd awaited all his life. A chance to prove his worth against the best.

FOURTEEN

3215 A.G. (After gods), Ankrit, planet An'kuruku.

The city of Ankrit was the oldest on the desert planet. A hallowed place where faiths and religions flocked once a year to profess their devotion to the gods. Banners fifteen feet tall in every color lined the main roads, marking out paths for believers to find their preferred temples. The smells of roasting meats, fresh baked breads, and spices mingled with human odors in a tapestry unlike anywhere else in the universe. Dejak watched Kaline as she took in pageantry, noting her responses to the sights and sounds of the holy city. For most, Ankrit was an experience. A transformational journey linking one's spirit with the natural world. While he had no issues with organized religion, Dejak never fully embraced the traditions or principles of worship. The impracticality of it disturbed him for reasons he wasn't inclined to explore. Picking a piece of lodged meat from between his teeth, he found Kaline a fascinating contradiction. She professed no individual measure of faith while espousing the glory of Rengu.

Dejak didn't know what Rengu was, or if he'd ever existed, nor did he care. Violent rhetoric threatened to collapse his society and, though he lured her to the holy city under false pretense, he expected to force her to recant through persuasion. If not, the desert had ways of balancing all matters.

It took almost half the day to reach his safehouse on the far side of the city center. Dejak's accumulated wealth enabled him to enjoy the finer aspects of life, building the reputation of a well-respected businessman and civil leader in the process. Granted, his interests were largely self-serving. The power vacuum left in the aftermath of the war exposed a great many flaws in the current regime's leadership structure. Most of a generation had been wiped out thanks to Kaline and the nightmare Amongeratix, allowing Dejak to slink in and accumulate power.

A trio of Prefects lingered on the corner across the street, watching his skiff pull into his expansive garage. Dejak scowled, daring them to cause a scene. It was because of the Prefects so many

An'kurukan men perished. The late Lezorsu followed his greed into the giant's dark embrace, plunging the planet into a consuming war. Dejak had been there. A willing soldier serving what he thought was the greater good. All he found was a lifetime of regrets. His friends perished during the onslaught, men and women he'd grown up with. Hatred formed in Dejak's heart. Revenge became his life's work.

Stumbling upon Kaline was no mistake. His network actively searched for those responsible for the war. Already, several enemy combatants were either missing or dead, removed from the equation as he took revenge in the name of the fallen. Yet for as much as he longed to run his blade across Kaline's ivory throat, his mind bore him down diverging paths. There was value in keeping her alive. She held many secrets and, though she was the catalyst responsible for nearly tearing his planet apart, the opportunity for Dejak to consolidate his grip on the desert and restore all to what he imagined the future should be.

Dejak wrestled with his thoughts as he spat in the Prefect's direction. They were wise enough not to react.

Once inside, he directed his people to ensure Kaline's needs were taken care of. He watched with amusement as she absorbed her surroundings. The open floor of his home was decorated with ornately carved pillars. Statues and sculptures sat on pedestals interspersed with the lounges and plush chairs begging to be used. Plants of all kinds filled the home with life. Sunlight poured in through a string of windows built into the roof. Linen curtains draped from ceiling to floor, billowing when a breeze managed to worm inside. What Dejak enjoyed most was the smell. That familiar fragrance of incense told him he was home.

"Welcome to my house, Kaline," he said. "Consider my staff at your disposal for as long as you remain here."

She turned from her inspection, searching deep in his eyes for duplicity that he knew she wouldn't find. "Why am I here? You have not told me, nor did your little cabal offer much when you kidnapped me."

He paused, reevaluating his estimation of her. He had not expected the challenge after seeing the depths of her defeat. "Very astute of you to piece that together. My colleagues insisted they took every precaution to ensure anonymity. I must address this with them. As for why you are, that is simple and complicated. The Prefecture knows you have returned, and you are a most hated woman. Removing you from the streets, and their purview, not only saves your life, it provides me with the opportunity to right old wrongs."

"What old wrongs?" Her stance changed, her body stiffening as she set her shoulders. "I don't recall our paths crossing before now."

"They have not. I knew of you, however. The woman with the flaming red hair and a tongue so sweet to lead all into temptation. We traveled half the world under your influence. Wide-eyed and naïve. Do you know how many corpses your honeyed tongue left in the desert all those years ago?"

"I was doing my job."

He forced a smile. "And a quality performance it was! Tens of thousands flocked to either banner. All eager to test their newfound courage."

"You don't understand," her voice dropped to a whisper.

"I think I do," he countered. "We each have a task to do with our lives. Yours was to subvert populations to the depravity of this Rengu. I cannot fault you for that, but much of those who survived seek your blood for what you perpetrated upon us."

Kaline met his gaze, trembling beneath her robes. "Why keep me alive? Do what you must and let us be done with this sad tale."

"Unlike you, I am no executioner. No, Kaline, I brought you here, to the heart of faith on An'kuruku, to help me rid the last influences of the gods forever." He sat back, a deceptive look brightening his eyes.

Ragan wiped his face and spat out a mouthful of sand. The fine particles whipped up in a frenzy around their transport as the pilot increased speed on what was supposed to be the main road between Tenemenah and Ankrit. Ragan had just enough experience from his travels to know road was a relative term. His one saving grace was the transport floated two meters over the sand. Ye their pilot failed to explain how the displacement would pelt them with unrepented fury… Ragan decided he hated sand.

Squinting in the hopes of reducing the impact, he stole looks at his companions. Only the Blood Witch appeared immune—another benefit to immortality and the protections of magic. He wondered if the Order was open to accepting males. He stifled a laugh at himself.

Seated beside him, Presha Von tilted her head and gave him a quizzical look. "What could possibly be so amusing?"

"This. All of this. We shouldn't be here. Since I joined Tolde I have been across half the universe. I've seen and done things no one back home would believe, except for maybe this."

"You are a strange young man, Ragan Sandinsol," she said and turned away.

He shrugged.

Presha's thoughts turned inward. Perhaps he had the right of it. None of them should be here. The deserts of An'kuruku were unforgiving, devouring all they touched with indiscriminate fury. She first contemplated disappearing, letting the sands consume her until naught but bones remained. But no, she'd given her word to help hunt down Kaline and claim a sliver of redemption for her sins. She left Ragan and moved to sit beside Sister Alessandra. The Blood Witch looked at her with a blank face.

"Are you prepared for what comes next?" she said.

Presha didn't know. She had been cast across the universe at the whim of another for so long she no longer knew what she was capable of. The thought of being reduced to anonymity after all her hardships and trial rattled through her like wind in a cave.

"How do you do it?" Presha asked.

"Do what?"

"Keep going after all that's happened. I'm trying to find a way through but every time I think I've rounded the final corner another block prevents me from moving forward. I fear I am to remain trapped in this cycle of hopelessness and despair."

Alessandra regarded her in silence.

Cheeks burning crimson, Presha dropped her gaze. "I'm sorry."

"It grows easier when you accept you have no choice," Alessandra finally said. "I was born for a specific purpose. I did not believe this at the time but have come to accept it the longer I live. My part in this story draws to a close."

"How can you know that? Amongeratix desperately wants your kind elminated. I heard him more than once lament his alliance with the Crimson Mistress." Presha failed to understand how she remained so calm. "It seems to me the only way any of us can know our tale is finished is by dying."

"Presha Von, you forget I have lived many lifetimes. The Grand Mistress believes in Tannus and what we seek to accomplish.

Now that Tannus is moving forward with his plans, Amongeratix has no time to hunt for our kin, or me."

Presha frowned. "Then why are we here searching for Kaline if the final battle is near?"

"Loose ends," Alessandra answered. "We cannot afford to leave her poisoned tongue free in the universe while everyone else is distracted. Rengu is the epitome of evil. His influence will core humanity from the inside, spreading rot and disease. The only way to prevent that is by removing Kaline from the equation."

"We are approaching Ankrit," Tolde announced from the front of the skiff.

Hearing bits of the conversation, Tolde Breed glanced back to ensure the others began their preparations. He did not know if they were going into a hostile environment and wanted to be prepared.

His gaze lingered on Von. Tolde failed to trust her fully, but he needed Presha to complete the assignment and hurry back to Tannus for the final campaign. The sooner this madness ended the sooner each could go on with their lives. It was only now he realized he never envisioned what the future might look like for him. So much of his life was devoted to the Inquisition then in stopping the greatest evil the universe had ever known from succeeding. With his brother dead, Tolde had no one but the people he'd come to surround himself with. *If only life had been different, perhaps I might find a measure of normalcy.*

A jab to his shoulder broke his thoughts. "Ow. What was that for?"

"Just keeping you focused," Luma Kai replied with a straight face. "Any idea where to begin once we get there?"

He didn't have much to go on. For as prominent as this Dejak appeared to be, much of his dealings remained concealed from prying eyes. He'd gone through great lengths to secure his fortune and build a quiet empire in the heart of An'kuruku. But to what end, he wasn't sure. Too much failed to add up for Tolde. There was no evidence of a man named Dejak before the last few years. Experience taught him everyone played angles. *What was Dejak's? What did the man want with Kaline?*

"Contacting the local Prefecture is out of the question. According to Matthias, they were too involved with the civil war here a few years ago. I have no doubt the man in Tenemenah has already sold us out and sent word ahead of our coming. With Paradise among us we cannot blend in. She will be spotted and remembered by any survivors."

Luma grunted.

"We may have bitten off more than we are prepared to handle with this one."

"Possibly, but my instinct tells me the sooner we remove Kaline from the board the sooner we can put a stop to this entire Rengu plague."

"She should have been dealt with sooner, but one question bothers me, Tolde," Luma said. "How can we be certain she is the only mouth of Rengu? It seems to me a vengeful god would have more than avenue available to spread his word."

Tolde paused. They never did learn the name of Tannus' race. He found it convenient his team continued referring to them as gods after discovering the truth. Some truths were too severe to accept. "One threat at a time, Luma. Eliminate Kaline and move on. That's all we can do."

Looking far from reassured, not that he could blame her, she still nodded her head in agreement. "We need to find the town recordkeeper. Force him to talk or steal what we need if we must," she suggested then. "Regardless, we are walking blind into enemy territory. I don't like it."

"Neither do I, but our options are limited. Tannus only agreed to this quest on the condition we made it quick and returned," Tolde said. "Naturally he said no more than necessary. I have come to accept their kind live in a world of subterfuge and half-truths. He did not say it, but I think he and Ruma Zzein know more about my future than either will say."

"Look at the bright side, you've already been dead once. What worse could happen?"

Eger City, planet Mannus Prime.

"I knew I was going to regret not killing you," the grizzled man in the screen said with a scowl. "What the fuck do you want now?"

Matthias maintained a straight face. Though they'd battled through their grievances during the campaign to liberate Mannus, he and Bootleg would never see eye to eye.

"I'm offering you a contract," Matthias said. "One last fight."

Bootleg rubbed the stubble on his chin and reached for a cigar, taking a dramatic pause to light it. "The last one was supposed to be it."

"Needs change."

Unimpressed, the mercenary exhaled a cloud of smoke. "What's in it for me? I'm still trying to rebuild what I lost on your little planet. I'm short personnel and vehicles. As fun as it was to kick the shit out of a real Guard unit, I'm in no position to take a second crack at it."

"This one comes from above me," Matthias half lied. "If all goes according to plan, you won't need to cut your teeth. We have a major operation unfolding and I have a team in need of protection."

"You want us to babysit your brats? The Shadow Hammers aren't interested."

Letting out an exasperated sigh, Matthias said, "At least hear me out before you say no."

Another cloud of smoke. The creak of an old metal chair. "I'm listening."

"I have a company of commandos on a small moon in the Occanum System. They've been deployed to secure a weapons system and keep it operational for the duration of the campaign. While they have enough manpower to operate the platform, they don't have anyone to watch their backs."

"Word is you have plenty of units on Mannus. Throw one of them at the problem," Bootleg countered.

Matthias shook his head. "Can't. All available ground forces are deploying to the planet. I can't share all the details over this channel, but I will say we are planning for this to be the final battle. One way or another the war is going to end."

Bootleg coughed and spat out his cigar. "Sounds to me you're expecting this unit to get hammered. That's a death mission, Matthias."

"I didn't know your outfit was so cautious."

"We're the best damned merc outfit in the universe and you know it," Bootleg sputtered. "Say I consider your contract. What's in it for us? You have to be expecting heavy casualties if you need outside help. No one deploys and armored brigade for a babysitting op."

"Name your price."

"You don't know what you're proposing, old man."

The tone turned serious. All banter faded as the prospect of the mission drowned reality.

"If we decide to do this, and I do mean if, I want each of my people to earn enough to last them for the rest of their lives."

Matthias didn't think enough were going to survive long enough to collect and that sinking feeling in his stomach returned. "Done. Hells, I'll set you up with your own small planet if you want it."

Bootleg scoffed. "You don't got that kind of pull."

"You'd be surprised what I can do now that I'm a member of the Confederation Council."

The cigar dropped from Bootleg's mouth as his eyes widened. "No shit?"

"No shit."

Bootleg snatched up his cigar and popped it back into his mouth. "If you can do it, I suppose I can too. Being governor of my own world sounds about right. When do you need my answer?"

"I'll settle for receiving word you are in transit to Ferom," Matthias replied with a weary sigh. "I've already transmitted coordinates and routes to take to avoid enemy contact. Bootleg, don't mistake this for a puff assignment. We're expecting it to be bad. Maybe the worst we've seen."

"Maybe for you, but my boys are tougher than that," Bootleg affirmed in a mocking tone. "Besides, we don't have to play by Guard rules. One of the perks of being in a merc outfit. I'll be in touch. When is the drop dead time you want us on station, if we decide to throw in?"

Matthias told him and cut the feed. He didn't care for the mercenary outfit but there was no denying their efficiency in battle. Throw in the fact they fell outside traditional military structure and they might have a shot after all. Now all he had to do was wrap up the debacle with the disgraced Cardinal Seniorus and convince the rest of the council to let him deploy.

Sewage tunnels, Eger City, planet Mannus Prime.

They'd been on the move nonstop for two days. Since having their cover blown at the last meeting. They were desperate in hopes of outrunning their pursuers. None but Dowan Mun knew they remained just out of reach by design. A tracking beacon attached to the bottom of his boot relayed their precise location to his warders. Oblivious to betrayal, Tinnus Har expounded a relentless tirade against the upstart Confederation, further swaying the locals seeking to return Mannus to the Conclave. Dowan listened without paying much attention. He'd heard the rhetoric too often since freeing the former Cardinal Seniorus and decided the best outcome for them all would be for the man to lose his tongue. Dowan had acquired just the right knife for the job.

"Inquisitor! How much longer do you intend on keeping us down with the shit and filth of Eger City?"

"Until I am certain we are no longer being followed and can go with these fine people back to their group to prepare for the next phase of your plan," Dowan replied.

Tinnus scowled, tugging at his sewage coated robes. "We've been down here long enough. It's been days and there has been no sight or sound of pursuit. How could anyone know where we are? We don't even know! Take us back to the surface."

Dowan set his jaw, glaring at the Cardinal through the gloom. "Rest here. I will scout the way forward. Once I find the path to the surface, and determine there is no enemy nearby, I will return and lead you up."

He sloshed off, Tinnus' protests wasted on the fetid air. A foul stench kept his nose permanently wrinkled. No matter how kilometers they marched through the detritus his senses failed to come to terms with the stench. Dowan vowed to burn every stitch of clothing he had on at the first convenient moment.

Rounding the first bend in the line, the Inquisitor exhaled. His body relaxed, if slightly. Tracing the route like an old friend, he moved with surety, having kept his companions moving in circles for the better part of their time below the surface. Nonstop movement left him sore. His back ached from being on his feet for so long. The protests in his stomach a constant reminder they hadn't had time to secure food during their flight.

Leaning against a green slime covered wall, Dowan dug into his breast pocket and produced the last cigarillo from a pack he confiscated from one of the dissidents. Placing the tobacco to his lips, he lit up and inhaled, eyes closing.

"If I can smell that, so can they."

He froze, a small part unwilling to open his eyes, but no one accused Dowan Mun of not being a man. Slowly, he opened them and was shocked to find a figure standing nearby. The voice was familiar, if somewhat foreign in the subterranean space. "Who are you?"

The man stepped forward, revealing his face.

Dowan jerked. "What are you doing down here? I thought we had a deal?"

"We do. I'm here to change plans a bit. Is Tinnus still with you?" Matthias asked.

"He is. There are five other civilians with us. All claim to be part of an underground movement to overthrow the Confederation. Once we return to the surface, they will lead us to their safehouses. I anticipate wrapping this up within the week." Dowan paused, suddenly unwilling to share more. Something felt off with Matthias. The man sounded the same, displayed the same mannerisms, but an alarm went off in the back of Dowan's mind.

"We may not have a week. Other agents are scouring the city for additional dissidents. The tide of rebellion must be eliminated, and in short order. Tinnus Har is dangerous. His forked tongue will turn many to his side if this fiasco continues," Matthias pressed.

"Who are you really?" Dowan asked, unable to contain his suspicion. "You're not Matthias. He doesn't talk this much."

To his horror, Matthias' face appeared to melt. Dowan pressed against the wall as the man transformed into a foreign face defined by hard edges and a withering glare. "You have no idea how difficult it is to assume another's face. The pain is … exquisite."

"Demon," he whispered.

The man smiled. "Far from it, though I've been called worse. While you do not need to know my name, for the moment, you should know I have been assigned to personally ensure your mission is successful. You have agreed to a task of great importance. I am here to prevent failure."

"How-how do I know I can trust you? Your face just melted. For all I know you're leading me into a trap."

"The First Counselor's word is good. Complete your assignment. Root out the insurgency and you will be allowed to disappear as agreed. Funds are waiting to be transferred to an account in your name. A new identity will be provided. But only after you bring this clandestine cabal down. Am I clear?"

Licking his lips, Dowan muttered, "I suppose I work for you now?"

A nod. "Get these people to their safehouse and report back to me directly."

Dowan accepted the transmitter that was being held out to him, tucking it into his pocket. "I'll be in touch."

I'll be watching.

Gedrick Silk watched the wayward Inquisitor stalk back to his group. The first part of his task accomplished, he ran through the endless list yet to be acted upon.

Brightstar, deep space transit line.

Sitting cross-legged on his favorite cushions, Tannus placed the backs of his hands on his knees and closed his eyes. The smell of incense filled his nostrils, a reminder of simpler times. Tannus slowed his breathing. In his mind's eye he replayed events from three thousand years ago.

A soft chime popped his eyes open. He looked through the darkened chamber before remembering where he was. Tannus rolled the stiffness from his shoulders. Muscle and bone creaked with the groan of millennia. Rising slowly, he dressed in a plain robe. The cleansing ritual rejuvenated his spirit, much as it had all these long years. Yet for the wonders it worked on his body, his mind remained troubled. The impossibility of the moment taunted him.

Thoughts twisted, Tannus slipped into a pair of sandals and went in search of answers. He found instead his brother's image waiting for him on a holoscreen in his office. Sorrow looked tired, worn down. A reflection Tannus assumed all three brothers wore. How or why they'd survived this long riddled him. Their violence toward each other had torn worlds apart, ended countless lives. He recognized each of them needed to be removed from the universe. They were a stain and only Tannus had the foresight to admit it.

"Brother, I trust all is advancing on schedule," he began without salutation.

Sorrow offered an unreadable look. "When did we lose all sense of civility? Have we ever been this crass? No wonder Father kicked us out."

"I am in no mood for games, Sorrow." Tannus bristled. "My fleet will soon depart for Inselcor for the automatons. Is there anything else you require from my end?"

"Are you certain this is the correct path?"

"We have been over this. Your Paladin has mastered *Grimfurvor*. Amongeratix is now in command of the human empire. This is the moment the Oracle has long prophesized."

Sorrow shook his head, tiny drops of blood shaking free. "Prophecy is a dangerous game. One misinterpretation and all is lost. The finality of what you propose will have far-reaching ramifications none of us prepared for."

"Brother, we cannot allow Amongeratix to continue his reign of terror. I trust you have seen the events transpiring on Vau Prime."

"The humans have never been more than a passing fancy for me, Tannus. You know this. Their short lifespans ensure most will not be remembered," Sorrow lamented. "Are we to grieve for them all? Despite the name I have given myself, my heart is not so big."

Tannus contemplated the words. Thought he'd come to accept many of the mortals into his inner circle over the years he used them like pawns to achieve his goals. Except this time was different. His relationships with Fistel and the librarians awakened a sensation he hadn't felt since before the Three were cast from their father's kingdom. Humbling and disconcerting, Tannus struggled with finding the perfect balance.

"It is not about grief, though we have suffered our share," Tannus started slowly. "How are we to expect these humans to willingly sacrifice themselves in our names when we shove them aside like chattel? I am done pretending to be a god, Sorrow. We never were and it was my greatest mistake in allowing the first humans to worship us. That false faith might now prove their damnation and we are the architects."

"You place too much on your shoulders. Let this gambit run its course but do not trust fate for answers. As you said, we are not gods."

Tannus frowned. "Can we defeat him?"

"We will soon find out." Sorrow shrugged. "To answer your question, I have no additional needs. My army is awaiting your ships. Let us gather one final time on our homeworld and settle old scores."

The feed ended, leaving Tannus more confused than before. Enough time passed that he no longer thought of Occanum as home. The once rich world of sprawling temple complexes, gardens, and prosperous cities teeming with life and joy was little more than a wasteland now. He seldom returned to those blasted plains, the grief too much for him to bear.

He developed a healthy sense of loathing for his family as the centuries crawled by. Their deviousness, spurred on by the circumstances of their creation, twisted the entire race in ways few fathomed. Tannus never knew how the originals were chosen. His father once mentioned some nonsense about a white dragon heralding the change, but Tannus failed to look closer. With no way to relate to the originals, he turned his inquisitiveness to other pursuits. It was those pursuits which led his brothers down their unique paths.

Perhaps Sorrow had the right of it the day he took a blade to his flesh. If the anguish inside his brother proved so powerful he not only lived through the deed he found a way to thrive, how could Tannus do any less for his own convictions? Yet he couldn't dwell on this further. Clarity of mind was needed now, more than ever. To defeat Amongeratix would take all his skill, experience, planning, and cunning. Even then, they were too evenly matched. Sorrow had his automatons, but Amongeratix had the skulldaerth.

Faced with a slaughter of humans on unprecedented levels, Tannus stalked back to his chambers to dress. He was scheduled to rendezvous with Admiral August and the *Solstice* in a few hours. Then the game would begin in earnest.

FIFTEEN

3215 A.G. (After gods), Former Conclave Headquarters, Krenz, planet Vau Prime.

Unspoken fear rippled through the menials assigned to the former heart of the Conclave. None raised their heads, walking in silence through once hallowed halls of authority and guidance. Entire floors of the building were gutted and renovated to fit Amongeratix. Casualties mounted as accidents plagued the workforce. Some claimed it was ghosts of the past returned to torment them. Others quietly suggested it was Amongeratix himself continuing the slaughter begun upon his arrival.

Statues of his likeness were already commissioned. Paintings and tapestries depicting the giant in all his glory decorated scores of halls and small buildings. His domination of Krenz became thorough. Those unwilling to cooperate or proclaim themselves his vassals were never seen again. Hundreds of priests and cardinals swung from the streets. The great purge continued. None of it mattered to their master that watched him and the witch that soon joined his side.

Algiss Her glanced away from the humans and cleared her throat, making a show of letting raw magic drip from her fingertips. "My lord, I was unaware you were in this part of the complex," she said, cursing herself for supplicating before him.

"Mind yourself, witch. I am not in the habit of broadcasting my movements."

"Forgive me. This has been a trying day," she said, unwilling to provoke his ire, at least for the moment. "I trust you have reviewed the reports on the slain assassin."

"Disconcerting, but little more. All signs point to a single god hunter operating in the city," Amongeratix dismissed. "I am confident our combined forces will eliminate the threat in short order, though I now question the timing of his arrival."

"Nothing is coincidence."

"No, it is not. There is the real possibility he seeks to draw me out. Lure me to a battle not of his choosing. I think the god hunter was sent to force my hand."

"What makes you suspect this?" Algiss asked.

"My scouts have confirmed the intelligence from this upstart Confederation."

"You suspect your brother seeks to force a final confrontation?"

Amongeratix nodded. "This has been a moment I have long anticipated. Ever our paths cross at odd intervals. We rise and fall on whim. Each side has been balanced, until now. Today, I stand in the heart of the human empire. All their tools, weapons, and manpower at my fingertips. Tannus has a portion of my strength. I will meet him and crush him at last. When he is kneeling before me in chains, a pet to decorate my throne room, I may at last find a measure of peace and begin my true destiny."

"True destiny?" Algiss questioned.

Amongeratix gestured to the city below. "This is but a steppingstone. The foundation required to reshape the universe in my image. Once Tannus is removed, I plan on converting Sorrow to my cause. Together we shall awaken the remnants of my people and ignite a new empire under my rule."

The Crimson Mistress froze. Amongeratix was a proven liability. A venom rampaging through the stars unapologetically. The prospect of hundreds more at his side inspired true terror in her for the first time since Ruma Zzein nearly killed her. She retreated within herself, determined to create a counterplan capable of preventing Forever Night from devouring the universe.

His voice dropped, almost nostalgic as he continued speaking. "It will be a grand new era my father would have been proud of. You will see, Crimson Mistress. Today is naught but the trials necessary to achieve greatness. Long shall my name be remembered."

For the first time in recent memory, she had nothing to say.

"I have already ordered General Kale to ready his army to meet my brother. The fleet is preparing to deploy as well. Have your witches spread across the combined forces," he ordered at her silence. "No doubt your meddling founder will throw her weight into the fight."

"My Order will deal with those cursed witches, but we are too few to protect the entirety of the landing force," she protested.

"My skulldaerth will be more than enough to negate the Oracle's witchery," he said. "Once more Occanum shall tremble beneath the fury of my army. This will be a moment unlike any the universe has witnessed or shall again. Perhaps I should have a chronicler to mark the final campaign."

"But why meet Tannus where he expects you?" she asked.

Amongeratix rose to his full height, looking down on her with consternation. "Because I don't back away from a challenge. Now go, prepare to depart."

As he stalked off, Algiss had never felt so small. She had much to do and no time in which to do it if her fledgling Order was to survive the approaching storm.

Wheels in constant motion, Amongeratix felt the tides drawing him toward a conclusion. The end of his long war with his brother appeared upon the horizon and, for the first time, he held a definitive upper hand. He allowed his thoughts to range ahead of the present. With no one to stand in his way, he could resume the cleansing of the universe, removing the human vermin wholesale until all was reshaped in his image. It began with his army.

The skulldaerth, for the most part, remained in suspended animation in their deployment crates. Though less than ten thousand remained in his service, they were deadlier and more efficient than any human force in existence. A force to be wielded at discretion and for maximum result. Amongeratix found them in the old Conclave private hangar bay, arrayed in perfect ranks. Their warder, a green skinned goblin sat on the back ramp of one of the transports. He eyed Amongeratix's arrival with casual indifference.

"How are my children, Isnas?" Amongeratix asked.

The goblin flicked an impossibly long tongue over his chin. White hairs protruded from his nostrils and ears in clumps. A broken incisor jutted from his upper lip, gnarled and gangrenous. Enslaved by Amongeratix centuries ago, Isnas and his tribe were forever indentured the giant.

"Just like when you saw them last," the goblin replied in a rasping voice. "They grow restless. Many are attempting to awaken."

"Soon they shall all be awake and set loose upon my enemies," Amongeratix confirmed. "Has there been any loss since departing Braewynd?"

The goblin bobbed his head. "A few, but nothing out of acceptable ranges. These nightmares are most hardy."

"The loss of a single skulldaerth is unacceptable," Amongeratix scolded, choosing to forget the hundreds slain during the Resurrected Man's quest. "Begin preparations. I want the entirety of the brigade ready for battle the moment we touch down on Occanum."

Isnas gawked. "You mean to return to that dead world?"

"Tannus tests me. I shall give him the battle he has long craved. It shall be the annihilation I have sought for millennia," Amongeratix confirmed. "Rouse the skulldaerth, Isnas. Do this one last task for me and I shall set you free."

The goblin stared at him questioningly before nodding. "It shall be done, my lord. The skulldaerth will march one more."

Satisfied, Amongeratix gave his creations a final look before leaving. The wheels of war ground into action. His step was light. His blood quickened as thoughts of the future collided with the visceral core of his being. After so long, all finally turned in his favor. He would grind the universe to heel under the sword and gun.

Zevistya Spaceport, low continent.

Sergeant Icarn stared out the viewport as their transport crossed the ocean to reach the low continent. He'd heard the stories from those who fought against the Rengu uprising several years past. Stories of fire and wanton death. When he looked down, he saw endless fields of green rolling across gentle hills. Certainly nothing to suggest the cleansing fires. Another hour showed him how wrong he was. Grasslands turned to abandoned husks of villages and cities. A blackened wasteland where nothing lived. Icarn's jaw dropped as the string of transports raced through mountain passes to their debarkation point. He hadn't wanted to believe the rumors. Refused to accept his fellow Guards were capable of such wanton devastation. A sinking feeling awakened in the pit of his stomach. For the first time in his career, he began to think he might have chosen the wrong side.

The transport slowed. They were close to the spaceport. Icarn settled back into the mesh webbing of his seat and clutched his rifle. He rocked as the transport touched down, winced as pale light flooded the interior as the back ramp dropped. Senior enlisted barked orders. The company surged to their feet, collecting weapons and assault kits. Icarn adjusted the pack on his back before ensuring his platoon followed suit. Strapped up, he waited until the front ranks deboarded before waving his people forward.

They touched ground, noting the ash beneath their boots, and were immediately swarmed with heat. Murmurs rippled through the platoon; Icarn ignored them. The spaceport showed signs of battle despite the quick work of Guard engineers establishing a tent city and logistics base for deploying troops. He knew this was the last stand of the remnants of General Strannan's army. Icarn spied the cemetery on the far side of the flightline. Endless rows of headstones. Part of him wished he'd been part of that army, though the quiet corner of his mind whispered it was best he wasn't.

Icarn's boots hit the deck and he stepped out of line to direct his platoon. "All right, shitbirds! Form up. Double time!"

"Get these troopers off the flightline, Sergeant! We've got more transports incoming," a flight officer barked.

Icarn bit back the curse on the tip of his tongue and turned back to his people. "You heard the woman. Right face. Forward, march!"

Following directions from ground crews, Icarn led his platoon to their tents. He ordered them to claim their bunks, keeping squad integrity. He didn't anticipate staying long. Word came down of a massive fleet building in Vau orbit. The big campaign approached, and every available combat unit was being pushed to the frontlines. Until now, Icarn never fought in a pitched battle. He doubted any of the Guards in his division had. The scope and scale of this deployment went beyond anything in the Prekhauten Guard's storied past.

The immensity of what they sought to accomplish thrilled him. Icarn considered himself a true professional. Yet for the bluster providing courage, he saw through the cracks command presented. A moral decay spread through the army, beginning with the enthusiastic purge of all former clergy in Krenz. Icarn felt the vitriol among his leaders, though his status as training cadre on Tatarast Island protected him from the brunt of depravity. But with no one to confide his fears in, Icarn kept his thoughts to himself.

Inquisitors swept through the building army, seeking signs of heresy against the new regime. Icarn chilled in their presence. Though the branches were designed to work hand in hand, he found the Inquisitors sinister. That sensation deepened the longer Amongeratix reigned. Icarn, like the others around him, gasped when video feeds showed the giant murder the former Inquisitor General in broad daylight. Never in his short life did he envision working for one of the

Three, and the worst one at that.

Icarn grew up a man of faith but found himself pulled further away the older he got. Perhaps the gods were returning to punish those like him. The prospect chilled his soul. During those brief times of perfect solitude, Icarn turned his thoughts inward and prayed. It distressed him to see so many of his platoon abandon their faith in favor of devotion to Amongeratix. Legends proclaimed the giant a villain. The despair of the universe. He failed to understand how any of them blindly followed Amongeratix's will, begrudgingly accepting the Conclave might have lied to them for generations. The closer he looked the more confused he grew. Icarn preferred taking matters at face value. The question of faith disturbed him far greater than he was comfortable with. Yet any thought he had of resigning his position faded under the weight of uncertainty. Obligation demanded he remain with his troops and keep them alive as long as possible.

"Squad leaders, put your people to work. Chow is at 17:00. I want gear laid out on their racks and weapons cleaned," he ordered. "Make it happen."

Icarn watched them move. In garrison, his platoon appeared competent enough, though much improvement needed to be done if they were going to survive. Command anticipated massive casualties, estimating over fifty percent in the first days of the coming campaign. Icarn found the idea of losing so many disgusting and a disservice to his level of competence. While he didn't know his current batch of recruits well, the thought of them lying dead and forgotten on the battlefield twisted him.

"Sergeant Icarn," a deep voice rumbled behind him.

Icarn spun and froze. The last person he expected to see, or know his name, was General Mobus Kale. The one-armed commanding officer of the Guard appraised every ounce of him, from the cut of his uniform to the lone string hanging from his collar where he'd recently sewn on his new rank. Icarn stiffened and snapped a salute.

Kale returned the gesture. "Stand easy, Sergeant. It has come to my attention you are proving an outstanding training instructor. I wish I had more of you to spread around."

Icarn's eyes widened. "Sir, I … I'm just doing my job. If I can prevent even one of these recruits from dying a pointless death, I'll consider it a success."

Cocking his head, Kale's eyes glassed over. "Aren't all deaths in combat pointless?"

Unsure how to respond, Icarn remained at attention. Instinct screamed for him to look around, desperate for eye contact with another soul. Discipline forced him to remain still. Kale's fierce reputation suggested what might occur if the general thought he was being disrespected.

"Keep up the good work. You have a few days to whip these recruits into shape. Then I expect to deploy to the greatest battle of our time. Carry on, Icarn. I'll have my eye on you." Kale did an about face and went in search of his next victim.

Icarn's knees trembled long after the general disappeared from sight.

Tannus' flagship, *Brightstar*, in transit to planet Inselcor.

No matter how hard he tried, Vicente Blackheart could not grow used to walking the enormous corridors of August's new dreadnaught. The pristine condition made it difficult to accept the ship was thousands of years old, or that an entire fleet of them flanked *Brightstar*. Lost a dozen times already, the pirate made his way through the endless passages, into empty holds twice as large as his ship, before reaching the bridge. There he found August and Odir conferring over a table full of old star charts.

"I'll never get used to this monstrosity," he announced.

Odir glanced up, the perpetual scowl on his face darkening. August nudged him.

"Vicente, I hadn't thought to see you again so soon," August said.

"You almost didn't. This is one damned big ship."

She grinned. "You get used to it after a while. I've already integrated half of your crew to their new positions."

He looked around, spying Sedge and a handful of others scattered across a bridge easily a hundred meters wide. Blackheart readied a quick remark but bit his tongue when a shadow fell over him from behind. Turning, he saw the largest being in his life.

"What do you think of my ship, pirate lord?"

Blackheart swallowed. "A very fine vessel indeed. Just, a little large for my tastes."

The giant laughed, breaking the tension. "Good. Good. I

appreciate a little humor from those I go to battle with. You will fit in nicely. Admiral August speaks highly of you."

And I don't know why. Clearing his throat, Blackheart said, "You humble me, sir."

"Please, no sirs. I am Tannus. Nothing more. The Prekhauten Guard may retain their ranks, but I am just a passenger on this voyage."

Blackheart shot August a worried glance, silently pleading for a little help.

August dropped her grease pencil on the chart and looked up. "I find that a little hard to digest. This is your ship. Your fleet. We are proceeding on a heading you prescribed. Tannus, we are every bit under your command."

"Destroy *Behemoth* and this fleet is yours to do whatever you wish with it," Tannus replied. "Our forces will be sorely outnumbered. Ten dreadnaughts will prove more than enough to break the enemy fleets and establish domination surrounding Occanum."

Blackheart leaned closer to August. "I take it this *Behemoth* is an equally large piece of nightmare made real?"

"Nightmare is the perfect term," Tannus said. "My brothers have a proclivity for the dramatic. Amongeratix's flagship has roamed the universe for centuries despite my best efforts to find and eliminate it before he reclaimed it. There are some creations that should not have been allowed to pass. *Behemoth* is one. Fortunately, I have a most capable tactician at my side." Tannus paused, eyes boring into Blackheart with withering fury. "Admiral, now that you have him, where do you see Blackheart fitting in?"

"I was hoping to make him part of my command team for the time being. Once he is up to speed with how these ships operate, I was going to transfer him to his own ship," she said. The pirate jerked back. "Blackheart may be a rogue and wanted by the Conclave, but he is cunning enough to see things I may miss. His experience will prove invaluable."

"With no danger of him absconding one of my fleet?" Tannus asked.

Blackheart cringed. "You have my word." The last thing he needed was to be hunted down by Tannus and the rest of the dreadnaughts. "Not that it is required. Admiral August has already broken my crew down across several ships. Even if I wanted to, it is next to impossible to pull them all together."

Tannus regarded him for a long moment before grunting. "I expect great things from you, Vicente Blackheart. Should we survive, you will be rewarded handsomely for your deeds."

"Most generous of you," Blackheart replied.

The giant seemed satisfied with the reply and focused on August. "How long before we arrive at Inselcor?"

"Some hours yet."

"Push the fleet. The engines need a good test before we reach Occanum."

Blackheart flinched, mind drifting forward to the inevitability of battle when August asked, "What are we expecting to find here?"

"My brother has developed a secret weapon to throw against the worst of Amongeratix's forces," Tannus admitted after a pause. "There are forces in play humans should not tamper with. Ancient and wrathful. I hope to even the odds. With both forces removed, the battle will fall to the human equation. Man against man."

Tannus left them envisioning a cruel fate. One filled with unending civil war.

"Not exactly a social butterfly, is he?" Blackheart said, clearing his throat.

Odir's snort earned him an elbow to the ribs, Blackheart grinned.

Ferom, planet Occanum.

"How the fuck am I supposed to know what this does?" Annalilly bellowed and threw her datapad against the nearest wall.

Someone chuckled from the far side of the room. Her scowl deepened. She hated relying on ancient schematics provided by Paradise Tear to guide her through each task. The woman was already spread thin, moving throughout the facility's many cavernous chambers and operating systems. Designed without human influence, the station operated solely on antiquated technologies of Tannus' time. Using a company of Guards, infantry at that, to get the station online was the most idiotic thing she'd done in uniform.

"Who laughed?" she demanded, knowing she wasn't getting an answer.

At their silence, Annalilly balled her fists and stormed off to clear her head. She failed to understand why they were on the moon instead of joining the main army. They stood on the cusp of the battle for the soul of the universe, and she was going to miss it, trapped on a moon with little strategic significance and no tactical advantage. Pointless.

She soon found herself in the command center and went directly to Fies. "I want a transfer."

Fies blinked. "Good to see you too. Is the main docking bay operational?"

Annalilly took a step back, suddenly remembering her hands were still fisted. "Did you hear me?"

He turned away, back to the console he'd been working on. "I did, and like any good commanding officer, I ignored you. Is there anything else?"

"You're joking."

"Look around you. I don't have time to joke. We've only gotten this station half operational. According to the timeline, I'm expecting the first screen of ships from Mannus Prime any moment. The armies and fleets will soon follow. I need that bay up and ready to receive ships ASAP."

Pursing her lips, Annalilly asked, "How can you ignore we've been sidelined? After all we've done throughout this war we're punished and forced to watch from this godsdamned moon!"

"Keep your voice down, Sergeant," he snarled. "You are a senior leader in this company. Act like it."

"You're avoiding the answer." She narrowed her eyes. The unspoken threat blazing.

He leaned close. "I don't like this anymore than you, but don't you think we've earned a break? We've left a trail of bodies across half the universe, too many of them ours. These people deserve a cush assignment, if for no other reason than their mental health. How many of your people are hiding their symptoms?"

Annalilly blushed. Too many was the obvious answer. A nervous twitch here and there. Guards jumping at the slightest sound. Some crying throughout the night. Others turned to drinking, when they were able. Aggression rose through the ranks. She'd addressed as much of these issues as possible but without the benefit of having a medical professional, her efforts fell flat. She agreed many of her platoon needed help. She had no way of delivering it. Maybe Fies was right after all. Maybe being off the line was the best thing for them.

"Sorry," she mumbled. "You know I act before I think."

He gripped her by the elbow. "I know, and that's fine. Just do it when we are alone. The last thing either of us needs is one of these miscreants talking behind our backs." Louder, he said, "You hear me? Keep the scuttlebutt down and get back to work! The clock is running."

Annalilly watched as no one did anything they hadn't already been doing. The power of true leadership, she mused. That anger fading, she decided to run down Paradise Tear and get her to show her, again, how to activate the atmosphere cylinders in the main docking bay.

Fies stopped her. "Annalilly, this stays between us for now, but I received word from Matthias. He's sending that merc outfit to watch our backs."

"The Shadow Hammers? I thought they took the money and ran," she said with a frown.

"They did, but he convinced them to jump back in."

"What does he know he's not telling us?"

Fies raised his eyebrows. "Sounds like we need to stay vigilant. It's a good bet that if Tannus remembers this place Amongeratix will too."

"None of it makes a damned bit of difference if we can't get the firing platforms online," she snapped. "What are you going to do with the mercs?"

"Depends on how amiable Bootleg is to following orders. Ideally, I'd like half of them arrayed strategically across the surrounding area protecting every avenue of approach and keep the rest in reserve. They don't bring too much to the table, but an armored brigade comes in handy. Especially when the enemy isn't expecting it."

She wasn't sure about that. They were about to face another force of Guards. Men and women with the same training and tactics. If Matthias managed to think ahead surely one of their counterparts would as well. Suddenly, Annalilly didn't feel as confident as she had a moment before.

"Keep your people at it," he told her, his tone warming. "We've already gotten half this place operational, but I don't know how much longer we're going to get."

"I get it. No one tells me anything either." She slapped his shoulder and offered a mock salute before departing.

*

"I can't even read this," Palco grunted.

Hollis set her wrench down and laughed. "I didn't know you could read."

"What's that supposed to mean?"

"Nothing," she lied. "Just didn't know being in the mines taught functional skillsets that translate to successful careers."

"She's fucking with you," Desril chimed in.

Palco rubbed his head, feeling an ache coming on. "What?"

"Big words and shit," Desril said with an exaggerated huff. "Try to keep up, man. We've got a war to win."

"I shoulda stayed in the mines. Least there everyone thinks like me."

A chorus of laughs rippled through the squad, eventually making the way back to Haggle and Quint. The senior leaders let the banter go, knowing it was the best remedy for the remaining sanity they had. Soldiers were expected to perform the impossible, often being thrown into desperate situations without proper intelligence and lacking equipment. This qualified as one of those times. If the squad wanted to blow off steam by ragging on each other, so be it.

Quint spliced a trio of wires and was rewarded with a flickering light on the control panel before him. "I think I got it." Sparks erupted from the wiring, dancing across the backs of his hands. A frown spread across his face.

Haggle tried and failed to conceal his grin. "We all weren't cut out to be electricians."

"Nope," Quint replied as he rubbed the singed hairs from his hands. "But you put a rifle in my hands, and no one will question me."

"Have I thanked you?"

Quint paused. "For what?"

Blowing out a deep breath, Haggle rose and leaned against the console. "For taking over this squad. I was never made to be a leader. Not at that level. I like where I'm at. If Jers hadn't resigned none of this would have happened."

"Buddy, whether you know it or not, you're a leader. These people look to you for advice, to see how you react to situations. I'm the new guy. The outsider with a nasty attitude and too much experience. At the end of the day, this is still your squad," Quint rebuked. "Now if you're done yapping, we have work to do."

"Roger that, Sergeant."

Annalilly passed by, choosing not to stop. Doing so would show them the smile creeping across her face.

Outer edge of Occanum System.

Captain Drukali made that odd clicking sound in his throat his crew came to understand meant he was nervous. Knowing no officer worth his salt would dare admit such, they left him to his mannerisms, comfortable he shared their sentiment. The *Vitriol*, renamed by popular vote in the wake of the betrayal at Hawker's Gate, slowed to real speed as she entered Occanum space. A full squadron of support craft blinked into reality a moment later. With his right arm across his chest propping up the left as he tapped a finger on his cheek, Drukali stared at the orb of the dead world drifting in the distance.

Like most, he'd heard of Occanum. The lifeless world where the final battle between the gods took place. Recent historical revelations suggested the planet was far from the sacred site once proclaimed by the Conclave. The belief that the gods weren't gods spread across the universe, leaving many rocked in disbelief. Drukali cared little. His focus was on preparing the battlespace for the coming fight.

"Captain, all ships reporting in. We are at full strength."

He grunted, expecting nothing less. So far as any of them knew, they had the advantage. But any good commander understood war was fickle. Tides shifted on whim. The sooner he laid the minefields and scouted the entire system the sooner he could assume orbital positions over the moon Ferom.

"I want First Flight to deploy a fighter screen for the minelayers. Second Flight is to begin sweeping the system for enemy craft," he ordered.

The bridge went into action. Orders were relayed and Drukali watched as his squadron set about their tasks. New Annihilator class fighters poured from their carrier. Sleek and near impossible to detect with the naked eye. Laden with kinetic bullets designed for deep space fighting and missiles, the fighters had heavy armor around the cockpit and engines. They were top of the line but had yet to be fully battle tested. They fanned out in standard formation, flanking the larger, more ponderous ships.

A flight of corvettes broke away from the main squadron. These were his hunter-killers. Combined, they had enough firepower to take down a battleship or carrier. Faster and designed to get out of trouble as quick as they got into it, the corvettes comprised the bulk of his command. His own cruiser maintained tactical dominance of the battlespace, at least until the rest of Khe-Zhehan's fleets arrived.

Part of his assignment was to find adequate space for large scale ship warfare. Big ships needed maneuverability. Thankfully Occanum was a largely empty system. Just three planets circled the distant sun, each with a scattering of moons. Drukali absorbed it all, noting gravity wells and potential dangers lingering in the cold dark.

"Tactical, enlarge quadrant thirteen," he said.

The image filled the main screen. Halfway between the system edge and the first planet was an area large enough to funnel an entire fleet. It was also the main entry point to the system from subspace routes. His mind raced through deployment schemes and potential ambush points. Given the proper leverage and enough firepower, he could destroy a healthy portion of the enemy fleet before they became battle ready. A grin split his hardened face.

"Dispatch the minelayers there. I want that entire area saturated."

SIXTEEN

3215 A.G. (After Gods), Eger City, planet Mannus Prime.

Gunfire echoed through the courtyard, displacing a family of red bills from their nest. Feathers drifted down to lay in the carpet of white blossoms in the grass. A second salvo, more deliberate and better aimed followed. Then another. A small crowd gathered. One and two at first. Smaller groups arrived. All eager to discover the source of the commotion. None were surprised to find two grizzled Prekhauten veterans exchanging salvos of blaster fire into a pair of target practice dummies that had seen better days. Murmuring began, followed by wagers on who shot best.

Torgast listened to them with interest. He was never one for putting on a demonstration, but morale needed bolstering. He glanced at Matthias, unsurprised to find the same thought playing out in the retired Sergeant Major.

Matthias reloaded his power charge, placing a hand over the end of his barrel to ensure he wasn't overheating the weapon. "Best five out of seven?"

The click-slap of Torgast doing the same rippled through the gardens. A determined look twisted his features. "You go first."

Grinning, Matthias took aim at his target and fired. The head exploded in a shower of plastoids and filler, much to the applause of the small crowd surrounding them. He jerked around, surprised to find what he assumed to be half the government building watching. *When did that happen?* Credits exchanged hands. Losers tossed their hands up. Winners offered consolatory pats on backs as they pocked their earnings.

Matthias decided to play into it. "Looks like they already know you lost, old man."

"Nobody loses until the last round is fired," Torgast grumbled. "Plug your ears."

His aim was true. A line of ion rounds tracked across the dummy's upper torso, shredding the material in a straight line. The crowd erupted in wild cheer when the head rolled off the shoulders and hit the grass. Torgast made a show of blowing the smoke coming from the end of his barrel. "Never take the sucker bet," he said, laughing.

Chagrined, Matthias had no choice but to accept. "I let you win."

Laughter circled the garden. With the show finished, everyone drifted back to their offices, meetings, or worse. The Guardsmen waited until they were alone before breaking down their weapons to clean.

"You're going, aren't you?" Matthias asked as he slapped his upper receiver back into place. "I don't blame you. Sitting here while the largest battle of our lifetime rages without us goes against every professional grain in my body."

"But?"

"I'm too old for this. I've been running the universe since before you slipped into a uniform. I'm tired. I have aches in places I never knew I had. My bones hurt and don't get me started on getting up in the middle of the night to hit the head," Matthias joked. "War is a young man's game. I meant it when I retired a few years ago."

"Therein lies the difference between us. You are retired, a respectable member of the council and a leader in the Confederation. I am still a commissioned officer and general of the armies. Staying behind is a complete disservice to everyone I order forward," Torgast said.

Matthias understood. He was torn between his body telling him to quit while he could and his mind screaming to sneak aboard a ship and steal a rifle. Between them was over one hundred and thirty years of military experience. Leaving that life behind had been the toughest act Matthias ever performed. He'd grown to love his subordinates, treating them like family. That, he knew, was a deadly evolution. Too many leaders made that mistake and broke when casualties occurred. He got out before the inevitable. He also knew Torgast had no business being on the front line. As general of the armies, his place was in the rear command center or aboard Tannus' flagship. Convincing him of that was another matter.

Torgast frowned. "I figure on hopping the lead transport when the first divisions roll out. Matthias, I'm not a politician. Never claimed to be. My life has been behind a uniform and by the gods, that's where I'm going to finish it."

"You don't plan on making it back?"

"Eh? What nonsense is that? I didn't say anything about dying,"

Torgast sputtered. "I'm thinking a vacation is in order once this mess is wrapped up."

"Even if we win there will be years of smaller brush wars and mopping up to handle," Matthias cautioned. "The war will effectively be finished, but there is still much to do before the universe accepts our little Confederation. You're needed here, with the rest of us fools tapped to be the leaders of the new universal order."

"People like you and I will be mostly obsolete by the time politicians are ready to shine," Torgast said. "We're already past our prime. With the promise of peace spreading across the stars there won't be any need for veterans or soldiers. Maybe it's for the best. We've been tainted by this war. How can any of us return to civility? What of those against us? Will they let go of their hatreds and emotions, throw down their weapons and accept the future with blind optimism?"

"One can hope."

"Hope doesn't better life," Torgast countered. "This is a war for ideals. For a way of life. I don't profess to understand why or how so many of our brothers fell sway to such evil. Perhaps the rot was always there, lurking in the distance for the opportunity to spread. It doesn't matter. We will either kill them or they us. Once the dust settles a new way of life must be found to restore balance to the universe." He caught Matthias' smirk. "What?"

"You just countered your own argument," he said. "You say we will be obsolete in one breath and describe the reason for our continuing to serve in the next."

Torgast paused, eyes narrowing. "Yeah, I suppose I did. Which brings me to my point. This war is never going to be finished with us, Matthias. We are constant reminders of violence to the politicians and forgotten clergy struggling to find relevance. The sooner I can take my ass to Occanum the better. At least there I'll feel useful."

"And leave me here to fend against the wolves alone?" Matthias teased. He received a pat on the shoulder accompanied by a barking laugh.

"You should have shot better, my friend. Maybe I'd have given you that seat on the transport."

"Like I said, I let you win," Matthias reiterated.

Torgast winked. "Sure you did."

"Wouldn't look good for an old retiree like me to outshoot the hotshot general who's going to win the war. Besides, I make you look good."

Repressing a scowl, Torgast ignored his barb. "Come on, I'm hungry. Might as well face the council on a full stomach."

"You're certain this is the right play?" Adris asked, eyebrow arched.

"I am. The campaign needs me to oversee it. You don't need me here."

A scattering of council members decorated the room. Adris and Virom sat beside each other, while Matthias leaned against the door beside a pillar containing the bust of man, he had no idea who it was. Seated on the edge of the large footstool beside the table was Standou. His look of relief was evident for all to witness.

"I wish you'd reconsider. This is a delicate moment for the Confederation," Adris said. "We are scheduled to vote of several key pieces of legislation."

Standou waved off her concern. "Let the man do his job. He is a soldier, after all. The council will be fine without him."

"Minister, I am not debating his services to our cause," she started, tone low. "Torgast engineered the campaign to secure Mannus Prime and defeat one of the enemy's largest field armies in the process. Not to mention converting at least half that force to our side."

"Precisely why he needs to continue his exemplary service," Standou quipped. "I am no great fan of the military war machine. I believe my position is well documented in that regard, but I also understand the necessity of putting the right people in the right jobs. Torgast is a proven commodity. We need him at Occanum. Besides, we have Matthias here to offer a voice to military support when the council next meets."

Matthias held his tongue by grinding his teeth. Instinct screamed for him to cross the room and break Standou's nose, or jaw, but his position as council member pinned him into a diplomatic corner from which there was no escape. Decorum took precedence over all else. *Doesn't mean I won't knock you down a peg or two given the chance.*

"I mean no disrespect, Matthias," Standou said. "Your military history is well known. Your deeds taught at the vaunted Prekhauten Officer Academy. But we are living in the moment, not the past. The time has come for you to set aside your rank and become an active part of the council. Or stand aside and let politicians do their jobs."

"You'll find I'm more than up for the challenge," Matthias growled. His clenched fist trembled at his side.

"Very good. I knew you were a man of remarkable talent."

"You have no idea."

"If we're done kissing ass," Torgast called out. "I'd like to get to the heart of the matter. I intend on taking the command shuttle to Falchi's fleet and pressing forward. At no point do I envision picking up a rifle and charging into the fray, but my experience and tactical mind are both needed to defeat Mobus Kale. You don't need me here." He looked at Adris. "This is your arena. Not mine. You do your parts, allow me to do mine."

"Well said," Virom said before anyone else could respond. "General, I think I can safely speak for all of us when I say best of fortune to you. We bestow our full trust and confidence in you to see the job done. Thank you for placing yourself once more in harm's way. You serve as an inspiration for us all to ensure the citizens of the Confederation are seen to with love and care by all parties."

Satisfied, Torgast gave a nod. "If there is nothing else? I need to ensure my affairs are in order before I leave."

He left without being stopped, leaving behind an envious Matthias dangerously close to making his final decision.

Abbey of the Order of Blood Witches, Acumensiis Comet.

An inexplicable energy resonated throughout the abbey. Ah'muf felt it surge from his fingertips to the core of his heart. The desert dweller couldn't recall the last time he felt this … alive. Magic and authority were evident everywhere he looked; he stood in awe in the presence of so many witches. With awe came a wave of fear, just enough to keep him honest. His experiences around Sister Alessandra were limited, their only conversation in passing, but it was enough to leave him afraid of the power each witch held and what might happen should they lose control in a fit of rage.

Shimmering walls stretched deep into the cosmic rock of the comet. How anyone managed to tame a comet to the point of established atmosphere and a working sanctuary was beyond his ability to comprehend. Ah'muf thought himself a simple man, as far removed from the mysteries of the universe as the next man eking out a living in the deserts of An'kuruku. Leaving at Elisa's side proved eye opening in many ways, but none more than by the feeling of smallness assailing his mind since arriving on the Acumensiis Comet.

"Stop acting like a tourist," Elisa scolded from his side as they were led down a wide passageway by one of the novices.

He noted how the young woman walked rather than floated like the rest of the Order. A sheepish grin spread across his face, Ah'muf muttered, "I cannot help it! Have you not witnessed the wonders of this place? *Farisi*, none of it should be possible. This building should not exist, yet here we stand. Wonder upon wonders. They will never believe me when I return home."

Her hand slipped into his. A subtle reminder that she did not expect either of them to see home again. She had said as much before. Not after the inevitable confrontation with Amongeratix.

"Yes, Ah'muf, there will be stories to tell," she said.

His innocent smile, infectious from the first time he flashed her with it, reminded Elisa that there was good in the universe. She just had to look to find it. The novice led them to a small room off the main meeting hall. Ushering them inside, she departed with a bow and returned to her duties.

Elisa looked the room over with casual interest. Nothing stood out. Nothing caught her eye. It was a plain chamber with no decorations on the walls. No collected items from a lifetime of travel and adventure. She wondered how anyone lived as long as Ruma Zzein without amassing anything.

A woman was seated with her legs crossed on a luxurious couch centered on the far wall. "Welcome, my friends."

Elisa cleared her throat. "You would be the Grand Mistress I take it."

A smile. It was only then Elisa realized the woman's hood was lowered. Her face on display. "I am, but you may call me Ruma while we are in private. I stand on ceremony but there is a time and place for everything. Your travels were satisfactory?"

"They were," Elisa replied, overcoming her initial shock at seeing a witch's face so clear for the first time. "Ishis Gul led us unerringly."

"The man has his uses, though we have never permitted him to set foot in the abbey," Ruma explained. "We seldom offer outsiders succor, Paladin. You and your, consort, are special exceptions. I must insist, however, you tell no living soul what you witness within our walls. We are mistrusted across the universe. Any knowledge you share can be used against us by the wrong people."

"Who is powerful enough to attack you?" Ah'muf blurted out. "I have seen what one of your kind is capable of. Here must be thousands! Surely no power in the universe is strong enough to bring the fable Blood Witches to their knees."

Ruma's thin smile caught Elisa off guard. "If that were true, we might all be comfortable spending our days in peace, but there are ancient evils lurking throughout the stars. Each more than enough to bring my Order to ruin and claim our power for itself. Against that we must ever be vigilant."

"True words for us all," Elisa jumped in before Ah'muf embarrassed himself, and her, again. "Gran—Ruma, why did Tannus have us come here? I was not under the impression your Order was directly involved in the war."

"Child, we have been involved since before Tannus dared question his father and began their terrible war," Ruma said. "Long have traveled the stars. Preparing for this final struggle. In a dream, I saw the universe burn dark. Stars extinguished. Life smothered into oblivion. Forever Night. With Amongeratix released and in command humanity's heart, we hurry to that demise."

Elisa whistled under her breath. "You think we will lose."

"I am prepared to ensure we do not."

Tensing, Elisa took the offered seat across from Ruma when the Grand Mistress motioned for her to. "Why do I get the feeling you aren't telling me everything?"

"No one in this universe knows the ravages of Amongeratix more than I, Elisa. Our history is one of mutual hatred," Ruma admitted. "Yet for all that, he has slipped away time and again, forcing us to this moment in time. You are the first Paladin since Sorrow created the line to reach this far. Hope rests on you and that dagger at your hip. Evil is ever powerful, often daunting, but good strives to restore balance. You, Elisa, are that balance."

"Can I kill him?" she asked, unsettled over the implications.

"That remains to be seen. Amongeratix and his kind are not mortal, nor human. They are … something else. An ancient race born through primordial magic. No mortal has succeeded in killing one, leastwise none without the gift of magic and transhumanification."

"What?"

"Altered humans through magic and imbued with supernatural powers. I called them god hunters after humanity turned to worshipping their old masters. It was a disease that never should have been allowed to take root." She winced, remembering her arguments with Tannus all those years ago for allowing such behaviors.

"What happened to these god hunters? I'm pretty sure one of them could do a better job with the dagger than me," Elisa suggested.

Sadness filled Ruma's face. "Gone. All but one and he is currently wreaking havoc on Vau Prime to lure Amongeratix to Occanum."

Elisa ran a fingertip over the ancient hilt at her hip. "How do I know if I have the ability to destroy the bastard?"

"My Order will protect you when the time is right," Ruma said with finality. "Do not worry over that. All will be as it should." She paused. Rising to her feet. "But come, you must hungry and tired after your journey. And, if I'm not mistaken, your companion I more than curious about the wonders of the Acumensiis Comet."

A rumble spread through her stomach at the mention of food. Elisa hadn't given thought to food or drink since boarding Ishis Gul's ship. Despite the ethereal energies swirling through the abbey, Elisa felt drained. She hadn't slept right since returning to Wexanos with the dagger. Her dreams, troubled and disturbing, ensured an endless string of restless nights despite the warmth and comfort Ah'muf provided. The lullaby in Ruma's voice promised her first peaceful night in months.

"A meal and a pillow sound pretty good right about now," she admitted.

Ruma raised her hood. "Good. Follow me. And let us change the topic of discussion. I find the gloom of war depressing. Tell me more of yourselves."

Lady, if you think war is depressing, wait until you hear my story.

Krenz, planet Vau Prime.

They crept like shadows through the night. Twenty armed figures in dark clothing and painted faces. Each moved on cue, hurrying to their targets. Armed with confiscated weapons from raided security stations and ambushed Guard units while Julian and his people were still in the city, they were the best Edam Boone had left. Hardened by years of guerilla warfare, the commandos hurried to their target unopposed.

Half the city was abandoned. Those with enough wealth secured transport offworld in the hopes of finding a better life. Those too poor hunkered down, securing what food they could find while praying Amongeratix's forces did not hunt them down. Gangs roamed the streets now. Disassociated youths eager for blood and to claim their share of the future while the world burned. Anarchy gripped Krenz, tearing the fabric of society and reality asunder.

Their target was a small security station in the heart of one of the more prominent housing areas, now empty save the squatters and filth looking for any advantage. Ringed with heavy security cameras and detection devices, the station was fully manned and a hub for Guard activity in the sector. Edam found no reason why, until Porii surmised it was one of the prime holding points for captured clergy. She implored him to act, to save her people and, after much deliberation and planning and against his better judgment, Edam Boone launched his raid. Thopos being the one to lead them.

Thopos ran at the head of the column. His gaze focused on the building ahead. Two stories with enough lights to prevent any possibility of sneaking up to the walls undetected. He reached the closest street corner without giving away their position and whistled. A ragged young woman, barely old enough to be called such, hobbled forward, out of breath and sweaty.

"Are you sure this is going to work?" he asked in a low voice.

She shook her head. "Not even a little"

Thopos shot his tech specialist a withering gaze. "Lovely. Do it. We don't have all night."

Grunting, she punched in a series of codes into her datapad. The exterior lights dimmed before extinguishing. "Ready."

Thopos scanned the target through enhanced night vision, confirming the power was out. He broke into a grin and slapped the woman on the back hard enough she dropped the datapad. He keyed the commlink attached to his collar. "Everyone, we only have minutes. Get inside, eliminate resistance, and secure the package. Rendezvous at the safehouse." Thopos drew a calming breath. "Ready? Move."

They burst across the street—Thopos led, praying none of the defensive measures were still active. He started up the small flight of steps as the first pair of security guards emerged. Both were gunned down immediately. The door opened, and Thopos rushed inside.

Setting his rifle down on the scarred wooden table, Thopos ran a hand through his sweaty hair and breathed a sigh of relief. The raid proved successful. Once all enemy forces within were eliminated, his people discovered almost thirty former clergymen and several family members. Their praise and cheers felt wrong considered how the gods outright abandoned them, but Thopos allowed the prisoners a moment of joy before breaking them into small groups and herding them back into the night.

An hour later, the last of his team slipped into the safehouse but he couldn't relax. They still had a long journey to reach the exit points he, Porii Daam, and Edam Boone established. Scores of clergy and their families funneled out of Krenz daily, escorted to distant cities less tainted by Amongeratix. As the numbers rose so did the dangers. Ever present was the anticipation of one of their own being captured and talking. Edam ensured the exit avenues were known only to a handful. No one had every piece of the strategy.

One of his lieutenants, having appropriated the rank system from the Guard to simplify things in the field, approached. A worried look crossed his face. "I think the last team had a tail."

"How certain are you?" Thopos asked.

"Couldn't confirm it but every time I looked over my shoulder, I saw the same figures in the shadows. Could be Guard. Could be anyone looking to join the cause."

"Shit. We can't afford to get pinched. Not here. We're too exposed. All right, get them up." He reached for his rifle. "I want this place cleared out in ten."

"We don't even know if the transports are lined up," the lieutenant protested.

Thopos reached for his rifle and shook his head. "Doesn't matter. We can't stay here. Have three men stay behind. Everyone else split. With a little luck I'll see you all back at base."

Thopos issued instructions and the group slowly got moving again. They were tired, malnourished, and abused, but they had their first taste of freedom since being captured and refused to return to that hell. Thopos didn't blame them. He'd rather die fighting than rot in an Inquisition prison cell.

When the last of the refugees was escorted to safety, he and the remaining three men took up defensive positions overlooking the safehouse. They were rewarded a short time later when a half squad of Guards in civilian clothes headed to the safehouse. Rifles rose. Knowing this location was burned, Thopos waited until the Guards headed for the door before opening fire.

The enemy died without knowing how or by whom. He smiled.

Capital District, Krenz.

Akin Brohl studied the reports flooding his tracking system. Hundreds of Guards and Inquisitors fell to his bombing campaign. There was nothing personal in his actions. This was war and he had one specific assignment. An assignment he had not accomplished. That infuriated him more than any response from the Inquisition and led him to silently question how much more it would take to lure Amongeratix into Tannus' trap.

There'd been a time when his efficiency went unquestioned. Time in stasis, frozen where he'd fallen asleep while the rest of the universe progressed, left him a constant step behind his prey. Amongeratix surrounding himself with unique weapons and allies made the task more difficult. Akin struggled with accepting the splinter fragment of Blood Witches working in concert with the terror. They always arrived too late and repeatedly lashed out. He took no amusement at their childish reactions each time. They may be incapable of killing him, but they were currently making Akin's mission miserable.

A clap of thunder trembled the buildings around him. Rain began, drizzling at first before opening in a rare storm. Akin stared out at the sheets of water, plotting. No matter how many he eliminated, his enemy refused to bite. A change was needed.

Amongeratix would come forth. The giant had no choice.

The Crimson Mistress watched with bemused interest as Amongeratix hacked and slashed his way through the chamber. Wreckage littered the floor. Smoldering bodies, both human and automaton, twitched beneath a flurry of sparks and leaking fluids.

Large sections of the ceiling swung from cables. A gouge ran the length of the floor, burrowed by one of the massive alabaster pedestals once containing the bust of a former Cardinal Seniorus. Chest heaving, Amongeratix ceased the destruction, as if suddenly becoming aware of his audience.

Turning on her, he sneered, "Satisfied?"

"Why would I be?" Algiss replied, cautious. Despite her growing powers, she had nothing capable of countering the whirlwind of devastation standing before her.

"You play coy now, witch? I should have thought you enjoyed seeing me lose my temper. Doesn't that fit into one of those contemplative narratives you construct?" His voice rose. "I should have killed the Oracle when I had the chance."

Algiss pretended to smooth a ruffle in her dress, ensuring she drifted a few inches higher. "I betrayed Ruma Zzein and allied myself and my Order with you. So long as this war lasts, we are attached to each other's fates."

"Come what end awaits," he added.

"This is ever the way of alliances forged through necessity," she said, suddenly unsure how much longer she should tether her future to the madman.

He gestured to the damage. "Perhaps you can explain why I am venting my anger on defenseless items instead of breaking the last god hunter? You assured me he would be handled."

Algiss pursed her lips, choosing her words carefully. "Sister Evangaline has been diligent in hounding your god hunter throughout the capital district. Her efforts narrow his avenues of escape, reduce his ability to rearm or hide. We will soon have him."

"You underestimate him, witch," Amongeratix rolled his eyes and pinched the bridge of his nose. "Those monsters slaughtered hundreds of my kin. They are unstoppable killing machines, and this one is here for me. I think the time may have arrived where I follow my brother to Occanum."

"You seek to meet him in open battle," she echoed.

"The choice was taken from me long ago. Let the god hunter murder this world for all I care, though I suspect he will hound my steps wherever I go."

Algiss worked through the information, seeing the sliver of possibility in the fires of his rage. Arrogance was the downfall of many and not even one of Amongeratix's race proved strong enough to outrun the god hunters forever. "I shall redirect my Order. We deploy at your side."

An eyebrow arched. "You already have orders. I want you with the Mobus Kale's army."

"He has rebuked our aid," she replied. "The great general believes magic has no place on the battlefield and is willing to risk the lives of his army on it. I will not send my Sisters where they are not wanted."

"Let me deal with Mobus Kale. Prepare your Order to deploy," he commanded. "But first, I think the god hunter needs to be taught a lesson. Summon my guard and that useless Inquisitor General."

Algiss Her made an effort to bow just enough not to rouse suspicion and drifted off in search of Ezekiel Goethe. *Finally.*

SEVENTEEN

3215 A.G. (After Gods), Ankrit, planet An'kuruku.

Luma Kai rubbed her eyes, making the burning sensation worse. Fine particles of sand too small to be stopped by her face covering drifted through the fabric. Nothing in the breadth of her experiences infuriated her more than the inescapable feeling of sand on her flesh. Near permanent scowl settling into place, Luma placed the binoculars up to her eyes and continued scanning the compound.

Large enough to be considered a small fortress palace on many worlds, Dejak's home was one of unparalleled splendor in the district of wealth merchants, politicians, and lobbyists. She found it odd how any could throw their wealth in the face of such abject poverty as seen across the desert planet. Why hadn't the people risen up? Rebellions occurred throughout the universe when the system became unbalanced. Surely the people of An'kuruku saw the disparity? Especially after the disaster war in the desert from a few years ago.

Palm trees towered over the cluster of buildings, waving lazily in the warm breeze. The smells of the city assaulted Luma's nose. She realized she disliked spice just as much as sand. She truly found nothing appealing about An'kuruku. If ever a planet existed where all wars should be fought, it was here. Toying with the notion of a dedicated war world, Luma swept her gaze across the sand-colored rooftops. A trio of armed guards patrolled with little situational awareness. Had they been paying attention one would have alerted the compound to Luma's presence. She detested sloppy work. Putting a round in each would be too easy but she didn't. She had specific orders to avoid detection.

Grumbling under her breath, Luma continued with her reconnaissance. A small pack of children under the age of ten emerged from the main building she guessed was Dejak's true home. One carried a ball he dropped and kicked across the compound. The others scampered after it with cheers. A smile broke her scowl. War raged around every corner but there were still places in the universe where children could be children without reprisal.

About to shift focus, Luma caught a glimpse of the unmistakable shock of crimson hair in a tail running down a woman's back. She clicked a button to zoom in, but the woman disappeared around a corner before Luma got a look at her face. Still, what she saw was proof enough. The average citizen of An'kuruku had olive dark skin with black or brown hair. Luma hadn't seen any natural variation since arriving. *Got you, bitch.*

"You're certain it's her?" Tolde asked once Luma finished her report. "We can't afford to screw this up."

Luma nodded. "Positive. Tolde, how many redheads have you seen since we landed? You can tell she attempted to die it black, but streaks of red are shining through. That's Kaline holed up in this Dejak's household. We should move quick before they get wind or that bastard from Tenemenah sells us out."

"We can't risk innocent lives."

Luma found herself growing angry. Years following across the universe like a loyal pet, enduring hardships, watching him die, for what? For him to spit in her face when she brought him the most important piece of information they'd obtained since reaching An'kuruku? "You're kidding, right? We've been risking every life since we chose our side in this damned war. Every time I strap on my armor and leap into another shitstorm is a risk of life. Tolde, we are talking about ending one of the two most serious threats in the universe. Think of all the lives that will be lost if she completes her purpose here and unleashed the fires of Rengu."

He shook his head. "I'm not willing to place children in harm's way."

"What about the rest of us?" she demanded. "Are you willing to throw us into danger, again?"

"Is there a choice? All reward comes with risk."

"So you're saying—"

A snap thundered. Smoke issued from the fresh hole still burning. The Blood Witch floated to the middle of the room. "This infighting is pointless. We have come to perform a specific task. How does not matter. Time runs short while you dither on the moral ambiguity conflicting you. Our orders are clear. Capture or kill Kaline and return to Tannus."

"You don't understand." Tolde's protest came out weak and

Luma gritted her teeth. The weight of all he had done and was expected to do threatened to drag him down.

"I understand more than you know, Tolde Breed. For centuries I have trained for Forever Night and now it is upon us," Sister Alessandra corrected. "Set aside these foolish differences and focus on what lies before you. Tannus expects us on Occanum shortly."

"Excuse me, but couldn't you do something about the children?" Ragan asked after clearing his throat. "I mean, you're the only one with magic. Isn't there a spell that doesn't result in total destruction?"

"Ragan," Tolde began.

Sister Alessandra leveled her gaze on the boy from Rastarok, a newfound respect twinkling in her eyes; one Luma felt as well. "Ragan Sandinsol, you are a wonder. Yes, I am much more than a force in battle. My Order was established to counter Forever Night, but we are imbued with compassion." She looked at each of them before continuing. "The boy is right. I may be able to render all within the compound unconscious long enough for you to enter, secure Kaline, and escape back to the skiff. With luck we will be well on our way to the rendezvous before Dejak awakens."

"Enough talking already," Luma added. "Let's get this over with."

As the group settled into planning, Tolde noticed the dejected look on Presha Von's face. Once their meeting concluded, he pulled her aside, leading her to the small terrace balcony overlooking one of Ankrit's countless public fountains.

"You are worried," he said.

She nodded. "Shouldn't I be? While none of you have warmed to my presence, I have come to view you not as enemies but as something else. Listening to the way you discussed capturing Kaline, like she was naught but an animal on the run, leaves me questioning my place in this group and..."

"Yes?" he prompted, noticing the tear trickling down her cheek. He felt nothing.

"Is this what awaits me?" Presha asked. "Will you turn on me for my crimes? Swing me from the same gibbet as Kaline in the name of order and justice? A prize for the universe to see?" Her voice broke. "Tolde, I promise you this, I shall not allow myself to suffer such indignity again. For too long I have debased myself before others. My father. The dark council. Amongeratix. Now Tannus. The only way for the cycle to end is by discovering my true voice and making a stand."

"And you choose to do this now?"

"I am left with no choice, am I?"

Tolde cocked his head, looking for the truth in her eyes. "Few of us are. But you cannot remain beholden to your past. We've been through this, Presha. Both you and I carry silent demons we cannot escape. The only way to break free is to push forward, forge a better life. Stopping Kaline is the important piece."

"You don't get it." Locks of hair swept across her face. "How could you? I've been on the wrong side of this war from the beginning. I see in Kaline so much of myself. It aches."

Tolde folded his arms across his chest and asked, "Why? I can understand your motives for your past but this Kaline is a cancer. You are not alike."

"Because I know she had been duped into serving a wicked cause. We can't just kill her and wipe our hands as we barrel into the next scenario," Presha explained. "We owe her at least the opportunity to recant. Like you said, we've both had second chances. Why does she deserve less?"

"Assuming she seeks redemption," he countered. "Not all villains repent."

"I refuse to accept that."

"Why does it matter so much to you?"

"Because I have to know if I can be redeemed as well."

Tolde closed his eyes.

Sitting at an impossibly ornate antique night table, dressed in soft silk robes, Kaline brushed her hair and stared at herself in the mirror. Old. Tired. Lines crowded the corners of her eyes. Still uncertain of Dejak's true intentions, Kaline felt a noose slipping into place.

She set the brush down and resisted the urge to scream. Since arriving in Ankrit she'd been presented before several small groups of influential locals. Dejak prevented her from speaking, claiming the reprisal would be more than his people could handle without proper planning. After each engagement he sequestered her in an empty wing of his palatial home. One question burned in her thoughts afterwards.

What did Dejak truly want with me and how soon would it all collapse?

Sighing, she rose and went to the balcony overlooking the interior courtyard—Dejak refused to allow her any view of the city proper. For the first time in as long as she could remember Kaline longed for basic social interaction free of agenda or purpose. A chorus of nightbirds sang to her from the boughs of a palm tree. She smiled. Simple pleasures were all but forgotten since becoming the mouth of Rengu. Kaline found their call pure, refreshing. Closing her eyes, she tilted her head back and listened.

Their songs awakened passions she'd long forgotten. The simple enjoyment of life stolen so long ago. Kaline's shoulders trembled. Childhood memories rushed in, breaking through the mental barriers. She saw her mother picking flowers. Her father bouncing her on his knee as she giggled with delight. Life had been simple then. Innocent. Kaline couldn't remember much. Those times had been robbed from her by her service to the death god.

Somewhere in the midst of her rumination Kaline realized the birds had gone silent. An eerie calm settled over the compound. Kaline's eyes snapped open. Without moving, she searched the far shadows. A sliver of pale moonlight illuminated the night, just bright enough to leave most of the world bathed in darkness. Nothing moved. Not even in any of the rooms she could view from her balcony.

Then the slightest flicker of movement. She tensed. Narrowing her gaze, she tried to get a better look. A compound this large demanded staff at all hours. Too late for the evening meal and still too early to begin preparing breakfast, the kitchens looked to be dark and empty. Perhaps it was a guard roaming the halls. Men like Dejak didn't get where they were in life by taking unnecessary risks.

Another movement from the opposite side of the first drew her attention. Kaline knew a trap when she saw it. Dejak no doubt had many enemies, but the coincidence of them attacking here, now, was too impossible. No. Whoever lurked in the night had come for her.

She rushed back inside, threw on a heavier robe and a pair of slippers, and hurried into the empty halls in search of one of the guards. The compound needed to be warned.

Rounding a corner, she gasped as she discovered a pair of armed guards slumped atop each other. There were no blood trails. No signs of violence. To all appearances, the guards seemed asleep. Heart racing, Kaline dashed past them. She discovered a second pair in another corridor. Every shadow became an enemy. Every soft sound whispered in the night the voice of malevolence come for her.

She was indeed the target. Why else would Dejak's people all be unconscious? *They had come for me at last!* She resisted the urge to shout for help. The odds of anyone responding were slim and it might only serve in giving her position away. Unfamiliar with the compound and the city, she couldn't run. But she could hide.

She rounded the last corner leading to her hall and skidded to a halt. There, at the far end of the hall blocking her door was a figure hovering off the ground. Millions of pinprick lights glistened off their robes in a whirlwind of colors. Kaline's heart clutched. *Death. This is death.* "Who are you? What do you want from me?"

The figure raised an arm and pointed.

Darkness swept in.

Confederation Staging Ground, planet Mannus Prime.

The newly constituted Confederation Army surged to life in the predawn hours. Hundreds of thousands of personnel slipped into uniform, packed their kit, ate a final meal in the hundreds of chow halls spread throughout the staging area, and reported to company rooms to draw weapons.

Torgast stalked through one of the camps. He stopped at warming fires, bantered with as many of his Guards as possible before moving on. The skittish banter lingered as he moved on. Unlike many, he found himself more alive during these difficult mornings. Deployments were hard on everyone. The fear of not knowing whether you would return home or not permeated everything. No one thought about what might happen once they were boots on the ground. What was the point? War did what war wanted.

First Sergeants began barking for troopers to fall in. The army groaned into ranks for their final precombat checks. Manifests were called, each Guard responding to his last name with first name, middle initial, and identification number. Once called, they filed into the pre-deployment sheds to await shuttles to the main transports.

Torgast's mind drifted back to his first deployment and the youthful vigor surging through his body. The ignorance of youth inspired foolish deeds. Torgast often felt surprised he'd survived those early days, though, in truth, combat losses were far fewer than the general public thought. Watching the holovids, one easily assumed war was gore and destruction on incomprehensible levels. Torgast, like the men and women surrounding him, knew better. War was one of the most human endeavors. Endless stretches of boredom encased in fleeting moments of sheer terror.

At least it had been, until Amongeratix decided to make his play for the universe. The old rules of war were cast aside in favor of an unrelenting campaign of horrors stretching the vastness of the stars. Torgast never imagined entire planets dying nor the Conclave collapsing beneath the burden of corruption and greed, yet here they stood. The impossible dominated all he surveyed. He wondered what it would all look like once the ashes settled. Would there be enough left of humanity for a civilization?

Cheers rose from those Guards boarding the transports. Others watched, struggling to control their fears as the first wave lifted off. Soon, the entirety of the army would be barreling through space. The campaign for the fate of the universe had begun.

Torgast caught himself grinning. By the gods, there was no other place he wanted to be right now.

Tempest watched the first wave of hundreds of shuttles light the night sky with their blue-white engines. Awed, she was witness to one of the grandest events in all of human history.

"Pay heed, my friend. Never again will be see such a sight," Adris Moscasco said from Tempest's side.

Together, they and the rest of the council, came to see their forces off to the grandest battle. Tempest heard the whispers. Some wished they were boarding the shuttles. Others saw this as a waste of resources and life, claiming the Confederation was not prepared for the immensity of what followed, and the campaign would expose Mannus Prime to unexpected assaults from different quadrants. But their opinions were for private meetings behind closed doors. Here, now, she saw them all beaming with pride, showering their military with praise and well wishes.

"This is indescribable," Tempest uttered. "Never in my life could I have imagined."

Adris gave her a gentle pat on the arm. "We honor these brave men and women boldly marching into the unknown dangers of a universe gone mad. My heart is heavy, Tempest, yet filled with hope for the first time since accepting this position."

"Can we succeed?"

"We damned well better," Standou said coming up on them. "Else this will be the end of us all."

Adris chose to ignore the statement. She led their group through the massed ranks to a command and control station where a young tech sergeant escorted them to General Torgast. Adris thanked the man and went to stand beside who she considered her closest ally.

He turned with a surprised look.

"What? You didn't think we'd let you depart without a proper sendoff, did you?" She smiled. "You are a ranking member of the council and the future head of all military operations. How could I let you deploy without the proper respect?"

Torgast offered a clipped nod. "I wouldn't dare presume, Adris."

Side by side, they watched as a now constant stream of shuttles came and went.

"It will take most of the day, perhaps longer to ferry the entire force up to the fleet," he explained. "My shuttle doesn't depart until later tonight."

"Yet here you are," she mused.

"I wouldn't be worth my salt if I wasn't here to send off the first units. Morale determines conflicts, Adris. These troopers need to see their senior leadership among them, now more than ever. It is good you wrangled the entire council for this."

She snorted, her voice dropping low. "More like wrangling snakes. Too many of the council have different views on this. Fortunately, each understands the importance of visibility at this critical moment."

"You allude to a coup the moment the army departs."

"I don't believe it will come to such, though we have seen the possibility lingering below the surface," she admitted. "What do you suppose we should call this military might? Prekhauten Guard feels wrong."

"Confederation Army sounds treasonous," he replied.

"Perhaps it is a matter for another time."

He nodded. "Any word on Tinnus Har? I don't like leaving with him loose in the city. He was one of the architects of Alain Nye's rise to power."

"He is being dealt with," Adris assured. "You focus on the war. I'll ensure all falls in line here. By the time you return I'll have Eger City cleaned up and representing the ideals of what we stand for. You'll see."

"It would be a shame to have to undertake another combat operation here otherwise," Torgast joked. He extended his hand. "Adris, it has been my pleasure serving with you. I don't know what future awaits either of us, but rest assured I will do all in my power to break the enemy threat once and for all."

"You carry the pride of us all on your shoulders, Torgast." Her words hitched, forcing her to turn away and leave him before sentimentality washed over her.

Torgast said his goodbyes to the rest of the council one at a time. Aliz stood on her toes to kiss his cheek in parting. Soon only Virom remained. They'd grown into fast friends over the past year and it was in the former Cardinal he placed his trust and inner thoughts.

"I suppose this is the conclusion to our grand designs," the Cardinal said. "Who would have imagined all that's happened since I first came to Mannus Prime and you took action to preserve the integrity of what the Conclave represented."

Torgast grunted. "Not the picturesque meeting I would have liked, but one I wouldn't trade for all the wealth in the universe."

"I shall miss our conversations," he admitted. "Take care of yourself, Torgast. Heroes may get statues, but they seldom return home to appreciate them."

"Who said anything about dying?" Torgast retorted. "Virom, it's been my pleasure. I never cared much for the Conclave but you are a man worth knowing. Let me end this and I'll tell you all about while you buy me endless drinks as we admire my statue."

They clasped hands.

"Deal."

Safehouse, Ankrit, planet An'kuruku.

Presha Von stared at the unconscious redhead stretched out on the bed. Her face twisted as she considered slipping a knife in Kaline's side, if only to save her from the public humiliation to come. The least she could do was spare the woman the hardships Presha endured since defecting.

"A snake ever sheds its skin to stay alive."

She studied Kaline, searching for signs of Rengu inspired rot. To all appearances, Kaline appeared nothing more than a woman trying to make her way through the universe. "How could one person be so filled with hate? Are we inherently flawed creatures to fall so far?"

Tolde crossed his arms. "You speak specifically to yourself and Kaline."

She nodded. "I do. I know I'm going to die before this is finished. I think I've come to terms with that, but I must know it has all been worth it."

"I wish I had answers for you," Tolde said, shifting his feet and unable to meet her gaze. "Nothing makes sense in this world, Presha. Look at me. You killed me yet here I am, in a different body but still the same man. A twelve-foot-tall man perpetually weeping blood after skinning himself alive three thousand years ago is our ally and we are in the presence of a powerful witch struggling with her disassociation to humanity. Let's not forget our benefactor who is driving his war against his brother. I don't think we're supposed to know if it has been worth it or not. Not until our time arrives and even then, the gods are not gods at all. What is there to pray to or believe in after that revelation?"

Kaline stirred before Presha could respond and she saw Tolde's hand drop to his blaster. She gestured at the sleeping woman. "She is still ensorcelled," Presha reassured. "Has the Blood Witch snipped her golden tongue?"

Looking reluctant, Tolde removed his hand from his blaster. "So far as I know. We must not take anything for granted. The longer that woman sleeps the easier our task will be."

"You still think to sneak her offworld?"

"It is the best way. With the Conclave dissolved and Vau Prime in chaos, there are no more courts capable of holding her trial," Tolde replied. "I think our best opportunity to remove her from the field is to hand her over to Tannus."

Presha snorted. "You expect him not to show prejudice?"

"I expect him to show restraint and use logic," Tolde said after a pause. "This is a delicate matter. She cannot be allowed to go free nor am I willing to suffer the loss of the moral high ground by summarily judging her. We will take Kaline to Tannus. Perhaps he will show leniency, possibly placing her in stasis next to her master. First, we must escape this planet undetected.”

“Find who did this and bring me their heads!” Dejak roared.

His bark caused his lieutenants to jump. Tensions were high in the compound. Though no one was injured, his prize was missing. Stolen from beneath his sleeping nose without so much as a hair left behind. Dejak did not believe any of his rivals could invade his home with such skill. Messengers were already dispatched to the major houses and local Prefecture offices demanding answers.

“We have searched the premises and Kaline is not here,” his chamberlain reported. “Whoever did this was not from Ankrit, or An’kuruku I’d venture.”

Dejak’s gaze narrowed. “Find Kaline! I don’t care what it takes.”

The chamberlain remained unphased. “I have had my people watching the star fields. No ships have departed since last night, and those were scheduled trade transports.”

“Meaning our foes are still among us, hiding like cowards,” Dejak concluded. “Send more troops to each of the major ports. No one departs without my say. Bribe the administrators. Threaten their families. Whatever it takes. Whoever did this will soon learn Ankrit is mine.”

“There is a note from one of the caravan departure points. They note an unusual group of offworlders on a single skiff.”

Dejak leaned forward, knuckles pushing into the soft wood desk. “Where?”

“Tenemenah. They left at dawn.”

Dejak broke into a toothy grin. “Summon my personal guard and ready my skiff. We take the side passages to cut them off. If they have my prize, they will pay dearly. Go. No more delays.”

“Shall I continue surveillance on the star fields?”

Dejak paused, drumming his fingertips. “Yes. We can ill afford to be wrong.”

Sorrow’s Castle, planet Inselcor.

Giants stood beside each other, lost in separate thoughts as they watched the army of ten thousand automatons march up the ramps to their boarding shuttles for transport to the dreadnaught fleet hovering in high orbit. Volcanic winds swept Tannus' hair, lending him a maniacal appearance, which in retrospect, he supposed he must be. No other reason compelled him to visit Sorrow in the heart of his madness.

"I have never understood why you insist on calling this rock home," he said disapprovingly. "The very air is toxic."

Sorrow fixed him with a bemused look. "Tannus, when have you known me to act rationally? Not since I flensed my flesh have I born traces of sanity."

Tannus tensed, the subject still sore after centuries. Guilt gnawing at him.

"It seems none of us deserved to survive the final purge."

"Yet here we are. Standing amongst a rain of ash watching an army of machines prepare to wage war against our brother. Tannus, we have lived long, and I believe I have never seen a stranger time. What do you think father might say?"

To that, Tannus barked a laugh. "No doubt he'd admonish us in front of the high court. 'You three have been nothing but a thorn in my side since your mother spawned you.'"

Sorrow laughed "Father never understood how to love," he admitted. "We are the victims of that ignorance."

"Love," Tannus mused. "I sometimes wonder how much more mother had to give. She had a kind heart. So unlike the others of our blood."

"And humanity worships us as gods." Sorrow snorted. "Fools. If they only knew we were naught but a race of assholes determined to rule over all as tyrants. Why did you let the Oracle convince you?"

"It seemed prudent," Tannus replied after some thought. "We were on the precipice of doom. The humans desperate for a chance to break free. They needed a higher power to look to. The Oracle and I deemed worship the lesser of evils."

Sorrow dropped the matter, commenting instead, "The last of automatons will be loaded within the army. They should be more than enough to negate Amongeratix's skulldaerth."

"I hope so," Tannus said. "Our brother now has a contingent of rogue Blood Witches at his side."

"I imagine the Oracle is fuming."

Tannus snorted. "For all her psychic prowess, she failed to see any of her chosen turning traitor. Especially not this close to Forever Night."

"This changes matters, Tannus. Why didn't you order the god hunter to finish our brother?"

"It didn't feel honorable. We are the last of our kind wandering the stars. If any of us are to die it should be by the hands of another, not a witch's dark creation."

"The old ways are fading. It is time for us to slip back into the ether as well," Sorrow voiced. "Once this matter is resolved, if I survive, I mean to disappear and never be seen again. It is only right. You should consider this as well, Tannus. We do not belong in the human universe."

Tannus eyed him with newfound respect. He seldom knew the inner workings of Sorrow's mind. None did. Since skinning himself, the younger brother traveled in a dark realm, straddling the boundary of sanity and madness. He never suspected Sorrow of having the desire to leave this universe behind. To abandon all they'd known.

Once they were to be heirs to the universe. Kings to rule through eternity. Tannus now believed that was nothing more than a lie they told themselves. The longer he lived, the more he suspected they were born to pave the way for a new age, and it was only through stubborn persistence that none of them fulfilled their purpose.

"Will you come with me to Occanum?"

Sorrow turned, a grim look on his face. "I will stand beside you when we confront Amongeratix."

EIGHTEEN

3215 A.G. (After Gods), Confederation Picket Screen, edge of Occanum System.

"Enemy ships entering real space."

Drukali leaned forward in his command chair. "Arm all weapons and prepare to engage. Pattern Alpha."

"Aye, sir!"

The *Vitriol* bridge crew went into action, sending similar orders across the small squadron of corvettes. A glance at the tactical screen showed him friendly icons drifting into position without engaging their main thrusters. He'd ordered all ships to go dark in the hopes of luring the enemy in. The first prong in his strategy. Knuckles bleeding white from his grip on the armrests, Drukali watched as the first enemy ship blurred into reality.

The cruiser was much larger than his ship, but it hopefully lacked proper knowledge of the battlefield. Drukali used every possible moment in the Occanum System to map out favorable routes and ambush points relative to system entry positions. He had laid, in his estimation, the perfect trap but knew better than to expect matters to go according to plan.

"Have they seen us?" he barked.

"No, sir. The cruiser is approaching as if the system were empty."

Drukali bobbed his head. "Good. Order all corvettes to target enemy weapon and engine systems. I want that ship dead in the water before the rest of his fleet arrive."

Blips on the tacscreen showed his forces spooling up their drives and moving forward. Accordingly, the enemy cruiser slowed, unsure what it had stumbled into. Drukali ground his teeth as the ships pushed closer. Moments later the first lance of ion rounds slashed across the field of vision. All five of his ships opened fire simultaneously. Chunks of the cruiser broke away.

"Hits on multiple decks!"

Drukali grinned. "Keep firing! We won't hold the advantage

long.”

His corvettes unleashed a barrage on the stricken cruiser. Drukali watched as the engine lights flickered and dulled before going dark. Crippled, the ship was dead in space but still had fangs. A ship to ship missile screamed across the void for him. *Vitriol* rocked under the impact. Warning sirens engaged. Paneling dropped from the ceiling. Smoke poured from a handful of computer terminals. Drukali was knocked from his chair.

“Direct hit two decks below the bridge. Void crews are moving to stabilize.”

Pulling himself up, Drukali wiped the blood from his lower lip. They wouldn’t survive another strike like that. “Target missile bays.”

A wave of missiles from three corvettes replied in kind. The cruiser rocked under the impacts. He watched part of the hull collapse in on itself, bending the central frame. Oxygen vented into space alongside a handful of unfortunate souls too close to the impact sites. Drukali’s blood raged. “Keep firing! We have her!”

He was rewarded by a series of internal impacts blowing several sections of the cruiser out. A handful of escape pods jettisoned. He ignored them. The cruiser sustained crippling hits up and down its hull. Drukali watched with a wicked gleam as the larger ship nosed down.

“Kill her.”

His corvettes complied. The cruiser died when the bridge was blown out. He briefly wondered if he knew the enemy captain or any of the officers but then remembered it didn’t matter. They were enemy combatants, and it was his duty to eliminate as many as possible before the rest of their fleet arrived.

“Cruiser kill, sir!”

Cheers rang across the bridge. His next set of orders died on his tongue when a second cruiser blurred into the engagement zone. Unable to slow, she plowed into the wreckage of the first ship and immediately came under fire. Drukali’s attention focused solely on the action before him, he failed to spy the third cruiser until it was too late. She blazed into the firefight, having been warned by her companions. One of the corvettes exploded as the cruiser unleashed every weapon it had.

“Helm, come about and engage that third cruiser before we’re all dead!” Drukali ordered.

Vitriol slowed and turned, seeking to come up on the cruiser’s blindside. The ships exchanged blows, each sustaining damage. Sparks showering from drooping cables, Drukali brushed the smoke from his line of sight. From what he could tell, the remaining three corvettes were holding their own against the second cruiser, dismantling her integral systems with precision and leaving him to face the unexpected cruisier alone. He had a trick for that.

"Tactical, send orders to Bravo Flight. Now."

He was rewarded a moment later by the second half of his squadron jumping into real space behind the cruisers. Missiles and ion rounds flared at the moment of entry. Caught off guard, the cruiser was unable to defend her exposed engines from the ambush—she died quickly.

Drukali adjusted his uniform, needing to look the part of a field commander, and focused his attention on what remained of the second cruiser. His ships poured fire into it and received none in return.

"Long range scanners are picking up multiple enemy signatures. Enemy fleet approaching Occanum System."

Blood up, Drukali resisted the urge to stand and fight. His ambush worked as designed, though losing one corvette was more than he wished for. Damage control teams arrived on the bridge and began putting out the fires and repairing potential structural damage. He strode to the tacscreen and frowned. Close to a hundred vessels were preparing to drop in on them. There was no way his tiny squadron had enough to do more than slow them down.

"Order all ships to fall back to secondary positions. We did our job. They won't be so quick to reach Occanum now," he ordered.

"Captain, do we stop to take prisoners?"

Drukali rubbed his chin. There was little time to pause and recovery the life pods and, knowing a limited supply of oxygen was in each, he couldn't help but feel a twinge of guilt as he issued the next order. "No. Let the enemy worry about that. Order the group to displace and pick up any of our own survivors."

Ferom, planet Occanum.

"Recon squadron reports multiple enemy ship kills," Hollis announced to the rest of the command staff.

Grins and jokes spread through them. Most infantry had little concept of space battles, viewing any ship kill as a good day. Fies scowled. The last thing he needed was his people growing over-confident and losing focus.

"Tone it down, people. Those sailors drew first blood, but we are still all alone out here," he barked. "Med bay, prepare to receive casualties."

Doc Little's voice came over the intercom, "Roger that."

Fies wasn't sure how many people his lone medic could treat, praying the corvette screen had enough surgeons and medics aboard to lighten the load. He turned to Annalilly and asked, "Any word on the rest of the fleet?"

"Admiral Falchi insists they will transit in system by the end of the day."

"They damned well better, or our friends from Vau Prime will be landing their armies unopposed." He shuddered at the thought of what would happen to the Confederation army if the enemy got here first.

"Fies, relax. Those ships are still almost a full day's burn away from Occanum," Paradise Tear said softly. "There is still time."

Instead of responding, Fies took a deep breath. He wasn't a large-scale warfare commander. His experience was in small actions. His company wasn't designed to take on armies, nor was he comfortable being the senior commander on the ground at the start of the battle. He wished Matthias or Torgast were here already. Hells, he'd settle for the resurrected Inquisitor. Anyone but himself.

Unsettled, Fies returned his attention to the impossible amount of intelligence pouring in from satellites, ships, and motion detection sensors scattered across the system. More data than he'd ever siphoned through before.

"Captain," Hollis announced distracting him. "Our pickets have fallen back to secondary positions. Enemy fleet continues transitioning in system. Standard Prekhauten deployment."

"Casualties?"

"Three cruisers, two frigates, and a handful of fighters. Several ships show battle damage."

Fies knew it wasn't enough. "The minefields are doing their jobs. Where is *Vitriol* now?"

"Moving to secure the outer approaches between the second planet and Ferom."

An alarm chimed and he stiffened. "Hollis?"

She typed furiously. "Another fleet just translated in our rear. They are on direct approach for us."

Fuck. "How many ships?"

"Thirty. No transponder signals."

"No signal? That's not SOP," he mused. "Open a channel and bring our defenses online. Let's hope these old guns can hold off an armada."

"We'll soon find out."

"Lovely. Hollis, get me that fleet commander," Fies ordered.

"Fies," Annalilly cautioned.

He waved her off. "Do it, Hollis."

"Channel open."

"Incoming fleet this is Captain Fies of—"

"Did anyone ever tell you that you talk too much, Fies? I thought noncoms knew better."

Cocking his head, Fies tried to place the voice. "Who is this?"

"Come on now, don't tell me you forgot your old pal Bootleg already. We just liberated that planet together."

A weight slipped from his shoulders. For the first time since deploying, Fies felt not everything was a disaster waiting to happen. "You could have given us a heads up when you translated into the system. We're in the middle of a battle here."

"So I see, but it doesn't look like those Guard boys are interested in pushing yet. My scanners show them taking a pounding on the far side of the system," Bootleg replied.

"I'm transmitting docking coordinates to you now. Get your people in quick. We're trying to keep this place secret for as long as we can."

"You show us where to go and we'll be there," Bootleg confirmed.

The line died before Fies could reply. Rubbing his chin, Fies told Hollis to transmit then turned to Annalilly, "See to the docking bays. I don't want any surprises."

"You don't think they'll betray us, do you?" she asked.

He shook his head. "I don't know anything anymore. Best not to take chances."

Annalilly pinched the bridge of her nose. "You know Matthias sent them to us."

"How in the hells do you know that?"

She smirked. "While you've been busy collecting grey hairs on this rock, I've been taking in all the intel communications from Mannus. We received word yesterday."

"Why didn't anyone tell me? I'm supposed to be in charge here."

"You seemed busy."

He jabbed a finger at her. "You and I need to talk."

Her smile threw him off guard. "Later, Cap. I've been given an important assignment."

Annalilly sauntered off, making a show of taking her time in front of the rest of the platoon manning the bridge. None were foolish enough to look up from their terminals. Fies huffed out a deep breath.

Fies glared after Annalilly before turning to the others. "Get this station ready to accept the Shadow Hammers and continue monitoring the battle. I don't want any surprises."

Upper orbit of planet Vau Prime.

Hundreds of smaller ships swarmed around the ancient dreadnaught like insects. *Behemoth* dominated the skyline over Krenz. Ugly and twisted, the ship inspired nightmares and despair. But to Amongeratix, it was a thing of raw beauty, a reflection of its master.

Algiss Her found it crass and void of unique characteristics; Behemoth was endless kilometers of spiraling madness. Human crew depravity was evident in every hall she strode through. Paintings in blood decorated bulkheads. Murdered civilians were nailed to doors and ceilings. She ignored the misery, choosing to focus on her ends rather than the depravity of the man they followed.

Algiss came upon a trio of menials systematically dismembering another. They laughed manically as their cutting tools plunged down into raw flesh. Blood sprayed the area with reckless abandon. Disgusted, the Crimson Mistress unleashed a torrent of wild magic into the murderers. They exploded in a hail of bone and blood that evaporated before touching the deck.

Drifting closer, she discovered the victim mercifully dead. Algiss snapped her fingers and the body collapsed on itself, dissolving into a pool of corporeal matter. A look of disgust twisting her face, Algiss hovered higher to avoid staining her robes. She left the scene, expecting to find a dozen similar incidents on her route to the bridge.

At the end of the long corridor, Algiss found Sister Ibrest waiting. The older witch idly picked at the corner of her mouth with a wickedly long fingernail.

"What news from Krenz?" Algiss demanded.

"Evangaline reports Geres Auk has recovered and is most interested in getting back to the task of hunting down the god hunter. I consider the man a waste of time. We should eliminate him and be done with it."

"Agreed, but Amongeratix claims to have designs on the barbarian," Algiss said. "Has there been any new activity in the hunt?"

"More casualties with nothing to show for it. We waste our time, Crimson Mistress. Our talents are better suited for confronting Ruma Zzein's ilk. I question the rationale behind joining forces with Amongeratix."

"So you've said," Algiss replied and resisted the urge to lash out. "For now, we stay the course. I expect to engage the Blood Witches at Occanum. The new Sisters must be prepared for combat before we arrive in system."

Ibrest bowed. "As you command."

"Where is Evangaline now?"

"Continuing the hunt with Geres Auk. She has been given orders to report to *Behemoth* but declines to acknowledge."

Impudent bitch. I should have clipped her wings long ago. "I shall handle her disobedience. Prepare the coven to deploy." Screams echoed from the corridors. A chorus of misery clawing at her soul. "Ibrest, I want this ship cleansed of all depravity. A ship of the line has no place mired with filth. Not even one so twisted as this. Kill the culprits on the spot and dispose of their corpses before Amongeratix arrives. It wouldn't do to be seen killing his new subjects on whim."

Ibrest bowed again and left.

Algiss continued to the bridge where she found a cadre of Prekhauten Guards acclimating to their new workstations. *Behemoth's* operating systems were outdated and far beyond anything in their experience, causing delays in training and combat preparedness. Whipped into frenzy by their officers, the crew diligently worked through the night to learn the new systems.

She found the stern figure of Grand Admiral Achen Tuth on the command bridge. He posed a striking figure with massive frame and close-cropped hair akin to the true Guard standard. Hands clasped behind his back in a classic pose, Tuth stretched each finger one at a time as his hawk-like gaze absorbed every detail on his new command. Algiss found him impressive, by human standards.

"Crimson Mistress," he said upon seeing her. "I hadn't expected you on the bridge this soon."

Her appraisal rose. Most mortals cowered from her. Grand Admiral Tuth accepted it in stride. The strength of his will prevented her from piercing his mind. Perhaps Amongeratix chose wisely in this fleet commander. Algiss was careful of how she approached him. She might have need of the man in the future and found it prudent to gain his confidence.

"Grand Admiral, my name is Algiss. I think at this point we can pass on formalities. We are to be traveling companions," she said.

"Indeed, but I stand on ceremony. No member of my command is allowed any degree of insubordination," Tuth replied. "What can I do for you?"

Seeing no point in beating around the point, Algiss said, "Are you aware of the acts of depravity occurring throughout this ship? On my course here I came upon a trio of menials murdering one of their peers."

"This is not an isolated incident. Reports of similar acts are coming in from all sections," Tuth replied with a dour look. "I have dispatched a full company of Marines to deal with the situations as they arise. My fear is they too will succumb to the madness."

"Perhaps my coven can help."

"How so?"

Algiss raised herself to his eye level. "We can weave protective spells around your people to ensure they are safe from *Behemoth's* afflictions."

"I'm sure Lord Amongeratix might have something to say about using his forces to kill his own people."

"Needs must, Grand Admiral."

He shifted, turning just a fraction of an inch toward her. "Why not cast your spell over the entire ship? Why waste lives? I have need of every crewer I can get. The fleet is already consuming most of my resources. Amongeratix ensures me *Behemoth* can handle itself without a full complement, but I have my doubts."

Algiss suppressed the smile threatening to break free. "You do not trust our noble lord?"

"I am a professional. I know what I know, and the sheer size of this ship demands a massive crew unlike anything in the Guard inventory," he replied. "Crimson Mistress, we are racing into the defining battle of our time. I refuse to do so with anything less than a full crew. As it stands, many of these men and women will not be returning once the last round is fired. I need to give them their greatest chance for survival and that means a full crew."

"I shall see what we can manage, but I make no promises. Magic seldom conforms to the whims of men."

He offered a clipped bow. "That is more than I can ask. Thank you."

Eger City, planet Mannus Prime.

Days of shuffling between safehouses and clandestine meetings with what Tinnus Har deemed less than desirable allies left him exhausted. He felt the noose tightening, despite not having encountered additional signs of being watched. The former Cardinal Seniorus grew gaunt, more from excessive worry than lack of nourishment. He found his stomach a bundle of nerves growing more unsettled as time passed. New spots decorated his face and hands, accentuated by dark veins protruding from his arms. He almost longed for obscurity, almost.

"We are getting nowhere with these meetings," he snapped at the taciturn Inquisitor nearby. "The allies you promised a little more than disgruntled peasants content with voicing their displeasure rather than acting on it. What have you brought me into?"

"Cardinal, you wished to integrate into the local dissidents. Those men and women you've met are that group. I'm afraid Mannus Prime has nothing left to offer unless you can turn this rabble into an angry enough mob willing to take on the Confederation after the bulk of the army deploys."

"To what end? I need fighters, not fodder!" Spittle flew from his mouth. "Where are the fighters?"

"This planet fought a sustained campaign lasting almost a year. Mothers and wives buried too many sons and daughters. The people are not interested in fighting. War claims more than just lives," Dowan offered.

Tinnus waggled a bony finger. "You promised me support."

"I provided you the opportunity to sway those interested to your side. You're not exactly a people person," Dowan countered. "I never said you would have the support to topple the Confederation and return to power."

Eyes narrowing with suspicion, Tinnus searched through his memories for the words Dowan Mun presented. A veiled threat lay hidden behind the admission, but what? He failed to identify the true threat. Could it be the rogue Inquisitor plotted against him? Seeking to dethrone his attempt at recreating an empire? Tinnus trusted no one.

"The entirety of their network consists of laborers with little to no exposure of politics," Tinnus said after careful thought. "Has not a single member of the military come forward to voice displeasure under the current regime? I would think more families simmer in rage at seeing their loved ones marching off to war and possible doom."

"I'm not a soldier. My experiences during the campaign were far different from those in the Guard."

"What did you do during the war?"

Dowan cleared his throat, running his tongue over his bottom lip. "Bela Cass and I attempted to enforce the Inquisitor General's will among those opposition forces."

"Cass being the other Inquisitor?"

Dowan nodded. "She was the more fervent of us. Bela made a coup attempt against Commander Torgast resulting in both of us being imprisoned. It wasn't until she tried to eliminate the Commander she was killed, and I was shuffled away to rot in a cell."

"Tell me what you saw of the battle. Of the people."

"Nothing in terms of battle. We were never allowed on the front lines, though there was no escaping the effects of the carnage. Artillery shelled both sides constantly. Morale dipped until a counteroffensive behind enemy lines opened the way for Torgast's army to conduct their final assault," Dowan explained. "Bela Cass and I often spent time roaming the city streets, working with the office of Cardinal Virom. His office was less than forthcoming."

"Naturally." Tinnus recalled his contemporary. "Virom seldom returned to Krenz, even for the most important matters. Some considered him a firestarter. No wonder this planet fell away from the Conclave so quickly. Is there nothing else?"

"What else can I say? Inquisitors do not belong in combat nor are we mandated for it without specific Conclave orders."

Displeased with the lack of initiative, Tinnus clasped his hands behind his back and began pacing. Events continued spiraling out of control, leaving him against the wall with nowhere to turn. His allies proved nonexistent, and he suspected the Inquisitor of leading him into a trap.

"Tell me, Dowan Mun, who do you really work for?"

"What do you mean?" Dowan betrayed no emotion, no change in stance to indicate a difference in nerves.

Tinnus stopped pacing. "It occurs to me an Inquisitor in enemy custody could not easily escape without striking a bargain with his captors. I know Virom well enough to know you could not sway him once he committed to a course of action. Torgast is an unknown to me, but the devotion shown by his army suggests he is a strong figure with little room to maneuver against. Your colleague is dead, yet you still draw breath. Why? Why were you arrested instead of suffering a similar fate?"

"I don't have the answers you seek, Cardinal," Dowan replied. "I escaped and took you with me. There is no conspiracy here. Not from me, leastwise."

"Not from you," Tinnus repeated. "You present a unique problem for me, Inquisitor. On one hand, I am to trust you to fulfill your oath of duty to the Conclave. But the other tells me you are not to be trusted. The lack of character among these dissident cells all but confirms such. So, I ask again, why should I trust you?"

Dowan Mun considered his options. Putting a round in Tinnus Har and ending this nightmare felt right but he'd find himself locked in a cell in short order. His new handler was a shapeshifter and the thought of him being anyone at any time chilled him. Lying to Tinnus wouldn't work either. The man may be on the run and desperate, but he'd kept his wits and remained dangerous.

"Who else do you have? I've led you away from your enemies, keeping you from harm's way while your perfect world devolves under its own weight. You have no one but me. It might serve to remember that."

Tinnus turned his back. "Necessity does not demand trust, or even confidence, Inquisitor. You are charged with specific purpose and have failed to live up to expectations. You say I am trapped at your side. Perhaps the time has come to prove you wrong. I was the most powerful man in the universe. Finding new followers of quality and potential is not so difficult as you assume. Tell me, Inquisitor, what keeps me from walking out on you?"

Closing his eyes to calm his rising nerves, Dowan replied, "Because I would either shoot you in the back or turn you in to the Confederation. You speak from both corners of your mouth, praising me in one breath and cursing me in the next. Your power stemmed from having a robust network at your disposal and the inherent fear established over centuries. Now that the Conclave is disbanded, who will respect you for what you were?"

"And just what was I?"

"The man who allowed the Inquisition to destroy all you stood for in the span of a few years."

"Perhaps shooting me is best," he murmured and resumed pacing.

Dowan watched him for a while longer before heading for the door.

"Where are you going?"

Dowan paused. Was that desperation in his tone? A spark of humanity Tinnus hadn't shown yet? "I need some fresh air."

NINETEEN

3215 A.G. (After Gods), Zevistya Spaceport, low continent, planet Vau Prime.

Icarn awoke to raised voices. The lights in their bay flickered on, bright and overpowering. A metal trash can was beaten repeatedly before being thrown down the aisle. Rubbing the sleep from his eyes, Icarn, like the hundreds surrounding him, witnessed a trio of master sergeants force marching through the bay with the ferocity of a tempest. They barked orders at the top of their lungs, each overpowering the other. Icarn scowled at the senior noncom when she kicked his bunk and yelled at him for still being in the rack.

Dragging himself to his feet, Icarn slipped into his trousers and added his voice to the confusion. "Let's move it, people. Dress out and prepare to deploy. Formation in ten!"

His platoon groaned into action. Nervous banter passed between them as the master sergeants exited out the rear and moved on to their next victims. Icarn envisioned similar scenes playing out across the marshalling area.

Soon his company chain of command started making the rounds through the bay. They checked with each platoon sergeant and squad leader while the company commander pulled his lieutenants aside for private briefings. Good riddance. Junior officers tended to muck things up. Best to leave daily operations to the noncoms.

Icarn finished lacing his boots and slung his rifle over one shoulder. After stuffing his gear into his assault pack, their larger duffel bags were already palletized and loaded on the troop transports waiting to leave Vau Prime, he started counting heads.

Nervous energy filled the bay. He watched. The next step after formation would be early chow. He didn't see how anyone could eat. He never did, instead stuffing packaged rations into his trouser pockets for the trip. Icarn felt off this morning as he watched his people. Far too many troopers hurled insults at their opponents, vowing to wipe them from existence. War, Icarn found, should never be personal. Enemy soldiers were there to perform the same job as his people. Killing wasn't the objective. He always thought survival should be the first priority. The rest would handle itself.

There was a certain cruelty in command's actions. Icarn heard the rumors of General Kale losing his grasp on civility in his quest to hunt down General Strannan. The insurrection continued through Krenz's subsectors, practically unabated. Isolated on Tatarast Island with the rest of the new divisions, Icarn caught brief snippets of newsvids depicting slain cardinals and dissidents despite the news blackout for all training units.

The thought of abandoning the Guard's founding principle of defending the people sat ill. He didn't know what followed, but a sinking feeling suggested the worst was yet to come.

Icarn followed his last trooper out the door and took in a sight he never thought to see. Tens of thousands of Prekhauten Guards filled the airfield, standing proud in resplendent armor and new uniforms amidst the backdrop of wrecked shuttles and fighters. Pennants waved in the predawn breeze. An entire division on parade, waiting for their orders. Icarn whistled under his breath. No one back home would ever believe him.

"Company!"

Icarn snapped from his musings and barked, "Platoon!"

"Atten-tion!"

Heels snapped together. The company commander issued the orders they all knew was coming. Chow first. Then transports. They had fifteen minutes before the next formation and final manifest. Icarn spun in a crisp about face and ordered his squad leaders to march their people to the field mess tents after being dismissed. Hundreds of tents were scattered throughout the staging area, one for each battalion. Cooks slaved through the night to ready the final meal on Vau Prime. Each tent held a full kitchen capable of feeding hundreds on short notice. Icarn found the food less than appetizing, as usual, and joined his fellow platoon sergeants drinking their morning caf.

"Icarn, some spectacle, eh?"

He took the first, bitter sip and winced. "It's something, Avis. Where do you suppose we're headed?"

Avis shrugged. "Does it matter? Scuttlebutt thinks we're heading to a major operation to end the war. I don't care, as long as we get the chance to plug a few bad guys."

Taking issue with the term, Icarn found it wiser to remain silent. He took another drink of caf instead.

"You ask me, this was a long time coming. We've been pussyfooting around the enemy for years without making a stand," Avis boomed. "After the debacle on Mannus Prime they've been asking for payback. I say this it! Let's hit the dirt and start punishing."

Sergeant Krilo shook her head. "You forget they're still Guards. We all have the same training, Avis. Whatever we have, they have. Those aren't the odds I'm looking to take into a fight."

"We got something they don't," Avis insisted. "We got a twelve-foot-tall ball of wrath with a private army. I heard they are unstoppable."

Icarn had no knowledge of that. Rumors ran wild as they did before every combat deployment. He learned not to listen. Expectations produced as many casualties as poor training.

"You're forgetting another thing," Krilo replied.

"What's that?"

"Amongeratix is just one of the Three. There are two more out there. Who's to say they don't have one or both on their side?"

Avis shot her a disturbed look. "Now who's talking nonsense? If they had any of the Three on their side this battle would have happened a long time ago. Trust in General Kale and Amongeratix and this war is as good as done. What do you say, Icarn?"

"As long as we all come home," Icarn said. "That's what matters."

"You know we're going to suffer casualties," Krilo cautioned. "Command is estimating as much as fifty percent in the first wave."

"How? We don't even know where we're deploying to," Icarn fussed.

Avis jumped in. "They're practicing good Opsec, is all. The fewer of us who know, the less chance of enemy spies finding out."

Downing the last of the caf, Icarn asked, "Do you suppose there are spies in the ranks?"

"Seems the prudent thing, given the circumstances," Avis confirmed. His quick delivery rankled Icarn but he refused to rise to the bait. "Wouldn't mind a few Inquisitors hanging around to root them out."

Avis was bullheaded but a good leader. They got along well enough. His current attitude left Icarn grasping for conclusions.

"Maybe," Icarn said after some thought. "I haven't seen any since we left Tatarast."

"Oh, they're here. You can bet on that. Ditched the uniforms and slipped into the ranks. Maybe not at our level but certainly at the company CP."

If the Inquisition was indeed spying on them, the implications were worse than anyone was willing to admit. Icarn let out a low whistle.

"Look out folks. Icarn stumbled onto a thought," Avis taunted. He chuckled, quivering his jowls. "Go on, Icarn. Share with the rest of us poor slobs."

"Speak for yourself, Avis," Krilo snorted. "I bathe regularly."

Icarn stifled a laugh. "If the Inquisition is embedded among us, what's to say we're not all under scrutiny already? Makes me think command doesn't trust us."

"Bah! Trust is overrated in times like this," Avis said too quickly. "We stick to each other, watch out for heresy and we'll get through this just fine."

"Formation in five! Move it, people. Those transports aren't going to wait forever," a master sergeant barked in passing. "We're at war! Time to act like it."

Avis grunted and spat. "Huh. Best we get to it. I'll see you on the transport."

They exchanged farewells and hurried to get their platoons loaded up. Nerves threatened to empty Icarn's stomach on the deck.

It was time to go to war.

Confederation Naval Vessel *Indomitable*, edge of Occanum System.

Admiral Falchi stared at the viewscreen, his gaze unfocused. With Occanum off limits, all but revered in the Conclave's annals, he had no actionable intelligence to formulate a battle plan. Though Falchi was second in command of the Confederation Navy, he had an entire fleet at his fingertips. Somewhere, lurking in the unseen distance, was Khe-Zhehan with a larger fleet. He admired the Admiral for her prowess and friendship but thanked the council for giving him his own command. Falchi spent years operating under Tannus' authority. Returning to a static military system felt just wrong.

"Admiral, all ships have translated to real space and have checked in."

He tore his gaze from the depths of space. Captain Samuel sat in his command chair. Though *Indomitable* was commissioned under Falchi's command, the ship belonged to Samuel.

"Very good, Captain. Run deployment pattern alpha."

"Aye, sir," Samuel said. "All ships, execute deployment pattern alpha. Time now. Gunnery Sergeant Asom, all shipboard Marines to battle stations."

The mixed collection of cruisers, frigates, a lone battleship, and smaller escort vessels broke into squadrons and began their sweep of the system.

Falchi shifted his jaw back and forth to relieve the tension aching his teeth. "This is an unprecedented moment, Samuel. I trust you have the ship historian recording everything."

"She is," Samuel confirmed. "We've been collecting interviews since leaving Mannus."

"Good. It wouldn't do to let this moment pass. They deserve that much." Falchi wanted as many personal stories recorded as possible before the first shots were fired.

"Admiral, have we any idea how large the enemy fleet is?"

"Your guess is as good as mine, old friend." Falchi's smile was sad. "I'm afraid, for the moment, we're going into this blind."

Samuel grunted. "Drukali reports a sizeable force already attempting to force it's way into the system. I've studied the casualty lists. Ours have been sustainable thus far. The enemy has lost almost a full squadron."

"Not enough to win this campaign," Falchi admitted. "Did you ever think it would come to this? So much has transpired since Hawker's Gate."

"None of us are the same, Admiral. This war changes us all on fundamental levels," Samuel said. "The Gate was long ago. Working for Tannus awakened new possibilities in us, though I don't know if it is for the better. I admit to bypassing many Guard regulations."

Falchi's laugh turned heads across the bridge. "That may be the understatement of the year, Samuel. It might also be the secret weapon we need to overcome our foes."

"God willing."

"Well, best not keep our infantry counterparts waiting. Let's sweep the system and bring the army in. We do have a war to win."

"Aye, sir. All ships, advance."

Asom seldom wondered what it looked like from the bridge. Content with his place roving the vital corridors of *Indominable*, he was where he belonged. True Marines went where they were ordered, did as they were told, and fought like the gates of hell opened before them. He liked his job and that was enough. His previous assignment in Eger City left him anxious. Too many wide spaces inspired paranoia. Asom couldn't control what he couldn't see, and the city streets held far too many concealment positions for his liking. He thanked the gods when reassignment orders came in for the *Indominable*.

Buckling his helmet chinstrap, Asom surveyed his Marines. They were some of the finest men and women he'd had the privilege of serving with. Command hadn't said where they were deploying to, but he learned enough from working alongside Matthias—Occanum. The dead world. The site of the final battle in the war of the gods. A small piece of him wished it would be equally epic in scale and definition. The rest of him wanted the war to end so he might slip away into retirement. Both parts agreed being relieved of his watch duties over Tinnus Har was the best thing to happen to him.

"Listen up, Marines. We've done this before. You know the drill. Boss man says move and we hit that section with everything we have," he barked.

"Is it true the enemy hasn't arrived yet?" a young private with wide eyes asked.

Asom forced himself not to scowl. "Don't worry about that, private. That ain't our job. We fight where we're told to. That's it. Watch your battle buddy's six. Don't let anyone get through and this ship stays in fighting condition."

"Any idea where we are, Gunny?"

"Right damned here, that's where. If the Admiral wanted you to know he'd have called you to the bridge already," Asom barked. "Any other dumb questions?"

The platoon effectively shut down, Asom nodded and gave them a thumbs up. "Good. Now, focus up. I expect things are about to get hairy fast. Doc, you got the aid station up and running?"

"Roger, Gunny. Corpsmen are dispersed to their squads. The surgeon is on standby near supply bay three."

"You get that? Supply bay three. Team and squad leaders, I want casualties triaged on site and transported back as necessary," Asom explained.

A haggard sergeant caught his attention and asked, "And the enemy?"

Asom put on a show of staring into as many of his Marine's faces as possible before answering. "Leave them where they fall. Our people come first. There's no room for traitors in the Confederation. Understood?"

Heads bobbed. A few grunted.

Asom snatched his rifle from against the wall. "Move out. I want all squads in battle positions ASAP. Report in when ready and prepare to repel boarders."

Asom stomped off to inspect his domain. Once his rounds were complete, he reported up to the bridge.

Indominable was ready for war.

Brightstar, departing Inselcor System.

"Hey, don't touch that!"

Krimpen Mass feigned a shocked look, going so far as to place his palm on his chest. Time's punch in his shoulder pulled him away and the pair continued touring their new ship under the gaze of several naval officials.

"You touch everything," Time grumbled.

"How else am I supposed to figure out what it does?" Krimpen replied. "Besides, its not like any of us have ever seen a ship like this before. I bet one of these could destroy and entire Guard fleet."

Time grunted. "I don't like the ceilings."

"Eh? What?"

He gestured up. "The ceilings."

Krimpen looked at the overhead pipes running the length of the corridor. "What about them?"

"They're too high. What happens if one of those pipes cracks? No one can get up there to fix it."

"You do remember this ship was built for giants."

"I don't see any," Time replied.

"That's because they're all dead but three. You didn't think Guard engineers capable of lowering the ceilings to make your experience more pleasurable did you?"

"Don't mock me, Krimpen. I'm making an observation. We don't have to agree on everything." Bristling, Time's muscles rolled and flexed under his sleeveless tunic.

Krimpen peered closer, surprised to find the tiny hairs on the back of his friend's neck standing on end. *Maybe the man has a point. I've been spooked since we boarded. None of this is natural. Not one damned rivet.*

"Your mother always did say you spent too much time looking at the sky," he teased. "Now look at me, Time. Focused on what's in front of me. Why, I don't see anything on this ship escaping my attention. No sir, not one thing."

"Tell me again why we're still friends? I should have drowned you when I had the chance."

"Fine way to speak to a friend. How many times have I saved your life?"

Time held up his hand. "All right, fair point, but your mother knew we were trouble together from day one."

Krimpen barked a laugh that echoed down the empty corridor. "That she did. Warned no good would come of hanging around you. Guess we proved her wrong."

"Did we?"

"What do you mean?"

Time gestured to the ugly metal walls of an age gone by. "Look at where we are. Trapped in the bowels of a ship that shouldn't exist and heading into what Blackheart promises to be the most important battle of our lives. Doesn't sound like we're living the high life, Krimpen."

"You're forgetting the part where he promised us enough to become lords of our own moons," Krimpen reminded. "That's the important part."

"Not if we don't survive."

Krimpen rubbed his jaw. "Eh, that's a fair point. We might have bitten off more than we can chew with this one."

"I've been saying that since the little rat sniffed us out on Solecca."

Krimpen lowered his voice and asked, "Do you suppose it's too late to get off this crate? You know, go home?"

"It was too late the day we let Vicente Blackheart back into our lives."

"That man is nothing but trouble. Three times now we've just been minding our business, and he drags us into another of his improbable adventures," Krimpen agreed and kept walking. He'd never admit it aloud, but the steady banter soothed his nerves.

Halfway down the corridor, Krimpen turned to his lifelong friend and asked, "What do you suppose they're up to these days?"

"Who?"

"Our mothers. Do you figure either ever found that love they were looking for?"

Time paused, his features twisting. He suddenly slapped a hand on Krimpen's back. "I don't know, my friend. I like to think so."

Teary eyed, Krimpen nodded. They had buried their mothers a long time ago and never looked back. "Come on, let's find something to eat. There has to be a chow hall around here somewhere."

"Are you sure I can't have one of my own?" Blackheart asked again, repeating his attempts to wear her down.

August fixed him with a withering glare. "You're not up to speed for that yet. We've been over this more times than is worth repeating, Vicente. Hasn't anyone ever told you no means no?"

"You have a whole fleet!"

"On loan from Tannus," she countered. "Perhaps you forgot that part?"

The pirate waved off her concern. "Ok, fine. He might not take kindly to me absconding with one of his babies, but you have to admit, I'd be the most feared pirate in the universe with one of these at my command. Just imagine it!"

"As well as being the biggest target either the old Guard or the Confederation labelled. Are you prepared for the entirety of humanity to hunt you down?"

"No one wants to die, Sharlyn," he replied.

"That's Admiral." She pressed her lips together, rage simmering in her dark eyes.

"The way I see it, Sharlyn—"

"Admiral."

"Is we need a little more flair for the dramatic. This war isn't going to last forever. What happens in the aftermath? Your precious Confederation could hire me on as a privateer to combat the lawlessness in those systems most depleted by the war. Imagine that, me a hero in all but name!"

She snorted. "Replete with statues worshipped by throngs of adoring sycophants, no doubt."

"That's rude, but yes. Why not? Lesser men have had more," Blackheart said. "Am I really asking for that much?" Her silence rebuked him. He waved off her dismissal, continuing. "Fine, be that way, but don't come crawling to old Vicente Blackheart when your ship is disabled, and you need help. Pass the wine."

She slid the bottle of Mannus red to him.

"This stuff isn't very good," he admitted after a swallow. "You could have mentioned it. I have better aboard the *Shrike*."

"I'm surprised you still have that bucket of bolts," she quipped. "My memories of it are not favorable. A battered vessel long past her prime. You should sell it for scrap and move on."

He beamed. "Right after you give me one of these."

She screwed her face up as she took a swallow of the watered-down wine. "Fine. Let me ask Tannus."

"Really?" His eyes widened.

She snorted, shaking her head. "Not going to happen. How are your people integrating with my crews?"

"Well enough," he replied after consideration and a scowl. "Most of my people were professionals in one manner or another before signing on. Sedge is the only one born into a life of piracy. I plucked the rest from merchants, a few Guard ships on shore leave, and shipyards. They aren't the best, or brightest, but I trust each of them with my life."

"You are certain?"

"The traitors and the weak were rooted out long ago," he replied. His voice dropped, memories of the Kharsis ordeal resurfacing. "No, Admiral August, my crew is the best I've ever had. I am proud to serve beside them. You will be too."

"I hope so. Tannus assures me we are more than a match for Amongeratix's long dreadnaught, but I'm not so sure. That madman built his ship and, from what I've heard, has twisted it into a vessel of darkness unmatched by anything the rest of the universe has to offer."

"You worry too much. Let the Three handle their business and we paltry mortals can deal with the rest."

"I am an Admiral. My job is to worry." She finished the last of her wine. "Remind me to tell the Quartermaster to jettison the rest of this into space."

He broke into a toothy grin. "I mean, if you truly feel that way, I can liberate the rest of the bottles from you. Wouldn't want them to go to waste."

"You're insane."

"I'm a pirate. My job is insanity."

Garbed in full length robes complete with hood to prevent the human crew from being disturbed by the sight of him, Sorrow padded through the heart of *Brightstar*. He recalled with fondness the day he first dreamt of the design. Memories of the building process and commission brought a smile to his tired face. Created for deep space exploration, the dreadnaughts were meant to take his people to the distant reaches of space on a voyage of discovery. He never envisioned them being turned into instruments of war.

The universe had Amongeratix to blame for a great many wrongs, this one of them. Sorrow ran a bloody hand over the paneling, smearing red. Feeling the end approaching, after so long, threatened to paralyze him. Sorrow never understood why his mother whispered the secrets of *Grimfurvor* at the first hint of schism. A weapon so powerful it could kill their kind with a prick. He questioned why anyone would create such a thing and leave it concealed in the very location his ancestors were created in.

Alas, the answer became evident.

Abbey of the Order of Blood Witches, Acumensiis Comet.

"Again."

Elisa planted her right foot forward and stabbed at Paradise's exposed stomach. The giantess eased back, slickly deflecting the blow with the back of her hand. Grunting, Elisa swept backward. Another blow avoided. Sweat coated her body. Her muscles ached from endless hours of training, Elisa admitted defeat and stepped back.

"You have mastered the dagger but have yet to master yourself," Paradise chided. "Control your emotions. You attack like an impetuous child."

Having arrived in the middle of the night, Paradise made her rounds through the abbey before seeking out the Paladin to complete her training. Though it was a necessary chore, Paradise longed to be with her cousins on Occanum as the first shots of what all hoped was the final battle were fired.

"How in the hells am I supposed to get close enough to kill one of you? You're twice as tall and twice as fast."

"Size matters little to a true fighter," Paradise replied. "Perhaps I was too harsh. I forget humans are made differently. We will resume when you are properly rested."

"I can go again," Elisa insisted.

"No. Eat and recover your strength. There is yet time."

Paradise started to walk away without so much as a single drop of sweat on her.

"You didn't answer my question!"

"Elisa, you are the Paladin. If you cannot do so, no one can."

"She has much to learn and no time in which to do so," Paradise told the Grand Mistress.

"Distressing, but not the finality you report, Paradise. Like most of her kind, Elisa is young, brash, and confronted by the frailty of her limitations. She will not fail."

"How can you be sure?"

Ruma offered a conspiratorial smile. "My efforts for the past three thousand years have guided us to this point. She is the Paladin, as I'm sure you have reminded her. A chosen one of Sorrow's design. We have all done our parts to get her prepared. The rest is up to her."

"It is unfair what my cousin did to her." Paradise softened her stance. "No child should witness her entire family being murdered in a blind fit."

"Destiny seldom consults with us before acting, Paradise. Just as you lament Sorrow setting Elisa on her path there are those who would offer condolence for your role in the final battle," Ruma offered.

Her words were unsettling. "Don't make this about me, Oracle. We were all there at the beginning."

"Which makes it fitting we have assembled here at the end."

Paradise peered into the gloom under the hood, searching for the words not spoken. The Grand Mistress was a wily woman with closely guarded secrets, surrounded by more walls than any other being she had encountered.

"You are worried," she guessed.

Ruma stopped hovering, lowering herself to the ground. "I not only have to worry over the actions of those chosen few throughout the course of this war, but I have the treacherous Algiss Her to deal with. I had not counted on fighting former members of my Order."

She bit off the last sentence, unwilling to tell Paradise of the concerns raised by Sogress or Deius Mlth. She considered the achedaetha prophecy an ill-conceived bane to all her daughters but never imagined it might come to fruition. While Ruma did not believe she would succumb to the cruel temptation, she could not help but wonder if Algiss Her would abandon all her principles in favor of bringing ruin to the universe.

"What do you plan on doing once we arrive at Occanum?" Paradise asked, changing the subject. "You have enough magic collected to obliterate half the enemy forces without deploying to the surface."

"Tsk, Paradise. You of all people should know simply having great power does not give one the authority to wield it unchecked," Ruma admonished. "I already have one Sister attached to Tolde Breed. Others will be deployed to counter this new Crimson Sisterhood."

"Will they be enough?"

"This is not our war, leastwise not on the surface. Ever have we, yourself included, been relegated to acting behind the veil. No. Occanum is a human war, and they must wage it within their means. We shall confront those who are considered supernatural," Ruma said. "Besides, the humans have always viewed my Order with a simmering mistrust. They fear what they do not understand, even if we were once mortals ourselves."

Paradise ran a finger over the obsidian edge of the lone table in the chamber. "This will not be an easy fight, though I suppose it is best we have returned home after so long."

"Why do you say that?"

"What better place to fight the end battle of our time than on the exact location of the first such battle." Paradise's voice dropped to a whisper. "You can't kill a planet twice."

Ruma's glance went unnoticed.

TWENTY

3215 A.G. (After Gods), Road to Tenemenah, planet An'kuruku.

Luma Kai pushed the skiff for all it was worth. The deck trembled as if threatening to break apart over the dunes. Smoke poured from the right engine. Metal twisted and screamed as the transport craft rocketed north to Tenemenah at almost dangerous speeds. She feared it wasn't enough. Pressure dropped on all gauges.

"Tolde, you need to figure something out or we're red splatter on the rocks!" Luma shouted over the engine whine.

They were several hours out from Ankrit, hurrying back to Tenemenah and their ride offworld. And they were being chased. Three skiffs filled with armed men taking shots at them appeared not long after escaping the holy city. Shadowing at first, they hovered just beyond identification range.

Not long after the sun broke the plain did the skiffs close and open fire. Tolde grabbed Ragan and headed toward the back with a pair of aged rifles to return fire. None of the rounds struck true. The gap closed. Slowly. Steadily.

Luma pushed the engines beyond their specs, cursing their choice of transport. She remained professional, insofar as to not point out the obvious.

The chase rattled on, kicking trails of sand in its wake.

"We can't fight them," Tolde shouted back. "Keep us moving."

Mouthing a silent retort, Luma cranked the engines again and was rewarded by a short burst of speed. She heard Ragan's cry of fear and turned to see Tolde catching him before he pitched overboard. The distraction was enough that their assailants took advantage. Incoming fire cracked into the hull and cabin. Wood splintered, slicing clothes and flesh. Pressed down over Kaline, Presha Von screamed in fear and rage. Luma tried to get them to go faster.

The skiff sputtered, jerking violently. Black smoke billowed behind them.

"That's it. She can't take any more," Luma called and cut the engines back.

Tolde scrambled over. She knew what he saw: one or more of the rounds successfully hit the engines. The skiff was almost dead.

He placed a hand on her shoulder and said, "Keep us moving as far as possible. Try to get inside that canyon."

"It won't be enough," she said, hair blowing wildly over her shoulders. "They have more guns and know the terrain better."

"True, but we have a witch."

Not waiting for a response, Tolde worked back to Sister Alessandra, noting the strain in her eyes for the first time. He often wondered if she had physical limitations and was dismayed to discover the truth at this moment. Yet magic wafted off her robes in shimmering waves.

"Alessandra, we need you," he told her. "Kaline can wait."

"Are you sure?"

Tolde flinched as a pair of rounds struck the stack of wooden crates strapped down next to him. "If we don't get these bandits off our tail, we're not going to have to worry about it."

Fixing him with a glare, Alessandra relented. "I hope you know what you are doing, Tolde Breed."

"So do I," he muttered before hurrying back to Ragan.

He sensed Alessandra at his back. Her presence buoyed his confidence. Once, long ago, he found work with the Blood Witches almost reprehensible. Now, he relied on them to resolve impossible situations. She settled in a step behind him and studied the approaching bandits.

"If I am not mistaken, these are no ordinary bandits," she commented and flicked her wrist, deflecting a pair of kinetic rounds from striking true. They splashed on the nearest rock.

"Dejak," Tolde concluded.

"That would be my guess. How do you wish to proceed?"

He hadn't given it much thought. Survival was his only priority. With odds decreasing by the moment, they needed an extra boost to get them into the canyon far enough ahead of Dejak's forces to set an ambush. "Can you screen our retreat?"

"Screen how? It seems more prudent to destroy their craft and be done."

Normally, he might agree, but their skiff was in sore condition and wouldn't carry them the rest of the way to Tenemenah. He needed at least one operable. "Slow them down without damaging the skiffs. We're almost where we need to be."

"I disagree with your rationale but shall do as you request. Are there limitations on harming the men aboard?"

He broke into a grin. "Just don't kill the pilots."

Electricity sparked from her fingertips, dancing between her hands. Alessandra turned her gaze on the fast-approaching skiffs through the wall of black smoke. Using her right hand, she directed loose sheets of magic. Sand melted where they passed. One skiff veered off before the sheet struck, pitching several gunmen overboard where they were consumed by magic. They died without a sound, their petrified arms raised skyward; Tolde bit back a groan.

Enemy fire intensified. Muttering an incantation, a wall of sand, hardened and thick, rose between them. The sound of metal screaming as it slammed into the sand wall echoed over the area.

Tolde winced, praying only one of the skiffs met an end as they raced into the canyon opening. Sand clouds lifted as they passed, spectral fingers questing for fresh victims. Tolde raised the cloth to cover his nose and mouth and bade Ragan to cease fire. With shadows pressing down from the canyon walls, darkness settled over them.

He worked his way back to the pilot station where Luma's face remained locked in a grimace. She vibrated with the skiff, so much so Tolde feared she might break apart with it. "Find a place to hide!"

Luma glared. "Are you mad?"

"Just do it!"

Luma jerked the controls and pointed their skiff to a lee behind a large outcropping of calcified sand running down from an overhang. They reminded Tolde of the teeth of an ancient monster long turned to stone. The skiff settled onto the hardened sand and died with a sputter when Luma cut the engines. Hurrying, he grabbed a weapon and took cover behind the sand teeth, motioning for the others to follow.

Tolde settled in behind his rifle and sighted in. The first skiff entered range, but, outgunned and with nowhere to run, he wanted them to draw closer before opening fire. Ragan and Luma settled with their weapons on either side of him. A glance behind showed Presha sat with the still unconscious Kaline. Of Alessandra, Tolde had no clue. The Blood Witch had disappeared. He cursed before returning focus on Dejak's approaching gunmen.

Waiting until he saw the looks on their faces, Tolde squeezed. The round struck the lead gunman center in the upper chest, pitching him back with a grunt. Luma and Ragan hit their initial targets and began shifting fire through the rest of the first skiff. Desperate, the pilot jerked the controls hard left and tilted the deck to prevent others from being killed. His actions resulted in equipment and people toppling overboard and a pair of rounds striking the skiff's exposed underbelly. A lucky round caught the main fuel line charging the suspensor lifts and the skiff pitched to the sand in a cloud of black smoke. The second skiff appeared, the gunmen unleashing a withering barrage in their general area.

Tolde sniped another man and rolled to his right. With the first skiff destroyed and half the crew presumed dead, their odds of reaching transport in Tenemenah increased. Seizing the opportunity, Tolde burst across the brief open space to the damaged skiff, ignoring the cries of disbelief from his companions. Tolde methodically eliminated the survivors as he came upon them.

The skiff was done. Fires sprang through the control panels. Sullen, Tolde popped his head high enough to view the engagement area. Cold realization settled in when he discovered how far from the others he'd run and, to his dismay, there was no way to make it back without being gunned down by the now furious gunmen on the second skiff.

He was trapped.

Dejak unleashed a full power charge on the lone man scrambling over the downed skiff. Metal evaporated but his target remained unharmed. Seething with rage, the merchant watched, helpless, as the stranger murdered his men in cold blood. Ordering the pilot to swing around hard right, careful to stay out of range of whatever creature had been throwing magic at him, the skiff hovered in for the quick kill. One man against twenty was odds any man worth his salt took advantage of. Dejak dropped the empty power pack and inserted another.

His rescue operation, initially conceived to be quick, efficient, and placing them back in his compound before midday, devolved into a nightmare he might never recover from. Wolves circled his estate already, sensing weakness. Whispers circulated the city, suggesting Dejak had finally gone too far. Pushed himself beyond his means. The only way to maintain his status was by recapturing the woman Kaline and asserting dominance over the would-be rulers of the desert.

"No one shoots that bastard but me," Dejak growled, knowing most of his people would be unable to hear him.

The skiff slowed, banking enough to provide adequate cover from small arms, and swept around the backside of his downed craft. Bodies littered the scene. Dejak might have been appalled at the casual disregard for life if not for the anger in his veins. Security personnel were easy to replace. Returning to Ankrit with the offworlder's head and his prized possession back in custody would not only cement his reputation but grow his standing in the right circles.

Movement caught his eye. Dejak crouched behind his rifle, sweeping the scope over the wreckage. He fired. Sparks danced off metal as the man ducked in time. Dejak fired again before the rest of his skiff opened fire. Succumbing to the madness, he watched as his gunmen reduced much of the skiff to slag, yet there was no body. Dejak barked for them to ceasefire.

A trio of guards dropped to the sand, weapons raised as they approached the skiff from the blind side. Dejak searched the wreckage for any sign of life, but thick plumes of black smoke occluded his line of sight. The snap-hiss of a round cracking the windscreen beside his head made Dejak crouch. He spun, cursing himself for forgetting the others hidden in the rocks. Desperation settled in as he realized his mistake. Focusing on a lone gunman opened the way for the others to reengage their ambush.

"Swing us around! Kill everyone you find but bring me the woman," Dejak barked.

One way or another, Kaline would be his and, through her, he planned on reshaping An'kuruku in his image.

Presha Von watched the battle unfold with dispassion. Her experiences since leaving her homeworld of Crimeat left her numb to violence. Bodies in the sand did little to arouse her imagination or spark a modest measure of fear for her own safety. She viewed life with no regard, knowing each soul lost now was simply one less to be ground into the dirt when Amongeratix finally got his way. Dust and sand blew in her face as she watched Tolde sprint across the open field of fire.

Presha ducked as streams of white-blue rounds slashed her way. Outnumbered, she realized it was but a matter of time before they were overrun, or their opponent brought in reinforcements. She longed for the feel of a blaster in her hand, if only to pretend to care. The wild thought of standing and extending her arms to embrace the withering fire teased her psyche.

The Blood Witch appeared and swept forward, arms dripping power. Presha peered into the cold shadows of her cowl and flinched. At her feet, Kaline groaned.

A scream grabbed her attention. Flesh and bone melted from their attackers before they broke apart into dust drifting across the sands. Those fortunate to have cover increased their rate of fire as desperation settled in. From the corner of her eye, Presha caught Kaline shake her head, greasy locks of unkempt red hair sweeping across her shoulders, and stagger to her feet. The mouth of Rengu stumbled off before Presha could stop her.

"Kaline, get down!" Presha snatched her pistol from the sand and moved to chase after the dazed woman.

She scrambled to her hands and knees when a single shot changed the world. Presha choked back a scream as half of Kaline's head evaporated and her corpse dropped to the sand.

And like that, the battle ended.

Dejak coughed a mouthful of blood. The dark liquid spilled over his chin to stain his tunic. He couldn't feel his arms or legs. Only the intense pain radiating from his chest. Remnants of dreams swarmed him, teasing the merchant with thoughts of what might have been and reminding him of the arrogance of his beliefs. Dejak wanted to laugh but the pain grew unbearable.

Through the black smoke and haze he spied the lone man who'd defied the odds to reach the downed skiff. Dejak's eyes narrowed, even as tears flowed. The man strode toward him. Confident. With purpose. So unlike the men of An'kuruku, who acted through subversion and backhanded politics. He wondered who this man was, to come boldly from the wreckage and hand down judgment through the barrel of a gun. If he had just a handful of such men …

The thought ended as the man halted a step away. Dejak's vision swam, darkening around the edges as a coughing fit racked him. Weakly, he stretched forth a hand. Dejak felt cold. His body numbing. When he managed to speak it was strained and but a single word.

"W…ho?"

"You should have stayed home," Tolde said quietly.

Tolde kicked the hand of the dead man away before hurrying over to the remaining skiff. Knowing better than to study the scene, he climbed aboard the second craft and inspected the control panels. He let out a sigh of relief when the engines gunned to life. Brushing off the thin coat of sand, Tolde activated the controls and took the skiff to the rest of his team.

He found them standing over Kaline's corpse. Only Alessandra remained indifferent. He hadn't known what to expect upon capturing Kaline. No matter how far they devolved from their original intent, part of him knew the moral obligation lie in putting her on trial for crimes against humanity. A new order was rising on Mannus Prime. One capable of ensuring justice. The human aspect, often dominating and overpowering, felt justification for her fate.

"What happened?" he asked when none withstood his gaze.

Luma lowered a torn jacket over the body. "Stray round to the head. She never felt a thing."

"She was supposed to be incapacitated," he pointed out.

Alessandra stirred, or perhaps it was the wind shuffling her robes. "Other matters of greater importance needed my attention."

Tolde paused. He wanted to say more. To expound upon the callous nature of the moment but lacked the tongue for it. All that mattered was a great evil had been neutralized and their mission reached conclusion. He debated burying her. Shadows circled overhead. Carrion birds summoned to their next meal.

"We need to go," he said after some thought. "Tannus will be expecting us."

"How can you be so cold?" Presha asked through her tears.

Ragan's hand rested on her shoulder though Tolde noticed the boy hadn't yet looked away from the body at his feet. Pressing his lips together as disparate thoughts warred in his head, he became aware of his lack of humanity since his resurrection.

"It is a matter of prudence. Stopping Kaline was the mission and, though it did not end in the matter we intended, the mission is complete. There is nothing more for us on this world. Our destiny is elsewhere," he explained. Even to him the words rang hollow.

"We should at least bury her," Ragan muttered.

"There is no time. Dejak likely will have summoned

reinforcements. Any delay places us in danger," Tolde said. "Come, let us go."

He stalked off, uncertain if any would follow.

A glance back showed Ragan and Presha had remained behind. Both kneeling and scooping sand over Kaline's body in a final act of dignity, one of which Tolde doubted she deserved.

Luma resumed her position as pilot while they waited. No one spoke as Presha and Ragan climbed aboard the skiff, their hands and clothes stained from the rich redness of the sand. A gesture from Tolde and the skiff resumed course for Tenemenah and the uncertainty of the future. For better or worse, the mission to An'kuruku ended.

Eger City, planet Mannus Prime.

The planet buzzed with activity. Fresh recruits continued pouring in from the far reaches of the universe. Diplomats and politicians from a hundred worlds swelled the ranks of the Confederation as new worlds petitioned for inclusion. Commerce and production increased on unprecedented levels. Those members of the council who did not deploy were threatened with being overwhelmed by the creature of their creation. The strain was felt from the highest level down.

Tempest found herself sleeping more nights than necessary in her office—a knocking now awakened her with a groan. Squinting at the chrono on her desk and the darkness of city life outside, she tossed her head back to strike the wall with a dull thud. Her muscles ached. Her mind reeled. Adris accused her of working too hard, insisting she take longer breaks between shifts. The universe, Adris declared, would handle itself. Tempest, being no fool, knew better than to leave fate to chance. The knock repeated, forcing her from the hard cushions. She staggered to the door.

"Do you have any idea how late it is?" she fumed after the door slid open. Tempest found herself staring into a strange face. "Who are you?"

The man smiled. An oddly hollow gesture. "Ah, my apologies. My name is Gedrick Silk. I am in the employ of Adris Moscasco."

"Aren't we all." Tempest rolled her eyes. "Why don't you go find her?"

Gedrick remained nonplussed. "It is far too late at night for such. Besides, it is my understanding you handle her more, how shall I say, delicate affairs."

Tempest paused, reconsidering her thoughts on the man. "Make it quick."

"Perhaps we would be better in your office," Gedrick suggested.

Suppressing another groan, Tempest stepped aside and gestured him in. She paused to check the hall, surprised to find it empty. Mind swirling with conspiracy theories, she closed the door then stalked across her office to slump in her chair.

She met Gedrick's stare with her own. Neither flinched. Neither balked. Tempest wanted nothing more than to sink into the depths of her dreams and start the next day fresh. Tracing her tongue across her bottom lip, she reached for the half-filled glass of water she had left on her desk.

"Again, my apologies," Gedrick began.

Tempest held up a finger for him to wait as she emptied the glass. "You said that already. Who exactly are you again?"

"Gedrick Silk. Adris Moscasco made me her spymaster."

The statement jarred vague memories of an earlier meeting. "You look different."

He smiled. "A trait you will get used to. I seldom carry the same image from day to day."

It all clicked for her. "You're the shapeshifter."

"The one and only," he said with a mock bow.

"I assume you're here to discuss our special problem," Tempest said as more pieces fell into place.

Gedrick bobbed his head. "The man we have following him has reported a sudden increase in followers."

Tempest was confused. "Isn't that the reason we have him in place?"

"True, but these new crowds are more violent," Gedrick replied. "The original rabble rousers are mostly gone. They were never a threat. Tinnus Har has collected the worst society has to offer. I fear for the safety of the new council."

"What proof do you have? I can't take this to Adris without evidence."

"Rumors only. My asset hasn't been able to confirm numbers or much of anything yet."

"That's not enough. I need as much intel as you can provide before we act," Tempest replied. "Gedrick, this is a desperate time. With the army deployed and the bulk of our attention focused on the coming battle we can ill afford to allow rebellion."

Spreading his palms, Gedrick said, "I have forces in place to mitigate any potential uprising. Tinnus Har will not be an issue."

"You can guarantee that?"

"No, but I can do all within my limits to ensure the former Cardinal Seniorus remains on the fringe."

"What of the Inquisitor? Can you trust him?" Tempest asked.

"In as much as he is worth, yes."

Tempest watched the conflict brew in his eyes, seeing his distrust. She'd never dealt with a shapeshifter, nor explored the possibility of doing so. Until now, they were little more than beings of myth. A childish desire to ask him to shift threatened to put a smile on her face. She shrugged off the idea, focusing on the moment. If she had her way Gedrick and a company of commandos would have already assaulted Tinnus Har and crushed any potential insurrection before it gained steam. She'd witnessed enough since their escape from Dalafar to dampen her normally cheerful demeanor. Adris called it the hardening of her shell.

"Keep pressing," Tempest said. "I need more before I take this to Adris."

"I shall," Gedrick vowed.

Gedrick rose, smoothing his tunic down. "I shall be in touch. Please give my report to Adris at your earliest convenience. Good night."

A glance at the chrono told her it was already well beyond that. She waited until he was at the door before instructing, "Get me names, Gedrick, and I will bring a hammer down on them."

Prekhauten Guard Spaceport, Krenz, planet Vau Prime.

Akin Brohl cared little for the human plight that had befallen the city. His focus remained on hunting down his final prey and fulfilling his purpose, avenging the spirits of his fallen brethren and, perhaps, finding the peace he had so long desired.

The hunt proved more difficult than planned. Witches hounded his movements, dispatching squads of Inquisitors and Prekhautens to slow his progress. Akin left a mounting body count in his wake. Yet for all his success, he failed to come within range of the one being his heart yearned to confront.

Creeping through the rubble of what had been apartments, Akin moved into a proper position with a clear field of fire. Smoothing over a small patch of ground, he slipped his rifle from his shoulders and affixed his scope. Each movement precise, the god hunter was methodical in his setup. A trio of powerpacks were laid out by his left hand, easy access for when the moment arose. Akin slipped a fresh charge into the magazine well, pausing to run a thumb over the timeworn metal. He pressed his forehead to the stock and muttered an ancient prayer before settling in.

Before him sat the main flight line for the Prekhauten Guard's primary spaceport. A dozen shuttles remained on the tarmac, awaiting their cargo before deploying spaceward. Countless specialized units had already deployed over the course of the last week. Akin noted their uniforms and designations and arrived at one inescapable conclusion. Amongeratix was preparing to deploy to combat his brother one final time. Should that happen, Akin's mission was complete and he would be free to pursue his purpose on his own schedule.

Armed patrols roved throughout the spaceport. Akin spied a pair of witches drifting between the shuttles. A grim smile crept across his face. His finger slipped into the trigger well. Lights announced the arrival of a small convoy. He watched the vehicles close on the shuttles. His heart rate spiked. This was it. Inquisitors and witches exited the convoy. There, looming over them, was Amongeratix. The terror of a hundred worlds. Akin exhaled and sighted in. He squeezed the trigger before inhaling.

The ion round crossed the distance in the blink of an eye, striking Amongeratix in the throat. Instead of dropping, the giant dissolved into wisps of broken matter. Akin's eyes widened as cold realization settled in—witches in crimson robes appeared from the night, surrounding him. Akin flipped his rifle to automatic and emptied a power pack on the closest witch. He was rewarded with a scream and the woman collapsing in on herself. Smoke steamed from her robes in death. He used the distraction to displace.

He scurried down the sharp incline to the ground and headed under what remained of an alcove. There a massive figure barreled into him and they hit the ground. The god hunter's rifle skittered away, forcing him to use his hands on his attacker. Blows hammered into his ribs. Grunting through the pain, Akin caught a glimpse of his enemy's face. Lifeless, dark eyes stared beyond him. Akin smelled magic on the air as he realized he had fought this man before. A giant among his own kind, his enemy this time no longer drew breath. Akin decided retreat prudent, for the blood magic of the witches often proved difficult to combat.

He wedged a knee between them and flipped the bigger man up and over. The body crashed in a cloud of construction dust. Akin rolled to his feet, spying movement through the haze. Flashes of crimson. Witches. Face darkening, the god hunter drew the dagger from his belt and charged the nearest one. Magic flared. Brilliant sheets of light striking his face and chest that failed to slow his assault. Akin crashed into the stunned witch, driving his dagger deep into her chest three successive times.

Bolts of magic slashed into his back, shredding his armor and clothing. Pain burrowed deep into his muscles. Fire burned through his blood, racing to his brain. Akin clutched his dagger tighter, twisting as he ripped it from the dying witch's chest. Ropes of blood trailed the tempered steel. A second witch added her magic, driving him to his knees. Smoke and evaporating flesh choked the air around him.

The sound of crunching boots on gravel drew his attention a moment before the giant struck from behind. A rib snapped. Blood filled his mouth. Akin switched the grip on his blade and drove backward. He was rewarded by the wet sucking of steel puncturing flesh. Hot fluids drooled over his fist, burning his exposed skin. Akin jerked blade and hand away. The giant continued his assault, forcing the god hunter to slam the back of his head into the giant's face. Akin felt bones breaking.

The witch assault intensified. Akin, a magical creature in his own right, shrugged off the destructive energy and used the distraction to escape his assailant. Sprinting, he snatched his rifle from the ground and exchanged power packs. Bolts of magic struck the ground around him. An acrid stench filled his nostrils. Mostly unaffected, Akin took aim at the raging giant stumbling toward him and fired. His rounds struck true, slagging the giant's head and shoulders. He ran before the remains dropped.

Akin had established a string of safehouses as he carved his way to the city center, each containing enough food, ammunition, and medical supplies to ensure continued mission success. The one aspect he failed to account for was the deception on the tarmac. *Where is he?* Akin slipped down a side street and clung to the shadows. He slowed his heartbeat the way they'd been taught in training, focusing his thoughts in a narrow channel. A trio of witches flowed past.

Akin waited, enjoying the crisp emptiness of silence, until he grew certain he'd slipped his pursuit. Confident he was once again alone, the god hunter surveyed his hiding spot. Narrow and with dual entry points. Akin reloaded his rifle, pausing to ensure his dagger was secured, and slunk down the passage. A pair of rats scurried away. Akin brushed webs from his face and continued. The area grew calm. An unprecedented twist. Fearful of an ambush, he picked up his pace.

He gained the end of the passage and poked his head out just far enough to ensure both sides of the street were clear. Weapon at the ready, Akin stepped into the open and dashed across the street. No bolts of magic tracked him. No shouts of surprise. His confidence grew. Safe for the moment, Akin took in his surroundings. The nearest safehouse was less than a block away. There he could regroup and resume his hunt. Akin Brohl stepped back into the street.

His last sight was of Amongeratix looming over him, a leering grin etched on his granite face as he held a sword.

Mission complete.

TWENTY-ONE

3215 A.G. (After Gods), Plains of Haddash, planet Occanum.

General Torgast surveyed the chosen battlefield. Endless kilometers of ash and dirt stretched as far as his eyes could see. Rolling hills and the spartan remains of a once proud civilization comprised his immediate surroundings. To his surprise, Occanum retained enough oxygen to breathe without aid. He didn't know how or why. It didn't matter. So long as his army could fight unhindered.

The ground rumbled beneath his boots as battalions of armor and artillery moved into pre-battle positions. Every inch of thirty-five kilometers from his position was covered by heavy and small arms. Anti-aircraft batteries deployed throughout the army, ensuring the entire airspace was protected from incoming artillery shells or rockets. More than two hundred thousand soldiers were marching into positions. Trenches and bunkers were dug. Millions of sandbags filled.

Torgast watched with rapt fascination. A lifelong military man, he never envisioned entire armies taking the field. Traditional Guard doctrine focused on small unit operations, not large-scale battles similar to that of Mannus Prime. That the entirety of the assembled forces on the plain belonged to him threatened to rob his grasp on sanity. An ache spread across his face, fading after he realized he'd been clenching his jaw. *Easy, old man. This is nothing new. You've led armies in the field before. Focus on the mission.*

"Impressive, isn't it?"

He found Matthias standing at his side. "Most. Was this what it was like on Mannus in the beginning?"

Torgast studied the man who was supposed to have remained behind to help guide the Confederation through the last phases of the war. How Matthias snuck aboard the fleet without anyone knowing until it was too late to turn back remained a mystery. One he didn't wish to explore.

"Yes and no. There, we didn't expect to engaged in a protracted campaign. I have no idea who first sprouted the idea of digging trenches and duking it out with artillery for the better part of a year." He ran a hand through his close-cropped hair. "We could have avoided countless casualties without those damned trenches. Will this hold similar outcomes?"

Matthias shifted his weight to the opposite foot. "I've seen and done things during this war I never imagined. The one constant I have learned is war is seldom static. We must be prepared to handle every contingency, even if we choose not to believe them possible."

"Says the man responsible for bringing Amongeratix to heel all those years ago," Torgast added with a raised eyebrow.

Matthias blushed. "That was, ah, a long time ago and I played a small part. It was the Inquisitor and the Blood Witch who did most of the work."

"How many others can lay claim to such exploits?" Torgast placed a hand on his friend's shoulder. "You are a legend among the ranks, Matthias. I am thankful you are here, if for no other reason than to boost morale."

"I expect morale to remain high until the enemy starts dropping whole divisions somewhere over the horizon," Matthias countered.

"Hopefully our gunships can blast most of them from the sky long before their boots touch this wretched soil."

Torgast knew though that the enemy would land in force, no matter how many shuttles were shot down, and they would be outnumbered. War, after all, often came down to a game of numbers.

"You are distracted," Torgast said to break the silence, noticing the faraway look in Matthias' eyes.

"We shouldn't have left Mannus with Tinnus Har on the loose. His influence can jeopardize all we've struggled to build."

"Little for it now. Our focus needs to be here. Now. Adris and the others can handle Har."

Matthias remained skeptical. Few of the new council understood the depths the deposed Cardinal Seniorus was willing to go to reclaim his authority. With forked tongue and barbed promises, Tinnus Har was a poison to all he touched. Matthias' brief interactions with the man conspired against any moral code. Har needed to be put down, like a rabid animal. Nothing else would stop his drive.

"Perhaps you're right," he conceded. "I've left contingencies in place to ensure his poison does not spread."

"Good man," Torgast said. "One less problem to worry about

goes far in helping maintain sanity. Leastwise that's what I've discovered over the past two years."

"How did you do it?"

"Do what?"

Matthias gestured to the army. "Keep it all in line throughout the siege. Most commanders would have broken at some point. I nearly did on An'kuruku when I faced off against Amongeratix's army. If not for Paradise Tear, I might not be here today."

"Simple. I made myself responsible for every casualty from day one," the general replied. "What's a paradise tear?"

"Not a what, a who," Matthias corrected. "She is Tannus' cousin."

"There's more than the Three? Gods, we're doomed."

Matthias didn't disagree. His experiences suggested a terrible conclusion approached. One neither of them were prepared to pay. "If it's any consolation, the only one we need to worry about is Amongeratix."

"No, he's not. Mobus Kale has twisted the Guard into his likeness and commands the bulk of Guard forces across the universe. Gone are the days of civility. We're in for one hells of a fight here."

"That we are," Matthias agreed. "It may look bleak at the moment, but you forget one important matter."

"What's that?"

Matthias broke into a grim smile. "We have reinforcements of our own."

Torgast grunted. "Let's hope they arrive in time to save at least some of us. I'd hate to be responsible for the second largest massacre on this blasted rock."

The sound of engines plummeting down from space drew their attention. Another wave of transports bringing in fresh infantry battalions burned toward the landing fields on the far side of the plain. Hundreds more awaited clearance to drop from the waiting carriers in orbit.

"So are you going to tell me how you did it?" Torgast asked without looking at him.

"Do what?"

"Escape Eger City and sneak on one of my troop transports undetected."

"I should be going," Matthias declared, knowing reports were waiting for the general. "There are other areas I need to reach before our friends arrive." He extended his hand. "Gods speed, Torgast."

"And you, my friend."

They parted, Matthias wondering if he had made a mistake in coming.

Ferom Operations Center.

"I need help," Doc Little said as he pulled the blood-soaked gloves off and tossed them in the trash. They'd been inundated with casualties since the space battle began in earnest. Far too many for a company medic to handle. Fies had feared this would happen.

"What do you want me to do, Doc? We're going to be outnumbered in every regard soon enough. Patch up the ones you can and ship them back to the fleet hospital ship."

"I'm doing that, Captain, but it's not enough. I have bodies stacked up throughout the hall. The screams don't stop." Little choked on a sob.

Fies wanted to reach out, to console his longtime medic but doing so, here in public view of both Guards and mercenaries, might send the wrong message. The station was ablaze with activity. Reports streamed in, relaying real time imagining of the battle edging closer to the planet proper. They were all strained, pushed to the limits. Food and sleep were forgotten luxuries. Even reinforced by the Shadow Hammers, Fies found himself strained to the breaking point. The last thing he needed was one of the most valuable members of his team to break.

Lowering his voice so those nearby couldn't hear, Fies said, "Do your best. I've put the requisition in for help. Last word I got was we've got medics and surgeons enroute. I know it's not enough, but it's all I can offer."

"What do you want me to do with the dead?"

Fies winced at the resignation he heard, knowing too that the morgue was already overflowing. "I'll detail a squad to help identify them. There has to be an unused refrigerator room somewhere in this monster. I've already placed the request for additional body bags." He paused. "Doc, remember, these were our allies. Friends and family. They deserve the utmost honor we can give them."

"That's what makes this so difficult." Little nodded. "Ok, I'm on it. Thank you, sir."

"What was that about?" Paradise asked Fies from the computer screen in front of him. She watched the beleaguered medic stumble back to the makeshift operating room.

Fies looked at the wall screen. "The usual. We're stretched too thin. Pushed to the edge and this fucking battle hasn't even started."

She cocked her head. "There are concerns over elevated casualties?"

"That's an understatement."

"Perhaps I can help."

"What do you know of human biology?"

"Not as much as I would like. I should have thought of this sooner, but many of our outposts contained automated medical bays."

"That would be nice, but we're not comparable in size or physiology," he replied.

"Send me Annalilly, and give me access to the operating systems," Paradise requested. "Once I locate the bays, I should be able to reconfigure the specifications to match your species."

"Will it be enough to save lives?" He refused to let hope in.

"Potentially," her image flickered. "As long as the power grid does not become overloaded, I should be able to get the pods working in short order. Give me a little."

"A little is all I can afford," Fies admitted.

"Fies! We got a shitstorm heading our way!" Annalilly barked from across the command room.

"Go," Paradise told him. "Leave your wounded to me."

Confederation Frigate *Vitriol*.

Sparks showered down, splashing Drukali's already burned face. His uniform was torn in several places. Many of his crew were dead. Many more would be joining them soon. Yet for the damages sustained, his ship still doled out punishment. The *Vitriol* claimed several enemy ships. Their corpses drifting across the edge of the Occanum system— Drukali had no intention of joining them.

"Helm! Plot a course into the minefield," he snapped.

A trio of corvettes hounded him, blasting away. Far from toothless, Drukali's gunners left a trail of wreckage in their wake. One of the corvettes pulled off course after a salvo of penetrator missiles exploded deep within her hull. Unable to kill the ship, Drukali had no choice but to run. Their survival depended on it.

Vitriol rocked as anti-ship batteries destroyed incoming fire. Drukali studied the rear screens, knowing his opponents were inexperienced captains following standard Guard doctrine. That, he decided, would be their doom. Drukali combined his efforts with the rest of his squadron, splitting the larger force into smaller two and three ship strike forces when the engagement allowed. This wild unpredictability resulted in almost a score of ship kills. None of those mattered to Drukali if he couldn't shake the three hounding his retreat.

"Distance to minefield?"

"Eight hundred kilometers, sir."

Too far. *Vitriol* needed help if she was going to use the mines to her advantage. "Increase speed. Where are our escorts?"

Vitriol rocked. Drukali stumbled, catching himself on his command chair.

"*Esteemed* is disabled. *Fury* is circling around behind our pursuit. She should engage momentarily."

"Open a channel to Captain Essle."

The helmsman punched in a series of codes and gave Drukali a thumbs up. Stretcher bearers arrived on the bridge, briefly grabbing his attention as they headed for the nearest casualty.

"*Fury* this is *Vitriol*," Drukali shouted above the chaos. "Are you with me?"

"Affirmative, *Vitriol*. We're still in the fight," Captain Essle's gravelly voice echoed. Frantic shouts of orders being given threatened to drown out her voice. "Where do you need us?"

Drukali grinned, licking the blood from his teeth. "Come up behind and target life support systems on that wounded corvette. I'm leading the other two into the minefield."

"Are you mad? Your ship can't survive that level of firepower in your current state."

"Let me worry about that. You keep these bastards off my tail."

At her pause, he winced, knowing the impossible scenario he'd placed his captain in. He also knew, as would any commander worth their salt, battles were often won at the height of desperation. With his task force sustaining heavy damage as more of the enemy fleets engaged, Drukali needed to make an example.

"Roger that, *Vitriol*. Moving into position now. Good luck."

"Thank you Essle. First round is on me if we make it out of this mess," he said. The line cut. "Helm, get us inside that minefield. I have a little surprise for our friends."

Vitriol rocked.

Confederation Frigate *Indominable*.

"That's the last troop transport. All ground units have deployed for the surface," Captain Samuel announced with a measure of pride. He hadn't known what to expect upon entering the Occanum System and was pleased their deployment schedule went off without delay. Now came the hard part.

Falchi rolled the stiffness from his shoulders. He hadn't slept more than three hours a day since departing Mannus Prime. Lines formed on his face and hands. Worry shadowed his eyes. As the second ranking fleet admiral in system and a member of the Confederation Council, Falchi wasn't expected to be anywhere near the fighting. That didn't preclude him from spending countless hours mired in doubt, second-guessing, and worry.

"Very good, Captain Samuel. Have we made contact with Admiral Khe-Zhehan yet?"

"No, sir. To my knowledge her fleet has not translated into the system," Samuel replied. "I have established comms with the base on Ferom. Fies and his people have done a remarkable job in a short period."

"Indeed. They are the nerve center of our entire operation, and a trump card should we need one." Falchi's head felt heavy. "Keep working on raising the other fleet. I want to know the instant they are in contact."

"Aye, sir."

Gaze locked on the massive viewport dominating the upper half of the bridge, Falchi let out a low whistle at the vast number of ships in sight. Corvettes, cruisers, frigates, a few battleships, and two carriers dominated his fleet. Hundreds of smaller craft flew between them, from fighters to shuttles and a privately registered craft he thought better of asking about. The unique aspect of this war combined friend and foe against a greater threat.

"Did you ever think to see such a sight?"

Samuel stepped to his side, hands clasped behind his

back in the traditional military custom. "Nor did I wish to, leastwise not under these circumstances," he admitted. "None of this is right. Brother kills brother while the puppet masters sit back in delight at the carnage they inspired. It is a shame the Inquisitor General is already dead."

"War has ever been a game of families, Samuel. Do not let that cloud your judgment," Falchi scolded without heat. "Soon this horizon will be filled with enemy ships crewed by people we once considered friends. The true travesty of free will lies in the amount of rot within our souls."

"You still believe in an afterlife?"

Falchi hesitated.

"I don't know what to believe at this point. The one thing I do know is we should all be free to worship and prepare for what comes when we close our eyes for the last time."

The veins in Samuel's neck popped. His gaze hardened. "Looking at it that way, I very much hope the hells are real. What more fitting realm for usurpers and betrayers is there?"

Turning to face his longtime friend and second in command, Falchi didn't like what he heard or saw. "Samuel, do not be so fast to dole judgment on our foes. Yes, we believe they have betrayed the tenets of the Prekhauten Guard and Conclave, but so too must they believe we are guilty of the same. This is a war of ideals," he reminded. "Of course, that doesn't make them any less of a threat, nor do I suggest offering quarter in any way. Alain Nye and Mobus Kale twisted far too many to their will to turn back now."

"Not to mention the monster loose upon Krenz."

Falchi lacked the desire to bring up Amongeratix. "I don't suppose the new Inquisitor General saw fit to deploy with his forces," Falchi said instead, puffing out an exaggerated breath.

"Cowards seldom do. Has the council learned who replaced Nye?"

"I have it on good authority it was one of Nye's senior people," Falchi answered. "Goethe, I believe his name is."

"Never heard of him."

"Nor do I suspect we had reason to. The Inquisition is renowned for keeping secrets. In the name of justice and order."

"Justice and order. How did we allow ourselves to be seduced by the lie?"

"Human nature is fickle. We tend to bend with the wind," Falchi explained. "How long did we serve without question while Nye played his power games?"

Samuel's eyes narrowed. "How long do you suppose he worked on the foundations of this uprising?"

"That is a question I fear may never be answered."

"Admiral! Contact from quadrant three. Incoming ships!"

The moment passed, Falchi returned to the stalwart officer. "Identify."

"Trying, sir. Transponders are transmitting a Confederation code, but their ship signatures are unlike anything I've ever seen."

The bridge fell quiet as the first images of a nightmare filled the displays. Falchi struggled to keep his mouth from dropping as he whispered, "Fuck me."

Brightstar, Tannus' flagship.

Sharlyn August listened to her new ship. The grind of metal as they prepared to enter real space. The smell of hydraulics and machinery forced into operation after thousands of years of inactivity. The buckle in the decks as the ship slowed. Her gaze never lingered in one place too long. So much of the dreadnaught's operating systems were foreign yet abstractly similar. She felt small, and not for the first time. The immensity of the bridge dwarfed her in unimaginable ways. Alien. Foreign. Her crew were never meant to man such a ship. Yet when the robotics entered and assumed positions throughout the fleet, she took offense.

Promised total command of the ten dreadnaughts, August wondered if the replacements were an indication of Tannus changing his mind. She'd done some digging and wasn't surprised to find Tannus offered with one hand while taking with the other. It took little imagination to see his betrayal and, she admitted with chagrin, there wasn't a damned thing she could do to stop him should he see fit to abandon his original plan.

Throwing doubt over all was the inclusion of the Bloody Man. Thought he had graciously confined himself to his quarters, August struggled with accepting his proximity. Just being in his presence inspired mild cases of madness. The Bloody Man was the most famous of the Three, even if the Conclave knew little about him. August found disgust in seeing a giant man perpetually weep blood after flaying himself alive. Anathema to all she held dear, the Bloody Man represented the dark soul of corruption heating at the fabric of the universe. She wanted him off her ship. Tannus refused.

The only one nonplussed by the turn of events was Blackheart. The former pirate lord took each new development in stride, as if he'd seen it all before. August failed to understand the man's complacency. She knew he played the game from multiple angles. Blackheart swore allegiance to her and the cause, but only so long as it fit his needs. She didn't doubt he planned on stealing one of the dreadnaughts at the first opportunity.

Movement drew her attention. Captain Odir left the command pit in the center of the bridge, making the long walk to her position. August caught his quickened step and braced herself.

"This ship was not made for humans," Odir said, struggling to get his breathing under control. "I know what it looks like, but gods be damned, no bridge should be this… massive."

He wasn't wrong. Though Tannus created the ship long before the Conclave's birth, many of the stations scattered across the bridge were clearly designed without humans in mind. "I trust you have something important to report, Captain."

Odir jerked to attention, remembering his place and role. "Sorry, ma'am. It's this ship and our special guest."

August dismissed his apology for she too felt the urge to lament. "Your report."

"We are entering the Occanum System now. Rendezvous with the fleet is expected within three standard hours. I have comms broadcasting our identity to any nearby friendly forces."

"Very good, Odir." The last thing she needed was to be mistaken for enemy craft. She doubted any ordinance in Falchi's fleet had the punch necessary to inflict damage to *Brightstar* but knew better than to leave such matters to chance. "See if you can raise the Admiral direct. And reinforce the importance of not firing on any assailant vessels to the gunners. This could get ugly fast."

"Already done. Gun crews have been suitably threatened if any decides to become trigger happy before the proper moment," Odir explained. At her snort, he added, "That includes our pirate friends, though I can't for the life of me figure out why we entrusted them with heavy weaponry."

"Pirates are notorious fighters," she said without conviction. "The longer we placate them with important tasks the longer we delay any mutinous attempts. Speaking of which, where is our favorite pirate lord? Still sulking after I changed my mind about giving him a dreadnaught no doubt."

Odir cleared his throat, lowering his head just enough to make August roll her eyes. "He, ah, has been called away by Lord Tannus."

"Has he now?" she asked in genuine surprise.

"I was instructed not to inform you."

A displeased glare slipped over her face. "I was under the impression this ship, and the entire fleet, was under my implicit command. Please tell me why my right-hand man of many years decided not to inform me of this?"

Fidgeting, Odir finally said, "Lord Tannus was insistent. He, ah, is quite intimidating, Admiral."

August found herself reexamining old sores between herself and the pirate lord, anything to keep her from confronting her feelings. Charming as he was, Vicente Blackheart remained one of the universe's most wanted criminals and, until recently, the focus of her attention. Did his golden tongue convince Tannus to his side or was this a matter beyond his control?

"Did Tannus explain himself?" She knew the answer before asking. Focused on defeating his brother, Tannus remained an enigma. "Never mind. I want Blackheart under surveillance from now on. If he makes any play I want to know."

"So much for allies," Odir quipped.

August wondered if they had ever been.

Capital District, Krenz, planet Vau Prime.

Rumors circulated through the city. Amongeratix, the tyrant of the ages, had gone. Some claimed he took his armies and headed across the stars to confront his brother in one final battle. Others said it was but a ruse. A small fraction believed the monster was dead, killed by the invisible assassin responsible for slaughtering hundreds of Guards and Inquisitors. With no way of confirming any rumor, the city waited, fearful of striking forth and unwilling to risk their lives should their favorite rumor prove false.

Hidden deep under the city proper in a network of tunnels and safehouses, Porii Daam could not care less which rumor proved true. Her contacts, by way of Edam Boone's organization, provided intelligence pointing to one inescapable conclusion: Amongeratix no longer controlled daily life in Krenz. That told her all she needed to know.

In his stead rose an equally deplorable monster. The new Inquisitor General, Ezekiel Goethe. What little she knew of the man suggested a shrewdness and cunning almost as great as Alain Nye's. Like most men who followed in a dictator's footsteps, Goethe's reign over the Inquisition and, now that the Conclave was officially disbanded, the universe tightened with each new mandate. He aimed to squeeze the population into submission. After nearly four years of civil war, the matter proved far easier than anticipated.

Porii saw it in the eyes of those she encountered daily. Broken. Hopeless. Pushed to the edge of submission, their fight having long expired. Rage fueled her. She knew she was once a key figure complicit to Nye's power grab. Most of the Cardinals were. Time showed her the errors of her ways, placing her in the position she found herself in today. Concealed among criminals while attempting to atone for her sins.

"He's gone," Edam announced upon entering the room.

Porii glanced up. "You are certain?"

Edam slumped onto the dusty couch across from her. "Yes. Two of my people watched him board the last shuttle. My guess is Amongeratix is headed for that big battle in the skies."

She refused to hope. "Your sources have been wrong before."

"True," he replied with no small measure of chagrin. "But multiple sources witnessed it. They also came upon the scene of another battle between those crimson witches and whoever was hunting Amongeratix."

"And?"

"He's not being hunted anymore. There were remains of at least two witches, a giant man missing his head and most of his shoulders, and a strange being cast in the rubble. Also missing his head," Edam reported. "Whatever happened, I'm glad I wasn't there."

"You saw the scene?" Porii asked. None of those described were known to her, furthering her lack of actionable intelligence.

He nodded. "Place looked like all the hells broke loose. I've seen plenty of destruction throughout the war, but nothing like this."

Edam paused, before muttering, "The answer is no."

"You don't know what I'm about to suggest," she replied. Creases deepened around the corners of her mouth.

"No, but I can guess based on that look and the honey tone you're using."

Leaning forward, Porii said, "This is our chance."

"For what?"

"To take down the Inquisition and restore order to Krenz."

Color left his face. "You're mad. There's no way our limited resources can take on the entire Inquisition. Not if any of us want to survive."

"We don't need to wipe out the entire order, just those in command," she insisted. "We'll never get another chance at this, Edam."

Exasperated, Edam threw his hands out before slapping his thighs. "How are we supposed to accomplish that? I've been in their headquarters. Security alone will be impossible to navigate."

"I can handle that."

Porii turned to find Thopos lingering in the doorway.

Edam sighed. "When did you get here?"

"Walked in right behind you," Thopos admitted. "Some of the boys used to work in a munitions plant. They know bombs. I reckon we could build a few large enough to take out the whole damned building."

"And die in the process," Edam snapped. "It's too risky."

Thopos shook his head, strands of greasy grey hair drifting in his face. "Not if we do it right. Use the access tunnels beneath the building. The ones servants and menials use. I can lead the teams to the right places once we secure accurate schematics of the place."

"What about the prisoners? You'll murder them as well," Edam pointed out.

Thopos shrugged. "I figure they're already dead. We'll be sparing the rest from torture, or worse."

Porii leaned forward. "How much time do you need?"

TWENTY-TWO

3215 A.G. (After Gods), Ferom Operations Base, planet Occanum.

The Shadow Hammers equipment filled a quarter of the massive landing bay. Over a hundred armored vehicles and short-range artillery capable of transitioning from indirect to direct fire sat in even ranks while mercenaries tended to them. Ammunition haulers sat behind each tank and howitzer. Infantry companies cleaned individual weapons and conducted maintenance on their light hoverjeeps. They were, in Fies' estimation, one of the more organized units he'd come across. They were also the force responsible for keeping him and his company alive.

He spied Bootleg conferring with his top lieutenants and headed that way. After the campaign on Mannus Prime Fies never expected to run into the mercenary outfit again. They'd done their part and were paid handsomely. Each survivor, all former Guards, took home a healthy paycheck. Several opted to retire, their thirst for vengeance slaked. Fies knew new blood filled the ranks. He didn't imagine any shortage in those willing to throw in for the right price. Desertion rates skyrocketed the longer the war drew on.

Bootleg saw him and dismissed his crew. Placing the half-smoked cigar back in his mouth, he said, "Well, well. Captain now, eh?"

"You know what they say, mess up and move up," Fies said without mirth.

"So I heard." Bootleg shifted the cigar to the opposite side of his mouth. "I've got the bulk of my people on the ground. We kept a small reserve in space. Where do you want us?"

Fies appreciated the direct approach the mercenary brought. Too many Guards stumbled under the multi-level command structure, leaving them unprepared. The Shadow Hammers had no time for pleasantries, though Fies suspected they'd be more than happy to take their pay for doing nothing.

"This bay is the largest entry point. Have your heavy armor and arty set up for any breach. You brought air defense?"

"Some. We're more of a smash and trash unit," the mercenary admitted.

Fies nodding, remembering their efforts on Mannus.

"Show me the enemy and unclip my leash. But yeah, I have a battery of AA."

"Keep them close to the main gates but not outside. This base has more than enough to keep any landing force away, for the time being. I anticipate having to get them involved though. Kale has more troops and more equipment. Sooner or later, they'll break through."

The cigar dropped as Bootleg's eyes widened. "Kale? Mobus Kale?"

"The same."

"Fuck all!" Bootleg gasped. "I thought he was dead."

"Far from it. He's the Guard commanding general," Fies said.

"And he's coming here?"

"What's wrong with you? He's just one man."

"Bullshit. He's a monster. Has been since he had his first platoon. I know more about Kale than I care to, and every instinct is screaming for me to cancel this contract, take my people, and forget this battle is about to happen," Bootleg said. "Look Fies, I like you. I do, but Kale is the sort who will expend every able body to accomplish his goal. Body counts don't matter. Once you become a target, you'd best start praying."

Fies cleared his throat, knowing praying wouldn't do much. "Relax. No one but us knows of this location. Even if Kale discovers our secret the main army will be too engaged with Torgast's armies to deploy a fraction of the strength needed to break us."

"You're not convincing," the mercenary retorted, attempting humor. "I only have five thousand combat ready troops. I can't fight an army."

"No one is asking you to." Fies folded his arms across his chest. With the space battle heating up, he knew it was but a matter of time before the ground war began. "What I am asking is for you to deploy your forces to best defend this base. Let me worry about the rest."

Bootleg's eyes darted back and forth. "Fine. I'll seal this base up and keep it that way. You have my word," he said. "Just make sure you leave a shrine for us if we don't make it."

"Biggest statue I can afford, paid for with your shares

naturally." Fies smiled. He made it a few steps before turning back to the mercenary. "Oh, and Bootleg, you might want to bring those space reserves down now. I imagine they won't last long once Kale turns his fleets loose on us. Just a suggestion. Let me know when you're in position."

A litany of curses followed Fies out of the hangar.

Far side of Occanum.

"Magnificent creations, brother." Tannus beamed.

Rank upon rank of automatons marched into the drop ships. Once deployed, they would form the heavy center of Torgast's armies. An anvil upon which the Prekhauten Guard would expend their lives and, if all went according to plan, draw Amongeratix to the front. The faceless creations carried quiet menace in their step. The march of steel shod feet echoed across the cargo bay. Instruments of war no human army had witnessed before.

"They will do their job," Sorrow affirmed. "Even against our dear brother's vaunted skulldaerth. Amongeratix will not expect such from us."

"Let us hope not. I want him focused on me."

Cocking his head, Sorrow asked, "Are you certain this is the best course of action?"

"No."

A single word. No fluff. No pretense.

Sorrow's gaze changed. Their exchanges through the years often involved fiery rhetoric and empty phrases as confusing as they were informative. The finality of Tannus' answer awakened a loneliness Sorrow hadn't felt since being abandoned by their father at the start of the Fall. A tremor nagged the back of his mind. "What are you planning?"

Tannus ran a hand through his hair, ensuring to scrape his nails softly across the scalp. His silence confirmed Sorrow's suspicions. Older brother or not, Tannus had a specific goal in mind. A destination from which repercussions would likely stretch across the stars for generations.

"Very well. Enjoy your subterfuge, brother." He resisted stating the obvious. That he would not be able to help. "Have you heard from the Oracle?"

"She is moving the comet into position. Your Paladin will be ready to strike when the moment calls for it," Tannus replied.

"I admit my surprise," Sorrow said. "She is a most sturdy character. The Forsaken Path has claimed all for centuries. For Elisa to come so far speaks of quality."

"Perhaps she will be the one to finally end our brother's maniacal reign."

"Then what?"

Tannus looked at him from the corner of his eye. "What do you mean?"

Rubbing his hands together, Sorrow said, "We have been trapped in a cycle of violence for so long. What happens once all of this comes to an end? Have you given thought to the future?"

"To what point? I seldom remember who I was before this," Tannus admitted.

"None of us are the same," Sorrow replied, then laughed. "If you recall, I once had flesh."

Tannus chose to ignore the comment. "I have long believed the universe will be best served without our interference, brother," he said instead. "We are relics of a bygone era, neither wanted nor needed. The last remnants of a race of tyrants. It has taken me long to come to terms with this."

"Allowing the humans to accept us as deities was a mistake," Sorrow said. The subject remained an open sore, even after all these years.

"It was."

The sounds of an army deploying across the plain took Sorrow back to the last lost to memory. Grand armies of their people facing off in a battle he nor his brother had imagined. The end of a species.

"It won't be long now." Tannus stirred, looking uncomfortable. "Amongeratix has departed his lair on Vau Prime. All the pieces are in play."

"Including your pet project?" Sorrow asked.

Tannus frowned. "He will arrive at the proper moment."

All Tannus had told Sorrow was that Tolde Breed was foreshadowed at the final battle.

"I see."

"Brother, I admit to looking forward to the end. My mind and heart have grown calloused since the Fall. I am so tired."

"As are we all." Sorrow ignored how Tannus never called him by name anymore. The slight lessened over time, to the point he found it amusing. Almost brotherly. "I must go see to my army. There is yet much to be done."

"Will you take the field with them?"

Sorrow fixed him with a gleaming smile. "I am not a fighter. You know that. Fear not. I have matters in hand, brother."

Abbey of the Order of Blood Witches, Acumensiis Comet.

"Wonder upon wonder, *farisi*! We have been aboard for days and yet I fail to process the greatness of all I witness!" Ah'muf proclaimed.

Elisa reached out, rubbing his back tenderly. "Never change, Ah'muf. I don't know how I would react."

He blinked several times before returning his gaze to the stars.

She smiled, her heart content for the first time in recent memory. "There was a time I looked to the stars and questioned everything," she said as a quiet reflection swept over her. "All the violence and bloodshed. Nothing made sense. Why me? Why at all? Have you any idea how long it took to accept this is the woman I was meant to be?"

"We do as we were created to do," he said, the words lacking conviction.

She fixed him with a queer look before breaking into a light laugh. "Ah'muf, what would I do without you? We have come so far, beaten and bruised every step and yet, no matter how daunting the task, you remain at my side."

A crimson tint flushed his dark face. "*Farisi*, I pledged myself to you. That oath remains. I will stand at your side from here unto your last breath. Though I confess to lacking the desire to confront that monster again."

"You and me both," she said. "It will all be over soon. I can feel it in my bones. We near the end of this impossible journey, Ah'muf."

"You sound sad."

Did I? Am I? Her eyes glazed over. "Perhaps I am. I spent years searching for answers after Sorrow left me alive. I was a child. Still innocent and filled with dreams. Now, here at the end, I feel… less. There is finality in what must come next, Ah'muf. Though the outcome is far from certain, I know I will no longer be burdened by the curse of the Three."

"That sounds like freedom to me," he whispered, eyes watery.

She nodded. "To whatever end. I wonder what I shall do once I am finally set free."

He reached for her hand, squeezing in silent reassurance. "We shall discover that together, my love."

The warmth in his tone was a blanket of comfort in her darkest hour. Could she dare? The future, ever distant and elusive, now sat upon the edge of a blade. A hunger arose, deep within the crusted edges of her soul. She yearned to be free. To know the truth of destiny finishing. Imbued by an endless stream of raw possibility, Elisa felt some of the weight burdening her for so long slip away.

Sister Deius Mlth, Mistress of Training, suffered beneath undulating waves of stress. Pressures intensified the closer they came to Forever Night. Achedaetha. The word froze her with fear. The possibility of Ruma Zzein serving as the unwitting agent of chaos, carrying the end of all things stripped Deius to the bone, tearing her certainties apart. The Order of Blood Witches stood on a precipice from which there could be no return. Tomorrow, she discovered, was never guaranteed.

Her earlier divinations with Sogress B'mn did little to assuage the anguish building. Deius knew what she had to do. What she must. Knew and was loathe to do so, for no one in their right mind stepped into the abbey's inner sanctum to confront the great mother. Yet what choice did she have? If the achedaetha had come, that ancient prophecy nearing fulfillment, the Order needed warning.

All she passed moved aside. Novices bowed in supplication. Sisters acknowledged her with smiles and warm words. An electricity lingered in her wake. A confirmation of dire moments fast approaching. Deius swelled within her robes. The situation demanded confidence, above all else, if she was to reach any form of conclusion. Stepping into the Grand Mistress' presence with a weak heart broke many Sisters through the years. Deius had no desire to suffer a similar fate. She reached the final corridor without incident, steadying her mind but failing to calm the turbulence in her soul. To her surprise, Deius found a pair of Sisters standing ward over the Grand Mistress' sanctum.

"I have come to seek audience with the Grand Mistress," she

announced.

Neither Sister moved. Deius felt their stares from beneath hooded veils. The silent scrutiny of her watchers.

"Is the Grand Mistress within?" she pressed. With Algiss Her turned traitor, Deius advanced to the second ranking member of the Order and, should it come to that, successor to the Grand Mistress.

A Sister stirred. "Yes, Mistress."

"I have urgent matters to discuss with her. Stand aside."

The Sisters parted to allow her access; Deius strained to learn their identities in passing. She had questions.

Once within the sanctum, Deius found the Grand Mistress staring into a cauldron of swirling colors and eldritch magics.

"Deius, I was expecting you."

Deius stopped short and clasped her hands before her. "Grand Mistress. I am afraid this matter must be addressed."

"Yes, I suppose it must." Resignation lurked within her tone. Ruma abandoned the spell, placing a keeping spell upon the cauldron to prevent days of work spoiling, and turned. "You come because of the prophecy."

"I have seen things, Grand Mistress," Deius admitted.

"And grow concerned for the future of the Order," Ruma finished. "The achedaetha is one of my greatest mistakes. Wrought from a time of vengeful ignorance tempered with the fledgling promise of liberation. Come, Deius. Let us discuss the future so I may assuage your fears."

"You have guards outside your doors, Grand Mistress."

"War changes us all, my friend. Algiss' betrayal continued reverberating through our ranks. I fear weaker Sisters will fall to temptation's promise. We must all take precautions in this perilous hour." She paused, studying her. "But this is not the reason for your visit."

Deius hardly limited this occasion to a mere visit. The future of the Order was a stake and, until she discovered the answers eluding her, the Mistress of Training could not rest or know peace. "Grand Mistress, I have foreseen the end of all things. After conferring with the Navigator, I have arrived at one inescapable conclusion. The time of the achedaetha has befallen. We are ripe for dissolution if this threat is not confronted and defeated."

"And you fear I am the architect of our demise."

Deius was shocked by the calm in her tone. The lack of venom or accusation. *Ever one step ahead of us all, Ruma Zzein. I admire and fear you in equal measure.* She nodded, not trusting her voice.

"Algiss Her is the other viable conclusion I assume," Ruma continued.

"She is. The way remained clouded, preventing me from ascertaining the truth," Deius said. "It would help if I knew the origins of this prophecy, Grand Mistress."

"Deius, you who have known me longer than most, we may dispense with formalities at this point. In here, I am Ruma."

Disarming smile aside, Deius struggled with the conflict of formality and friendship. She prided herself on her duty, seldom letting personal emotion interfere with necessity. When she spoke, the name trembled off her tongue. "Ruma, please explain the depth of my fears."

Smoothing down her robes, Ruma Zzein gestured for her to take a seat. "You, of course, know the history of our Order. Of what I was in those days before the Fall."

Deius did. They all knew the truth upon attaining the rank of full Sister.

"In those days, I worked hand in hand with Tannus and a select group of mortals to establish civility in a universe consumed with tearing itself apart. It was a frightening hour for all, myself included, for we did not know how much the humans, who had been reduced to chattel for so long, were willing to fight for themselves. Perched upon the verge of light and dark, I had many visions. From Forever Night to the achedaetha.

"Millennia passed without incident. My confidence in humanity strengthened and I built my Order. Some prophecies were forgotten, passed off as twisted dreams lacking fulfillment. Others came to fruition. I no longer controlled my thoughts. Yet for each passing hour I could not escape the burden of the final two. After a time, long after the rise of Conclave, much of what I once took for granted was forgotten. Unburdened by glimpses of demise, I allowed myself to dream again. Tannus always referred to me as the Oracle. In my heart I knew tranquility. Life flourished, as I envisioned long ago."

Her voice trailed off. "I forgot, Deius, my own warning. Forgot the ideation of one of us being the instrument of our demise."

"What changed?"

"Algiss Her. Had my thoughts been clear I would have

anticipated her betrayal. She has ever been a proud woman. Strong and charismatic in ways I never was. I should have seen the cracks. Noticed the quiet hunger for power simmering in her. I mistakenly allowed friendship to subsume common sense. Algiss' turn came at my weakest moment. She now has the strength to challenge me directly, and defeat me, Deius. That is important. She can beat me. We both know it. The only way to stop her is by ensuring the Paladin completes her destiny and Amongeratix is finally destroyed."

"You stray from my original intents," Deius reminded. "How can I be certain it is Algiss and not you who are the architect of our demise?"

"A test of loyalty, is it?" Ruma asked, a strange glint in her eye. She removed her hood and, for the first time, Deius saw the age in her face. "Very well. Come. I invite you into my mind. Search the fragments of my soul and discover the truth of the answer you seek. I lower my walls to you, Deius Mlth. Mistress of Training and, should ill befall, my most worthy successor."

Taken aback, Deius followed her example by lowering her hood as well. Trepidation trembling her questing fingers, fires burned within her veins. Sweat beaded upon her brow as she lost herself within the abyssal depths of Ruma Zzein's eyes. Life and death played out before her. Deius watched stars collide. Civilizations rise and fall and the glimmer of hope spring to life where none should exit.

There, in the infinite mirrors of eternity, Deius Mlth discovered her answers.

PGNV *Endless*, troop carrier enroute to Occanum.

Sergeant Icarn's disillusionment strengthened the closer they got to the coming campaign. Senior leadership cast a blind eye to the growing terror, swirling with depravity, among the junior ranks. He witnessed fellow Guards executed for expressing thought. Public punishments, which had been outlawed, were carried out daily in front of full battalions. Tensions rose. Guards were quick to sell out their companions in the hopes of retaining obscurity and remaining in Mobus Kale's good graces.

Determined to avoid scrutiny while attempting to maintain order in his company of recruits, Icarn watched and listened.

"Icarn! Stop daydreaming and focus."

Straightening in his seat, his gaze went to the massive sand table the operations staff built to detail the projected landing zone and initial engagement zone. Detailed miniatures of enemy troop placements and artillery positions dotted the ash-colored landscape. Icarn noted the desolate landscape, marred only by fragmented remains of buildings and gentle hills ravaged by time and orbital impacts. He found it difficult to believe a major civilization once occupied the planet, nor that he, of all people, was headed to the birthplace of the gods.

"The first wave will land in force here, establish and beachhead and push out to allow subsequent landings," the intel officer explained by moving his pointer from the center of the table to the flanks. "Casualties are expected to be high. Some units will suffer close to seventy percent in the first few hours."

Murmurs rippled through the leadership. Casualties were expected, but such rates would render those first units combat ineffective before the end of the first day. Those few survivors would be decimated. Icarn imagined few, if any, would be in any condition to return to the frontlines.

"Fleet is expecting stiff resistance from ground fire as we deploy," the intel officer continued without emotion. "Deflecting fire from atmosphere capable cruisers and frigates will attempt to eliminate enemy air defense capabilities to mitigate potential losses. Your key elements will be to push forward. Do not stop. Secure the landing zone and engage the enemy. Questions?"

Icarn had several, none of which felt appropriate to ask in present company. A resigned atmosphere lingered over the assembly. A finality in their eyes. Icarn watched his friends and comrades with interest. Some already believed themselves dead. Others worked through situations in which they might escape the coming carnage. For himself, Icarn felt numb.

"Study this map. Memorize every terrain feature. Your lives depend on it. Dismissed."

Icarn rubbed his jaw, mouth agape as the scale of the operation came into focus. One hundred infantry battalions, countless armor and artillery units. All scheduled to land on Occanum in three successive waves. He didn't know the Guard had so many active divisions.

"Fuck me, eh Icarn?"

Icarn closed his mouth to avoid looking like a fool. "That's one way to look at it."

Sergeant Avis sidled next to him. Massive in stature and personality, Avis was the quintessential Prekhauten Guardsman. Dedicated to the founding principles, he prided himself on putting the Guard first.

"A lot of people are going to get killed down there," Icarn added.

"More of them than us," Avis confirmed. "Fuckers should never have turned traitor."

"It's a crazy war."

Avis' head jerked back. "Crazy isn't the word I'd use. Have you heard how many people across the fleet the Inquisition has rounded up for suspected treason? We're riddled with poison. General Kale will clean it up. Guaranteed. Him and Amongeratix will cleanse the weakness from us and show us the path to true liberation. Imagine it, Icarn. A society operating the way it was meant to, without the stain of heresy."

"Good days," Icarn said without conviction. "If we survive."

Avis grunted. "We've been through tough times. Trust in the general. Trust in the plan. You'll see. Hey, you heard about Krilo?"

"No. What?"

"Executed in front of her platoon."

"What?"

Avis mimicked pulling the trigger. "Caught her with contraband traitor literature. She's been working with the enemy for a while now."

He didn't know Krilo well, nor Avis for that matter. They'd only worked together for less than a year thanks to the push to build combat ready divisions. What he did know didn't suggest Krilo capable of turning against them. She spoke softly, seeing to the needs of her people above all but the mission. Not necessarily kind, Icarn thought Juvan represented the best of them. And now she was dead.

Icarn glanced around to see if anyone else was eavesdropping or showing interest in their conversation. His mind raced. If the Inquisition latched on to any of them, they were doomed. It took little imagination to hear the sound of boots approach from behind. The stench of hot breath on his neck as the Inquisition set sights on him. "Are any of us safe?"

"Safe? This is war, Icarn. We've about to drop into the mouth of the beast. Pray to the gods your shuttle makes it in one piece. You ready for this?"

Am I? How can any of us be ready for something of this magnitude? "We'll find out soon enough. You?"

"I was born for this."

Doubting anyone but General Kale was born for war, Icarn bobbed his head.

Behemoth, enroute to Occanum.

Mobus Kale closed his eyes. The voices in his head raged. A cacophony of distraction when he longed for silence as Amongeratix's flagship marched across the universe. Peace nestled on the fringes of observation. A haunting reminder of the great trial his life had become as it neared fruition. Never in his life did he imagine such military might would one day rest at his fingertips. Power coursed through his veins, imbuing him with invincibility no enemy might break. Yet for all his desires, Mobus remained empty.

He caught the wisp of fabric drifting close, rousing him from his solitude. "You come unbidden, witch."

"When last I checked, I did not require permission from mortals to come and go as I please."

The sneer in Algiss Her's voice stained the air between them.

"Bother your master. Leave me alone. I have much to prepare for."

Algiss swirled around to face him, the power dancing off her robes forcing him to open his eyes.

"What do you want, witch?"

Nonplussed, Algiss folded her arms. "Wheels are turning, Mobus Kale. Much of what we once thought to be truth shifts in the approaching darkness. There is a new tide sweeping through your armies. You would do wise to listen to advice when freely given."

"I hear no advice. Just the flatulent taunts of a creature who should not exist."

"We are not alike, you and I, Mobus Kale, but we are aligned with the same powers," Algiss said. Oh how she longed to kill the man. "Amongeratix is strong, yet he is not infallible. He will require us to set aside our differences in the coming days if we are to defeat his brothers."

"Let them waste away on each other. I care not," Mobus snapped. "My test is against all those who thought themselves my betters. I shall break them without mercy. You shall bear witness."

"I care little for the whims of mortal men," Algiss replied evenly. "Already the weakness of our benefactor shows. He escaped the god hunter on Vau Prime, but I do not believe he has the strength to defeat both brothers and, if he should, Amongeratix shall be weak. Vulnerable."

"What are you saying?" Mobus cocked his head even as his mind began to race.

Algiss drifted closer. "Only this, the time of the gods has ended. Their pathetic reign faded under the despair wrought upon themselves. Should Amongeratix prevail, he will not be able to defend against our two great powers. Should we combine forces."

She left as swift as she arrived, leaving him mired in thoughts—an idea sparked. Should Amongeratix fall the universe would be at his fingertips to do with as he wished. He smiled for the first time in as long as he remembered.

TWENTY-THREE

3215 A.G. (After Gods), Confederation Headquarters Complex, Eger City, planet Mannus Prime.

Julian adjusted his tunic, trying his best to ignore the itch of the course fabric on his throat. A scowl etched upon his brow, he gave himself the final once over in the floor length mirror before strapping on his pistol belt and heading for the door. Dawn had yet to break, the first inkling of light a mere promise. Julian often found sleep difficult to attain, for the nightmares promised fresh torments should he close his eyes.

The horrors of Krenz followed in his footsteps. A bitter companion mocking from the edges of his vision. He continued losing weight despite the endless amount of food and drink at his disposal. Lines creased his face and hands, aging him beyond his years. His mind often wandered during those quiet moments alone, allowing him the sole opportunity to balance his mind and spirit.

He slipped into the hall, joining the Council guards already preparing for their day. Ignorant of the horrors happening halfway across the universe, they laughed and joked without concern. Julian envied them. He recalled those days of banter and mirth, when the war first started. The cocksure attitudes they all bore in thinking the war would not last to the end of the year. How many faces haunted his dreams now, years later? Julian found himself unwilling to grow close to anyone on Mannus.

"If I didn't know better, I'd say they made a mistake making you a fancy pretty boy."

He spun, breaking into a smile as he looked down at Sel's welcome face. "What can I say, they made me an offer I couldn't refuse."

Her grin mirrored his. They embraced. She was a valuable fighter and resource and, he reluctantly admitted, a friend. Several guards paused to stare.

"Sel, I didn't think I'd see you again so soon," he said.

"The Council keeps me moving around," she replied. "Unlike

you. How did they convince you to take up another command?"

"I owed a friend a favor."

Sel backed off. "Captain, it's good to see you, but I wish there were better tidings."

"What do you mean, Sel?"

Sel stepped closer. "There's talk about. Rumors mostly, but enough to get me on edge. Can we go to your office?"

"That bad?"

"Aye, that bad."

Julian led her through the corridors and ushered her inside his new office. Stomach growling, Julian wasted no time. "What's going on?"

"Remember the shape changer, Gedrick Silk? He's been given a job here in Eger City," Sel explained. "He's also on the hunt for Tinnus Har."

Julian stiffened. He hadn't been aware Har's location was common knowledge. "We've been tracking his movements for some time now. Have you contacted Gedrick?"

"I don't have that authority," she replied. "I only catch snippets in the ops center."

Julian frowned. It was all but impossible to prevent gossip from spreading, though the Council had taken great care to ensure all essential traffic was encrypted. False plays, under the direction of Tempest, kept enemy spies confused long enough for agents to intervene. At least in theory. Julian began having suspicions about the effectiveness of the plan.

"Sel, what I'm about to tell you stays between us," he began. The quiet consent in her eyes told him to continue. "The Council has given Tinnus Har just enough rope to hang himself. We are tracking his movements and who he meets with to root out any potential dissident cells capable of disrupting our operations. We have a man on the inside funneling information back to us." He felt guilty not telling her the full truth. Sel had been there through his darkest moments and deserved to know, but orders were orders. The less who knew of the fallen Inquisitor's involvement the better.

"You're worried about dealing with a bunch of people like us," Sel concluded. A glint of mischief flashed in her eyes. "Do I need to be concerned?"

"Not at the moment," he said, surprised she took the exclusion so well. "Everything is in place for when Har makes his move."

"Or you let me make a move and save the resources for more important issues. I only need a clear field of fire and one shot."

He smiled. "I'll keep that in mind. What brings you back to the palace? I didn't think being in the heart of government suited you."

"A few of us were called back for special assignment. With so many of the Council deployed forward to the coming campaign they deemed it prudent to heighten security ahead of the next voting session."

Julian winced. Security was already tight. The revelry of a new government forming had faded, allowing the hard work to begin. Fresh recruits continued pouring in, volunteers from across the stars willing to stand up to tyranny and secure their way of life. Julian envied their youthful ignorance. Politicians and diplomats from a hundred worlds crowded in for an audience, many petitioning to join the Confederation. Julian's crews were overworked and pushed to the edge of exhaustion. With no sign of let up, they were forced to hire too many raw recruits without undergoing the proper background checks.

"I'm glad you're back," he admitted. "I can use your talents."

"I'm sure I can dedicate the time." Sel cracked her knuckles. "What do you have in mind?"

"There's a big vote later today. Something about new planets joining our little escapade. I don't have the manpower I trust to secure the council chamber and ensure the complex is secure from potential threats. Too many of the new hires are green. Keep your ear to the ground. Watch and listen for anything threats," he said. "If you can."

"Shouldn't be a problem. I have a solid team working for me," Sel said. "I'll make sure this place is sealed tight and, if Tinnus Har happens to show his face, well…"

"Thank you, Sel," Julian said. "Now, I'm starving. Want to catch chow?"

"Sure," she replied. "It's been a while since we got the chance to catch up. Without anyone shooting at us that is."

"Is everything in place?"

Dowan Mun tensed as Har's question. He counted more than twenty men and women crowding around Tinnus Har. They were more rabble than gathering. Instincts screamed to turn them in. But there were others, others that had already gone to their assignments, though where and what was kept hidden from him. He shifted, impatient to learn more.

"Aye, Cardinal Seniorus," a man missing his right eye confirmed. "The boys are moving into place now. Sure promises to be a red day."

Tinnus Har lacked the man's enthusiasm. A string of defeats and near arrests left his confidence shaken. Local jails were filling with the man's compatriots, threatening to derail Tinnus' plans. Revenge smoldering in his soul, the former Cardinal Seniorus ached with resolve. He needed the new Council toppled, capitulated in the least, to begin his new universal order capable of challenging Vau Prime and restoring his name to grandeur.

Though his rival and erstwhile ally, Alain Nye, was dead and forgotten, the stain of his actions reverberated across the stars. Entire worlds burned, fanned by the flames of prejudice. While Tinnus desired to rule above all else, he needed as many worlds under his thumb for a true powerbase. Arthritis locked his hands, twisting the fingers and shooting intense pain up his forearms. The stench of roasting fowl further added to his misery. There's was a hominess he never cared for among these people.

"You are certain they cannot be traced back to me?" Tinnus asked.

Heads bobbed. "Aye, sir. Scrubbed them clean, we did."

Doubting their efficiency, Tinnus began pacing. Smoke drifted into his nostrils when he passed the open fire. He frowned, waving the odor away. Tinnus lacked any knowledge of Eger City, relying on the Inquisitor and his local gathering to move him through a string of safehouses. The Confederation security teams drew closer, each escape proving narrower than the last. Suspicions bloomed. Tinnus learned long ago to never accept a man at his word, but so far from home, and in an alien environment, left him with little choice.

"What do you think, Inquisitor?" Tinnus asked.

Startled, Dowan ran his tongue over his lower lip. "Well, it seems to me this is the perfect time to execute our plan. We cannot continue evading their guards without suffering casualties. Half the Council is rumored to be deployed to the war, leaving the rest scrambling over the scraps. This is the hour to strike."

Tinnus grunted. "And if not? I am risking everything on this, Dowan Mun."

"All reward comes with risk, Cardinal Seniorus," Dowan replied. "The question needing answers is whether you have the stomach to do what must be done."

"Indeed. I have played this game long before you were born, Inquisitor," Tinnus barked. "Do not seek to question my resolve." He turned on those pledging themselves to his cause. "What of you? Are you willing to give your lives if needs be to see me restored to power and usher in a new age?"

The mention of death clearly rattled some, leaving others more resolved than before. Madness lingered in their eyes. Tinnus huffed. "Then we must prepare, for the swift tide of vengeance shall descend upon this town with the fury of the new day. This day, my friends, we take back what was always our and begin the long crusade to dominate the universe."

Cheers sounded as he raised his hands.

The first golden rays of sunlight crested the eastern horizon, bathing the land in warmth and promise. At the heart of Eger City, in the newly christened Capital District, gathered those men and women sworn to restore order to a universe gone mad. The Council of the Confederation finished their morning rituals before heading to the conference chamber to debate the issues of the day. The palace was abuzz with anticipation as reports from Occanum streamed in. Battle was engaged. Soon the final answer would be laid bare.

Aliz longed to be on Occanum with the others. She desired to see the end with her own eyes. Perhaps then the nightmares would end.

Peeking between the ceiling height curtains circling the room, she spied several familiar faces already assembled and many more she didn't recognize. Aliz spent her life behind the curtain and now that she was forced to stand before the masses, unmasked and bare.

"We have to stop meeting like this."

"Captain," she replied without looking as footsteps came up from behind her. "I welcome the opportunity. Perhaps we can find a quiet corner of the universe untouched by war or human corruption. I can disappear and retire a simple old lady and you can at last open that bakery you've dreamed of."

"I admit the smell of fresh baked bread outdoes weapon grease and combat boots," Julian said, coming to stand at her side. "But our time is not yet finished here, Aliz. We've only just begun I am afraid."

She faced him. "Julian, once the hands of power sink their claws into you, they seldom let go. We've both seen this."

His head dipped in acknowledgment. "Are you ready for another day of boring meetings and endless debate?"

"How can anyone be ready for such? You know, after all these years I still can't understand why Lorenu did it," Aliz lamented.

Another group of diplomats and functionaries entered, taking their seats along the walls. Aliz found them no different from any one of a thousand she'd witnessed during her time in Krenz. Fresh faces filled with youthful ignorance. She wished them well, knowing the path forward was anything but guaranteed.

"Look at them, Julian. So young. So oblivious to the game they are entering. Was I ever that young?"

"War makes us older than our time, Aliz," he replied. "This will pass. The war won't last forever. One way or another there will be peace and you and I will benefit from our struggles, the losses, and the grieving. Somewhere in the future is our opportunity to heal. Perhaps with a little flour on my hands and a fresh loaf in the oven."

She gave him a light tap on the shoulder and a conspiratorial wink. Julian tensed, giving Aliz concern. She opened her mouth to ask what she did wrong when he pushed her to her knees.

"Get down," he said and drew his blaster.

"What is it?" she whispered.

Placing a finger to his lips, Julian slipped the safety off and stalked forward. A split-second later the chamber erupted in a hail of gunfire.

Screams drowned out the rising chaos. Bodies littered the floor, their blood mingling in pools. Sel gunned down as many of the enemy as she could, firing until their riddled bodies cooled on the once pristine marble. Flanking her was her handpicked squad of former Guardsman, all survivors from the Krenz insurrection. Their fury bleated out under the report of short rifles. Sel spied the first dissident drawing his blade and approaching the Council table. He died with a gurgle, blade clanging to the floor.

She moved, years of discipline in her actions. Trusting her people followed, she carved a path through the men and women attempting to storm the council members now huddled together in the back of the circular chamber. She spied movement on the parapet and took aim. Sel caught a glimpse of her attacker and stilled when Julian's face came into focus. She returned her attention to the last few dissidents.

"Keep one alive," she barked. "We need answers."

Her squad followed orders with ruthless enthusiasm. Soon the smoke weeping from the barrels of their blasters was the only thing moving in the chamber.

"Clear!"

"Clear!"

Sel kept her blaster trained on the sole survivor, delighting at the fear in his eyes as he trembled. A wet stain spread down his right thigh. *Good. Fucker. Thought you were coming in here and getting away with it. I'm going to enjoy this.* "Who sent you?"

His lower jaw quivered but no words came forth.

Sel crossed the space between them, jamming the hot barrel under his chin. The sizzle of cooking flesh turned her stomach. "You have one more chance. Tell me who sent you or you join your friends. Simple as that."

"Sel!" Julian shouted.

A dozen guards surrounded the Council in an iron ring.

She pressed harder. "I'm handling this, Julian."

Reaching her side, he laid a hand on her forearm. "Not here. Not like this. Take him to an interrogation room and do what needs to be done. We need to secure the chamber first."

Rage filling her, Sel relented. She wanted nothing more than to fire a round into the man's skull and be done. Leering at the man, she whispered, "You are fortunate he's here to stop me." Louder, she said, "Lup, Balk, secure his hands and get him somewhere we can have a quiet conversation."

She watched her men drag the dissident away before asking, "How did this happen?"

Several heads turned their way.

Julian ignored them and answered in a soft tone, "Doesn't matter right now. Get the answers from him any way you can. I'll see to the Council. Meet me back in my office in one hour."

"I want him arrested and brought before the Council immediately."

Concerned looks met Adris Moscasco's fierce demeanor. Blood

stained her tunic, her tussled hair lent her a wild look.

Gedrick Silk, sullen with guilt, nodded. "I will issue the warrant at once."

"Do we know where he is?" Standou asked, tweaking his mustache. "Clearly there has been a failure in information for so many of his hired thugs to have infiltrated our inner circles."

Gedrick ignored the barb. His confidence was already weak. "My inside man reported their location last night, though I doubt they have not moved since."

"Isn't there a way to track our man?" Tempest avoided naming the Inquisitor. But a handful knew of his role.

"I have teams scouring the city for their whereabouts. We will have Tinnus in custody by the end of the day."

"It would be a shame if he resisted," Standou suggested.

"Which brings me to another matter," Adris said ignoring what was being implied. "Few know Tinnus Har is on planet. Do we put the former Cardinal Seniorus on public trial and risk the good will of the people or try him behind closed doors and be done with the matter?"

"You know my answer," Standou replied.

Julian scratched flakes of dried blood off the back of his hand. "That makes us executioners. I didn't sign up for that."

"We are elected to keep the people safe," Standou scoffed. "Eliminating the threat that is Tinnus Har falls under that charter. What we like or want is irrelevant. The man is dangerous and, as long as he draws breath, a threat to all we seek to accomplish. I shall not lose sleep over one villain hanging. Neither should you, Captain."

Adris turned to Aliz. "What say you? He has proven a thorn in your side far longer than the rest of us."

Pursing her lips, Aliz replied, "Tinnus Har represents all that is wrong with the universe and surely deserves whatever fate this council decrees. But I question the moral authority of this body if we reduce ourselves to his tactics. Executing Tinnus Har, by whatever means we choose, renders us no better than him. I will have no part in that. Not after all I've suffered."

"He plotted to overthrow the Conclave," Standou pointed out. "You were there, Aliz. I should think you, of all people, would want revenge."

She fixed him with a sharp smile. "I prefer to go to the afterlife with a clean conscience."

Standou snorted.

"I fear none of us are worthy of that," Adris interjected before the conversation devolved. "Captain Julian, Gedrick, do what you can. Get us answers. You have the full authorization to requisition whatever forces necessary. Do not stop. Do not tire. I want this man brought before us."

They rose, preparing to leave when the door slid open and Sel burst inside.

"We have him!" she announced.

Gedrick straightened, eyes bright with relief.

For the thousandth time, Dowan Mun ran a finger over the stock of his blaster and contemplated putting a round in the decrepit old man's skull. He longed to be done with this assignment.

"We need to move," Tinnus Har whined. "It's been too long. Word would have reached us by now if they were successful."

"Give it more time. Surely the chaos and confusion will take time to sort out," Dowan replied. *One shot. A heartbeat and that's it. One of the great villains is no more. Give me a reason, old man. I beg you.*

"No. We must move. Now. The attempt has failed. Gather what little we have and get me out of this city," Tinnus demanded.

Several men rushed to obey, leaving Dowan staring at Tinnus with undisguised hatred. He drew his blaster. Slowly. The sound of metal scrapping worn leather. Tinnus' eyes widened as his body tensed. He mouthed the word betrayer.

Chaos erupted.

A door opened. Three loud bangs concussed all within the abandoned house. Smoke followed. Shouting. Tinnus and Dowan were shoved the floor under the unforgiving press of rifle barrels.

Bang.

Choking on the smoke filling the room, Dowan's last conscious thought rattled through his head. *Finally.*

Tenemenah, planet An'kuruku.

Uneasy silence choked them. No one spoke in the aftermath of the battle of the pass. Not when they buried Kaline. Not during the rest of the journey to the spaceport.

Fighting the demons in his mind, Tolde failed to shake the accusatory stare in Kaline's dead eyes as he lowered her into her sandy grave. He never wanted her dead, despite the spur of the moment fury almost responsible for tearing his group apart. Kaline best served the universe as a reminder of humanity's fragility. Of the impossibility of halting the forever war between good and evil. Though she was responsible for countless deaths across the stars, she was as much a victim as the rest of them. And now she would never know the sweetness of redemption. He wept for her and, perhaps, himself.

He decided to break the silence and, if done right, breathe fresh life into the beleaguered group. Casting his gaze over his now beleaguered friends, Tolde reconsidered the cost of all they sought to achieve. *Is the price worth all this*?

"Alessandra, where do you come from?" he asked. Sister Alessandra had been with him the longest and he knew nothing about who she was, what made her. Plus, out of their group, she seemed to be unaffected by the lingering grief.

Heads lifted. Sister Alessandra cocked her head, the shift of her robes focusing on him. "What do you mean?"

"I mean before you became a witch," he pressed. "We all come from somewhere. Had a family. A life before being dragged into this tale. Where did you come from?"

"I fail to see the relevance of your question," she replied. "All that matters is I am a loyal daughter of the Grand Mistress. My humanity is a relic, buried deep in the recess of forgotten memories."

Presha slid across the bench to come beside Tolde. Streaks of dried tears marred her face as she caught the silent relief in his demeanor. "Tolde is right. Our humanity is what makes us who we are. You were not always a Blood Witch."

"This questioning is pointless," Alessandra reaffirmed. "I belong to the Order. There was no life before that."

"Aren't you curious about your past? Who your family was?" she asked.

Ripples of power danced over her robes. Alessandra raised her arms. Tolde tensed, expecting a flush of power. Instead, Alessandra surprised them all by lowering her hood to expose her face.

"Very well. I came from a small farming family on one of the moons of Severus. I was the youngest of three daughters and the only one born with my gifts," she said, ensuring to meet their awkward stares.

"Once I began exhibiting signs of being different from my sisters, things changed. My parents became desperate to get rid of me. Or so it seemed at the time. A witch came not long after, though the damage had been done. Words spread through the community and my family was threatened with being turned outcast over me. I was a small child. All I wanted, all I knew, was family. Now, at the edge of despair, I became abandoned. The Order took me in. Trained me. Gave me a new home. I have not seen any of my blood kin for close to one hundred years and, before you ask, do not care to. That life ended for me long ago. All that matters is fulfilling my oaths to the Grand Mistress. Any other questions regarding my personal life?" She looked each in the eye. "Or shall we focus on the final task awaiting us?"

"Final task?" Ragan chimed in after clearing his throat.

"We are to rendezvous with the comet and provide escort for the Paladin when she attempts to fulfill her destiny and destroy Amongeratix," Alessandra announced.

Tolde's face twisted. "How long have you been sitting on this? I wasn't aware of this."

"Tolde Breed, you have been bestowed the gifts of the Grand Mistress, but you are not privy to our inner workings," Alessandra said. "My orders come directly from her."

Unsatisfied with that, Tolde searched his fragmented memory for any clues he might have missed. Frustration settled in, for so much had happened over the past four years he often forgot all but the prominent moments. Certainly his quest to discover his brother's killer, followed closely by the hunt for Kaline, contributed to his mental fog. He gasped.

"Tell me what you see," Alessandra said. "Where are you, Tolde Breed?"

The skiff rattled on.

Tolde blinked. "When I look too deep into memory I stand before a door. Steel, with no handle or hinges. I know I need to go through but I ... I am afraid to. As if a secret I am not meant to know lurks behind."

A softness overcame her, making him suspicious as he blinked again and fully cleared his mind. "Some doors are not meant to be opened, Tolde. You must look to your friends for what comes next. Focus on the moment. Our journey is nearly complete."

"Easy for you to say," he said, voice lowered in shame over the past.

"We're at the spaceport," Luma called from the pilot seat.

New life swept over them. The promise of leaving An'kuruku and returning to the fold invigorated them in unique ways. Ever the optimist, Ragan failed to keep his grin from filling his face. His infectious enthusiasm spread as the skiff pulled into an empty slot outside the main terminal. Tolde nodded at him in thanks.

Hurrying, they gathered their belongings and marched through the crowds to their landing pad. Instead of finding relief, they found their shuttle surrounded by a squad of Prefects armed and expecting them.

Tolde unsnapped his blaster. "What is the meaning of this, sergeant?" he asked. He felt the others fan out behind him. The raw power of Alessandra tingled the air.

"This your shuttle?"

"It is. Is there a problem?" Tolde asked. He ensured his hands remained in the open. The last thing he wanted was to shoot his way out of Tenemenah.

"I'm going to need you all to come with me."

"We are rather pressed for time, sergeant. If there is a fine, we will gladly pay it and be on our way."

The Prefects readied their rifles in unison. Emboldened, the sergeant said, "It's not that easy. See, there's been reports of a group of offworlders assaulting merchants down south."

"Is that so?" Tolde replied. "We've been on the far side of the city trying to secure a deep desert mining contract. Don't know anything about the south."

The sergeant gave them a knowing look. "I don't see any mining equipment and none of you look like miners. I'm going to need you to lay down those weapons and come peacefully."

Tolde sighed. "I'm afraid that's not going to happen. It would be best if you took your men and forgot you saw us."

A nervous rippled twisted through the Prefects. Fingers slipped into trigger guards. Barrels waved between targets.

Tolde's right hand dropped, lingering just above his blaster. "Don't."

The first shot went wide, sparking off a mechanical hauler. In that split-second seven men were gunned down. Tolde and Luma swept through the Prefects with military precision, ensuring none remained to shoot them in the back. Ragan and Presha hurried aboard the shuttle with the gear.

Sister Alessandra glided to the pad's entry and, muttering a spell, placed a hand on the cold metal. "I've sealed the doors, but it will not last. We should be gone from here."

"I couldn't agree more. Luma, are you finished?" Tolde asked.

Alessandra climbed aboard the shuttle as the engines began to whine. Luma Kai holstered her weapon. "Done. Fools should have read the situation before opening fire."

He agreed. Violence had become the currency of the age. "They were green. Too many died here during the first war. People are growing desperate the longer this civil war stretches. Maybe stopping Amongeratix will restore a measure of order and civility."

Even as he said the words, Tolde knew the power vacuum left in the wake of the Conclave threatened to devour entire star systems before the Confederation gained enough steam to return law and order to the population. If they won. Victory felt far from certain despite the assurances Tannus offered on Wexanos.

"Get us airborne. I want to be away from here before the rest of the city discovers what happened," he ordered.

Luma gave a clipped nod and hurried aboard.

Tolde stood alone in the center of the carnage.

TWENTY-FOUR

3215 A.G. (After Gods), *Brightstar*, Confederation Defensive Line, orbit over planet Occanum.

"You know, the longer we stay aboard this ship the more I'm having doubts about your decision-making capabilities," Time announced as they passed through *Brightstar's* dorsal section in search of a meaningful task up to their standards.

Krimpen Mass waved his concerns off. "We've been over this, Time. You need to get over your past. It's the only way to move forward."

"Dumbass," Time muttered. "Now what? We're here. Got nowhere to go and no way to do it besides. Might as well find something useful to do."

"Admiral did say she wanted us to stay out of trouble," Time said. "Where are we anyway?"

They looked around, learning the corridor they walked down looked exactly like every other one they had been through since boarding *Brightstar*. An endless maze of twisting passages painted gunmetal grey and void of characteristic.

"I think I can help with that."

Captain Odir appeared, striding down the corridor toward them.

"Cap'n, sir! Didn't expect to find you down here with the gearheads," Krimpen offered a sweeping bow successfully prompting an eye roll. Time elbowed him.

"August may have command of the fleet, but this ship is under my command. I think I have the perfect place for two strapping lads like yourselves." Odir beamed. "Gentlemen, follow me."

"Ah, mind if we ask where to?" Time asked as he fell in line and followed Odir. Krimpen on his other side.

"You are requesting positions of relevance, yes? Meaningful here at what we pray will be the final battle in this endless war." Odir turned the corner, leading them closer to the outer hull. "I have the perfect assignment, and it comes with a window view."

Time's dark face blanched. *How much did he overhear?* "We're not pilots, just so you know."

"Doesn't mean we can't learn," Krimpen added too quick to be casual.

Time rolled his eyes.

Odir halted before a wide double hangar door and gestured them forward. "No pilots required. Admiral Falchi deployed more than enough for the limited number of fighters and shuttles in the fleet."

They entered and paused a step inside the chamber. Stretched along their line of sight in both directions were massive cannons. Banks of ammunition, each shell larger than three men, sat nestled in storage containers behind each gun.

Krimpen offered a whistle, certain there was enough firepower to break a planet.

"Welcome to the combat heart of *Brightstar*," Odir said. A measure of pride in his voice. "With a little good fortune, this will be the hammer that breaks *Behemoth's* back and wins the battle. Your help will be much appreciated. Perhaps even necessary. Think of the stories they will tell. Of Krimpen Mass and his stalwart companion. Champions of justice." His demeanor changed, growing serious. "Make no mistake. This will be the toughest fight in modern history. Victory is anything but certain. Your help here could well turn the tide should matters go wrong."

"What do you want us to do?" Time asked before Krimpen had the opportunity to mess things up. Again.

"Integrate into battery command. Help when needed. Do this and I shall be eternally grateful, provided we live to tell about it."

Time nodded. "You can count on us, sir."

Odir turned to leave, pausing to look upon his gun crews.

"Think we'll get statues out of this?" Krimpen asked Time looking around with wide eyes.

From the door, Odir called, "The largest you can imagine, Krimpen. Choose a planet and I'll pay for it myself."

"Shit," Krimpen replied so only Time heard. "We really are going to die."

"Yup."

"I should have stayed in bed. Maybe joined the ground forces."

Time fixed his friend with a curious stare. "What would you do there? You're not a soldier."

"No, but at least if I get shot, I just have to fall a few feet." He shuddered. "Up here … How long do you suppose we can hold our breath?"

"Idiot," Time slapped him on the back of the head. "Who's in charge here?"

Heads turned, all with the same thought. Who in the gods were these people?

Blackheart kept walking. His heart thudded in his chest. A tingle electrified his right hand. The whisk of military trousers chasing him down the corridor threatened what little hold on reality he had. Impressive as Brightstar might be, Blackheart swore he heard the ghosts of crews long past chiding him from the bulkheads. The last thing he needed was a mental drubbing by the one woman he considered a friend.

"Vicente, wait!"

He threw up a hand and walked faster. "I said forget it, Sharlyn. This is my problem, not yours. Just let it rest."

"How am I supposed to do that when we stand on the eve of battle, you damned pirate?" she fired back.

The insult halted him. Blackheart spun on her, wounded. "That's all I am? A criminal. Murderer. Worse? I thought our shared experiences meant something."

August flexed her hands in frustration. "Did they? I trusted you. Brought you into my confidence and requested permission to seek you out because I knew I was going to need your help in this fight."

"You're not wrong there," he said with a hint of snark returning. "But you can't fight my battles for me, nor are you privileged to know everything I say or do. Not even on your ship."

He fumed, impotent with his emotions and realities. He thought there was a spark between them. An opportunity to escape his current life and start anew. Hurt seeped into his eyes.

"I… I was wrong. Forgive me. I spoke in haste," August said, rebuked.

He stared at her, caught off guard.

Awkward silence settled between them as a pair of crewers rounded the corner, jerking to a complete stop before reversing their direction and hurrying from the line of sight. August almost laughed.

She remembered her early days, fresh in uniform and in the fleets. Stumbling upon a senior officer proved a terrifying moment. If only those two knew the ridiculousness of the moment. Had they been just a little earlier they would have witnessed her apologizing. The thought of that tale spreading through the ranks as *Brightstar* lurked in the dark space behind Occanum amused her to no end.

"Did you just apologize?"

"You'll never hear it again."

He made a face of concession. "Fair enough, but I'll always have this moment."

"You're still not going to tell me?"

He shook his head. "Tannus told me not to."

August hadn't expected Tannus' interference. Command of the fleet belonged to her, but this was still his ship. Their interactions proved limited, especially now he had his brother at his side and a war to wage. In fact, she had no idea whether they were still aboard.

"I know that look." Blackheart waggled a finger. "We have more important tasks at hand. Tannus can handle himself. You and I need to figure out how to get this bucket of bolts in the right position to counter whatever Amongeratix throws at us."

"Precisely what I'm trying to do," August replied. "I need you on the bridge with me."

"I'm flattered."

"I'm not asking."

He stiffened, squaring on her with pinched eyes.

"Look Sharlyn, you're a capable military commander. You know doctrine and how to fight what we have coming. I'm a pirate. Stand up fights aren't in my best interests," he said, the words ringing hollow. "You need Odir. You don't need me."

"That's where you're wrong," she said. "We've been through this. You bring a rogue element to the fight our enemies won't expect. Why are you insistent on hiding now the storm has begun?"

He shifted his weight to the other foot, refusing to meet her gaze.

August tensed. *Enough is enough.* "Speak up. I'm done playing games, Vincente. Answer the question or spend the rest of the war in the brig."

"Fine," he snapped and threw up his hands. "What do you want to hear? That I feel inadequate? That I'm worried about failing, of letting you down when you need me the most? Sharlyn, I'm not cut from the same cloth as you. I'm … I'm scared."

She softened. "You fool, we're all scared. I wouldn't trust a sailor under my command if they weren't. But it doesn't matter. All you need to do is let instincts take over and push forward. We don't fight because we want to. We fight because we must."

"But I'm not a soldier," he pleaded.

"Like I said, it doesn't matter. You may not have the training, but you've been in thick of things before. Or have you conveniently forgotten your role in the battle of Hawker's Gate?"

"No one can change the past," he whispered. "But I can hope for a measure of redemption."

"Let's find out together," August offered.

Hurried footsteps echoed down the corridor, sliding to a halt not far from them. August turned as the young sailor snapped a rushed salute.

Chest heaving, he reported, "Admiral, Captain Odir requests you return to the bridge. Enemy fleets are arriving in force."

August returned the salute and gave Blackheart a careful look. "Well, pirate, are you ready to do this?"

He offered a wry smile. "No, but I don't suppose the enemy is going to change his mind. Might as well get it over with."

"That's the spirit. Sailor, please inform the Captain we are on the way."

Indominable Bridge.

"Order the fleet to deploy in combat formations and prepare for engagement," Falchi ordered. "Samuel, I want task force commanders free reign to engage as prudent. Overall command remains with *Indominable*."

Samuel clasped his hands behind his back and relayed the orders.

All intelligence pointed to their fleets being outnumbered three to one and twice again as many ground troops. Fears ran through the Confederation ships. Furtive glances at commands issued. Knuckles whitening as engines gunned. Sweat pouring down faces and backs among the gun crews as they loaded their weapons and prepared for the greatest battle of their time. Falchi did what he could to instill confidence among the crew. They looked to him for guidance, now in their darkest hour, and trusted in his ability to keep them alive. Additional pressures placed on him by the Council and the declining Khe-Zhehan forced him to take on more than he was prepared for.

"Fleets are deploying into strike forces, Admiral."

"Very good, Captain. Tactical, bring up all the current engagements on the system edge. I want ship and casualty counts. Enlarge enemy deployments and plot predictions," Falchi ordered.

Experienced eyes poured through the data, noting the increasing size of the enemy force pushing into the system. His initial screen fleets were not intended on delaying the entirety of Vau Prime's navy. Still, he found encouragement in noting the number of wrecks and dead ships drifting at the edges of the minefield. *Would that they were troop ships instead of warships. Perhaps then Torgast would stand a better chance.*

"No troop ships though," Samuel mused.

Sadness filled Falchi's eyes. "A shame, isn't it?"

"Admiral, all of this is a shame. Brother fighting brother, and for what?" he replied. "One thing is for sure. I wouldn't want to be on the ground when Amongeratix brings his armies."

"I concur, but we must focus on what is heading our way," Falchi reminded. "We have enough trouble barreling at us. I must admit, I am surprised with the number of ships we still have in the fight."

He saw Samuel's surprise from having admitted that it aloud. Drukali's task force wasn't necessarily a suicide mission but none in command expected many survivors. That any ships remained in fighting condition came as welcome relief. He was grateful.

"Drukali reports four serviceable ships. The others are combat ineffective," Samuel added. "Sir, the last two ships are holding the line. What are your orders?"

Studying the graphics, Falchi saw a desperate situation. Debris fields scattered between the opposing forces, occluding scanners and intercepting much of the exchanging fire. A large portion of the minefield was gone, detonated by Drukali's maniacal ploy to lure enemy ships in. Smaller vessels unleashed withering fire on the outskirts, but the mines were spaced far enough apart to prevent a chain detonation. Falchi admired Drukali and promised to promote the man, should any of them survive.

"How much longer can they hope to hold?"

"Calculations suggest a few more hours," Samuel said. "Sooner or later Amongeratix is going to throw his heavy ships into the fight."

"And those corvettes won't stand a chance," Falchi replied. "Samuel, order them back. I'll not waste lives for no reason."

"Aye, sir. Comms, issue the order. Get those ships out of there and regroup with the rest of their task force at Ferom to refit and rearm."

Warning alarms filled the bridge—a dozen capital ships were entering the system.

Capital District, Krenz, planet Vau Prime.

Edam Boone watched with rapt fascination as Thopos and a select handful assembled the components to what they promised to be the mother of all bombs. He expected an explosion to end this endeavor in short order and struggled with the notion of fleeing before the inevitable. Only the stern presence of Porii Daam prevented him from turning coward in front of his people. The smell of gunpowder and chemical choked the air, furthering his misery.

Forced to contemplate his life's decisions, Edam cursed the late Zoraq Darc for ensnaring him while he was still young and allowing the cruel bite of temptation seep in. He'd leapt with both feet, uncaring where he landed. Criminal enterprise remained strong in Krenz's underworld and Edam did his part. His efforts resulted in enormous wealth and influence among the organization. So when it came time to appoint a successor he was the logical answer. Little did he guess he assumed command of a dying beast struggling to stay one step ahead of the end.

"Shit! Look out!"

Edam flinched. It took every ounce of control not to hide behind the fallen Cardinal. Laughter broke out among the workers. Edam's fright turned to anger. He glared at them. A toothless bite serving to increase the laughter. From his side, Porii broke into a fit of laughter.

He pouted. "Funny."

Thopos strolled over. "Just a bit of fun the boys cooked up. We all agreed you look too tense. You're making us nervous."

Nervous? You fucking idiots. You have enough explosives here to take out three city blocks. You should be nervous! "Am I supposed to be anything else? This isn't the sort of thing we are known for."

"It will be," Thopos replied with a shrug.

"He's right," Porii added. "Should this succeed, our efforts will be remembered for generations. They may not record our names, but we shall forever be known as the ones responsible for ending the tyranny of the Inquisition and giving the people of Vau Prime a new hope."

"And if we fail?"

"Then it won't make one bit of difference. Ezekiel Goethe and his nest of villains will maintain their iron grip until nothing remains but the dust of broken dreams."

"You're not lessening the sting," he remarked with a raised eyebrow.

She fixed him with a level stare. "I wasn't trying to. Edam, you are a good man. I realize that now. But good men need more than intentions to make a difference. You must be willing to sacrifice if true salvation awaits. We all agreed this is our best course of action, in fact our only one. It is far too late to turn back now."

"She's right, boss. This is the only way. We do this right and no more Inquisition. Folks can be free again," Thopos added.

"I understand that, but it doesn't help much," he admitted. "Say this works. What then? Who fills the power vacuum we're creating?"

"Such matters will resolve themselves," Porii said. "I fear there is no return to the way things were. The universe has shifted. The old power constructs collapsed under their own weight. If humanity is to evolve it must be through politics and the good will of the people, not religion or fear."

Edam puckered his lower lip as he contemplated this. Porii Daam had devoted her life to ensuring adherence to the gods and, when it proved necessary, the decrees of the Inquisition. For her to abandon all she once stood for humbled him. He seldom considered others before being thrust into the heart of this by Aliz. His original sole purpose was to look after his people, the rest of the universe be damned. What a difference a few years made.

"We've seen what internal politics accomplish, Porii," he replied. "They helped bring down the Conclave."

"Did they?" She cocked her head. "Or was it Amongeratix's continued influence over those in power who swallowed decency and the rule of law?"

He'd done his best to forget the twelve-foot-tall relic from humanity's grim past. "How long do you suppose he worked to twist those in power to his will?"

"Who can say? Surely as long as I have held my robes," she replied. "Amongeratix has ever been a thorn in our sides. History and legend collided somewhere the day he was captured and imprisoned. I managed a little research before the collapse. It appears he has been prevalent in our politics for the past fifty years, though I cannot say to what extent. What I do know is he has corrupted the minds of many over the years, pushing us into this impossible scenario from which, I fear, there is no return."

"You're full of cheer," Edam commented.

Porii bristled. "This is no time to balk. We stand upon the precipice of irrevocable change. With no way to go back, we must press ahead and shape this new universe in the image we wish."

"You're suggesting we attempt to assume control if this works?" He gestured toward the bomb. Thoughts of power often entertained his dreams, but he never once imagined making them reality.

"When," she corrected.

"Porii, we're criminals, not leaders."

"Are you not?" she asked. "Who has stepped up in the absence of order? Who goes out of their way to ensure the people are fed, have a safe place to stay or medical supplies? Who, in this wretched world, continues giving more than they have to keep the people alive in the strained hopes of outlasting the chaos and violence?"

"I—"

"You, Edam Boone. It has always been you and your predecessors."

"And for it you branded us criminals," he snapped, uncomfortable. "I never understood what Zoraq found in allowing Aliz to infiltrate our ranks the way she did. Even before the war she helped place us in position to execute our current operations."

"I admit I do not know Aliz, only her reputation. She found something in you everyone else overlooked."

"What would that be?" Edam asked. He held his breath, eyes boring into the Cardinal. The bustle behind them as the others continued assembling the bomb that would alter the face of Krenz authority forever drowned out to a low murmur. They all sought answers. A purpose. A meaningful existence, especially now. If it came from a woman once considered their enemy, so be it.

"Quality."

He saw the single word answer strike chords in those within earshot. Postures straightened. Heads held higher. Porii nodded at him before she returned her attention to the operation.

"Let's end this," Edam declared, conviction in his words. "I am tired of cowering beneath the blanket of fear the Inquisitor General smothers us with. Let the three of us usher in a new age. One where peace and justice may take root."

Porii gave him an appraising smile.

Thopos chuckled.

Quality indeed.

Abbey of the Order of Blood Witches, Acumensiis Comet.

Magic wove between her fingers and hands in ribbons of multi-colored patterns. Sonic vibrations danced in the air, striking deep into the very heart of their souls with limitless inspiration. Joy passed, imbuing those precious few seated in a semi-circle in ways neither explainable nor deniable. This, Ruma Zzein promised, was the true way of the universe. If only others understood the way she did.

A honeyed aroma kissed the air, seducing them with hints of paradise. Elisa didn't know whether this was possible or not but, for the briefest of moments, allowed her heart to reach for the tranquility among the patterns. Fresh strength flowed into her, woven from the Grand Mistress' care. She closed her eyes, allowing the magic to consume her mind and frame. When next she opened them, Elisa felt like a new woman.

"How?" was all she managed.

Ruma's eyes remained closed. "We are symbiotes with a higher power. The universe shares its gifts with us, and we accept with open hearts and clear minds. Few outside of the Order know these ways."

"Is that because they do not understand magic?" Elisa asked. She blushed immediately after, lowering her gaze.

Ruma's golden laughter bore an infectious taint. "No, my dear. It is because so few bother to listen. Humans are creatures of great strengths and equal weakness. Seldom do they look beyond the frayed edges of their own mortality, even as they dream of eternity. If you close your eyes and open your inner being you too will hear the universe whisper to you."

"What does it sound like?"

Ruma's eyes opened, and she smiled. "Like a song."

"It sounds perfect," Elisa whispered.

"And so much more," Ruma agreed. "But we are not here to discuss the nuances of my haggard Order. Elisa, we are little more than relics of a time when humanity struggled to find purchase among the stars. Once this war ends, I intend on taking what remains and exploring the uncharted regions of the universe. Perhaps even finding a measure of solace I have lacked for so very long." Her smile weakened. "It is but a dream."

"An old friend once told me he dreamed of winter. I never knew what that meant. I think I don't even as I say it." Elisa shook her head, the ghostly image of Mollock Bolle grinning at her from the dust of time.

"Winter lies at the heart of every trial," Ruma said. "We have entered the long winter, so many dread and so few are equipped to handle. But you, Elisa, you have at last come into your own. Soon we shall arrive at the transfer portal where you and a team of select individuals will travel to Occanum to fulfill your role as Paladin. What happens after you leave my sanctuary is beyond my ability to keen."

Absorbing the words without comprehension, Elisa was desperate to learn more. To know what was expected of her when she at last confronted Amongeratix. An unending stream of questions assaulted her, threatening to undo all Ruma sought to strengthen her with.

"I see the turmoil in your eyes and would offer what comfort I may," Ruma soothed. "Elisa, I cannot say how you will accomplish your task, only that you must use the dagger to finish Amongeratix by your own wit and strength. Nothing you are about to attempt will be easy. You will soon discover unique torments await and I am unable to assist directly."

"Can I really kill him?"

Ruma considered the question. She appreciated Elisa's directness though worried it might come to cause her harm on Occanum. *And I shan't be there to help. Ah, the cruel vagaries of life. You give with one hand and take with the other.* "If you can't, no one can. Destiny is at your back, Elisa. And you will not be alone."

"I would not take Ah'muf with me," she replied. "Not for this. He is a dear man and wears his heart on his sleeve, but I fear that devotion will only get him killed."

Though she longed to tell him to stay away, Elisa knew the words would fall on deaf ears.

"I was not referring to your love interest," Ruma countered. "I speak of those who are coming to your aid. Heroes rise from among our ranks. They will do their part to ensure you get close enough to use *Grimfurvor*."

"What heroes?"

"I, for one," Paradise Tear declared from her place in the corner of the dark room.

The giantess sat with her legs folded beneath her, hands open and upside down on her knees. Her eyes were closed, head tilted back as she bathed in the glory of the universe.

"I am thankful, Paradise." Elisa bowed her head. Having one of Amongeratix's kin at her side bolstered her confidence even if they were not close. "But I doubt even you and I are enough to combat the entirety of his devilry."

Ruma placed a motherly hand on Elisa's thigh. "Others are coming. Soon. All loose ends are raveling again. The tapestry of space and time shall once more be whole. This I have foreseen. All it takes it a spark of hope and faith in yourself."

Easy for you to say. I've spent a lifetime mired in doubt. How much more do I have to give? This precious universe of yours has already taken so much from me. Come on, universe. Give me a sign.

As if on cue, the great oculus on the roof of the inner sanctum opened. Elisa gazed upward and felt her jaw drop. There, in the near distance, sat an undulating maw of reds and greens.

Ruma beamed. "Elisa, welcome to Kar-edora. The Heart of the Universe."

Elisa wasn't sure if the whistle breaking the scene was hers or not. Regardless, she had never felt smaller and stronger at the same time. Perhaps she had a chance after all.

TWENTY-FIVE

3215 A.G. (After Gods), Plains of Haddash, planet Occanum.

They marched. Twenty thousand armored creations stomping in unison across the ash covered plain. Soldiers paused their preparations to watch, for never had such a sight been seen. A clarion call, gilded and inspiring, broke across the horizon, lifting spirits and providing hope.

Torgast watched with rapt fascination as the army of automatons marched across the plain, ghosts from a bygone era. Watching them inspired visions of what Occanum must have looked like when the armies of the gods took the field for that fateful battle. Torgast suddenly felt small, as if the entirety of humanity was little more than a jest. His left hand trembled. Minute at first before spreading up his arm. His breath caught as the clarion roared, louder. Stronger. He wondered if human endeavor might ever be capable of producing such a sight. As if to emphasize his emotion, the first golden rays of light crested the horizon.

"I never thought I'd see the day," he murmured, bewitched.

"Magnificent, aren't they?"

Torgast turned, surprised to find Tannus behind him. Lurking just beyond was the Bloody Man. He offered the man a sidelong glance, even as his mind failed to reconcile the concept of surviving perpetual bleeding for millennia.

"That they are, my lord."

Tannus waved him off. "I am no lord. Leastwise not over humanity."

"Habits," Torgast admitted. "Military men tend to look to higher authority hoping it might ease the burden of leadership during trying times."

"These are nothing if not trying," Tannus mused. "Sorrow and I have decided to take the field in the hopes of drawing our brother forward."

Torgast's stomach clenched. "You truly think Amongeratix will meet you on the field? It seems far easier to bombard all of this out of existence and go home."

"He's dour," Sorrow spoke up. "I like him."

A dark look passed over Tannus' face. "Forgive my brother. He tends to enjoy the dramatic, though his automatons are a stroke of pure genius. They will do well to even the numbers when Amongeratix lands." He paused. "To answer your question, yes. Bombing us out of existence would be prudent, if not for his ego. Amongeratix was ever consumed with pride. He allows it to slander his opinions and obfuscate situations. He will come. The need to finish out long battle is too strong, within us both."

Torgast's thoughts turned inward. Somewhere, amidst the endless backdrop of space, General Mobus Kale burned with similar intensity to get even with Torgast. What Torgast knew of the man suggested he too longed for personal combat. The strategy for Occanum depended on it that fanatic arrogance. Torgast ran through the numbers of anti-aircraft batteries deployed across the continent. Enough to down a fleet of ships. The enemy army would pay dearly for that arrogance.

"I never imagined witnessing the Three do battle," Torgast replied, his voice dropping to a whisper. "Now I stand among two titans and fear the arrival of the third."

Stuffing his hands in his jacket pockets, Sorrow glanced at Tannus and commented, "You should tell him about the witches."

Torgast didn't want to know and chose to cut in with another question. "With those machines be enough to break the enemy lines?"

"I am afraid their design is for something far sinister," Tannus replied. "Amongeratix has a host at his back. They are genetic mutations crafted over centuries and sworn to his service. They will not tire nor cease until they fulfill their master's desires. They are the skulldaerth. An army with but one purpose; break the enemy. Sorrow's automatons will counter their strike. Renegade Blood Witches will be countered by the Grand Mistress, though I assume random casualties will sprout from that engagement. General, it is for human to fight human."

The last rank of automatons halted in position and powered down. There they would stand until the hour of their need. Torgast failed to envision their might sweeping through enemy ranks. His gaze fell upon those battalions assembled on either side of the phalanx. Armor and infantry massed. Unlike the campaign on Mannus, there would be no expansive trenches dug on Occanum. Minor defenses were erected to take the brunt of incoming fire, but Torgast argued against the digging. He wanted to avoid the long stalemate of the Mannus campaign and be free to wield his army as needed.

"Are you prepared for this?" Tannus followed his gaze. "They are a fine army. One of the best I have witnessed."

"Can any of us be prepared for what is to come?" Torgast said. "I have no idea how large the enemy force is, only that we will be severely outnumbered. My one hope is General Kale will fight with standard Guard doctrine, thus allowing us to counter with unpredictability. The air defenses should eliminate a healthy portion of assault craft. Who knows, maybe enough those who manage to land will lose heart. Wouldn't that be a day?"

"Better armies have broken for less," Tannus agreed. "You know my brother and I shall not fight with you. We are here for specific purpose."

Torgast fixed the giant with a baleful look. "What chance have we without your might at our side?"

"Fear not. This is the hour we have long awaited."

Torgast considered the words, struggling to find meaning among them. He had seen and done things his younger self would never have imagined. Each deed a step in the long march to this point. How would history remember him? The hero of the Confederation or a failure responsible for dooming humanity?

"You speak in riddles I am not equipped to unravel," Torgast said. "Yet what else can I do? I will trust in you to see us through this. The army is as prepared as it can be, given the circumstance."

He paused as a hoverjeep soared up to them. A young captain dismounted, rushing to his side.

"Captain?" Torgast prompted when the man just stared.

"Ah, yes. Sir. Admiral Falchi reports the enemy fleets have arrived in system and have begun conducting assault operations to reach the planet," he said with a salute. His gaze never wavered from the Bloody Man.

Sorrow enlarged his eyes and popped his head forward. Laughter sprang from his lips upon seeing the man stagger back. Tannus glared at his brother, who shrugged innocently. Torgast ignored them.

"It appears the battle has begun," Tannus said.

"So, it has," Torgast agreed. "Thank you, Captain. Dispatch this through command headquarters. It won't be long now."

Another salute and the man hurried back to the hoverjeep. Torgast watched him speed off, his mind already racing through what must be done.

"Gentlemen, I will leave you now. My work is just beginning," he said.

"Fortune follow you," Tannus replied.

"And you."

Tannus waited for Torgast to depart before addressing Sorrow. "Come, let us finalize our preparations for Amongeratix. Once more Occanum will ring with the sounds of battle. I pray our ancestors forgive us for what we are about to do."

"I don't see that happening," Sorrow quipped.

Confederation Flagship *Indomitable*, planet Occanum.

Falchi watched as an endless tide of warships entered real space. Unwilling to allow his enemy time to gather tactically, he ordered his fleets to engage at will. Ships burned from missile and laser strikes. Others detonated, casting their debris into the cosmos. Not a single enemy ship entering the system went unscathed, yet more funneled into the engagement area. Data flowed in increasing flurries, so much he failed to keep track of it.

"Admiral, we are holding the line but there is a danger," Samuel reported.

"I see it. The enemy has yet to throw the full weight of their capital ships at us." Falchi ran a finger across his chin. "What is the minefield's strength?"

"Eighty-seven percent, sir. More than enough to stall what we have facing us."

Unless it was a trap. "Captain, do you remember the derelict ship in the Mannus battle?"

"Sir?"

Falchi gestured at the minefield on the main star map. "What is to stop them from executing a similar maneuver and wiping out the mines and whatever screening ships we have too close to the location?"

Samuel blanched. "Tactical, order all covering squadrons to

pull back to secondary positions. Get them away from that minefield immediately!"

As Samuel gave the order and Falchi turned back to the data, a monstrosity from their worst nightmares emerged into real space and plowed into the minefield at full speed.

Hands clasped behind his back, Grand Admiral Achen Tuth watched with delight as the minefield detonated. The rippling explosions caught every ship in the area, from small fighters to beleaguered corvettes and cruisers on both sides. He deemed them acceptable losses. The freighter was a space hulk. Engineers worked tirelessly to join seven massive cargo haulers into one monstrosity and then pack it with enough explosives to destroy a planet.

"Order Group Alpha to engage. I want the battlespace cleared," he barked to the bridge crew.

At his side, Mobus Kale watched with disinterest.

"You see, Kale, the system will soon be ours," Tuth boasted. "I will control the space lanes in short order. You may prepare for deployment."

"The battle is not won yet, Tuth." Sister Evangaline, now assigned as Kale's liaison, casually announced before Kale could reply. "You would do well to remember Lord Amongeratix's orders."

He shot a fierce glare at the Crimson Sister. "When last I checked you fallen witches held no sway over my command. Go back to your master where you belong and leave the fighting of war to men."

Power cackled off her crimson robes. Achen met her stare for stare, unbending.

Evangeline cocked her head, the shift of her robes the lone sound on the now silent bridge. "You play a dangerous game, Admiral."

"Grand Admiral," he corrected. "As it stands, this is my bridge. My fleet. I have been given full authority to conduct this campaign as I see fit by your Lord Amongeratix. I suggest you take up any issues with him. Now, if there is nothing else, get off my bridge."

Evangeline raised a bony arm, the fingers pointing at his chest. Despite his bravado, Achen Tuth flinched. Her laughter danced across the open air, wicked and filled with dark promise.

"General Kale is your army ready to deploy?" she asked without taking her gaze from the admiral.

"It is," he replied.

"Prepare to deploy. Lord Amongeratix wishes to establish a landing zone immediately."

Kale ignored her to instead remark to Tuth, "Enjoy your space toys, Tuth. I go to make war like a real man."

Achen Tuth contemplated having their shuttle destroyed the moment it cleared his bays. Doing so would send a clear message to both Amongeratix and those meddling witches. He was a man of destiny. One unclaimed by wild powers having no place in the mortal universe. Resuming his gaze at the last remnants of the minefield erupt. A scattering of Confederation ships limped away.

"Order all heavy ships to push forward," he barked, ignoring the witch and Kale as they left. "Clear a path for the troop transports." *The sooner they debark the sooner I can return to wiping out the rest of this pathetic fleet.* "Open a channel to *Behemoth*. I wish to speak with Amongeratix."

"He will betray you should you provide a long enough leash," Algiss Her said.

Amongeratix did his best to ignore her. The witch grew more arrogant the longer she stood at his side. He'd seen the kind before. Ambitious and treasonous. Her would do anything to usurp his authority the moment he showed weakness. Beset by vipers, Amongeratix chose to focus on the one power capable of thwarting his plans. Somewhere on Occanum's surface awaited his brothers. Amongeratix was surprised to find Sorrow joining forces against him. Their wayward brother seldom aligned with one side or the other.

Oddly, this pleased Amongeratix. For he would at last rid the universe of his plagued kin. But not before learning of Rengu's hidden location. His plan to murder those Tannus hid at the end of the last war did not extend to their hated filled uncle. He needed Rengu to enact the second phase of his plan.

"He is one man. Small in every regard," he replied when she cleared her throat. "I have need of him to complete his mission."

"At what expense?" she pressed. "Tuth commands this fleet, not you. His ships will not hesitate to obey his commands. They will turn their guns on *Behemoth*."

Amongeratix closed his eyes. "You think this ship matters? Is it a symbol of my authority? Do not mistake strength with power. This, all of this, is a mere extension of my might. Long has it served me, bearing me through many wars and conflicts. Should it be destroyed, I will not weep, nor will I abandon my purpose. My brother demands I come to him on Occanum. This is undoubtedly a trap. One he will regret laying."

"You would waste resources for vanity's sake?" Algiss refused to relent.

"I am not in the habit of repeating myself, *witch*. You tested my resolve once before. Do not make me kill you," he snarled. "This is my hour. All that matters is landing on Occanum with my skulldaerth. We will break the enemy lines and reclaim this universe in my name. Human loses are secondary, as you are well aware."

Algiss folded her hands within her sleeves. "You underestimate these humans. Long have they plotted against one another, always seeking to gain power while driving their opponents into submission. There is wrath buried among them."

"A hate from old times," Amongeratix mused.

"I don't understand."

His eyes slowly opened. "My people bred humans for chattel. Generation after generation born to serve. Is it any wonder they now harbor animosity toward me? Given the opportunity they would tear me limb from limb in blind rage without knowing the source. Ironic, isn't it? They fought for their freedom yet remain enslaved by their past."

"Ah, look!" He gestured to the main viewscreen. "General Kale prepares for the invasion. Summon your sisters. We go to war."

"Yes," Algiss replied, adding after, "my lord."

"Grand Admiral, prepare the skulldaerth for deployment and ready my shuttle. The hour for brotherly reunion has arrived."

Confederation Operations Base, Ferom.

"What the fuck am I supposed to do with that?" Bootleg shouted over the roar of engines and clamor filling the landing bay.

Dozens of wounded ships from fighters to corvettes docked, desperate for repairs and rearming. The Shadow Hammers, those not engaged in fortifying defenses, were hard pressed in keeping up with increasing demand. Bootleg felt overwhelmed. He longed to be back in the turret of a tank, leaving the engineers and mechanics to do their jobs. The only problem was his outfit had a small platoon. Nowhere near enough to handle the surge of wounded vessels.

"Boss, this is shit," Asher called, throwing a grease smeared wrench to the deck in disgust. "How are we supposed to get these birds patched up and back in the air before the enemy gets here?"

"Keep working. Use all hands," Bootleg snapped even if he sympathized with the man. They were one of the top mercenary units in the universe, but even they threatened to be overwhelmed by the amount of work being cast upon them. "We need to get these ships back in the fight before our position is compromised. I need clear fields of fire so we can put these fuckers in the ground where they belong."

Bootleg snatched up the wrench and handed it to his second in command who accepted the tool with chagrin. "Sorry, boss. My nerves are getting the best of me."

"You and me both." Seeing the number of wounded and dead left him rattled, awakening doubts of his decision-making skills. *How many of my own will I be placing in body bags? More than my conscience is willing to accept. That's for sure. I don't know why I let myself get talked into this. No reward is worth the shitstorm we have coming... Well, maybe.* "Now get back to work. This is only going to get harder."

"As long as we get to fight," Asher said. "The guns are thirsty, boss."

"There's a fight coming all right," a dark-skinned naval officer announced as he walked up to them. "One neither of you wants if you have any sense about you. Who's in charge here?"

Bootleg studied the man, noting the torn uniform and bloodstains. He toyed with admitting ownership to the landing bay but thought better of it. Discretion kept mercenaries alive. "Fella by the name of Fies. He's up in the command deck directing traffic."

"You are former Guard," the man noted the way Bootleg carried himself. Soldiers had an uncanny knack of recognizing each other regardless of how long they had been out of service. He extended a scarred and calloused hand. "Captain Drukali. What's left of my ship is over there still smoking. I'd appreciate any help your people can do in getting her back into space. My fight with those fuckers from Vau Prime isn't over yet."

Taking an instant liking to the man, Bootleg accepted his hand with a grin. "How bad is it out there?"

Drukali fixed him with a look that turned Bootleg's stomach.

The mercenary gave the stricken cruiser another glance before gesturing to the main doors leading deeper into the base. How the ship remained space worthy was lost on him. "If you don't mind, Captain, I'll escort you to Fies," Bootleg offered. "He's a good man, even if he still clings to the old rules of war."

"I appreciate that. and I didn't catch your name."

"I didn't give it, but my people call me Bootleg."

Confederation Operations Center, Plains of Haddash.

Matthias slid his bolt forward with experienced hands. His ion rifle had already been cleaned and readied, but he preferred the intimacy of the gunpowder relic. A dozen drums holding several hundred rounds each, all he could scrounge during a sweep through the camp, sat on the ground beside his cot and a stack of fresh power charges. A combat dagger and bayonet rounded out his kit. Matthias lifted the rifle to his shoulder. His finger slipped into the trigger well and he lightly squeezed. The click reverberated through his tent with a satisfying report. Final preparations complete, Matthias went to check the closest lines one final time.

The distant skies, on the edge of sight, were filled with residue from countless explosions. He, and the those in the army daring enough to glance upward, tried to imagine the carnage and mayhem ripping through both fleets. His own nightmare would come soon enough. The volume of enemy ships pouring into the system would eventually break through and the ground invasion would begin. The slaughter, he predicted, expected to be beyond mortal comprehension.

"Councilman!" a young page waved him down as he wormed through the camp. "Councilman!"

Rolling his eyes, Matthias snapped his holster, ensuring the blaster was secure before halting to await her. His mood soured with cold contemplation, he needed time alone, not cornered in the command tent with men and women who hadn't seen the frontlines in decades. Those nearest stopped what they were doing, eager for any snippet of how the war progressed.

She was out of breath by the time she slipped through the ranks to meet him. "Excuse me, sir, but Field Marshall Torgast has requested your presence."

Of course he has. The man has three hundred thousand soldiers at his disposal and feels the need to keep me on a leash. "Please inform the general I am touring the lines while there is still time. I will be back at my earliest convenience."

If he expected her to depart without putting up a fight, he was disappointed.

"I'm sorry sir, but he says it is most important," she stated with the haughtiness only professional politicians attained. "I am instructed not to return without you."

Impressed Torgast knew him so well, Matthias rested his hand on the blaster's handle. "Well, if that's the case, I hope you have a good pair of boots on. We're going for a walk."

Confused, she stammered, "But sir, I … I don't understand."

"You said you weren't to come back without me. Well, I have a job to do. That means you're coming with."

He caught the faint snicker of laughter from those troopers close by. Matthias fought to keep a grin from showing. Soldiers never changed.

Without waiting, he continued his trek through the lines, pausing to offer words of encouragement to sergeants and privates alike. He asked of readiness and spoke of the dreams of the future with countless soldiers. They greeted him like an old friend.

Spirits rose in his wake, even as word spread ahead of him. Matthias prided himself on being a relatable leader, something those in the higher levels often forgot. When the time came, he promised he would stand among them and face the dark tide rising. Once more he vowed to join the battle and, should the fates decree, aid the army to victory. From his side, he saw the page nodding more than once. Morale high, he did not stop until the first sounds of distant thunder broke across the plain.

"What was that?" the page jumped. "There are no clouds in the sky."

He gestured skyward. "That is the sound of all the hate in the universe barreling our way. Come along. It appears we are about to have company."

Hesitant cheers followed his passing.

Confederation Flagship *Revengence*, outskirts of Occanum

System.

The warning sirens were silent. It was well past time for that. Every man and woman aboard the massive ship knew the enemy had arrived in system and in force. Scores of smaller ships already drifted through the system, waiting to be sucked into a gravity well and lost forever. Countless souls lost to a madman's aggressions. A debris field the size of a small planet scattered between fleets in a protective barrier made larger with each shot fired.

In the midst of it all sat might *Revengence*. Once the pride of the Prekhauten Navy, the ship had taken a continual pounding since the ambush at Hawker's Gate several years ago. Resolute in their resolve, both captain and crew cared for her with love, for she was both their salvation and deliverance.

But a secret worry rippled through the ship—rumors of Admiral Khe-Zhehan's loss of faith in her purpose and a falling out with the fledgling council on Mannus Prime. Those of strongest composition squashed the rumors immediately, but damage had been done. Several crewers privately questioned whether the admiral was the right person to lead, especially after learning of the rise of Admiral Falchi to supreme fleet command.

Captain Affernee heard those rumors, absorbing them with stoic distaste. Nerves already high, punishing those dissenters served little purpose. He needed every available hand at their positions and ready to fight when called upon. Striding through the worn decks and corridors, Affernee inspected gun crews, maintenance teams, and medical bays. His hands ached from turning wrenches. His back sore from putting endless kilometers on his boots. His eyes burned from the lack of sleep. Yet he kept going, if for no other reason than to prove to himself he did all within his ability to ensure his beloved ship stood prepared.

Stopping for a quick bite in the crew mess, Affernee seldom took to the officer's mess, the captain of the ship ate with sailors and Marines. Scuttlebutt suggested today was the day *Revengence* unleashed her mighty weapons and reminded the universe of her bite. He slapped several crewers on the back as he left, offering grim words of encouragement while wondering how many would not survive the day. Emboldened by their fierce pride and steadfast loyalty, he made his way back to the bridge and discovered the universe had devolved into chaos.

"Captain," Khe-Zhehan greeted. Loose strands of hair gave her a wild look. Her uniform bore a mild stench, prompting him to question the last time she bathed. Not that he was in much better condition.

"Admiral, the ship is in order," he reported with a crisp salute.

"I expected no less. It appears our mettle is about to be tested sooner rather than later. Tactical has picked up engine signatures splintering from their main fleet. They will be within range of our anti-ship missiles within the hour."

"At last," he replied. "Revenge for the Gate."

"Indeed," she echoed. "Captain, I know I have not been the shining example expected of me. I apologize. I allowed the situation to get the better of me, much to my shame. Know I shall not fail you or this crew. You, who have given their all for almost five years. If not for you…"

"Admiral, no further explanation is required," he interrupted, his cheeks burning red as he lowered his eyes. "We stand before you prepared to give our all. The past is the past."

She laid a hand on his forearm as she turned her gaze back to the display screen. "I hear Falchi's squadrons are taking a beating."

"Fighting is heaviest in his sector," he confirmed. "Actual numbers are not confirmed but I would not want to be in his position right now."

"He will hold. He must. The hopes of the Confederation rest on his ability to outwit the enemy," Khe-Zhehan said without pause. "Intel confirms Achen Tuth is our opponent."

Affernee stiffened. He knew the name. They all did. "Tuth is a wily combat leader, but he suffers from vanity. We could turn that to our advantage."

"You anticipate his arrogance getting the best of him," she concluded. "A worthy goal but one we cannot count on. Tuth was an established admiral before the war. He earned his pips through blood and sweat. We must watch for potential traps, or it will be our funerals."

Affernee's mouth went dry. "I am confident in our fleets, Admiral."

"Send a communique to Admiral Falchi. Inform him we are set to engage and will hold our part of the line."

"Aye, Ma'am," Affernee replied. He turned to relay the orders when a rash a red blips emerged on the main screen.

"Enemy ships in sector seven!"

"Magnify," Khe-Zhehan ordered.

Tactical enhanced the image for the bridge crew to see. Dozens of targets entered the engagement zone. True to their training, none of the crew gasped or showed emotion.

"Tactical, pull up schematics of those ships" Affernee said. "I want to see what we have coming at us."

"Aye, sir."

Data scrolled beside the holographic image of one of the ships. The ship had minimal armament and heavy armor. Eyes narrowing, he realized what he was looking at. "Those are troop transports," he muttered. "Admiral, the enemy army is moving through our line of fire."

"Tuth with not have left his ships undefended," she theorized. "Captain Affernee, order a strike by fighters and corvettes. Let us test the fangs of our enemy."

"Draw them out and then attack?"

She nodded. "I need to know what we are truly facing before committing our full resources. We have the chance to win this war right here if we play it right."

Affernee feared Khe-Zhehan might slip back into the doldrums of inadequacy, ruining their chance to alter the battlespace in the Confederation's favor.

"Admiral, this is what we have been waiting for." He lowered his voice and stepped closer. "I saw we hammer those ships until naught remains but debris."

Khe-Zhehan fixed him with an unreadable look. "Captain, I will not risk this command on impatience. We execute fully when I know what I'm facing. I want all fighters and strike craft on full standby. Weapons free on my command."

Bristling but unwilling to question her authority, Affernee barked the orders. On screen, his fleet moved into position. Across from them, several hundred kilometers distant, the enemy marched on.

TWENTY-SIX

3215 A.G. (After Gods), Confederation Operations Base, Ferom.

The dull thump of flesh striking metal echoed. Fies closed his eyes and knocked the back of his head against the wall again, lighter this time. Frustrations threatened to boil over. His crew had been on Ferom for a week and there was still too much they didn't know, couldn't figure out without help. Unfortunately, those capable of getting the base up to peak operations were all occupied. He needed help but none came. His Guards were on their own, trapped in a spiraling situation worsening by the moment.

A steady stream of wounded ships poured into Ferom's orbit. Fies knew it was a matter of time before the enemy turned their attention to the moon. Half a dozen batteries of ship killers dug into the moon's surface gave him teeth, but without proper guidance he doubted they'd do much good. His company struggled under mounting pressure. They lacked sleep and steadily pushed closer to the edge few soldiers came back from. Fies dreaded the inevitable mistakes. Accidents rendering his command ineffective, or worse. It was only a matter of time.

"It will take more than that to put a hole in the wall," Annalilly said as she walked up to him. "I know, I've tried."

"Remember when we were simple soldiers following a crazy Inquisitor? How did we get to this point?" he asked without opening his eyes.

"You didn't stop getting promoted." Her response, true as it rang, struck deep. "Maybe we should have done like Jers. He's got to be enjoying life at this point."

"I could use him right about now," Fies admitted. "I'm in over my head, Annalilly. We all are. Command should have sent a different unit for this assignment."

"But they didn't," she replied. "Now it falls to us to keep Occanum clear so the boys on the ground can win this fight. I'm just glad we don't have to tackle any of the Three again."

"You and me both," he said. "Any luck with the big guns?"

She shrugged, leaning against the wall beside him. "Some. Quint and his squad are down there arguing with ancient computers and corrupted automatons."

"Keep up the pressure. We're going to need those guns before long."

She squinted. "What do you know I don't?"

"Nothing, just a hunch. We're taking too many wounded ships in. This was supposed to be a secret base. Every vessel out there is like a beacon Amongeratix can't resist."

"Fuck," she said.

"Fuck."

Times like these Fies almost wished he smoked. He shoved off the wall, pausing to straighten his fatigues. "I think I need to talk to the admiral. We're going to need more than a troop of mercenaries and whatever defenses this base has if Amongeratix turns his focus to us."

"I don't see how he can help. The fleets are already hard pressed to hold back the enemy," she told him. "With the minefield gone the battle has devolved to chaos and Vau Prime continues funneling fresh ships into the system. We won't hold for long."

"All the more reason to call for help," Fies told her. "Press Quint. We need those guns up and ready."

"I'll see what I can do. Oh and Fies, don't get all heroic on me." She fixed him with a conspiratorial wink. "I can't afford to keep getting promoted. Think of my image."

Annalilly stalked off before his mouth caught up with his brain.

Watching her go proved easy. Despite their not so quiet romance, Fies and Annalilly had two distinct leadership styles. He preferred coercing subordinates into doing what needed to be done while she enjoyed jumping straight down the throat with both boots. Both worked, with varying results. He almost lost himself in memories when he spied the man marching straight for him. *Gods lament. Don't I get a moment's peace?*

"Captain, how can I help you?" he decided to take charge of the situation lest another obstacle get thrown in his way by addressing the naval officer heading toward him.

"I assume you're Fies? I'm Drukali. Captain of the *Vitriol*."

"I am. What can I do for you?" Fies asked again.

"You can start by getting my ship back in the fight. I need

repairs and a restock on ammo."

"I have plenty of munitions for you, but finding enough mechanics to dedicate to your ship is going to prove an issue," Fies replied. "We weren't expecting to be a refit base and I'm expecting an attack in short order."

Realization lighted Drukali's dark eyes. He hadn't considered the effects of so many stricken vessels seeking succor on the moon. "Perhaps I can help. Is your communications array encrypted?"

"It is."

A nod. "Good. Take me to your bridge, Captain Fies. I have a call to place."

Taken off guard, Fies tilted his head and asked, "Who are you going to call?"

"Admiral Falchi. If what you say is true, and I have no reason to believe otherwise, you're going to need all the help you can get. I'll make a deal. You get my ship back in the fight and I'll organize orbital defenses."

"Sir, that is the best thing I've heard all day." He sucked in a deep breath. "This way."

Plains of Haddash.

Chaos reigned as drop ships and shuttles plunged through the fading atmosphere. Burning wreckage crashed around the landing zones. Thousands of lives lost in a daring gambit to establish an area large enough to prepare for the coming campaign. Icarn risked a glance out the port window and instantly regretted it. Bodies tumbled amidst the wreckage. Most were already dead. Those unfortunate few still alive screamed until flames burned their lungs out. Icarn gripped his rifle tighter and screwed his eyes shut.

The shuttle rocked, desperate to avoid the endless streams of anti-aircraft fire filling the sky, but with so many vehicles choking the sky there was nowhere to go. Icarn began muttering prayers, adding his voice to the others. The smell of urine filled the cabin. More than one Guard vomited, setting off a chain reaction. Explosions intensified. Streams of ion fire opened up as the first wave broke through the lower atmosphere. The shuttle beside them was hit, tearing open and spilling flesh and flame.

"Get us on the fucking ground!" someone screamed.

Icarn lost his grip on the rifle when the shuttle took a hit. Warning sirens broke out. The screech of metal tearing free adding to the cacophony of destruction. A rent opened in the ceiling. Wires and cables dropped, dripping fluids and sparks throughout the cabin. Fires sprang up, engulfing those Guards nearest.

Icarn overcame his fear enough to shout, "Put those fires out before we all die!"

Guards rushed to obey. Icarn snatched his rifle from the deck.

"Brace for impact!" the pilot's shrill voice came over the intercom.

Settling back into his webbed seat, Icarn tightened his safety straps and prayed. He knew, if they landed intact, their troubles were just beginning. Another explosion knocked his head back.

Darkness filled the cabin.

The shuttle plunged into the ash and dirt of Occanum so hard the frame buckled. Men and women screamed. Icarn tasted blood. Spasms wracked his body. A sharp pain jabbed into his chest when he attempted to unbuckle the safety harness. Thunder pounding in his ears, the Prekhauten sergeant pushed through the pain and confusion as best as he could. Flickering lights bathed the cabin in half-light. He spied several unmoving figures, broken and twisted among the wreckage.

"Get out of the fucking bird! This thing is a prime target!"

He didn't know who shouted. It didn't matter. The signature thump of artillery rounds impacting compelled the Guardsmen to move. Icarn had never been under such intense fire, nor did he have any idea such was possible. Panic gripped him. He struggled with the safety restraints. The crash bent and twisted the shuttle's frame, locking him into his seat. Tears rolled down his cheeks. The harder he struggled the tighter the restraints became. Icarn managed to draw his combat blade, twisting the knife to slice through the strap and freeing him. The shuttle rocked as shockwaves from incoming fire threatened to crush what little remained.

On his feet, Icarn stepped over broken bodies. He tripped and fell repeatedly before being forced to climb over the wide-eyed corpse of his company commander. Icarn dropped to his knees and ripped his helmet off after touching the ash covering the planet. Other Guards scrambled over him as he vomited. Knocked down into his own bile, Icarn gave in to the rage building. He fought and scraped his way to his feet. His rifle butt found several ribcages. The venom in his tone roared over the screaming artillery rounds. Slowly, too much for his liking, the company survivors gathered their wits. All heads turned to him for orders.

I can't be the only NCO to make it. I can't. Icarn wiped his mouth with the back of a sleeve and slammed his helmet back into place before those Guards spied the terror rising in his gaze. A pair of artillery shells exploded less than a hundred meters away. Debris added to the shockwaves and shrapnel, knocking Icarn from his feet. He slammed into the shuttle's hull with a bone shattering huff and slid to the ground.

A quick diagnostic run showed his armor absorbed the brunt of the impact, but integrity was reduced. Icarn shook the stars from his vision, redoubled the grip on his rifle, and stumbled back to his Guards. The bombardment continued mercilessly. Bodies and wreckage were thrown into the air with each explosion. There was no safe place here.

Icarn looked up and watched with horror as dozens of burning shuttles added their carnage to the scene as they plunged down. Yet hope was not lost. He spied a growing number of shuttles successfully landing in the distance, disgorging their Guards. The second wave. He figured most of the first wave was either dead or beaten up too much to contribute.

"What do we do now, Sarge?" a rattled voice asked.

A flight of enemy fighters raced overhead to strike at the massing Guards in the rear of his position. Streams of ion fire rakes exposed soldiers. Icarn felt despair take over. His darkest thoughts were confirmed. Prekhauten command cared nothing for their lives. He and the others were little more than fodder for the bigger guns attempting to land. Bait. That's all they were.

"We need to get out of the kill zone and establish a defensive line," he barked over the screams of falling shuttles.

Soon, if the Guard managed to build a line, the armor and heavy weapons would be landing. He needed to find a way to give them every opportunity, if they didn't get killed first. Icarn watched as others began moving. Small groups of two and three at first, followed by larger clusters. He wanted to shout, to scream at them to disperse but helmet intercom transmissions were limited to company frequencies only. His worst fears were soon realized. Enemy forward observers began dropping high explosive rounds among the retreating clusters.

It was too much for his recruits. They broke and ran. Some for the perceived safety of their shuttles. Others toward the enemy in the confusion of battle. Icarn's pleas fell on deaf ears. Too late. All too late.

Incoming fire intensified, turning the landscape into a charnel house of nightmare and gore. Unable to handle the influx of events, Icarn unstrapped his rifle and cast it into the ash. His mind snapped. No sense of duty remained. Only survival. He gave the shuttles a final look, breaking into a crooked grin as several more were destroyed by the merciless artillery barrage.

They never had any hope. Not the first or second waves. Icarn struggled not to laugh as the realization they were never meant to dawned. Why else would command drop them into this scenario? He sat, for a time, as the sweep of artillery left his position. If the enemy had any sense of tactics they would send light infantry, scouts and spec ops, forward to clear the area. That's what he'd do—surrender. Icarn struggled with processing all he witnessed. No one back home would believe him.

Home. The notion mocked his senses. None of them were going to see home again. He pulled himself out of the ash and started walking. What was it all for? Years of service to the Conclave, to the universe, all mangled by the twisted desires of a handful. He once believed in their cause. Believed the new leadership meant to reshape the universe in a more efficient vision aimed at raising the standard of living for all citizens. Icarn offered to spend his life for such lofty ideals, but not this.

No sane man, in his limited opinion, willingly walked into this with good intentions. Command painted the insurgents as evil traitors. He saw them as men and women fighting for their lives against an oppressive regime willing to sacrifice all it stood for to accomplish its goals. Then came the sickening devotion to Amongeratix. Icarn believed in the gods and their roles in shaping human evolution. How anyone could bend the knee to the greatest villain in history puzzled him.

It wasn't until he was halfway through the kill zone that Icarn realized he'd been seduced by a lie. One responsible for countless deaths on the sad plains of Occanum. Black smoke and acrid haze obscured his field of vision. He lost track of time. The once crisp reports of cannon fire dulled. His weapon and helmet lay in the ash somewhere behind him. A trail of bodies marked his passing. Most, he noted, were shot from behind.

"Icarn? Is that you?"

He froze, not expecting any survivors this far forward. Through the haze he made out the bloodstained form of Avis, blaster in hand. Out of everyone in the company of course it was Avis who survived.

"Avis? What are you doing out here?" he asked.

Avis strode forward, stepping over a pair of Guards. A hungry look tainted his eyes. "They shouldn't have run, Icarn. Fucking traitors." He spat a mouthful of blood. "All they had to do was remember their training and do their jobs. We're Guards, right? Sworn to follow the orders of the officers appointed over us and all that."

Icarn tried to swallow but his throat was too dry. "You … you killed them?"

Avis glanced at the bodies. "Someone had to. I'm glad you're here, Icarn. Now you can help me hunt down the others."

He's gone mad. How long before he kills me too? "Avis, listen to me, we have to get out of here. Soon we're going to be caught between armor divisions. We need to find a safe place."

"You are here to help, aren't you?" Avis blinked rapidly, his face an unreadable mask. "I never liked you. I thought you were weak, unable to do the hard tasks. But you're here. Together we can regain our company honor and stand beside General Kale with our heads high!"

Icarn shook his head. "Avis, we need to move."

The sergeant's head slowly titled to one side. His blaster rose, barrel waggling. Icarn saw death in Avis' eyes and regretted leaving his rifle behind.

"What are you doing out here, Icarn?" Avis' voice turned dark. "Our lines are back that way."

Think, Icarn, think. "I… I got lost in the confusion. The shelling."

The barrel swiveled toward his chest. "You were trying to defect. You're a traitor."

"Avis, listen to me. It's not like that."

Avis slipped into a firing stance. "Liar! You are a heretic and a traitor. I should have known."

Icarn stood helpless as Avis' finger fell on the trigger. *Would my mother learn of my fate? Would anyone?*

He heard the shot. A rush of boots from behind.

Rough hands grabbed him by the shoulders and shoved him to his knees. Icarn didn't put up a fight. Shock numbed him. He stared into Avis' dead eyes glaring up from the ash. Accusatory even from the grave. Icarn felt the tension leave his body. His fate was out of his hands; hands being shackled behind his back.

"This one's an NCO. Blindfold him and get him back to HQ. He might know something."

Icarn snorted, the sound lost of the din of battle. Refusing to put up resistance as he was blindfolded, his captors dragged and pushed him across no man's land in silence. Cannon fire grew louder. His nose crinkled at the overpowering smell of so many men and women crammed together. Human waste from slit trenches and latrines roiled his stomach.

The whisk of a tent flap pushed aside told him he reached his destination. Icarn gasped when he was jerked into a field chair. The shackles remained but his blindfold was ripped from his head and tossed aside. He blinked to get acquainted with the change of light and found himself staring into the face of a haggard man who had seen too much action. Icarn's mouth dropped open as he recognized the face.

"You're—"

The man nodded with a look of mild disgust. "I get that a lot. Name and unit, sergeant."

"Icarn. 37th Infantry Division."

"That's a new division? I don't recognize it."

"Just formed on Tatarast," Icarn confirmed. "We were mostly recruits, Sergeant Major."

"I'm retired," Matthias corrected.

The pair of soldiers guarding the tent exchanged grins. Icarn's brows pinched together but he remained silent.

"Icarn, you put me in a difficult position. We have standing orders not to take prisoners. Fortunately for you those stripes on your sleeve are enough to make me suspect you might have valuable intel I can use."

"Sergeant Major, I'll tell you anything you want to know if I get to live," Icarn blurted. He stared pleadingly at Matthias, desperate now that he was so close to escaping the wrath of the gods ravaging his army just kilometers away. "Hells, give me a gun and I'll step in with one of your units. Anything not to go back to that nightmare."

Matthias hummed. "Very well. Wrap him up and get him over to the Field Marshal's command. I'm sure Torgast will love to know what our friends on the other side are cooking up for us."

"Th … thank you," Icarn managed as the blindfold slipped back over his face.

A chair slid. Boots crunched on the hard soil. Icarn flinched at the hot breath on the side of his neck.

"Don't thank me yet. You've got a long way to go before they shove you in a prisoner of war camp. Get him out of here."

Icarn went willingly. His war was over.

Behemoth, entering Occanum orbit.

"It appears General Kale has no concept of grand tactics," Algiss Her mused from Amongeratix's side. The Crimson Mistress viewed the data streaming in with casual disinterest. Her concerns were on her Sisters deployed with the various Guard units and ships. Several were already dead, lost to the vagaries of war. Helpless to prevent it, she needed her people on the ground, or away from Occanum altogether.

Amongeratix grunted. "Perhaps, though I see a certain genius to his incompetency."

"Genuis? He sustained over thirty-seven thousand casualties in the first hour. Both the first and second waves are all but wiped out."

"At what cost? Those units were recruits, barely out of training. He sacrifices those he does not need to the bite of enemy guns while landing the bulk of his veterans far out of range. It will take days for his main army to gather and prepare their assault."

Her refused to accept his answer. "That is two full divisions he will not have should the enemy prove a tougher fight than anticipated. The man is a fool."

"History will decide his fate, not your or I," Amongeratix cautioned. "You forget he will have my skulldaerth anchoring his assault. We will not lose, Crimson Mistress."

She bristled. "What of the Blood Witches? They have yet to play their hand."

He paused the data stream to glance at her. Algiss was convinced Amongeratix could pierce the shadows of her cowl and bore deep into her soul. The effect stimulated emotions she had not experienced since her early days as a novice. Her hands knotted under concealment. She wanted nothing more than to break his gaze and be free.

"Why else do you stand by my side than to counter the Oracle?"

he reminded her. "They cannot kill me anymore than you, but they will prove problematic before the end. Your time to shine approaches, Crimson Mistress. Are you prepared to eliminate your mentor and peer and know the true meaning of power? Or shall your fledgling Order collapse beneath the weight of its blind ambition?"

"My Sisters will do their parts so long as we live long enough to engage," Algiss affirmed. "None of this changes the fact we are sustaining too many casualties and losing too many ships."

"You are here for specific purpose, witch. Do not forget your place." His glare threatened to overwhelm her. "Are your witches where I decreed?"

Bristling as she attempted to retain the last shreds of dignity, Algiss said, "They are, though I must once more request caution. I have already lost several to this ill-fated frontal assault. We cannot sustain our strength and do as you request if we continue losing Sisters."

"Your hour approaches, witch. The moment when millennia of wanting concludes as you will meet your mentor on the field. This is the day in which old wrongs are righted and the eternal quest for revenge at last meets an end. Do not make me regret accepting you to my side."

She fell silent, rebuked amidst her internal scheming. Algiss prided herself on her ability to read situations and manipulate others. She ran into a stone wall, damaged but unbroken, when dealing with the giant. Never had she felt such raw hatred in a living being, prompting her to question how his flame hadn't burned itself out already. Frustrated and frozen in place, Algiss noticed Amongeratix shift his stance.

Gone was the casual regard in which he watched the battle play out. His shoulders squared on the screen. He stood taller; head cocked slightly to one side. She swore she caught the angry cadence of grinding teeth. *What steals your attention*? Wisely, Algiss held her tongue. Her patience was rewarded a moment later.

"Where are those stricken ships going? They retreat but not to safety."

"My lord?" she asked, failing to see his point.

"My fleets are punching holes in the center of enemy lines, forcing wounded ships to fall back lest they are destroyed," he explained. "Conventional wisdom says they should be retreating to the far edge of the system where our guns cannot reach, yet they cluster around one of the planet's moo—"

"Surely those ships no longer factor into the equation," she pressed. "They are out of the fight and, as you are quick to remind me, we outnumber our foes by three to one."

Amongeratix turned so she saw his eye. He gestured to one of the small moons orbiting his homeworld. "They regroup, but why?"

"You speak in riddles," Algiss said with distaste. She's spent a lifetime listening to Ruma Zzein's misdirection and veiled prophecies.

"Ah, brother. I see you have not forgotten all of Occanum's secrets," he mused, seemingly forgetting her. "Master of the Ship! Get Tuth and Kale now!"

A pair of flickering images came to life moments later, stealing focus away from the raw look of hatred Algiss shot toward Amongeratix.

"Your summons is ill timed, my lord." Achen Tuth frowned. "My fleets are engaging across the area of operations. We are driving the enemy back, but I need to focus on the situation lest they work around my strategies."

Amongeratix clicked his tongue. "You will redirect a strike force to the moon of Ferom immediately."

"To a lifeless moon? That makes no sense, my lord. I need every available ship where they are if I am to secure victory."

"There will be no victory if that moon is not subdued and captured, Admiral," Amongeratix retorted. "General Kale, I want a full division deployed to that moon. Your orders are to exterminate everyone you find."

"I don't understand," Mobus said. "I am scheduled to drop with the rest of the army within the hour. My forces are suffering heavy losses on their descent. I need every available rifle on the ground."

"Listen to me closely, before I turn *Behemoth's* guns on your ship," he growled. "There is a hidden base on that moon with enough firepower to decimate the fleets and end this war in short order. My brother has no doubt discovered this base and has forces deployed to bring it back into operation. I cannot allow this. You will follow my command and do so without question. Am I clear?"

Algiss shifted. *The man is mad. He is losing control of his army.*

Achen Tuth swallowed tightly. "Clear, my lord. I will reassign a task force at once."

"Kale."

Mobus Kale stared back at his master, the look in his eyes unreadable. "It will be as you say, though I have doubts. You jeopardize our victory."

The images faded, leaving Amongeratix seething. "I surround myself with lesser fools. Perhaps killing Nye was a mistake."

Algiss barely contained her mirth. "My lord, if this base is as much of a threat as you believe my Sisters will need to accompany the Guards."

He shook his head, long locks of oily dark hair sweeping across his shoulders. "No. As you say, your witches are needed elsewhere. They remain with their assigned units. Ferom will be dealt with. I do not believe Tannus has activated the defense grid. There is still time."

"How can you be sure?"

He fixed her with a cruel gaze. "We would already be dead if he had. You may make your final preparations. We deploy soon."

"As you command."

Kar-edora, Abbey of the Order of Blood Witches, Acumensiis Comet.

Tolde Breed stepped down the ramp and onto the comet for the second time. His skin crawled with odd sensations he could neither explain nor clarify. Shadows watched from the corners of his eyes. Yet each time he turned to get a better look they dissolved into nothing. The moment his boots touched the ancient stone he shivered as unfamiliar vibrations ran through his bones. He never professed to understanding magic. The concept went against every logical grain in his body despite having been entwined with it for decades.

Nor did Tolde understand the Grand Mistress' obsession with him. In his mind, he was just a man. A man who died and was resurrected to complete his task. Mired in internal conflict, Tolde slung his pack over one shoulder, his rifle in his other hand, and stepped aside so the others could join him. They were told enroute that time was of the essence, and they needed to rendezvous with the comet with all haste. Luma Kai pushed their battered shuttle as hard as it could go. Smoke poured from cracks in places Tolde feared it shouldn't.

Their mission to remove Kaline from the board complete, Tolde led his band of travelers back into the heart of a world none but Alessandra understood. She assured them all matters would be solved in short order upon their return. Tolde wasn't sure he believed her. Each turn of their journey led them down darker roads. He no longer understood his role in this war. He lacked purpose other than what Ruma Zzein and Tannus decreed.

The thought of being little more than a puppet in a cosmic game, a fear he had yet to overcome since his first encounter with Amongeratix on that derelict in the depths of space, burrowed into his psyche. While his own life or death meant less than it had before he died, Tolde longed to see his boon companions find the peace each deserved. They were among the best he had ever had the pleasure of knowing. Far better than he deserved.

Ragan was the last off. His youthful demeanor was worn thin after a series of misadventures. Tolde wondered if the boy thought he made a mistake in failing to stay behind on Romalle and pursue young Riles Tenaru's heart. Questioning if love proved stronger than all the hate and bile corrupting the universe, Tolde clapped the young man on the back and stepped in line. None spoke, though Ragan offered a grin. Tolde spied the dried remains of blood on the boy's sleeve. The last vestige of Kaline. Perhaps the Order had extra clothing.

Sister Alessandra led them through the winding maze to the rooms they previously occupied before making their assault on *Behemoth* last year. Damage from the attempted coup could be seen in several spots. Burn marks scoring the walls. Gouges in the once pristine floors where magic destroyed. Tolde frowned. How could such destructive power be considered good for any of them?

"You were reborn thanks to the gift," Alessandra said as he walked by.

Tolde paused. Could she read minds as well? Unsure if any thought remained safe, he swallowed the lump in his throat and kept moving.

Each entered their room, setting down their bags and weapons. Tolde entered his room to set his kit down then joined Alessandra in the hall where she waited.

"We need food and a chance to freshen up."

"There is yet time. Tell the others hot baths and fresh food will be available shortly."

"Where are you going?" he asked as she began drifting away.

"I must speak with the Grand Mistress. She will want to know all of what transpired on An'kuruku, and I must prepare for the next task."

"Alessandra, what does come next?"

She halted. Her robes shimmered in a cascade of colors. "That is not for me to say, Tolde Breed. Go, see to your needs. I will come when it is time for your audience with the Grand Mistress. You have my word."

TWENTY-SEVEN

3215 A.G. (After Gods), Abbey of the Order of Blood Witches, Acumensiis Comet.

"So, we have come to it at last," Ruma Zzein said as she raised her hood. "I did not think this Kaline would be taken alive. Not after her crimes against humanity."

"Crimes have a way of shifting with time, Grand Mistress," Sister Alessandra replied. "Presha Von has been nothing but penitent since joining us, albeit at Tannus' request."

"You suggest humans have redemption in their genes?"

"I am not one to know either way." Alessandra bowed. "The humans are a most interesting mixture of elation and regret. I confess I do not understand them well, even after so long among them. If possible, I would like to remain among them after the war. They have become… my friends in a manner."

"Ones who are more comfortable out of your presence than among it," Ruma corrected. "When I started this Order, I did so with the intent of bringing civility to the universe. It was shortly after the last battle of Occanum. Humanity was free from its foul masters for the first time and did not know how to behave. I thought, with my hubris, I might establish a permanent means of providing assistance in their fledgling universe. Time conspired against me, and our paths soon diverged down irreconcilable paths."

Alessandra listened with divided attention. She longed to return to her assignment, knowing time drew short and there was much yet to do. But an audience with the Grand Mistress, where the secret histories of the Order were laid bare, were rare for any Sister.

"Tannus argued against it all," Ruma admitted with sorrow. "He cited this would all collapse on itself and here we are."

Alessandra straightened. "Argued against what, Grand Mistress?"

"Everything. He thought allowing the humans to worship his people as deities was wrong. I argued they needed a beacon to guide them as they established themselves. Countless generations of servitude and they suddenly found themselves in a unique position none were prepared for. For my arrogance, the universe is paying the price." Ruma shook her head.

"Alessandra, I am old. Some believe me eternal, but I feel the scrape of time against my bones. I discovered an inescapable truth during Algiss Her's insurrection. I am fallible. The older I get the more mistakes I make. I fear I have led the Order to the brink of collapse and nothing I do will prevent that fall." She took a deep breath. "What would you have done in my position?"

"Excuse me, Grand Mistress?"

"We can drop the honorifics here. Were you the all-powerful head of the Order, how would you have handled the insurrection?"

"I… I do not know. It is clear Algiss Her had been compromised for years, perhaps longer, before launching her coup attempt. To have subverted so many Sisters would take time and no small measure of stealth."

"Indeed," Ruma said. "She was seduced by a lie. They all were. I should have seen it, but I was blind. I once considered Algiss among my closest friends. Her betrayal stings."

"You are the strongest of us all," Alessandra said with caution. "Mistress Her cannot withstand your power."

"Perhaps. Perhaps not. I do not know if I have the heart to confront her," Ruma admitted. "The cost of friendship."

"But the mortals lack the ability to battle one of our kind."

"In a direct confrontation, yes. You and I know there are ways to kill a Sister."

Alessandra shifted, unwilling to meet her gaze. Some truths were not discussed, even in closed circles.

"I trust the Inquisitor is well enough to perform his final task."

Alessandra fought to keep the scowl from her face at the change of subject. "He is. They each question their roles in this story. I fear there is not much holding them together. They run on a ragged edge even I am powerless to prevent."

"I wish to see him. One last time," Ruma said. "Will you bring him to me, Alessandra?"

"Yes, Grand Mistress."

A nod; a dismissal. "Go. We have much to prepare for."

Alone in the main corridor, Alessandra's head bowed. Knowing Tolde Breed must die weighed heavily on her.

*

She studied him from the sanctity of her cowl. Wizened eyes peering through his battered exterior, piercing deep into his soul in search of cracks. Ruma once considered herself a good judge of character, but recent betrayals rocked her foundational beliefs. At this stage, there could be no taking chances.

"You question whether I have the resolve to see this through," Tolde said, shifting under the awkward silence.

"Would you not if our roles were reversed?" she replied. "I don't know what makes you special, Tolde Breed. You were a normal Inquisitor before encountering Amongeratix all those years ago. That meeting changed you. Marked you for destiny's designs."

He wiped a hand through his unruly hair. "If I could go back and change that I would. I never wanted the burden on my shoulders. Not the Three. Not Rengu. None of it."

"Such choices are not ours to make," Ruma said. "The Three will sort themselves out, though you have yet a large role to play."

Tolde cocked his head. "And Rengu?"

"He is… contained. With Kaline removed there is none to spread his poison. You did well on An'kuruku. I must llay upon you one final charge, if you are willing to accept."

"What?" he tensed, anticipating the blow.

"Protect the Paladin. Elisa is the key to our success or failure."

The tip of his tongue snaked from his lips. "That will be no small task, Grand Mistress. We will be in the center of a war and the enemy now has your magic."

"A contingent of Sisters is already deploying to counter the renegades. Let them worry about magic, Tolde. You must promise me you will do all you can to protect Elisa. She must get close enough to use *Grimfurvor* and end this war."

He tried piercing the veil of shadows beneath the hood but soon found the effort pointless. Tolde bobbed his head. "I will do all within my power to see Amongeratix pay for his crimes. You have my word."

"Thank you."

She watched him go, contemplating telling him the truth of why he was spared and what was yet expected of him but the weight pained her heart too much. Some burdens were not meant to be shared.

*

"What is it?" Elisa asked.

Swirling colors collided in a circling eye. Trails of vapors and red tendrils poured from the center, stretching into nearby space. The twinkle of fading stars caught in the gravity well shone through massive gas clouds. A dark maw beckoned from the colors. Hungry. Devouring.

"Ka-edora. The heart of the universe," Ruma told them with pageantry she hadn't used in centuries. "Through there you will go."

"Through that?" Tolde Breed balked.

"It is quite harmless, I assure you."

Tolde shook his head. "That's a black hole."

"At one time, before it grew into an entity of itself," Ruma explained. "Long ago I discovered the paths through the Eye. I will not bore you with tales of my travels. Of the other worlds I bore witness to or the unraveling futures. No. There is a webway through the Eye none have utilized since I founded the Order. Through magic we shall send you through the Eye to the scene of your final battle."

"Who is to go on this little adventure?" Presha Von pipped up from the back of the group.

Ruma turned to her, the stiffness of her stance lessening. "Only those who wish to fulfill their destiny. I demand none go but on their own accord."

Tolde stepped forward, coming to Elisa's side. "Best we get this over with."

"Like we ever had a choice," Elisa muttered.

Ruma waited, watching.

Sister Alessandra stepped to Tolde Breed's side. Ruma looked at her Sister before nodding and glancing away.

Next came Elisa's lover. "I will not allow you to march into danger once more without me, *farisi*," Ah'muf called, though his voice trembled. He stepped forward.

Ruma saw Elisa pleading with her eyes b the desert dweller was not to be deterred and moved to her side

The biggest surprise came from Ragan Sandinsol. Youthful vigor no substitute for experience, Ragan exhaled a deep breath and stepped forward.

Luma Kai swept her darkening gaze over them. "You're all mad," she scolded. "Then again, I must be as well. If we're going to die, I wouldn't be able to live with myself if I wasn't there."

"Die?" Ah'muf squawked.

"It is a possibility, Ah'muf," Ruma Zzein said, studying the former Inquisitor. "There are no guarantees when you arrive on Occanum." Her gazed shifted, hardening. "Presha Von, the decision is yours."

"I have no desire to enter his presence again," she replied. "If it is all the same, I would remain here."

Ruma stared at the woman without comment prompting Presha to lower her gaze to the floor. Ruma saw the flash of shame and guilt.

"Raise your head, Presha. You have made your decision, and no one shall judge you for it," Ruma soothed. "I shall welcome your insight and companionship. You may be at peace in the abbey."

"Thank you."

Ruma glided forward. Her robes took on the hues of their eyes. "It is done. You are the spear upon which so many hopes rest. I bid each of you good fortune and fortitude to see your task through to whatever end you may. You may return to your quarters and make what preparations you deem best."

"What are we waiting for?" Tolde asked.

"For my cousin to let us know it is time."

They turned at the sound of Paradise Tear's booming voice. The giant leaned against the door frame, arms folded. Her golden hair framed the hard lines of her face, lending her a determined look few matched. She looked at each of them, silently searching for answers to questions only she knew. Her gaze last fell to Ruma.

"Tannus must engage Amongeratix first. They cannot kill each other, but their battle will provide the necessary camouflage to get the Paladin into position," Paradise continued. "For now, we wait. Recent intelligence reports say Tannus has landed on Occanum, with Sorrow, but Amongeratix has yet to make his appearance."

"I just want this finished," Elisa said through clenched jaws.

Paradise's glare softened. "Elisa, I shall be by your side to the end."

"So it will be," Ruma interrupted. "Sister Alessandra will summon you when the time comes. Until then, my friends."

One by one they filed out under blankets of hushed conversation, leaving Ruma Zzein the only person in the chamber. She swiveled to face the Eye. Memories rushed back, presenting her with a myriad of possibilities and awakening the sudden desire to leave the universe behind and seek out new worlds without the taint of magic or gods. But then, she had always been a romantic.

Krenz, planet Vau Prime.

The world changed the day Amongeratix departed. Nestled in his web of power, Ezekiel Goethe turned the screws on the city as he attempted to crush the rebellion for good. Inquisition shock squads scoured entire neighborhoods without mercy or remorse. Hundreds were rounded up and funneled to hastily erected prison camps north of Krenz. Torturers and questioners interrogated nonstop as executions mounted. All video and news communications were cut off. Goethe used his authority to bring the city to its knees.

Recruiting drives followed in the wake of abductions. Hundreds of men and women shipped to the Inquisition Academy to earn their roses and spread Goethe's ministry. Standing upon the ruined foundation of one of the universe's storied institutions, Goethe sought to recreate the universe in his image. It began with the lower class most likely, in his estimation, to provide safe harbor for the insurrectionists bringing anarchy to Krenz. With Amongeratix and those accursed witches offworld, Goethe found himself void of obstacles.

Burrowed deep underground in a string of rotating safehouses, Edam Boone and the remnants of his criminal empire hurried to complete the bombs. Engineers worked around the clock to meet the agreed upon deadline and liberate their city from a never-ending nightmare. Against his better judgment, Edam continued his raids. They funneled scores of former cardinals and their families out of the city to small starports to be taken offworld to star systems far from the fighting. It still wasn't enough to satisfy Porii Daam who hounded him for more.

"Another seven cardinals gone," she fumed. "How many must die to satisfy the bloodlust of this madman?"

Edam's eyebrow arched. He knew the answer, though wasn't eager to remind her. Every last individual who once wore the crimson robes of state would be dead already if Goethe had his way. "You must focus on the positives, Porii."

She spun, dull brown robes scraping through the dirt on the tiles. "Positives? You should know better. The Inquisition broke every promise to the people, becoming the very monsters they swore to defend against. We sit here playing at being soldiers while our enemy grows stronger. How many more loses must we endure before the end?"

"You're assuming there is an end favorable to our cause," Thopos cautioned. "We are pushed, herded into scenarios beyond our ability to rationalize. Stumbling on you was mere happenstance and it has turned into a boon for many. People who should be dead are alive because of you. Yes, Porii, there are positives. It just takes a little extra to accept them."

Rebuked, she shut her mouth with a click. Edam met her gaze, waiting.

She made a show of waving Thopos off. "Yes, yes. Fine. We have made great accomplishments, but unless we stop Goethe, they will all be for naught. We are running out of time."

"My people are working as fast as possible," Edam reminded as he plucked debris from his dark green tunic. "I have a score of spies inside the Inquisition. We have infiltrated Goethe's inner sanctum without detection. Once we gain access to the servant entry points, we can move forward. I know you are impatient to atone for your perceived crimes, but I am unwilling to risk the lives of my people by moving too quickly. Can you imagine the damning effect if we fail?"

"All reward is tempered by risk, Edam Boone." Porii straightened. "I have half a mind to storm into the Inquisition with a bomb strapped across my chest and end this now."

"Easy, lass. Suicide is no joking matter."

"Suicide or sacrifice, Thopos?" she countered. "I would not be the first to make a martyr of myself."

"Are you listening to what you're saying?" Edam threw his hands in the air. Pulling himself off a couch whose best days were long forgotten, he began pacing. "Our cause has no need for martyrs, Porii. The future can only be won by courage and cunning."

"We have no shortage of either and our enemy continues gaining momentum." Porii's voice bore a hard edge, filed and bitter. "Our future rests on those bombs doing their job. While I have no doubt they'll explode prettily, what guarantee Goethe and his senior staff will be slain in the blast?"

"Porii, there is enough explosives in there to bring the entire gods damned building to the ground," Thopos said.

"Thopos, you paint a dangerous picture. If one of those men grows careless."

He chuckled, causing Edam to stop in mid-step and fix him with a disparaging look. "The lads know what they are about. There won't be any mistakes."

"All of them are missing a finger or other body part!" she exclaimed.

"That's how you know they're the best. They've made their mistakes and learned from them," he said with a nod. "We're in good hands. I swear."

Swallowing his fears of all that might go wrong, Edam changed the subject before paranoia set in. "Porii is right about one matter. We need to ensure Goethe is present and as close to the blast as possible. That means getting close to him."

"Now that is suicidal," Thopos said. He shuffled to the wall of dusty, crude stained windows overlooking the old shop floor where the bombmakers toiled. "I'd rather take my chances with an accident."

Edam couldn't blame him. Marching into the heart of the Inquisition spelled doom for any volunteer. Security tightened thanks to increased raids and activity dating back to the late Davith Strannan's attempts at breaking the death lock on the city, the Inquisition had become a near impregnable fortress.

Despite this, Edam saw a way in. "Not true. We already have people on the inside, Thopos."

"Workers, Edam, not people posing as Guards or Inquisitors. I don't see a sanitation worker getting close to the Inquisitor General without rousing suspicion."

Porii chimed in, "He may be onto something. Let's hear him out."

It was Thopos' turn to scoff.

Edam exhaled the deep breath he'd been holding. "One of us needs to get inside."

Thopos shifted, looking uncomfortable. "Good luck with that. I'll stay here, where it's safer."

"I'm not asking you to go, old friend." Edam smiled. "I've already been inside, with Julian, and know the layout. No one will recognize me and, if they do, it will be from the last time I was there, in a Guard uniform. All I need to do is get close to Goethe and ensure he is front and center for our attack."

He paused, a stunned look on his face. *Where did that come from?*

"Everyone wants to become a martyr," Thopos groaned. "Edam, how in the hells do you expect to get clear before the bombs go off? They will be on set timers. Once we activate the bombs there is no turning them off."

Edam fixed Porii with his strongest look and said, "Risk and reward."

Plains of Haddash, planet Occanum.

"Field Marshal, the enemy is marshalling forces for an assault."

Torgast thanked the runner with a backhanded wave. Optics showed him entire divisions, largely unaffected by the initial artillery barrages and gunship strafing runs. His hopes for evening their combat strength dimmed. Mobus Kale had more Guards and better equipment. The battlefield stretched for fifty kilometers in either direction. A massive number of troops and vehicles. Torgast knew the hour approached when Kale's armies would take their turn and deliver punishment of their own.

He scanned the area of carnage. He estimated two full divisions lay slaughtered on the plain. Their broken corpses mocked his humanity. Torgast figured most were men and women doing what they thought was right. Disillusioned by their commanders and fed into a meat grinder. Thanks to the admissions of several prisoners, including a veteran sergeant named Icarn, Torgast knew those forces were undertrained and unprepared for the violence greeting them upon planetfall. His heart wept for the families expecting their children to come home.

The massing forces on the edge of his field of vision summoned his attention. Hardened infantry divisions, mechanized and light, gathered for the grueling march across open fields of fire. Behind them lurked tanks and bunker busters waiting for the breach in his lines. Enemy artillery, well out of sight, was no doubt adjusting their barrels at the direction of forward observers embedded in the infantry. The one aspect Torgast needn't overly worry about was an aerial assault. His anti-aircraft batteries and hunter-killer gunships scoured the skies of any enemy craft foolish enough to be taken unawares. Falchi's fleets ensured no enemy dreadnaught or destroyer entered orbit to deliver their bombardments.

"As long as I control the skies, I control the battlefield," he whispered.

"What was that, Field Marshal?"

Torgast flinched. He turned and found himself staring up at the giant Tannus. "I thought I was alone. My apologies."

"Never apologize for doing what feels right, Torgast."

Gone were his simple tunic and trousers. Tannus stood armored in battle gear unlike anything Torgast ever saw. Dark silver with golden hues, the armor encased Tannus from the neck down–no doubt it too was a relic from the old war. He noticed the massive sword at Tannus' hip. He was armed with nothing else.

"Will that be enough to kill him?" Torgast gestured at the sword.

"Kill him? No. It is not my destiny to slay my brother."

The admission, simple and plain, stripped Torgast of any illusion he held concerning the future. He wanted nothing more than the Three to disappear. Take their fight elsewhere and leave humanity out of it.

"Do not mistake my comment for defeatism. One of us, perhaps both, will die here today, but it will not be by my hands. Amongeratix and I have fought long and desperate wars across the span of time. Neither of us holds an advantage."

"How are we to steal victory from this madness if neither of you is capable of killing the other?"

"Help comes, Field Marshal," Tannus said. "This war ends today and, you have my word, humanity shall at last enjoy the freedoms promised three thousand years ago."

Unsure how to respond, Torgast resumed his watch on the battlefield. The dark lines of distant infantry were moving. The long march across the killing fields had begun. He didn't expect the enemy to break the way the first two waves had. No. These were the professionals. The real fighters. Mobus Kale's spearhead coming to claim victory.

"Runner!" Torgast barked. He heard the scuffle of boots and continued, "Send word to the artillery. Commence firing as soon as the enemy is within range. Bring them to their knees."

"Yes, Field Marshal."

"It will not be enough," Tannus said after they were alone again.

"No, I didn't imagine it would be," Torgast answered. "Hopefully I can even the odds a little before they get here."

"Courage, my friend. Bend. Do not break. The storm shall pass."

Torgast watched the giant walk away. Soldiers raised their rifles and cheered.

The first thump of cannons firing broke the silence lingering over the battlefield. Hundreds more followed, of every caliber. Soldiers watched horrified. Former guards dug in or pushed forward, desperate to survive and redeem the failure of the first wave. Drop shuttles continued falling from the skies in burning, twisted wreckage. Medics and surgeons, already overwhelmed by the extreme number of casualties, raced to pull survivors from the wreckage.

A cheer arose from the defender's ranks as a massive troop carrier pierced the planet surface like a dagger in the heart. The frame crumpled under the weight and velocity as explosions rippled in a chain reaction. The carrier exploded, molten shrapnel shredding nearby troop formations and slagging numerous armored vehicles.

Shockwaves blew rings of ash and dust kilometers in every direction. Helmets dampened vision, enhancing eyesight through thermal optics. The enemy war machine ground forward. Matthias surveyed the damage. Flashbacks from An'kuruku whispered promises of the nightmare to come. He tried placing himself in the boots of those Guards marching through the carnage, praying they made it close enough to engage with rifles before artillery devastated them.

"Order the artillery batteries to increase their rate of fire," he ordered the radio operator beside him. "We need to break the lines before they enter small arms range. What's the status of our armor?"

"Sir, the First and Second Armored Divisions are in position and prepared to engage as ordered," she replied without looking up from the table array of screens and radios.

Cannon fire roared across the battlefield.

Confederation Operations Base, Ferom.

"Captain Fies, we've got incoming!" Haggle shouted across the command deck.

The whirl and hum of antiquated machinery threatened to drown out the myriad conversations.

"Put it on screen," he barked.

His eyes popped at the armored spear driving hard through Falchi's fleet. Each ship had enough firepower to reduce the moon base to rubble without deploying ground forces. No naval tactician, Fies scanned the enemy force for any weaknesses. He spied several small troop carriers dropping behind. *Looks like they want this place intact.*

Fies opened a channel to the mercenaries. "Bootleg, this is Fies. We're about to have company. Looks like division strength at least."

"Let them come. We're tired of waiting," Bootleg's reply was scratchy. "How long do we have?"

"Not long. Are you sure you can hold?"

"Does it matter? We hold and live or not."

Fies admired the man's grim determination. "I'll try and whittle them down before they land," he vowed. "Fies out."

He returned his view to the screen, pausing to count the number of friendly ships in the area of operations. *Not enough to break the assault. Not by half.*

"Operations center, this is *Vitriol.*"

Fies' heart beat faster. "Go ahead, *Vitriol.*"

"Reading the enemy force approaching. I am marshalling all friendly forces for a strike. We'll be going dark for a few minutes as we round the far side of the moon and come upon them from behind."

"Affirmative, *Vitriol.* Coordinate your attack with our defensive barrage," Fies replied.

They'd gotten the heavy guns online and, thanks to a detailed block of instruction from Paradise before the comet passed out of comms range, stood ready to engage any hostile force. Annalilly whistled her appreciation for the sheer size of the armaments. Like everything else on Ferom, the weapons were built by Tannus' people, far exceeding any mortal capabilities.

"Annalilly, are the defense batteries up?" Fies called out.

"And hungry for their first kill," she replied. "Say the word."

"Target the troop carriers and that dreadnaught first," he ordered. "Time to even the odds—fire."

"Firing."

Flashes lit the screens as the ground rumbled, threatening to tear apart. The scream of plasma shells rocketing into space echoed throughout the base, a reminder of the power that had once dominated the universe. Fies shielded his eyes, spots dancing across his vision. Streams of vermillion fumes tracked across open space. He watched the enemy fleet attempt to disperse, but their ships were slow and bulky. Two troop carriers were struck and vaporized in the blink of an eye. His mouth dropped open as the dreadnaught was sliced in half.

The broken halves split open and drifted apart, a field of bodies and debris stringing between them. To Fies' surprise, the rest of the fleet increased engine speed instead of falling back. Part of him admired their tenacity.

Warning sirens went off.

"Talk to me!" Fies shouted over the din.

"Engines are fried," Annalilly reported. "I've got no controls. We're dead in space."

Well, at least we got rid of that dreadnaught. Now it's up to Drukali and Bootleg. "Do what you can to get us back up and running."

"No promises."

Bootleg nearly pitched to the deck as the guns fired. Ancient dust trickled down from the ceiling in brown sheets. Men and women scrambled to repair walls of fallen sandbags and heavy weapon positions.

"What the fuck was that?" Asher asked as he picked himself up.

Bootleg spat a mouthful of dust. "Looks like this old girl has some teeth left. Fies just told the universe we're here."

"Do you think they hit anything?"

"I hope so, for all our sakes," Bootleg replied. "Or this will be my dumbest mistake yet."

"You mean your last mistake," Asher pointed out.

The intercom blared to life, halting the retort stinging the tip of his tongue. "Bootleg, this is Fies. Here they come."

"About time," Asher managed. "I'm tired of waiting."

"Take your position. I'm making a final sweep before hopping in the turret." Bootleg extended his hand. "Good luck, Asher."

"I was born lucky, boss."

TWENTY-EIGHT

3215 A.G. (After Gods), Plains of Haddash, planet Occanum.

Nestled in his turret, Confederation tank commander Newon Gruv watched the enemy formations march inexorably closer. He marveled at their courage while questioning if he had that same grit. His moment approached. All questions and doubts were laid bare in the face of the armored wall drawing nearer. Newon didn't expect to survive. He didn't think any of them would.

A warning blip announced the front ranks had entered long barrel range. Newon repressed the urge to hit the firing pedal and remind the enemy of what they marched toward. "Heads up, people. It won't be long now."

Newon looked down into the belly of his metal monstrosity. He saw the gunner and loader looking back at him. Fear and hope in their eyes. The assistant track commander pressed his hands together, his lips moving rapidly. Newon couldn't see the driver or front gunner. He closed his eyes and offered a quick prayer to the gods.

The rumble of artillery no longer made them jump. Few on the front lines even heard the thunderous roars. Newon knew thousands were already dead. Many more lay wounded or maimed. He'd never understand what drove men to commit such wickedness on each other. Perhaps it didn't matter. He was here, on Occanum, ready to do his part to ensure it never happened again.

The spear tip of the Prekhauten armor became clear. Menacing vehicles bristling with guns and dark promise. Newon swallowed. Large armor battles were all but unheard of during the Conclave's reign. He swore the entire Guard inventory rolled his way. A tremor began in his left hand, spreading up his arm. Newon tried to imagine the other tank commanders experiencing similar emotions. Were they scared? Ready to break and run? Or did they tap into a measure of resolve none knew existed?

He never got the chance to find out. The red warning above his computer terminal flashed green. "Fire!"

The tank bucked from recoil. Newon placed his face in the

tracking viewer and picked out his next target. Tanks opened fire up and down the line. They were rewarded with several kills, tearing gaps in the advancing lines. Black smoke rolled across the plain. Newon trained the gun on a stricken tank still operable and repeated the command. His second round killed the tank, blowing the turret off to one side and melting the front compartment. Newon almost grinned, until he spied a dozen barrels swivel his way.

"Brace for impact!"

Iver Tier earned his commission following Mobus Kale's orders. First on the low continent and then Krenz, he carved a bloody swath through the enemies of the Conclave. Now a company commander, he roared as the armored formations engaged the enemy. It was the first strike back against the Confederation traitors. Morale nonexistent among the infantry thanks to merciless barrages and airstrikes, Tier needed a small victory to keep his Guards ready to fight. With the enemy lines too far for the naked eye to discern, Tier imagined burning vehicles and fleeing infantry. No fool, he went over tactics and the battle plan.

The rumble of tanks pushing forward lessened, signaling it was almost time to advance. Heart pounding, Tier rechecked his rifle, ensuring the power charge was full. Rushed orders filtered over the company net. Squad leaders and platoon sergeants conducted last moment checks in anticipation of their assault.

"All units, advance in line and engage."

Tier exhaled the breath he hadn't realized he'd bene holding and issued the command to his company. Tens of thousands of Prekhauten Guards climbed to their feet, formed ranks, and headed into the killing fields. Cheers rose from the second line. Guards waved their rifles in the air. Emboldened by the support, Tier raised his rifle over his head in reply. The traitors would break and run without support of their heavy guns and armor. There was a flash followed by screaming.

War. Raw. Total. Perfect.

Mobus Kale watched the two armies clash. His blood coursing at the carnage, Kale's mind raced through endless possibilities. Neither side held the advantage, despite what the traitors might think. His differences with Amongeratix aside, Kale knew all it took to break those lines was one solid push. The leading edge of the assault was already under the traitor's protective artillery blanket, though the cannons continued reaping a heavy toll on the follow-on assault elements.

Grumbling at the wanton loss of life, Kale turned his attention to the massed ranks of skulldaerth … standing there. Amongeratix promised their use at the proper moment. In Kale's eyes it was past time. He cared little whether men lived or died, but prudence suggested he had need of every soul in uniform once the war ended and the reconciliation campaign began. The Prekhauten Guard never maintained large standing armies. That changed with his ascension to command. Kale vowed to grind all heresy and resistance beneath his heel across the universe. It began here on Occanum.

"Keep that armor moving!" he barked at his command staff.

Radio operators, runners, and staff officers glanced up from their screens and monitors for additional clarification. He gave none.

Warning sirens blared an instant before the frontlines exploded in thunder, flame, and fury. Entire infantry regiments were pushed to the ground as the shockwaves rippled across the battlefield. Walls of smoke and fire licked high into the damaged sky. Kale turned sideways and braced as the debris field slammed into his command area. Tents ripped away. Tables and maps cast to the wind.

Brushing the ash and dust from his chest, Kale regained his composure and scanned the damage. His mouth dropped in horror. Of the two hundred heavy tanks and armored personnel carriers sent in the first wave, less than twenty retreated. The others burned on the plains of Haddash. Brutal reminders of the cost of war. For the first time, he found the possibility of defeat was real. He scrambled to issue new orders when a horn rang out across the plain.

Loud and burrowing into the very soul, the horn signaled at the last march of the skulldaerth. Kale watched as his army shied away from the nightmare creations. In step, the skulldaerth marched through the disheveled Prekhauten ranks. Guards were trampled underfoot. Their cries added to the screams of the wounded.

Metal arm whirring, Kale stared at the skulldaerth long after their last rank entered the open space.

Indomitable, orbit planet Occanum.

"Sir! New enemy ship signature entering engagement zone,"

the helm officer shouted.

Falchi leaned forward, eyes fixed on the main screen. In his heart, he knew what approached. Nothing else could inspire the fear he heard in the officer's voice on sight. His fleets were taking a beating. Dozens were eliminated, either destroyed or forced to retreat just to stay alive. Proud of each captain and crew, they did their jobs, but so much needed to be done if Vau Prime's fleets were to be driven to surrender. Rather than giving in to fear, Falchi adjusted his jacket and gave Samuel a knowing look.

"Well, Captain, we will soon find out if we've stung our foes enough they forget their lessons in standard tactics."

Samuel, face blanched, said, "Yes, sir. Tactical, bring it up. Might as see this monstrosity for ourselves."

"Aye, Captain."

Behemoth dominated the screen. Hulking and bristling with weapons, the ship defied odds by remaining operable. Falchi saw signs of unprecedented damage, wounds accumulated from across the ages. If not for the asset lurking on Occanum's far side, he might have given the order for full retreat. The ancient ship reminded Falchi of a rotted tooth, spreading disease and filth. His stomach roiled. Striking him most was how different *Behemoth* was from *Brightstar*.

"My gods," Samuel uttered, the sentiment echoing across *Indomitable's* bridge. "We don't have enough firepower in our entire fleet to bring that down."

"Not in our fleet, no, but do not forget the assets Tannus provided." Falchi kept his calm.

"Should we worry about repelling boarders?"

"I shouldn't think so, Samuel. Arrogance appears to have gripped our counterparts. They are abandoning traditional tactics in favor of madness," Falchi cautioned. "Still, it won't do for us to be caught unprepared. Are the Marines in place?"

"Yes, Admiral. Gunny Asom has his contingent in the standard breaching points. We are well defended should Admiral Tuth feel inclined to waste lives."

Falchi didn't take his eyes from the screen. "Can you imagine an entire navy of these roaming the stars? Humanity never would have had a chance."

"It's a good thing the gods battled themselves to extinction," Samuel concluded. "What are your orders, sir?"

Falchi pointed. "There, do you see that? *Behemoth* brings a fleet of escort ships in her wake. If we place our focus on that nightmare the rest of Tuth's navy will swarm us. We won't stand a chance."

"Neither can we engage *that*," Samuel added.

"Agreed. Order all fleets to pattern delta. Break off and fallback. Let's give our friends over there the joy of giving chase," Falchi ordered. "With a little luck we can get the smaller ships to break off and expose themselves the way that dreadnaught heading for Ferom did."

Falchi was thrilled when Ferom's guns split the top of the line warship in half. Now over a hundred dogfights filled this portion of Occanum's space. Countless ships, pilots, and crewers engaged in battle. It wasn't enough. They needed August.

"New signals entering real space at five thousand kilometers! Ships are firing!"

Falchi spat. Tuth proved wilier than he'd given him credit for. While all focus went to *Behemoth*, the Grand Admiral sent a smaller strike force around the outskirts of the system to ambush the Confederation from the flank.

"All ships, brace for impact!" Samuel barked. "Turn us around. I want to meet them head on. Full firing solution immediately."

"Aye, sir. Full firing solutions plotting," the weapon's officer replied.

Falchi gripped the arms of his chair as *Indomitable's* artificial gravity struggled to compensate for the pitch as she wheeled to face this new threat. He heard the engines scream. Felt the hull buckle under pressure.

"We cannot ignore *Behemoth*," he said through gritted teeth.

"Admiral, it may be time to bring Admiral August into the fight," Samuel suggested.

"Brace for impact!"

Red light bathed the bridge. A warning siren yawled. *Indomitable* rocked from both outgoing anti-missile fire and incoming ordnance blasting gouges in the hull.

"Damage on decks thirteen through twenty. Multiple hull breaches. Repair crews are moving into position."

"We won't need repairs if we can't stop those missiles," Samuel snapped at the voice who reported the damage. "All guns, fire!"

Indomitable engaged. Missiles and rockets exchanged from the ships blazed across space. Falchi watched the lead enemy frigate take a salvo across the bridge. The brief flash of flame as what oxygen remained vented into space told him the ship was dead. A dozen others fanned out in standard attack patterns.

"Ship kill!"

"Bring the rest of the squadron up," Samuel ordered. "We can't win this alone. I want targeting solutions interspersed among our ships. No one strikes the same target. Fire at will."

Falchi spied *Behemoth* powering closer to the planet. Should she break the defensive screen the dreadnaught had enough firepower to break the Confederation ground forces at will.

"Admiral, we need August. Now," Samuel pleaded as the ship rocked from another salvo.

Falchi, having seen enough, agreed. "Send the word and give her my compliments. We'll handle this mob."

Indomitable rocked again. *I hope.*

A screen of fighters raced past the bridge, blazing bolts of blue-white cutting across space to strike unseen enemy ships. Falchi strained with his inability to do more than shout orders with Samuel and wait.

"Ship kill!" Tactical shouted.

Falchi's attention went to the strategic screen. An enemy cruiser blinked from red to black. Any satisfaction proved short lived when he counted the remaining numbers. *Not enough. Nowhere near enough. Come on, August, where are you?*

Brightstar rattled as her engines powered. Crewers ran to battle stations, both eager and terrified of what came next. Adrenalin coursing through their veins, the heart of the Confederation navy surged forward.

Krimpen Mass and Time caught glimpses of explosions in the distance through the shielded bays the cannons protruded from. A Prekhauten corvette exploded in a flash, crumbled steel drifting away. A trio of starfighters shot down by fierce anti-ship fire. Capital ships showed damage up and down their spines. Debris and bodies floated through space, turning all into a hellish world of unimaginable proportions.

"Why the fuck are we here again?" Krimpen gestured out the bay. "This is madness."

"We promised Vicente we'd help," Time replied with a shrug.

Rolling his eyes, Krimpen growled, "I'm going to kill him."

"All gun crews prepare to engage!"

Disturbed by the call, Krimpen twisted his neck to both sides in slow, deliberate stretches. Thankful for the distraction, he decided the pirate could wait.

"Are you two finished whispering sweet nothings?" Sergeant Mobac snorted.

Krimpen opened his mouth to snip while Time waggled a finger at their gun crew leader.

"Fire mission!"

Mobac dropped his glare at the issued command and began shouting to the crew.

Krimpen and Time hurried to their positions, ensuring the magazine racks were operating. Each cannon aboard *Brightstar* held fifty rounds in standing tubes, gas operated and self-propelled, they ensured the cannons sustained a continuous rate of fire for as long as necessary. Behind each weapon system was a storage bay filled with hundreds of rounds. While Krimpen amazed at the volume of destructive potential, Time mentioned he found the withered age of the ammunition disturbing.

"Hey, what happens if they don't work?" Krimpen whispered after the clicking lock of the breech slammed into place.

Time fixed him with a scolding look. "You're the reason we can't have nice things, Krimpen." He leaned closer. "There has to be life pods around here. Keep an eye out. Things turn sour and we skip out."

"There's only one place to go."

Time shuddered.

"We're going to die here, old friend." Krimpen slapped his back. "Might as well accept it."

"Or we do our damnedest to stay alive," Time replied.

"I like that idea better."

"Prepare to engage!"

Krimpen and Time exchanged worried looks, pausing to clasp forearms one final time before assuming their positions.

Confederation Operations Base, Ferom.

Drukali's damaged fleet struck with as much force as they had remaining. Several enemy ships were damaged beyond repair. Others were forced to turn and run, but not enough to prevent the troopships from landing on the lunar surface. *Vitriol* stormed into the fray, firing every operable cannon and laser. Small escort craft and a flight of fighters caught unawares evaporated to the cheers of the bridge crew. Drukali allowed the break in discipline. Smoke and electrical fires plagued his ship. The hull was beaten to the point of cracks in several locations, any amount of motivation helped.

Slipping through the split halves of the dreadnaught, *Vitriol* pushed as hard as her engines allowed. The corvette, last of his original command, screamed through space. Drukali knew it was a matter of time before a lucky shot crippled her for good. Until then, he vowed to unleash every measure of punishment she had remaining. Alongside him stormed the scattering of battered Confederation ships once seeking refuge on Ferom. Drukali admired his fellow captains. All marched willingly into what he determined a suicide scenario. His fears were confirmed when three ship signatures winked out of existence on the tactical screen.

"Where are those shots coming from?" he shouted over the din of communications gripping the bridge.

"Sir, enemy frigate in sector two. We hadn't picked her up until now."

Drukali spat. "Spin us about and engage. She's fresh in the fight. If we don't take her out now there won't be anyone to save those people on the moon."

"Aye, Captain!"

The Prekhauten frigate hove into view. A bristling fang of weapons come to kill them. "Not if I kill you first," Drukali muttered. "All guns, open fire!"

He watched as lances of white-hot energy flashed from his bow cannons. Similar streaks raced from the frigate.

Drukali opened shipboard communications and shouted, "All hands, brace for impact!"

"Ferom base, this is *Vitriol*. We've done all we can. You're on your own from here," Drukali's broken voice crackled over the speakers. "Gods speed."

The remnants of Drukali's conscripted task force, less than a handful now, streaked away from the Prekhauten fleet. Drop ships roared down to Ferom's surface, depositing thousands of assault troops.

Fies made out *Vitriol*. Sadness took him as he saw the darkened hull. Streams of oxygen poured into space. A handful of escape pods rocketed away. The once proud corvette was dead in space and no help was coming.

"Annalilly, take a squad down to Bootleg and report directly to me once the enemy makes contact." His heart ached as he watched her snatch up her rifle and hurry out of the command deck, her chosen squad filing in behind her. *Is this the last time I see you? Did I just send you to your death?*

Bootleg covered his ears as his short barrel artillery dropped their barrels and fired a salvo of anti-personnel rounds point blank into the advancing Guards. Smoke filled the bay, the report echoed louder and louder until ears bled. Bootleg clicked the button on the side of his visor, changing the screen to thermal imaging. What he saw sickened him. He estimated over a hundred bodies, or parts thereof, littered the surface. Not a bad start, but far from the success he required to stay alive.

"Hit em again!" he bellowed as the adrenalin gripped him.

The thump of HE rounds slamming into tubes was the sound of music. Bootleg shifted his cigar to the opposite side of his mouth and grinned like a fool as the thunder roared again. Any elation he felt faded as he caught sight of the enemy surging forward. Any normal unit would have broke and run. The cigar dropped from his mouth. *What sort of animals are these Guards?*

"First company, open fire," he ordered.

A line of tanks and armored vehicles barked. Heavy machine guns added to the cacophony. Slaughter commenced. Bootleg dropped behind his heavy gun atop the turret of his tank and depressed the butterfly trigger with both thumbs. An automatic grenade launcher spit a hundred rounds in the span of three heartbeats before reloading. The Shadow Hammers unleashed their full fury on the Prekhautens.

Rank after rank fell and still the enemy charged. Brave men and women driven by the whips of insanity. The first cracks in his defense came after the enemy entered small arms range. Sappers dragged themselves through the dust, camouflaged with specially designed cloaks preventing standard helmet imaging from detecting them. Bootleg spied the first rocket scream into the bay, striking the engine compartment of one of his light armored vehicles. The explosion was followed by several dozen more.

Bootleg scanned the immediate area, unable to find the source until a second salvo launched. He swiveled his machine gun, dropping the barrel to compensate the angle of fire, and fired as fast as the weapon could cycle. The distraction allowed enemy hoverjeeps converted for fast strikes to race in and fire a smokescreen into the bay. Bootleg kept firing until his weapon clicked dry. He discarded the used powerpack and reached for another. Ion rounds pinged off his vehicle. He ducked. The heat of energy rounds sizzling overhead.

Asher's voice came over the helmet, "Bootleg, they're getting inside. What do we do?"

Popping back up, Bootleg gasped in shock as the first enemy infantry units, decimated from the Shadow Hammers, entered the bay. He ran through quick calculations and reached an inescapable conclusion.

He keyed the intercom, "All Hammer units, this is Bootleg. Fall back. The bay is lost. You know the drill. Fall back to secondary positions and make these fuckers pay."

Several vehicles roared to life and began backing away from the fight. Dismounts retreated in an orderly procession, bounding back by squad under cover. Bootleg loved his people and watched their actions with pride. Many fell, wounded or dead. He slammed the fresh powerpack in and began raking the enemy infantry. The artillery fired a last salvo before withdrawing. Bootleg and Fies made contingency plans to abandon the main bay without losing all their armor assets. Neither expected an entire division to come for them.

"Bootleg, all elements are out of the kill zone," Asher reported after a brief spat of heavy fighting. "Get out of there."

Enemy Guards poured into the bay in small squads and fire teams. Bootleg gunned those down he spied through the smoke. They kept coming. Hundreds. The mercenary swept the battlefield, ensuring his people were gone but for the last company punishing the enemy.

"That's it, fall back."

The last handful of operable tanks and vehicles slowly disengaged at his order.

Enemy forces, sensing a rout, poured in and formed defensive postures. Bootleg waited as long as he could before depressing the switch in his gloved hand. He was rewarded with hundreds of explosives detonating up and down the enemy ranks. Reinforced doors slammed shut as the flames swept through. Bootleg thanked the gods the doors blocked out the screams that had started.

Right. Round one goes to us. "Secure secondary positions and dig in. That little stunt won't hold them long."

Bootleg dug into a pocket for another cigar.

Annalilly halted her squad in an old storage unit along the main corridor leading to the landing bays. Echoes of gunfire vibrated the walls. She flexed her fingers, the old aches returning. Born for moments like these, Annalilly double checked her ion rifle. The others followed her lead.

"Right. Sounds like the mercs are deep in it," she said. "We're not enough to shift the tide. Not against the size of the enemy force."

"So, we turn back," Jelin Quint said. His deadpan look made it seem more than a suggestion. "Ten of us aren't going to put much of a dent in them."

"Who would have expected a full fucking division come for us?" Annalilly snapped. "They paid for it though. Fies figures between us and *Vitriol's* force over half the division is slagged."

Haggle swallowed; his throat dry. "That's not enough. We're going to get k—"

"Say it and I'll do you myself." Annalilly's rifle swung toward him. "Listen up, all of you. This is the battle we've been waiting for. One last fight to break the Guard and end the war. I'm not ordering any of you to proceed. There's no shame. You don't think you got it in you, fine. Turn back. This is the only chance you have. I'm linking up with the mercs."

She shifted her gaze through her soldiers. Guards and friends she'd spent the better part of her career fighting alongside. Annalilly had no desire to see any of them die, but the mission always came at the expense of the soldier. To their credit, each met her gaze, unflinching.

Jolent, the ever-taciturn sniper stepped forward. "I fight. We've been pushed around too long. Let's kill some Guards."

Or so she thought he said. His thick accent made it next to impossible to understand the man.

"Anyone else?"

Beve slammed an elbow into Haggle's ribs. The heavy weapons specialist broke into a toothy grin. "Never cared for traitors. Universe is better without em."

Glowering at the man, Haggle quipped, "Sure, LT. We're in. Not like we have anything better to do."

"Speak for yourself," Quint cut in. "I finally have something to live for and would like to make it home to see if I can make it work."

Annalilly's eyes widened. She, and a few others, suspected he nurtured a growing relationship with Adris Moscasco's aid, Tempest, but had only supposition to go off. Until now.

"We both do, Quint." She laid a hand on his shoulder. "I don't plan on dying."

He passed a glance at the others before settling on her. "Good. I don't either. Let's get this over with."

Annalilly clicked off the safety and led them back into the hallway. They moved quick, covering the distance in short order.

Corporal Yeves took point. She'd once fought against the men and women beside her, back when no one understood the significance of events unfolding on Crimeat. Sickened, she switched sides. Now she led the charge, though whether from a renewed sense of duty or the desire to right past wrongs remained known only to her Annalilly could only speculate. At her side raced Hollis. The slender ex-Guard proved an integral part of the squad starting with the Kharsis campaign. Annalilly thought it only fitting they were here at the end.

Following the twisting corridors, the squad went into the depths of the base, coming out along one of the main arteries the Shadow Hammers were using to funnel ammunition and supplies forward. The smell of blood and expended munitions filled the air.

Haggle spat a mouthful of bile as the moans and cries of the wounded grew stronger. Noticing his emotion, she went to reassure him when Jelin Quint spoke,

"Focus on us. Don't look at them. It won't serve you any justice, Haggle. Trust me."

Wiping the wet stains from his face with a sniffle, Haggle said, "Right. We're almost there."

A series of detonations sounded.

"Annalilly, I'll take the flank," Quint called. "You lead to Bootleg."

"Copy. Palco and Hollis go with him," she ordered.

The trio broke off, leaving her and six others hurrying to find the mercenary commander.

Annalilly found him not long after. Bedraggled and covered in smoke and blood, Bootleg was the picture of death.

"We have to stop meeting like this," he barked, a laugh following upon seeing her. "Fies finally get tired of you?"

"Something like that. How bad is it?"

He glanced back over his shoulder where several platoons were engaged in a fierce firefight. A handful of bodies littered the ground. A medic worked frantically to save the life of another.

"We're holding, but not for much longer without a little help," he admitted. "I figure we took out over a brigade so far but I'm starting to bleed people, Annalilly. Most of my equipment is down. I have three tanks left, no artillery."

"Is there no way to get around behind them?"

"Why?"

"Take out their command and force them to fallback long enough to resecure the main bay?"

"Lady, there's not much of the main bay left. The mines I planted ensured that." He scoffed. "But sure. I have a few routes mapped out. Won't be able to take too many but a good enough sniper will crack a few heads and give our friends pause."

Annalilly broke into a cruel smile. "I have just the man." She turned, saying, "Jolent, job opportunity."

"Good." His dark skin glowed in the flickering light. "Who do I kill?"

"Anyone field grade and above. You shoot, the rest of us will provide cover," she said. "Bootleg, lend me a guide."

He nodded, though the look in his eyes lacked confidence. "Asher, get your tail over here. You ain't out the fight yet."

"Thanks, boss." Sarcasm dripped from the man.

Annalilly liked him already. "Alright, let's move. Beve, you and Desril take point with Asher. Haggle, bring up the rear." She gave Bootleg her sternest glare. "Hold the line, mercenary, or we're all dead."

"No pressure."

TWENTY-NINE

3215 A.G. (After Gods), Krenz, planet Vau Prime.

Night bathed the city. A blanket without comfort. Porii Daam hurried across the last main avenue on foot. She was part of the advance party, against Edam's wishes, and responsible for securing entry into the maintenance tunnels crisscrossing the entire capital district. Hundreds of hover trucks ferrying endless streams of supplies and food filled the tunnels daily. Three were laden with enough explosives to destroy half the city if not controlled. She wondered if the others were as concerned. So much had gone wrong.

"How much longer? The trucks are already in the queue," Edam panted.

Sweat beaded across his brow, emphasizing the labored rise and fall of his chest. Porii marveled at the man. How had the fate of Krenz fallen to the whims of a notorious criminal enterprise? She vowed to find and thank Aliz for the years of developing relationships with the man when no one was looking. If she survived.

"Not much. The access point is less than a kilometer ahead," she replied.

Edam and Thopos drew alongside her. "You are certain it's still there?"

"Your people confirmed such last night," she replied. "The gate has been used by the Conclave for decades whenever we did not wish prying eyes to know our goings on. Goethe may have tightened his hold on the city, but the old Conclave buildings are largely abandoned."

Thopos grinned. "Giving us the perfect opportunity to drive a dagger into the Inquisitor General's plans."

Porii raised an eyebrow. She found the man almost fatherly, in a rogue sort of way. "Right. We can end this tonight."

"Not if we don't get there," Edam warned. "We need to keep moving. The longer those trucks are waiting for us the better chance they are discovered."

"Let's go."

They reached the abandoned gate not long after. Vegetation had grown over most of it. Rust showed in several places. Porii had used this entrance twice in the past, never questioning why the Conclave hadn't invested in a proper gate. Iron bars built into what appeared a derelict building and surrounded by shrubs lent the appearance of an area people chose not to linger.

"This is it?" Edam balked. "We have tighter security than this."

"Sometimes hiding in plain sight is best. No one has ever entered the Conclave through here. Only the Forum and a select handful even know this exists," she said. Her voice dropped off, knowing she was one of the last alive.

Thopos snatched the gate and pulled. An agonizing screech sang out. "Just like home. Come on. The trucks are in position."

With Porii a step behind providing directions, they filed into the tunnel. Edam brought twenty of his best, leaving orders for the rest to disperse if their plan failed.

"This way," she urged when Edam fell back, his hand trembling. "We're almost there."

They reached the far end without detection, slipping into a small room containing an arrangement of office furnishings. Cobwebs decorated the corners. A layer of dust covered the floor. Porii marveled at their luck. This was it—Ezekiel Goethe had much to pay for.

Once in a secure location, they dropped the packs and started changing. Most wore traditional Guard uniforms. Edam and Porii slid into crisp Inquisition clothes, the blue tinged roses stark against the black background. Porii felt dirty.

"Are you sure about this?" Edam asked. "There's no turning back from this point."

"The Inquisition falls tonight," Porii confirmed and opened the door leading into the Conclave without pause.

Muttering, Edam and the rest followed.

"Stay calm, Edam," Porii soothed at seeing his hand going to his blaster. "We are almost there."

"Easy for you to say," he whispered back.

Porii ignored him, choosing to focus on the task at hand. They were as deep into enemy territory as they could get and had no time for distractions. She took them down a long staircase and into the main artery supplying the complex. Armed Guards patrolled the area, though the ones she saw bore disinterested looks. It was then she came upon the first checkpoint.

"Inquisitors, identification please," a grizzled sergeant missing her right arm said.

Porii handed over the fabricated chips, holding her breath as the Guard scanned them.

"What about them?" she gestured at the men behind Porii.

"They're with us. We are on special assignment from the Inquisitor General." She leaned conspiratorially close. "Between you and me I think it's overkill, but we've captured a high ranking Cardinal. The Inquisitor General is going to make her pay tonight."

"Damned red robes should all be strung up and executed for what they did," the Guard agreed. "We're better off without that stain. Enjoy it for me."

"Oh, I shall," Porii confirmed and led her team past security.

One step done.

"Are you certain they are positioned correctly?" Edam asked for the fifth time.

Thopos clasped his friend on the shoulder and said, "Relax. The last thing we need is someone making my guys jumpy. Remember, one little mistake and boom."

"We are in the right place. The bombs are positioned to bring the entire center of the building down," Porii added. "We need to set the timers and get out before it's too late."

It was well beyond too late in Edam's opinion. What little courage he had remaining threatened to flee, robbing him of both strength and sound judgment. His legs wobbled. His vision clouded. Edam admitted he wasn't made for situations like this. Now that he was here, the criminal mastermind struggled with the urge to break and run. He glanced as Thopos set the last timer and wiped his hands on his trousers.

"That's the last of them. We have fifteen before the bombs go off."

Several of their people broke up into groups of two or three and headed for the exits.

"Let's move," Porii prompted.

They turned to leave and stopped in their tracks as soon as they rounded the corner leading to the main corridor. A squad of Guards stood, weapons raised and pointed at them. Several of Edam's people were already on their knees, hands behind their heads. Three Inquisitors stood with the Guards, blasters drawn and glaring at the trio with unmistakable sneers. Eyes flitting between the Guards and his people, Edam toyed with doing something stupid.

"Well, well, I hadn't thought any of the Forum remained at large," a thin man in a white uniform stepped through the ranks to confront them. "Porii Daam. You didn't honestly believe you could sneak into the depths of my domain without being recognized, did you?"

"Ezekiel Goethe," she snarled.

He titled his head, eyes never leaving her. "At your service. If you would be so kind, lay down any weapons you may have. Slowly. It would be a shame to kill you here when so many of the adoring public clamor for your head."

Edam and Thopos obeyed, making a show of their compliance. Helplessness filled Edam's eyes. Ezekiel watched with casual disinterest. He then pointed at the nearest Inquisitor. The man placed the barrel of his blaster on one of Edam's men and pulled the trigger.

"No!" Edam shouted, horrified as the body slumped to the floor.

Ezekiel leered. "I said it would be a shame to kill you, not them. If anything, you have done me a great favor, Cardinal. I assume this is the mysterious head of our secret criminal underground. You have plagued this city for too long. A new order of justice reigns. There is no room for the likes of any of you."

"You'll pay for this," Edam said through his teeth. "I'm going to kill you."

"Quaint," the Inquisitor General replied, focusing on Porii "Tell me, Cardinal, why are you here? What is your scheme?"

"You'll have to torture me to confess," Porii snapped.

"Oh, I shall," he told her without raising his voice. "I shall and you will beg for death before I am through. Your death cements the last fall of the Conclave. I win. Now, hands above your heads and join your companions."

"How did you know I was here?" Porii asked.

"The Guard at the security station was once assigned to your detail, but I don't suspect you recall. Clergy seldom took time to know their subordinates," Ezekiel explained. "She reached out to my office the moment you passed her desk. I knew I had to come personally, for you are the last. The end of the Forum. The others are dead and soon you shall join them."

"Now who has hubris?" she taunted,

Edam met her gaze seconds before she shoved him back and tossed a pair of grenades into the massed Guards.

The explosions sent bodies flying.

Confused, he struggled as Porii shoved him a second time and shouted, "Go! Get to the trucks and get out of here while you can."

Edam stilled, watching as she scooped a blaster from the ground and began firing. He stepped to follow her, unwilling to allow another to die in his place when Thopos stopped him. The grizzled old man snatched Edam by the collar and spun him back toward the loading docks. Several of his people slipped by, following Porii's last command. He was swept in the tide of escape. He couldn't go back now if he wanted to. The rest engaged the Guards with hands and teeth.

Come on, you bastards. Cut your teeth on this! Porii opened fire.

Thopos grabbed the blaster beside Porii and added his fire to the battle. He was rewarded by two rounds to the chest. Porii reached for him out of instinct before taking a round to her shoulder. The impact pitched her to the ground beside him. A second and third round hit her back and leg. Tears streamed down her face from the pain. She reached out a hand to caress Thopos' cheek, noticing the life was already gone from him.

"Thank you," she whispered.

Ezekiel Goethe stepped from the chaos. His uniform smeared with black stains, hair out of place. Blood trickled down his cheek. Fury enlarging his eyes, the Inquisitor General aimed his blaster at Porii and slipped his finger on the trigger.

She refused to close her eyes. He didn't deserve it. Porii Daam spat a mouthful of blood at Ezekiel right before the world exploded. Hatred blazed in her eyes. One final look of defiance. Then, nothing.

Eger City, planet Mannus Prime.

"Kill me now and be done with it!" Tinnus Har demanded.

For days he railed against the fractured dissidents of Eger City. Tinnus vowed to slaughter every last one the moment he broke free. The people of Mannus Prime would never forget his name. The aggression soon whimpered out. A flame snuffed in infancy. No visitors came. No captors to gloat. He was forgotten. His worse fears realized.

When the door creaked open, showing him light for the first time beyond reckoning, Tinnus' legs went out. Collapsed in a puddle of storm water and human waste, he shielded his eyes from the obscene glare.

"Get up."

Harsh. Removed. The woman's voice barked a simple command he struggled obeying. Rough hands jerked him to his feet when he failed to comply fast enough. He cringed, fearing the inevitable beating, but none came. Other than a steadying hand, no one laid a hand on him. Gradually, the stars and black lines dancing across his vision cleared and he looked upon the stern face of Adris Moscasco.

"You were given one chance to prove yourself," she began when he opened his mouth. "A final opportunity to prove you were not the snake the universe remembers you as. Clearly that was a mistake, but I felt obligated to try."

"More the fool you," he wheezed. "Have you come to kill me, Moscasco? Are you my executioner?"

"Nonsense. We are not the same, Tinnus Har. You may have been neglected since your capture, but you were never harmed. My guards were specifically instructed not to touch you," she said, her tone measured. "It is certainly more than you deserve, but I am no killer. The Confederation operates under different principles, Tinnus. It is a shame you never gave them a chance before launching your insurrection. I should thank you. Without you we wouldn't have had an in with the local dissidents. Those who survived are being rounded up as we speak. Your coup has failed."

Tinnus swallowed the little saliva he had. "What do you plan on doing with me? I've shown my colors. You can't keep me here, not without compromising your lofty moral principles. Nor can you set me free. I pose too much of a threat, even in this pathetic condition."

"You will be cleaned up, dressed in fresh clothes, and taken to a shuttle. There you will be deposited on a small planet far from the reaches of power to die an old man," Adris' gaze sharpened when he whimpered. "Never again will the universe suffer your indulgences. You are banished from the Confederation upon penalty of death." She stepped back. "Guards, clean him up and escort him off my planet."

Tinnus Har was strapped in and blindfolded. He shifted awkwardly in the web meshing as the shuttle vibrated on takeoff, breaking through the atmosphere and into space. Unseeing and unable to move thanks to the restraints locking his hands in place, the former Cardinal Seniorus accepted the indignity of his situation, barely.

The thought of a fresh start enticed him. Tinnus failed to comprehend how the Confederation had anywhere in the universe untainted by the Conclave, however. Religious fervor ran high among the seven hundred worlds. He and his predecessors ensured that.

The flight smoothed as the shuttle broke free of the gravity well. Quiet settled throughout the cabin. No one spoke. No one came to him with promises of violence. Tinnus eventually drifted off to sleep.

He awoke a short time later, muscles stiff and sore. A foul taste lingered on his tongue.

"Water?"

Footsteps edged closer. He felt calloused fingers fumble around the edge of the blindfold. Tinnus flinched when a few short hairs by the tops of his ears ripped out. His scowl turned to outright disgust when he looked up.

"Traitor," he hissed.

Dowan Mun, dressed in civilian clothes lending him a trader's appearance, folded his arms and leaned against the nearest bulkhead. The shadow of a beard decorated his face. Wild knots of hair sprawled from his scalp. If Tinnus didn't know better, he'd never suspect the man of once being an Inquisitor.

"That's all you have to say?" Dowan asked.

Tinnus knew better than to struggle. A sinking feeling crept in. "Why are you here? Completing the dirty work Moscasco assigned?"

"Don't place yourself on a pedestal," Dowan cautioned. "I was sent to babysit you. Make sure you either played by the rules or broke them. You chose to break them. Turning you in ensured my freedom. You were just an assignment. Nothing more."

"And she assigned you to take me to my forever home?" Tinnus sneered.

Dowan loomed over him. "Actually, I decided to take matters into my own hands. You see, she gave me back my life, but I knew I was never going to be free. Not with the stain of serving the Inquisition marking me. I needed to find an out. A way to disappear without worrying about the Confederation coming after me.

"Then I realized my business with you wasn't finished yet. I have a score to settle with you, Tinnus Har. You almost got me killed, for no reason. So, I did a little digging and found out what shuttle you were on and when you departed. It didn't take much to subdue the pilot and take his place." He grinned when Tinnus stiffened. "Oh don't worry, he's alive. Might have a headache when he wakes up, but still breathing. The only way for you to stop haunting me is from me dealing with you once and for all."

Tinnus flinched and began struggling with his restraints. "Coward and traitor! Let me go and face me like a man. Better yet, free me and I guarantee you will never hear from me again. I'll disappear and become forgotten. You have my word."

"Your word isn't worth shit."

Tinnus clamped his mouth shut, knowing the point in pleading was already past.

A red light blinked on, filling the cabin with an ethereal glow. Dowan's eyes lit up, sparkling with madness. "Time's up," he announced. "We're here."

"Where is here?" Tinnus asked.

"Your final destination—goodbye, Cardinal Seniorus."

"You can't do this!" Tinnus shouted at Dowan's back as the Inquisitor returned to the cockpit and sealed the door. "Mun! This is murder! Stop!"

A warning alarm chimed. Tinnus glanced around, frantic to break his bindings. The hiss of escaping oxygen filled the cabin with a roar. He watched in horror as the back ramp unsealed, opening to the endless maw of space. Tinnus opened his mouth to scream as he was sucked out the shuttle.

Dowan Mun turned the shuttle to watch the frozen corpse drift away. For the first time in his life, he was truly free, and a universe of possibilities awaited. The shuttle drifted as he contemplated his destination.

Plains of Haddash, planet Occanum.

They struck with unrepressed fury. Thousands of ancient monstrosities shrugging off ion rounds as they closed on the front ranks of Confederation infantry. Bodies littered the plain behind them.

Unable to repel the skulldaerth, the infantry fought to the last. Axe and sword slashed into Confederation soldiers. The skulldaerth struck with no sound. No roars or battle cries. They executed the sole task they'd been created for.

Until the Confederation front lines gave way to reveal a surprise of their own. Thousands of automatons marched at the skulldaerth. Monster and machine clashed.

Sorrow watched his creations take the field. A father's pride twinkled in his deep-set eyes. Though he longed for a time when violence proved obsolete, he roused to the challenge of defeating the elder magic his brother used in creating the skulldaerth. Sorrow spent decades studying the creatures. Dissecting stolen specimens, researching what little scraps of information existed. Once, long ago, Sorrow discovered the remnants of Amongeratix's labs and found enough to develop his counterpunch. Seeing them engage sickened and inspired him in equal measure.

"Magnificent creations," Tannus said as he strode to his brother. The wind swept his long, black hair. Smoke stained his armor. "You did well, brother."

"They should never have been forced into this situation," Sorrow replied. "I lament the twisted fate which perverted my designs."

"Needs must," Tannus grunted. "Amongeratix must be stopped."

"We have been through this before, Tannus. Forever trapped in an endless cycle. Look at them. Killing without regard. Abandoning the principles of life." Sorrow lowered his gaze, unable to meet the glorious demise of his hard work. "It won't be long now. Amongeratix will not be able to resist the call. He knows we are here. He will come."

Hefting his massive sword, Tannus fixed his brother with a menacing stare. "Good. Then we shall conclude our business."

Sorrow watched as he stormed off, slow, thunderous steps wading into the field of battle. *Fight well, brother. May this time be the last.*

Men and women ran at the sight of his giant frame. Tannus raised his sword over his head and roared. Confederation soldiers responded in kind, doubling their efforts. The front line bent in the center, folding back on the Prekhautens. Dozens of ion rounds struck Tannus' armor. Infuriated, the giant struck. His efforts were rewarded a moment later when the sky shimmered.

All around the battle froze. Fingers pointed at the disturbance. Tannus halted his strike, planting the tip of his sword in Occanum's ash. His chest rose and fell in great heaves. Thousands of years of regret led him to this point. The ghosts of his people watched from a distance, eager to see the inevitable conclusion to their sad tale.

Shockwaves knocked those closest to the ground. Hurricane strength winds swept across the plain, screaming and growling. Tannus stood firm. When light at last returned he stared at the stalwart figure of Amongeratix.

"Brother!" Amongeratix bellowed. "We meet again!"

"There will be no quarter for you, my brother," Tannus shouted back.

On cue, both armies began pulling back in a mighty circle. Brother circled brother. Skulldaerth and automaton battled to the last.

Amongeratix leered at Tannus. Wild, untampered. "Come, let us finish our struggle and see who is fit to rule the universe."

"This day shall be your last, brother," Tannus vowed.

Amongeratix raised his sword and beckoned Tannus forward to the roar of outgoing artillery. Feral look twisting his face, Tannus accepted the challenge.

Abbey of the Order of Blood Witches, Acumensiis Comet.

"Long has been your journey. Your trials are beyond compare, yet each of you has weathered the storm to this point. I do not envy what comes next, for evil ever hungers. Whether you have the fortitude to survive remains to be seen, but you go with the good wishes and preparations of the Order of Blood Witches." Ruma Zzein paused to sweep her gaze over the assembly as they gathered to leave. "I do not promise you victory. Amongeratix is a worthy foe. You have the tools, the training, and the knowledge to do what must be done. Go with the blessings and well wishes of my kind. Yours is the noble charge. A quest many before you have attempted without success." She stopped to meet each's gaze, settling on Elisa last.

"Use the dagger, Paladin. Strike Amongeratix down and free the universe from this endless cycle of violence and bloodshed. Only you can do it and that is enough. No charge is placed upon the rest of you. You are free to go at will, though I caution the success of the mission is in the balance."

Elisa shifted her weight to the opposite leg, lowering her gaze. She drew a deep breath and stepped onto the barge. The others followed one by one in silence.

Tolde Breed was the last to board. A somber pall cast upon his face. He settled a final look at Ruma Zzein before his gaze cast to the smaller Presha Von standing beside her. He nodded then turned and boarded.

Ruma Zzein watched them leave, a prayer on her lips. She had planned for this moment for centuries and now that it was here found herself locked in a cell of her obscurity as those precious few players prepared to fulfill her designs. The cruelty of not being able to help, here at the end, stung.

THIRTY

3215 A.G. (After Gods), Plains of Haddash, planet Occanum.

Torgast watched as the titans battled. Spark and flame danced from their swords. The ground trembled, breaking open with each thunderous blow. Both armies continued falling back, no longer as interested in slaughtering each other. He ordered the artillery and airstrikes to intensify, knowing better than to accept any lull. Somewhere across the plain, he knew Mobus Kale did the same.

"Matthias, this is Torgast. Do you have eyes on Kale?" he said after snatching a handset.

"Negative. The field is too distorted. I can't make out our lines from theirs," Matthias replied. "Hells, I can't tell who's winning."

Torgast winced at Matthias' intonation. He didn't think it much mattered if Amongeratix wasn't stopped.

Refocusing on the struggle between brother, Torgast spied the crimson figure of the Bloody Man wading through the armies to a point far from his brothers. "Where is he going?"

Tracking the giant's path, Torgast spied the very target he sought. To his surprise, the Bloody Man was marching into the heart of the enemy army where a trio of witches in crimson cast bolts of magic into the Confederation ranks. He reached for the handset again.

"Matthias, I found him! Plotting firing solution now," he called.

"Roger, artillery on standby," Matthias replied.

Now you pay for your crimes, you fucker. Time to die, Mobus.

Guards fell back as a creature torn from their nightmares waded into their ranks. Sorrow slayed all foolish enough to engage or were too slow to escape. A squad of automatons marched at his back, carving a path of damage no human could withstand. Mayhem gripped Occanum, much as it had three thousand years ago when the last of his kind waged war. While Tannus focused on Amongeratix, he left himself exposed to the traitor witches wreaking havoc among the Confederation.

The skulldaerth and automatons were whittled down to handfuls, having fought for the entirety of the day. Each served their purpose. Whatever survived wouldn't escape the planet. Sorrow pushed those thoughts aside. His initial surprise upon discovering a cadre of traitor Blood Witches exposed raw emotions. Any respect he held for the Oracle, including the debt incurred from her Order keeping him alive after the madness made him flense himself, diminished in the face of this new threat. Sorrow needed to eliminate the witches so the Paladin could fulfill her purpose unopposed.

Bodies trampled underfoot. Others sliced in two by his slender sword. Sorrow dripped blood in his wake. Some Guards stood fast, determined to win glory. They died like the rest. A bolt of magic, green-yellow in the fading light, slammed into his chest. Sorrow grunted and shook it off. Fools. Magic had no lasting effects on his kind. Snarling, he broke through the final perimeter. A light armored hoverjeep slashed across his line of march. Panicked Guards unleashed a hail of ion fire at point blank range.

Clothes scorched, armor blackened, the assault did little more than increase Sorrow's agitation. With a mighty bellow from the bottom of his lungs, the giant swung down and sliced the jeep in half. The wreckage crashed into the ash and dust, both Guards scrambling to get free. Sorrow moved with lightning quickness, grabbing the gunner by the throat and heaving him over the army. The engine exploded behind him, incinerating the driver.

Unaffected by the damage, Sorrow crossed the distance to the nearest witch. Magic splashed from his armor, dripping impotent to the ground. He flexed his grip and cut diagonally. The witch came apart in a cloud of vapors accompanied by a sonic scream only he heard. Sorrow wasted no time in moving on the next witch. His intimacy with the Order left no room for error. Any witch proved dangerous.

A wall of flames met his advance. Sorrow paused, throwing an arm to shield his face as the heat washed over him. He felt his scabbard melting. Sweat poured down his body. Undaunted, the giant broke through and came face to face with the remaining witches. To his surprise, he recognized one.

Algiss Her gawked at the Bloody Man carving a path through the Guards. She recalled their only meeting, now so distant cobwebs clouded the edges of her memory. Algiss played a large role in saving Sorrow's life. Those actions now mocked her as bodies fell like wheat to the scythe. She turned her focus to the weak assaults of Sister Ibrest against the giant. Algiss knew the outcome before Sorrow's blade flashed.

The repercussions of so much power unleashed back to the universe made her sag. At her side, Sister Evangaline dropped from the air, collapsing on her hands and knees. Ash clouds puffed off the ground, choking both witches. Algiss wiped the grime from her eyes and thrust both hands out toward the approaching giant, funneling her will and strength at him. It wasn't enough. Sorrow broke through and locked eyes with her.

Algiss snarled. "Bloody Man! You have come for me, eh? Ruma Zzein's dog sent to right old wrongs. Bah! Come and taste my fury!"

Her assault drove him back one step, then another. Smoke and steam billowed off him. Patches of blood flash dried only to weep again.

Evangaline picked herself up, lifting back in a hover and added her strength to the Crimson Mistress' magic. They watched Sorrow stagger under their combined weight. Thinking they'd stolen the advantage, the witches advanced–Algiss recognized their mistake as Sorrow broke into a rictus grin.

His sword flicked. Evangaline screamed as the ancient blade sliced through both her wrists, severing her link with the true power of the universe. A backhanded swing took her head.

Sorrow executed a riposte and struck Algiss Her in the chest as Evangaline's death scream rattled her. The Crimson Mistress slipped from his blade. A useless sack of flesh. Panting, struggling for each breath that came slower than the last, she watched her slayer step off to find new victims. The irony of being murdered by a man she once saved burned in her mind until darkness took her.

"That's it," Torgast slammed a fist on the waist high sandbag wall. "All batteries, open fire while they're distracted."

"But sir, the Bloody Man…"

Torgast fixed his radio operator with a grim look. "Will forgive us." *Or he won't.* "Open fire. I want Kale dead."

Mobus Kale growled from atop his vehicle. Unlike other commanders, he longed to be in the heart of the fight. That irrationality put him in place to witness a sight few lived to tell of. His heart hammered in his chest as he watched the Bloody Man step from myth to reality. Envy flared his cheeks. Oh how he longed for such power. Each step and cut the Bloody Man executed displayed natural artistry. If he had a tenth of such power at his command the universe would bend to his will. Marvel turned to shock when the hoverjeep exploded and the first witch died.

The Bloody Man killed Algiss Her, eliminating a threat and the main obstacle to his ascension to Amongeratix's right hand. Mobus roared to the skies in triumph and ordered his guns turned on the monstrosity marching his way.

Confederation Operations Base, Ferom.

"This is fucking nuts," Jelin Quint barked over the roar of gunfire. "We don't have enough guns to keep them back!"

"Keep firing! We need to buy Bootleg time to mount the counterassault," Annalilly shouted back.

Slamming a shoulder into the wall to avoid a pair of ion rounds, Quint grunted and returned fire. An enemy soldier pitched back but the hole filled immediately. The squad had regrouped at the crossroads of the two main arteries leading in and out of the base. Quint and his team secured a major side access passageway, allowing Bootleg to funnel fresh troops back to the front lines undetected.

Blood streamed down Asher's face. He sprinted to Quint, adding his fire to the hail repressing the Guards attempting to secure the entry point. "We need to keep pushing."

Quint agreed but failed to see how to proceed without suffering unacceptable casualties. "Give our man a chance. He's the best damned sniper I've seen."

Asher pushed forward, forcing Quint and the others to keep up. He spied the small cylinder flying from Asher's hand and warned the others to close their eyes before the flash bang went off. The enemy was not so fortunate. Asher and the squad fell on them with uncontrolled fury, clearing the position and securing it in short order.

Quint wheeled on the man, snatching him by the collar below the chin. "You play the fucking hero again and I'll kill you myself. We didn't come here to die because of some merc shithead who couldn't cut it in the Guard."

Asher grinned, maniacal and dangerous. He slapped Quint's hand and stalked away.

"Do that again, asshole," Quint warned.

Annalilly took his place. "What was that all about?"

Quint never took his eyes off the mercenary. "I'm just trying to keep everyone alive. That idiot too. Is Jolent in position?"

"And popping off heads," she confirmed. "He's reporting mass confusion among the junior ranks. Between their initial losses after dulling their teeth on the Shadow Hammers and now losing their leadership we have them ready to break."

He shook his head. "We don't have enough to keep them out. If they regroup…"

"Let Fies worry about. He has a few tricks up his sleeve yet. We just need to push these fuckers back into the main bay and keep them there."

"Haggle, get your ass up here," Quint barked.

The junior sergeant knelt beside him out of breath. "What's up, Sarge?"

"Take your team and cover Asher. Try not to get killed."

"No promises," Haggle quipped and rose again. "My people, let's roll."

Yeves and Beve followed in behind Haggle. They soon caught up with the mercenary, joining him on the mad dash to inner bay doors. Asher ducked, sidestepping the scattering of rifle shots meeting them, and leapt into one of the sandbag bunkers Bootleg constructed before the battle. Haggle and the others joined him, against his better judgment. They established a base of fire with Beve's heavy machine gun anchoring the center.

Haggle wanted to wait for Annalilly and the rest of the squad to arrive before engaging but Asher opened fire before he voiced his concerns. The mercenary unleashed his fury on the distracted Guards, felling several before others took notice and returned fire. Fragmented squads adjusted fire on the bunker, bounding closer with each salvo. Grenades exploded against the sandbags. Haggle fell back, ears ringing as Beve opened fire.

Return fire intensified. Haggle scanned the bay, dismayed to find over a full company advancing on their position. *Damnit, where is everyone?* He slammed his rifle on the sandbags and took aim. Haggle's eyes widened as he spotted a pair of rocket launchers zeroing in.

"Beve, get down!" he screamed as both rockets fired.

"Haggle!" Quint shouted, throwing a hand up to prevent the flames and debris from the explosion from striking his face. Rage and sorrow took over—he hefted his rifle and charged.

He made it one step before Annalilly jerked him aside. "They're dead! Get your head back in the fight. We've got a job to do."

"We don't know that!"

The stench of roasting flesh choked the rest of the squad. Quint felt his stomach rebel. Fingers of black smoke curled up over the bay door to run along the ceiling.

Annalilly softened her voice. "Quint, they're gone, but we can still win. Help me get the doors closed and we can avenge our friends."

He slowed his breath, pausing to close his eyes before bobbing his head. Sealing the bay was their only option now that the attempt at securing the entry failed. Quint and Annalilly, with the rest of the squad forming a base of fire down the center of the hallway, raced to each side of the bay door. They hit the controls, slamming the blast doors shut and locking them before the Guards in the bay reacted.

Annalilly made the call back to the command room while Quint placed a gloved palm on the door before they left.

"The gate's sealed. Do it now!"

The call came in and Fies hit the control on the main board, holding his breath. Warning sirens raged throughout the room. Soldiers paused their duties to watch the flames engulf the main landing bay, incinerating man and machine. A sneer filled his face. They'd won. Kale's division was decimated. Less than a battalion's worth was now moving through the base to return to their drop ships in a mad dash to survive. Gunships strafed them at will. The skies over Ferom were clearing of enemy ships.

Cheers rose from his company. Fies, ever reluctant to admit victory until the last shot was fired, felt the tension drain from his shoulders. He was about to order Bootleg to mop up the enemy and secure the base when the doors hissed open and Annalilly and the others strode in.

Fies scanned their faces. "How many?"

"Haggle, Beve, and Yeves," Annalilly replied, stone-faced. "Hollis is shot up. Doc's doing all he can to plug her leaks. He says she should make it.”

She kept talking but Fies stopped listening. His thoughts swirled around their lost comrades. Haggle's perpetual jovial attitude. Beve's solemn commitment. Yeves willingness to do whatever it took without being forced to. Friends. Boon companions.

“Bootleg, wrap this up,” he ordered, pausing to clear his throat and sniff. He glanced at Annalilly, “Go ahead and take your people to the aid station. I'm going to need you soon.” When no one moved, he tried again, “Hey, do you hear me?”

Frowning, Fies noticed the squad looking past him, to the main screen dominating the far wall. He turned, following their gaze. His mouth dropped open. Eleven massive dreadnaughts filled the screen.

Brightstar.

“*Revengence*, withdraw. Do not engage. This is *Brightstar*, I repeat, do not engage. We got this,” August pleaded. The flagship continued plunging into the heart of the battle and, to her dismay, a direct course with *Behemoth*.

“Negative, *Brightstar*. We are engaging. Let us soften them up for you. We have a score to settle,” Khe-Zhehan replied. She cut the channel after saying, “Gods speed, August.”

“Stupid woman,” August fumed with clenched fists.

“She's going to die,” Blackheart chimed in.

Wheeling on him, August shouted, “I know that!”

The pirate held his ground, holding up both hands in mock surrender.

August turned to her bridge. “Helm, can we intercept before she engages?”

“Negative, Admiral. Best case we arrive just after.”

Odir leaned closer and whispered, “Admiral, she won't last that long.”

“All ships, full speed and engage at will. I want that ship out of my space,” she barked. Crewers executed her orders in total silence. August glanced up at Odir. “This ends now. Get me Admiral Falchi.”

Indomitable.

“Admiral, incoming transmission from *Brightstar*,” Samuel

announced. "She is engaging with *Behemoth* now. She requests support with smaller ships and fighters and, ah, rescue operations."

Falchi pulled his gaze from the tactical screen. "Rescue ops? For whom? Her ships have enough firepower to wipe out both fleets."

"It appears Admiral Khe-Zhehan is attempting to make up for past mistakes by taking on the dreadnaught solo." Samuel's face blanched. "She's committing suicide."

The sound of Falchi's fist slamming down caused several of the crew to flinch. The battle raged around them. Ships from both sides dying. Enough debris choked the airspace that several of the smaller ships risked damage navigating the area. A quick calculation showed *Indomitable* too far from the dreadnaughts to matter.

"Order the fleet in. We can't abandon her like that, Samuel," Falchi said through clenched teeth.

"All ships, prepare to shift engagement and clear a path to those dreadnaughts," Samuel ordered. "Ensure to stay out of the line of fire. Do not engage *Behemoth*."

Grand Admiral Achen Tuth reveled in watching *Revengence* explode. Khe-Zhehan served as a thorn in his side for too long. Removing her stain from the universe proved mildly satisfying. Dozens of escape pods plummeted away to the safety of the planet's surface. He cared little for them, knowing Kale's armies would make short work of them soon enough. Instead, his focus lay on the ten massive ships barreling through the battlefield. Dreadnaughts in the same make and model as his ship.

"All batteries open fire! Bring those ships down!" he bellowed.

The space between the ships erupted.

"Gods damn it, get up Sharlyn!" Blackheart grunted as he tried pulling her free from the melting beam covering half the bridge.

Smoke filled the area. Several crewers and bridge officers lay dead. Red lights bathed the mangled bridge. Work crews struggled putting fires out. Medics and corpsmen treated the wounded, pausing to cover the faces of the dead. Blackheart ached from burns down the left side of his body. None of that mattered. August was still alive, though her breathing was shallow. Blood covered her face and hands. Odir lay dead by her side, all but crushed under the weight of the beam.

"I need help!" Blackheart shouted over the chaos. Blood flowed down his right sight, aggravated by his need to rescue August.

Two shadows fell over him. Blackheart looked up to find Krimpen Mass and Time bending down to lift the beam.

"What are you doing here?" he asked.

"One. Two. Lift," Time strained. The beam rose just enough for Blackheart to give a final pull. August's body slid free a moment before the beam crashed back down.

Krimpen extended his hand to the kneeling pirate. "Our gun was destroyed in the fight, but we got a few good licks in on those fuckers. *Behemoth* ain't troubling anyone anymore."

"Figured we could do more here on the bridge than down there," Time added. "Besides, no one will miss us."

Blackheart didn't know whether to cry or kiss both men. "Come on, help me get her to sick bay."

Time gestured to Odir. "Who's in command if they're not?"

Pausing, the pirate gave Odir a final look before taking in the rest of the bridge. Blood thundered in his ears. His mouth went dry. "Well, I suppose I am. Get her patched up, boys. Please. I'll handle this."

Blackheart watched as Krimpen Mass and Time carried the stricken admiral to a pair of nearby medics, forcing them to set aside the wounded crewer for August. Neither medic appeared pleased, though both thought better of interfering. With August on her way to medical treatment, Krimpen and Time ambled back to the captain station where he waited.

"She's good. Where do you need us?" Time asked with a smile. The tattoos on his face wrinkled. "There's still plenty of ships to kill out there."

Absconding with *Brightstar* would never prove easier, but Blackheart knew there'd be no living with himself if he did. He clasped both men on their shoulders; an old spark igniting. "Pick an empty spot. Let's get this ship back in the fight."

Plains of Haddash.

Tannus lowered his sword. He breathed heavily, as did his brother. The armor slowed them, making each swing an effort. Blood dripped from dozens of cuts on both brothers. Bruises marked their exposed flesh, for there were no rules of engagement. For the first time since engaging Amongeratix, Tannus paused to look around the battlefield. Human armies ceased fighting to watch them struggle. Wind swept the plains, carrying the stench of battle far and wide to the song of the wounded. Amongst the near endless crowds of watching soldiers stood the Bloody Man. An old pain dating back to the fateful moment they were cast from their father's presence marred his face. Tannus looked away.

"Had enough, brother?" Amongeratix sneered through a mouthful of blood. "You never did have the willpower to match your lofty convictions."

Tannus raised his chin, pulling at the cut running down his cheek. "Ever have you talked when you should fight. This ends today. One of us shall stand. The other falls."

"I look forward to it." Amongeratix pointed his sword at Tannus. "Your head will decorate my throne room. A fitting tribute to the new master of the universe."

Sword dragging from the ash, Tannus stalked toward his brother. There were no tricks for either. Amongeratix met him with the clash of steel. Sparks dripped from their blades. Small fires sprouted from the ash at their feet. The planet rumbled as if remembering the past.

Tannus blocked a cross body blow, dipping and spinning. His blade whistled through the air as he drove down. The blow caught Amongeratix unprepared. He barely brought his blade up to deflect. Shards of steel flew from his sword, embedding in his face. Pricks of blood blossomed. They exchanged a series of blows to the tune of Amongeratix's wild laughter. A lifetime of misery poured into every strike. An uppercut sliced through the tightening straps of Tannus' armor, forcing him to backpedal and remove the hanging armor before it became a hindrance.

Sweat stung his eyes. Tannus gasped. An inkling of doubt crept into him. To his surprise, Amongeratix followed suit. His armor dropped to the ground with a clang. Tannus charged. They met in the middle under a furious assault. Slowly, Amongeratix began to push his brother back. The balance shifted.

Amongeratix glared at Tannus. Unbridled hatred, raw and uncontained won free at last. He struck harder, faster. Each assault bending Tannus. Soon, he would break him. He felt it. A final two-handed blow drove him to his knees, gasping for air. Their gazes remained locked, neither willing to give.

"It's over, brother. All these long years and you've not improved. When last we met, I was the victor. You could not defeat me then. You will not now. There will not be another chance. Today, I kill you, brother. Give Father my regards."

His great sword raised for the killing blow. Tannus held his breath. *This is how it ends. After so long, I have failed.*

Night darkened, blackening out all sight. An audible pop sounded. Amongeratix roared and staggered back, sword dropping from his grasp. When the artificial lights of army vehicles blinked back Tannus stared at a handful of humans and his cousin. Hope swelled, filling him with revitalized energy. A grin spread, cruel and promising. The battle was not lost after all.

"The Paladin arrives," Sorrow uttered.

Stars dazzling his vision, Amongeratix caught the blur of movement in time with a blast of magic. A Blood Witch! He threw an arm up to block the power. Pain lanced his arm and chest. Smoke poured from his clothes as they caught fire—the witch unleashed her full power on him. Distracted, Amongeratix lashed out at the last second, catching a human with a raised dagger aiming at his side with a backhand that sent her sprawling.

He sneered as she crashed into the ash, left curling around her side.

"Pathetic scum!" he roared.

Elisa winced from the pressure of broken bones. Blood trickled from her mouth, mingling with the acrid sting of ash pasted to her lips. She vomited when trying to stand. Blinking away the wall of tears, she heard Ah'muf's strangled cry.

"*Farisi*! Are you hurt?" he asked, dropping to her side.

It was then Elisa realized she'd lost her grip on the dagger. Frantic, she searched the nearby area. Without *Grimfurvor* her role of Paladin ended in failure, like all those who came before.

"Ah'muf, the dagger! Help me find it!"

The desert dweller dropped to his hands and knees, sifting through the ash and dirt to his elbows. Behind them, the battle raged unchecked.

Elisa spied Tolde Breed stepping for a clear shot and unloading the full power charge of his rifle into Amongeratix's neck and face.

Amongeratix spun. "Bold human. So ready to die, are you?"

"You don't remember me, do you?" the man taunted. "Ever have you haunted my dreams. Decades I've spent tied to you, frozen in time as I hunted you from one Conclave prison to the next. I have dreamed of watching you die, and you don't recognize me."

Amongeratix paused in midstride, his head cocking as he studied the man's face. "I've never seen you before in my life."

Emboldened, Tolde glanced out of the corner of his eye to where Ah'muf helped Elisa back to her feet. The dagger gleamed in the dull light. "Not this face, but you know me, evil one. I helped put you in chains after you escaped from the prison on Keltoo. I hunted you from Crimeat to here. Now I get to see your stain removed from the universe once and for all. You and all the rot you've caused. No longer will humanity suffer your filth."

"You!" Amongeratix gasped. Tolde watched recognition grace the giant's features. "I thought you died long ago. No matter. Killing you now will prove more satisfying."

Amongeratix attacked—Tolde opened fire. He got off a string of shots in the time it took the giant to close the distance. Any thought of fleeing failed to form. He knew there was no way he could outdistance the monster. Yet instead of panic, Tolde found himself embraced with calm, as if he knew this was where his life meant for him to be. Emboldened by that knowledge, he stood his ground and fired. *Come to me, monster. You have haunted my dreams for far too long. Let us finish our game.*

The giant lashed out, snatching Tolde from the ground and crushing him with both hands. The audible snap of bones breaking echoed loudly. He couldn't figure out why the human smiled as he died. Amongeratix gave the broken corpse a final shake before casting the body to the ground.

"Who's next?" Amongeratix shouted.

His chin rocked back from a blow with a rifle. The weapon shattered from the force. His cousin dropped the remnants and followed up with a series of punches to his face. Broken teeth flew with spittle and blood. *How?* Magic blasted Amongeratix's body as the witch renewed her assault. Ion fire from two other humans dug gouges in his exposed flesh. None of it was enough. Amongeratix fought like a caged monster even as the first hints of fear arose deep within.

He shifted, using Paradise to block the waves of magic from hammering him. The rifles dried up, their power packs dead. He smiled.

Across the plain he saw Tannus rise and reach for his sword on unsteady feet. He blinked through the blood flowing from a score of wounds. Half his face burned thanks to the Blood Witch. Weakened, Amongeratix fought for his life.

Limping, Elisa made her way to the giant's side undetected. She grimaced with each step. Pain wracked her body. Her red hair clung to her neck from sweat. Elisa fought through the pain, ignored the tears. An errant step knocked her to the ash. She clung to the dagger tighter. Soft hands grabbed her when she tried to rise. Elisa looked into Paradise's eyes.

"Finish this," Paradise told her.

Elisa nodded, regretting the unnecessary movement. With a mighty heave, Paradise lifted her up and spun. Together, they collided with Amongeratix.

Roaring, Elisa stabbed *Grimfurvor* into the giant's chest with every last ounce of strength. The blow staggered him, causing him to lash out, catching Paradise in the side of the head. Elisa screamed as she fell.

Reeling, useless hands fumbling at the dagger in his chest.

The universe paused. A held breath of uncertainty.

Panic filling his eyes, Amongeratix mouth opened wide in a silent scream. Surprise. Fear. Shock. All crashed within the demented confines of his mind. He fell to his knees. Rot spread through his body. Flesh turned purple black. His hair fell out in clumps as the flesh on his scalp burned. Muscles desiccated as the magic imbued in *Grimfurvor* poured into his soul. Amongeratix reached out a hand, skeletal and weak.

"Finish it, brother. Do not leave me like this. Not if ever loved me."

Standing before him, Tannus looked down with sadness. He raised his sword and swung.

The soldiers closest gasped as Amongeratix's head flew from his shoulders. When it came to rest naught remained but a battered skull. Smoke billowed from the neck. A popping sizzle loudened before fading. What remained of his body sagged, collapsing in on itself in a wasted puddle of ruined flesh and bone. *Grimfurvor*, its destiny fulfilled, disintegrated in the wind. Dust on the plains of the dead planet.

Amongeratix, the great enemy, was dead.

His brother was dead.

"It is done," Paradise said. Tannus could hear the shock in her voice.

Tannus dropped his sword. Three thousand years culminated in a heartbeat. He cast his head to the sky and wept, thankful for the cover of darkness. Some hurts weren't meant to be shared. He caught Sorrow drop to his knees and lower his head. Hair concealed his face, but it took little imagination to know how his brother felt.

He barely heard the whispers as they started. Word began passing through both armies.

Sorrow kept a watchful eye on what happened next—The Prekhauten Guard, seeing their champion and master destroyed, lost the will to fight. Those units furthest from the front retreated to their waiting drop ships, desperate to flee before the battle resumed. The rest threw down their weapons and raised their hands in surrender. Confederation soldiers swept through their enemy to establish control. The skies filled with aircraft. Guards were funneled into loose formations and marched to holding areas away from their weapons.

The war was over.

Turning away, Sorrow knelt beside Amongeratix's remains, scooping a hand through the remnants of clothing, lost in memories of a time before the hatred and madness gripped them. He wiped a tear from his eye, refusing to let it fall. Enough tears had been shed. Now was the time for healing.

He went to Elisa's prone figure. "Paladin, you have done what none could. The universe owes you a debt," Sorrow told her. "Amongeratix is no more. We are finally free."

"What happens next?" she asked, the word terse on her lips.

Sorrow had no answer. Kneeling beside her, his mind filled with his hand in directing the course of her life. Never before had he been faced with what came next. Now that it was here, he had no words.

"Now humanity will start over without our influence," Tannus replied. "The long war is ended, here where it all began. You have all proven yourselves worthy of immortality. I have had the pleasure of serving alongside many heroes, none on your levels. Thank you, my friends. The filth will soon wash free. Life shall continue the way it was intended. Without our interference. I…owe you all a great debt."

Luma Kai, choking back her tears, gestured to Tolde Breed's lifeless body. "Part of that debt goes to him. Without Tolde Breed none of this would have been possible."

Tannus hung his head. "We must ensure the universe never forgets his name."

They gathered in a circle around him, heads bowed.

THIRTY-ONE

3215 A.G. (After Gods), Plains of Haddash, planet Occanum.

Occanum teemed with life. Units consolidated. Armies reorganized in preparation for redeployment. Sprawling prisoner of war camps stretched across the plains of Haddash. Pits were dug for mass graves, the names and units of the fallen recorded for next of kin notification. Days passed since the last shots were fired and the threat of disease spreading increased. Once the formal surrender of Prekhauten Guard forces became official, both armies turned to healing. Soon would come a period of investigations, war crime tribunals, and forgiving, but those days were still far off. Today, they were all soldiers and deserved to be treated with respect.

Torgast supervised the transfer of power, forced back into dual roles as military commander and Confederation representative. Authorities from Mannus Prime were enroute to formalize the surrender, until then he alone controlled the situation. Eyes burning from lack of sleep, Torgast ran a hand over his rumbling stomach. He glanced up at the shadow falling over him.

"A week of this and I feel like the walking dead," he muttered. "You don't look any worse for wear."

Matthias entered the command center, a wry grin in place. "What can I say, retirement does wonders for the soul. Any word on the rest of the council?"

"Adris says they will be here within the next day or so," Torgast remained seated behind his field desk and offered, gesturing him to an empty seat. "I, for one, can't wait to be relieved. You know it won't be long before the idleness starts to get the best of the army. Soldiers shouldn't be left unattended."

"Relax. There's no alcohol and nothing to loot," Matthias said, then teased, "Running them through battle drills might take their minds off it."

"And risk an open rebellion? You have a death wish." Torgast barked a laugh. "They know the war is over. Some of the units will deploy to trouble spots across the universe. I imagine it's going to take years for life to get back to normal, if ever."

"I'd like to say that's for someone else to worry about, but it seems not." Matthias rubbed his jaw. He'd done his part. Played his role and now looked to the future and those golden years away from war and politics. "At any rate, I'm about to head down for the ceremony. Do you have all this under control?"

"Can anyone?" Torgast gripped. "Go on. We'll talk later. Hopefully I can find the time to rest, at least for a few hours before the council arrives."

Matthias offered a clipped nod and headed back outside.

Matthias' gaze immediately went to the multi-colored stream of cosmic lights trailing the Acumensiis Comet. Shivering at the thought of being so near the hub of magic, he hopped in his hoverjeep and began the long trek through the army and the ruins of a forgotten city. Once on the other side, he began noticing odd structures and impact craters from millennia of asteroid strikes. Time had not been kind to Occanum.

Parking the jeep, he donned his jacket and, choosing to leave his weapons behind, headed for an open passageway leading down. A pair of guards snapped to attention and saluted. Matthias reluctantly saluted in passing. Torches lined the tunnel wide and tall enough for Tannus' people to move about comfortably. He stared down the long tunnel, his imagination getting the better of him. The air stifled him, tightening his collar. A fetid smell drifted up from below—the place he must go. Footsteps in the dust marked the passing of the others, leaving him to assume he was the last to arrive.

Matthias still had no idea why he was included. His dealings with Tannus were few since arriving on Mannus Prime. Convinced humans should have no interest in the Three, he felt he was trespassing where he didn't belong.

So much changed thanks to that fateful mission to Keltoo when he was a young sergeant. Duty kept him involved, even when rationale demanded he abandon his path. His original squad, those few survivors of the mission, were all gone, as was Tolde Breed, a man he had never truly called friend but found no other description for him.

The tunnel started leveling off and his discomfort increased. Matthias summoned what confidence remained and strode into the chamber at the end of the hall. A pale green light bathed his surroundings, casting the world in an ethereal pall. Heads turned upon his arrival. Familiar faces and boon companions. A massive machine dominated the chamber, much like the one on Kharsis had before Presha Von killed the planet. An uneasy feeling tickled his stomach, clashing with the building fascination.

"Matthias, thank you for coming," Tannus announced, stilling all communication.

Unsure how to respond, he joined the others.

Tannus met his gaze for a moment longer before addressing the others. He had imagined this moment for so long and it still felt surreal. Rehearsed words and thoughts, random fragments of ideas, all rushed to his tongue as if eager to be set loose.

"None of this would be possible without you," he began. "The terrible legacy of my bloodline now comes to a close. I will not say my heart is unburdened, for great and terrible were the deeds of my kin. For those I make no apologies, but I believe my actions now will begin to make amends. It is has been my sincere pleasure coming to know you. Each of you has taught me what it means to be human. Perhaps I shall see you in my dreams." With a nod he turned to his cousin. "Paradise, it is time."

Ruma Zzein drifted towards him. Her hood down, she was weeping. "Tannus, are you certain?"

His gaze softened. "Oracle, this has always been the plan. With Amongeratix gone and Sorrow departed for the unknown reaches I am the last of the Three. My purpose has ended. Humanity does not need me. It never did. That is our greatest mistake, Oracle."

The words caught in his throat. "Ever have you been my friend. I shall miss you."

"And I you. Be at peace, king-son." Ruma bowed her head. "You have earned it."

He grinned. "Fitting our tale ends where it all began."

Tannus climbed into the last stasis pod that awaited. The whirl and hum and machinery bounced off the walls.

Paradise Tear finished a series of checks, ensuring the machine was prepared. A distant look clouded her eyes. "Tannus."

"Cousin, you were robbed of your life long ago. I would return those years to you," Tannus told her. "You deserve to find your peace."

"One day I shall," she vowed. "Fistel offered the Great Library to me. I declined. As you said, I have missed too much. This universe is foreign to me. It will take time to grow accustomed to the human empire and I intend on seeing every mystery and wonder there is. Perhaps one day our paths shall cross again, Tannus."

"You are the best of us," Tannus admitted to her. "Go in peace, my dear cousin."

"Goodbye, Tannus," she whispered.

Tannus laid down knowing he was at last at peace. The lid lowered slowly, sealing with a metallic hiss. Soon he would dream of better times and promises made.

Matthias and the others watched as gases and chemicals swirled in soft clouds, filling the pod. Paradise Tear strode to the side and inserted her right arm to the elbow in a small tube built into the pod. He saw her wince as the needles pricked her—the machine activated. A soft flash announced the pod was sealed and working. Tannus, fallen god-son, was encased in stasis like the hundreds of his surviving people.

The time of the gods had ended. Humanity was now free to pursue its own course for the first time.

"Now what?" Matthias asked.

Luma Kai and Ragan exchanged curious looks with him. The pair of Blood Witches held their silence and didn't bother to speak. He looked for Elisa before recalling she'd been transported off world with Ah'muf at her side to a Confederation hospital ship to recover. He suddenly felt smaller for reasons he doubted he'd ever be able to explain.

Ruma Zzein turned to him. The tears were gone, wet streaks drying on her aged cheeks. "Now we must move forward. Humanity must learn to handle the universe without my kind as well. I mean to take the comet and contemplate what this all means. But first, we must honor the memory and legacy of Tolde Breed."

Matthias dipped his head in regret. They never had the opportunity to say goodbye.

"I shall miss him," Ragan mumbled. "He ... he was like a father to me. The only reason I left home. Without him I never would have known the rest of you or discovered who I am."

"He was a good man," Alessandra said and then added, "for a human."

"As do I," Ruma consoled. "But some matters go beyond our

ability to control. The future is ever in flux. Our desires and wishes fall second to what will be. Tolde's sacrifice enabled the Paladin to fulfill her role. Without him none of this would have been possible."

"He was the last of his family," Ragan whispered. "Where will he be laid to rest?"

Luma Kai folded her arms across her chest. "He never spoke of home. I do not know where he was from."

"Sounds to me like this should be his final resting place," Matthias said. He was surprised when he saw their stares of confusion. "What? He is an integral piece of saving the universe from Amongeratix. What better place for the man than beside the son of a king?"

"Tannus always held a soft spot for Tolde," Ruma admitted. "I think he would approve."

"This spot shall be hallow," Paradise said wiping at the blood streaking down her forearm. "A shrine will be raised for all who sacrificed. I will see to it. The memory of Tolde Breed will not be forgotten."

"I would like to stay and help," Ragan said after a minute.

Paradise beamed down at him, having enjoyed his company from their first meeting. "You do him justice, young Ragan. I think he knew this from the moment he met you."

The discussion faded. One by one they filed from the chamber, heading back to the surface.

Paradise went last, pausing in the doorway to give her cousin a final look. She swore she saw a smile on Tannus' face, as if three thousand years' worth of weight was suddenly gone. She envied him.

"Farewell, cousin. You leave large shoes to fill."

She shut off the overhead lights.

Brightstar, high orbit over planet Occanum.

The whirl and hum of medical equipment drew her from the darkness of drug induced unconsciousness. Sharlyn August refused to move, fearing the pain and ache deep in her bones. Her legs were crushed, confining her to a hoverchair for the rest of her life. Medication kept the worst of the pain at bay, despite the trauma twisting her thoughts during those long moments when the medical staff thought she slept as she heard them discuss her condition.

August wept for her friends, Odir most of all. Her First Officer stood at her side for long years before the war and never once thought of leaving while the war raged. He paid for his loyalty, joining an endless list of comrades. At least he was in good company, she mused after the tears dried. A sharp lance of pain ran up her leg and into her hips. August winced and pushed the handheld button injecting fresh meds.

Her doors hissed open, and she opened her mouth to unleash the torrent of venom dancing on her tongue. August paused upon seeing the trio of men entering. Any animosity she had for the medical staff faded when she caught one of the orderlies sputtering from behind.

"Haven't you caused enough trouble?" August asked, her voice weak.

Blackheart pointed at his chest. "Me? Haven't you been lounging long enough? There is a fleet to command, you know."

Time elbowed the pirate in the ribs. "Don't listen to him, Admiral. We've had your ship on lockdown since you went down."

She glanced at the odd pair of Krimpen Mass and Time before settling on Blackheart. "Should I be concerned?"

"No more than usual."

"And my ship is still here? You haven't attempted to steal it yet?"

Making a show of rolling his eyes, Blackheart said, "What kind of man would I be if I did that?"

"A pirate."

"There's no challenge in it, my dear August. I'm already in command, by default you understand. If I wanted this ship I'd wait until you were recovered enough to steal it from under your nose." His smile almost succeeded in charming her. Almost.

Grimacing as she attempted to sit up, August asked, "What happened after I went down?"

"The fleet destroyed *Behemoth* and a fair portion of Guard ships before the call to ceasefire came in," Blackheart explained. "Seems our friends on the ground were successful in killing Amongeratix."

Her eyes widened. "So, the war is—"

He nodded. "Over … Well, this part is at any rate. I'm sure it will take years before the last brush fire is put out."

"Where is Falchi? Did he survive?" Emotion thickened her

voice. She wondered now how many others she had lost without knowing.

Blackheart held out a staying hand. "Easy friend, you're getting too far ahead of yourself. As far as I know Falchi survived. He should be planetside as we speak for the formal surrender of all Guard and Inquisition armies."

"I should be there," August protested.

Krimpen leaned over Blackheart's shoulder. "How do you propose to get there? You need rest if you're going to recover. Rumor has it the Confederation has big plans for your dreadnaughts, once they're repaired, that is."

"No rest for the wicked," Blackheart teased.

Imbued with their energy, August said, "I'm tired of resting. Medics and surgeons have been preaching this for days. I'm a fleet admiral, not a disposable crewer. There is too much to do. I have to schedule repairs, source replacements, and draft letters to the families of everyone we lost. Not to mention reorganizing the fleet and preparing for new deployment orders."

Blackheart feigned coughing. "I am a captain if you recall. What do you think I've been doing since you went down?"

"I hate saying this, but he's kind of good at it," Time added before she had a chance to protest. "The ship has been humming since he took over."

"Has it?" she murmured.

"Spare parts are hard to come by," Blackheart jumped in. "Engineers are cannibalizing unused portions of the ship to plug the main leaks. We lost a fair portion of our port cannons, and the engines suffered some damage. Another one of the dreadnaughts wasn't as fortunate. She's dead in space, which works in our favor. I convinced Falchi to authorize the full tear down so the surviving nine ships can get back to full strength. Your fleet will be ready to march in short order. Once the engineers gain a better understanding on this ancient technology that is."

A thousand concerns and questions clashed. She felt useless laid up like this, but no amount of rank or influence was going to free her from the ruthless medbay staff. Admitting the notorious pirate lord exercised his best intentions took effort. Admitting she was in no condition to command took more. Sharlyn settled back into the pillows and sighed.

"We won, Sharlyn. Accept it. Hells, enjoy it. You deserve that much at least. We all do. No longer will the Inquisition spread their brand of fear across the stars."

"What do you mean? What about the Inquisition?" she asked.

Krimpen groaned and covered his eyes.

Blushing, Blackheart said, "Word from Vau Prime has reached us. It seems some clandestine element destroyed the Inquisition headquarters, killing the current Inquisitor General and most of his staff in the process. The Inquisition is finished."

Her heart wept with joy. One of the worst evils to befall humanity was gone. Now the Conclave was abolished, their clergy dead or in hiding, and the Inquisition no more. Few obstacles opposed the Confederation from stepping in and restoring order and justice to the former capital planet. The immensity of it all overwhelmed her.

"Do you have any idea what this means?" she asked, struggling to choke back tears. "The tyranny is over. We no longer have to fear being prisoners."

"I seem to recall I was the only one bordering on being a prisoner," Blackheart said. "The Inquisitor General had no love for me or my kind."

"All hail the fearsome pirate lord, so eager and ready to retake his throne before the dust settles!" Krimpen announced with a smile, displaying the empty holes where his teeth once sat.

Blackheart spun, fixing the man with a venomous glare. "Shouldn't you be helping with repairs?"

"I'm not even being paid," Krimpen fumed. "Speaking of which, we should talk about compensation when you are feeling better, Admiral."

Time bobbed his head. "True. We may have big hearts, but we need financial compensation to fill our bellies."

August snorted, unable to contain her laugh. "You will both be paid handsomely for your work here. As will you, Vicente."

"See, I told you she was reasonable," Krimpen said to Time. "All it took was a little charm and a flashy smile."

"You're missing teeth, genius," Time reminded. "Thank you, Admiral. We'll be along now. There's plenty still needs doing on this tub. Come on, let's leave these two to their arguments. I can't handle Blackheart on an empty stomach."

"Scoundrels," Blackheart fumed after they left. "I regret ever hiring them.”

“Yet neither of you can quit,” she reminded. “Perhaps your fates are more entwined than you wish to accept.”

“Maybe,” he said, “Doesn’t mean I have to like it. They’ve been thorns in my side since Kharsis.” He shook his head. “I need a drink every time I am forced to deal with them.”

“You need more friends, Vicente,” she suggested. “Perhaps a change of pace.”

Blowing out a breath, Blackheart said, “That’s not such a bad idea. I’ve tried my hand at this pirating life, even gave some time to serving the side of order and justice, but I don’t know if I can go back. Not now, not after all this.”

“You could always go home, make a run at an honest living.”

“And beg my father to take me back? I don’t think so. I have him to thank for the Inquisition wanting my head.”

“He was that mad you abandoned the family business?”

“We are men of passion,” Blackheart told her.

“Truly?”

He gestured with empty hands. “What can I say. There is an irresistible charm the men of my family exudes.”

“Vicente.”

He jerked at her tone. “What?”

“Shut up and kiss me.”

Eger City, planet Mannus Prime.

With her great enemy destroyed and the remains of the Conclave in disarray, Aliz found herself lacking purpose. Instincts screamed for her to disappear, back to the shadows she felt more comfortable operating in. After all, she deemed she deserved a quiet life far from the public eye. Future in doubt, Aliz closed her last bag and headed out of her apartments. She found Julian waiting in the hallway, a wry grin on his face.

“Leaving without saying goodbye?” he asked.

Aliz studied the fresh scars on his face from the failed assassination attempt. “You and I both know I don’t belong here.”

“I’m not arguing.”

The rest of the Council had gone to facilitate the surrender of all Inquisition forces on Occanum and in system occurred without fanfare. Surviving enemy commanders were herded to a secure location in the center of the battlefield beneath a ring of fluttering banners. One by one they signed the official documents announcing the end of major fighting. Confederation Council members cheered and applauded their military war machine while secretly dreading the task of rebuilding. Logisticians and supply masters bowed under the weight of rebuilding an empire. Next of kin notifications were drafted by the thousand, those unknown fallen soldiers were interred in a massive grave on the plains of Haddash with full honors.

"I need a new beginning. I feel trapped in these walls. A prisoner in all but name."

"I might be able to help with that. Please, come with me."

She did, against her better judgment. "Why do I feel like you are leading me into a trap?"

"Me? Aliz, you are the only one I have told my deepest secret to. Why would I betray you?" he replied as they entered the Confederation communications room.

Aliz paused. On one screen were the faces of Adris Moscasco, Cardinal Virom, and Standou. The other had the battered face of Edam Boone. "What is this?"

"Aliz, you didn't think we would just let you slip away without at least a modicum of fanfare? Without you much of what we have achieved would not have been possible. Your work on Vau Prime after the Inquisition took over is one of the greatest accomplishments in recent history."

"Accomplishments? All I did was get people killed, Adris." She shook her head. "I deserve no accolades."

"Think about how many more are still alive because of you," Edam cut in, a disturbed look on his face. "We owe you a debt. I owe you."

"What happened to you?" she asked him, peering closer to see the damage done.

"A small explosion. Nothing to worry over."

Aliz jerked back. "You set the bomb that destroyed the Inquisition!"

"Had some help. A former cardinal named Porii Daam ensured the Inquisitor General died in explosion. We couldn't have done it without her," Edam explained.

"Which is why you were summoned," Adris said, resuming

control of the conversation. "Now that the peace treaty has been formalized, we find ourselves in the unexpected position of having to care for the people of Krenz again. I would like you to return to your home and, with the help of Edam Boone and his organization, begin restoration of that once great city."

"Our people need as much help as we can give them," Edam added.

She stiffened. "Why me? I don't have anything left to give. Leastwise not there. I did all I could, Adris. Vau Prime took all it could from me."

"I do not ask this lightly of you. As such, you will be the Confederation's official representative and all the pressures, complications, and problems you can possibly imagine will be thrust upon your shoulders."

"All the more reason for me to say no."

Edam cleared his throat. "Aliz, you would be doing our people the greatest service. You know the people. You know this city. I believe you are the perfect person for the job. Of course, you will have my entire network at your full disposal. Together, we can remake Krenz into the image of what it always should have been." His mouth moved for a moment, but no sounds came forth. "Help me. Please."

Torn between a future of endless possibilities and the torments of her past, Aliz slumped into a chair. She ran the tip of her finger over the desk, feeling the thin veil of dust. Her thoughts drifted back to that final morning with Lorenu.

"Even with the Inquisition toppled I can't imagine the danger has passed. Anarchy had set in by the time I left. We will need a large force to secure the planet," she concluded. Lorenu deserved that much and, maybe, she did as well.

"We?" Adris prompted.

"Some matters go beyond our wants, Adris," Aliz said. "I will go, though I have several small favors to ask."

Relief broke over Adris' face. "Anything, Aliz. You have the full weight of the Confederacy at your disposal. We have already directed Tannus' flagship, *Brightstar* to return for you and your staff. Admiral August is highly capable and the ranking officer in our fleets. She will see you to Vau Prime in short order. The rest of the dreadnaughts will be deployed across the stars as a show of authority and serve as a reminder that peace is our desired goal. You will have a division at your call along with all the resources and supplies we can scavenge to help the people of Krenz."

"A good start, but I require a few people for my command team," Aliz interjected.

"Who did you have in mind?"

Gedrick Silk stared at the rolling hills surrounding the western side of Eger City from the balcony running the length of the Confederation Headquarters. Despite the news from the front, Gedrick felt hollow, as if a vital piece remained missing. He stretched, frowning at his inability of reconciling who and what he was.

"Gedrick."

He turned, surprised to find Aliz' warm face smiling at him. "Councilor. What can I do for you?"

She gestured to the empty bench below a bay window. "Let us skip the formalities. I am just Aliz. Have you given any thought about your future?"

"Much. It is all I can think of," he admitted. "I have no home to return to. No allegiances beyond my own."

"What if I could give you new purpose? A true family."

Gedrick considered her, failing to work through any angle she might play. "I am listening."

Aliz broke into a wide smile. "Let me tell you of a dream of hope and the promise of a new dawn for us all."

EPILOGUE

Year 01 H.E. (Human Era), Eger City, planet Mannus Prime.

Matthias looked around the room, his gaze sweeping over the familiar faces of men and women. Empty chairs tugged his emotions. Faces no longer there but for memory's sake. Matthias saw ghosts lurking among the former Guards. Tolde Breed in his original body. A sad smile upon his face. At his side were friends now long dead. Kastor. Haggle. Beve. Davith Strannan. He missed them, each for different reasons.

"Sergeant Major," Fies handed him a mug filled with some of the best beer he'd ever had. "You'd never think a bunch of librarians could brew like this."

"Fies, one of these days you and me are going to take it out back."

Fies broke into a grin. "I don't know where you're going to find the time. Seems like the council is going to keep you busy."

"Since you bring it up, I've requested your company to be reassigned to the council in a diplomatic function."

"That can't be a good idea," Fies replied looking worried. "We spent the entire war at the sharp end. Transitioning to a peacetime environment won't be easy. It's all Annalilly and I can do to blunt their teeth."

"Relax," Matthias said. "The details still need to be worked out, but I imagine most of your role will be accompanying council members to different worlds seeking inclusion in the Confederation. Everything is different now. The old ways are gone, leaving us to pick up the pieces and figure out the future. The war may be over, but there's going to be no shortage of pop-up fighting, conflicts, and worse for the foreseeable future. We have a lot of work ahead of us. If you're willing to stay on."

Fies rubbed his chin, glancing across the crowded room to where Annalilly stood laughing with Quint and Doc Little.

Matthias followed his gaze. "Have you asked her yet? Not that you need to. You two have might as well have been married for years now."

"I love her, I do, but I don't know if marriage is high on her to do list." Fies snorted. "Might as well but shackles on a dog, for all the good it would do."

Matthias laid a proud hand on Fies' shoulder. "You'd be surprised. I suppose we should get the formal part of this over."

With a nod, Fies strode to the center of the room and barked, "Listen up!"

Conversations faded until awkward silence dominated.

Fies took a private account of those assembled. Jolent, ever silent and resilient, confirmed he would be staying on. As did Hollis and Palco. Desril contemplated going back home and starting a farm though no one believed he would. Annalilly vowed to remain by his side until the end, citing his inability to stay out of trouble as the reason. Jelin Quint decided retirement sounded good and gave back his stripes. Any loss he might have suffered was replaced by the not unexpected romance with Tempest. The ex-Inquisitor Luma Kai signed on to lead their misfit company into a new day. Fies didn't know if she fit in but was willing to give her a shot. Besides, he didn't mind taking second seat for a change.

"My friends, I raise my glass to you. You who stood against the tide and helped win this war. You who will never be known or recognized. No one who was not there will understand the sacrifice you all made, or the wounds you bear long after the last shot was fired. This will be our last official function as a unit, though I suggest we meet once a year to remember old friends and rekindle our bonds of fellowship."

"That's the smartest thing you've said in a long time," Annalilly chimed in with her usual snark.

Fies blushed. *That is it. The last straw.* "Annalilly, I have had enough of the constant snapping, snide comments, and attempts at undermining my authority. The way I see it, there is only one way to get you to calm down."

"Don't do it," she whispered. She tensed, unsure whether to hit him or accept the punishment.

"Will you marry me?"

For the first time in recent memory, she was speechless.

Cheers erupted when she nodded.

Grinning from ear to ear, Fies raised his mug once more and

shouted, "Let's drink!"

"Bastard. This isn't over," she sniped and kissed him.

Planet Wexanos.

The gentle lapping of waves upon the shore soothed her troubled mind. The war had been over for almost a year, yet the nightmares remained. Confederation officials continued expanding their reach, desperately attempting to prevent further bloodshed as the rest of the universe struggled with the power vacuum. With the influence of the Three finally removed, an unprecedented time of peace promised to guide humanity into the future. The war brought out the best and worst of them, forcing each to make choices they should never have been in position to do. For Elisa, it was the culmination of decades of anguish. At last freed from her obligations to Sorrow, she found herself in a new world she wasn't prepared for.

She tilted her head back and closed her eyes. Sunlight caressed her face. The warmth settled deep in her tired bones. Sea birds called and swooped down along the shore, close enough to the secluded villa to give her peace of mind. She'd never considered what life might be like after. Now, she stood upon a new existence without limits, or expectations. The scars remained. They always did. She cradled the stump of her ruined arm, often subconsciously, when in the presence of guests. It was a small price for helping rid the universe of its greatest threat.

"*Farisi*, we have company," Ah'muf called from inside.

Elisa smiled. Pushing herself to her feet with a tired groan, Elisa snatched her crutch and followed her love to the villa's entrance. Her face brightened upon seeing Paradise Tear standing in the foyer, hands clasped before her and wearing a warm smile.

"Elisa," Paradise said. "It does my heart good to see you again."

"I thought you were gone," she replied. Ah'muf's forced cough jarred her. "Forgive me, I am being rude. Please come and sit. Ah'muf, will you bring refreshments?"

"Of course, *farisi*." He slipped off, allowing them to speak in private.

Once settled, Elisa waited for Paradise to speak. They hadn't seen each other since that final day on Occanum.

"You will forgive my interruption, but I wished to see you

before I departed," the giant said.

"No apologies necessary, my friend. It is good to see you again. I admit to having sequestered myself to this quiet part of the continent until my wounds heal, both mental and physical," Elisa explained. "Between you and I, Ah'muf's steady devotion and pestering are seeing to my recovery far more than standing down."

"You are perfect together." Paradise smiled. "I'm leaving as I no longer have reason to remain here. Sorrow has gone, slinking off to uncharted regions where our influence does not exist. And with Amongeratix gone and Tannus in stasis I find myself suddenly free to explore this universe. Thousands of years were stolen from me."

"I hope Sorrow finds the peace he seeks," Elisa said. She had come to terms with the Bloody Man's influence in her life, choosing to look to the good over the bad. "We all deserve it."

"How is the leg?"

Elisa blinked at the subject change. "Better. It still hurts to walk but this planet has wondrous healing properties. I imagine it won't be long before I am back on my feet."

"You were always among the best of us, though you refused to believe it." She paused, studying her. "Elisa, have you given thought to my last request?"

"I have but will not lie and tell you I've decided one way or the other," Elisa confirmed. *I knew you were fishing. Don't think I'm going to tell you everything.* "I just finished being the Paladin. Jumping into another hefty assignment feels wrong. Besides, the Great Library is already in capable hands."

"Fistel is a wonderful man, for a human, but this is his first time alone in many decades," Paradise said. "You deserve a quiet life. The universe has already asked so much of you. Isn't it time to settle down, perhaps start a family?"

"This house craves the sound of children!" Ah'muf announced. He appeared and set down a tray of glasses on the table between them then sat beside Elisa, hand on her knee. "Think of it, *farisi!* A dozen happy voices laughing, playing! It will be a dream come true."

She fixed him with a withering glare as her face burned crimson.

Paradise coughed. "This is a conversation best had in private. I shall go now. Whichever you decide, know that will always be there for you. Just call. Goodbye Elisa."

Ah'muf beside her, Elisa watched Paradise walk away, perhaps for the last time. "I hope you find the peace you are looking for—Fare well."

"What was that?" he asked after they stepped back inside and shut the door.

Elisa leaned into him, pressing her head against his shoulder. "Nothing, love. Nothing at all. Now, let's discuss this matter of children."

The time of the gods ended. Years passed before humanity settled into a new peace. Wars and disputes spread as warlords attempted to seize power in the absence of Conclave rule. Slowly, inexorably, the Confederation spread too. Prosperity rose for all people. The dead planet Occanum became a pilgrimage. Thousands traveled to the planet to honor loved ones.

A hundred years after the war ended a miracle occurred.

Clouds filled the skies. Rain fell on Occanum for the first time since that last fateful battle millennia ago.

Paradise Tear stood below an overhang, marveling at the downpour stretching across the plains of Haddash. She returned to her cousin each year. Her friends and companions from the war were long gone. Once more she found herself alone. Saddened yet buoyed with newfound confidence, she left Tannus' tomb. She almost missed the sprout of green grass spiking from the ash and mud.

Life had returned to Occanum.

Paradise boarded her shuttle knowing her work was done at last. She punched in a set of random coordinates and departed her home for the last time. Somewhere, in the vast expanse of space, her sole remaining cousin needed her.

Here ends the 7th and final volume of the Forgotten Gods Tales.

Author's Note

Whew, it's finally finished. Almost 1.5 million words spanning a universe. I have always considered this to be my prized series. Originally, I planned on 10 volumes but felt trapped by the story. Hopefully I managed to bring this all to a satisfactory conclusion. And who knows, maybe one day I'll head back to my favorite universe and see what old friends are up to.

Thank you all for taking this journey with me. To date, I have almost 40 books in the wild. None have taken such and emotional toll on me as the Forgotten Gods series. Crafting any world is a labor of love and I gave this one all I had. I did my best to make the warfare realistic. (You didn't really think I wanted Haggle to die did you?) As a veteran of both Iraq and Afghanistan, I have seen war firsthand and understand how the unexpected happens. The good guys don't always survive. In this, I hope I did my friends who did not return from those distant lands justice.

After all, this is as much your story as it is mine.

Christian Warren Freed, June 2024

Check out these other great series by
Christian Warren Freed

The wolves are returning to war!

Peace in the northern kingdoms is shattered the night King Badron of Delranan finds his house invaded, his son dying, and his daughter kidnapped. All signs point to his longtime rival and neighboring kingdom, Rogscroft. Armed with vengeance, he orders his fear army, the Wolfsreik, to deploy east while simultaneously sending a covert team to rescue his daughter.

Led by his pariah brother, Bahr, the group slips into enemy territory only to discover all is not the way it should be. Darkness is afoot in the north. An ancient power stirs deep in the discontented hearts of men, for evil has ways of surviving.

It is a race against time to rescue the princess and, if Bahr can help it, prevent a war.

Fate is not on his side.

Welcome to the opening salvo of the Northern Crusade. The final battle between the forces of good and those who serve the dark gods. Heroes and villains rise to the challenge, for the fate of the world is at stake.

Not your father's Tolkien, the Northern Crusade is perfect for fans of Brooks, Martin, McKiernan, and more.

CHRISTIAN WARREN FREED
COWARD'S TRUTH
A NOVEL OF THE HEART ETERNAL

Welcome to Ghendis Ghadanisban. City of god-kings.
City in turmoil.

The god-king is dead! Whispers of murder spread through the city known as the Heart Eternal. His death allows an ancient evil Razazel to return and resume its quest to dominate all life. As if that isn't enough, warring factions threaten the jewel of the desert. The only way to prevent this is by a group of reluctant heroes to escort a young boy filled with the dying god's essence to the ancient mountain of Rhorremere so the god-king can be reborn. It is a quest bound to claim lives, for evil never stops.

Far off in the mountains, a squad of stranded space marines sells their services in the hopes of being rescued. Their search brings them in conflict with too many enemies. Forced to join the quest, it is a decision that may prove their ultimate doom.
Fate and destiny clash as agents of good and evil set forth to stake their claim.

Welcome, friends, to the Heart Eternal.

THE
LAZARUS MEN
A LAZARUS MEN AGENDA

CHRISTIAN
WARREN FREED

Welcome to the world of the Lazarus Men.

A thrilling sci-fi noir adventure combining the best mystery of the Maltese Falcon with the adventure of Total Recall and suspense of James Bond.

It is the 23rd century. Humankind has spread across the galaxy. The Earth Alliance rules weakly and is desperate for power. Hidden in the shadows are the Lazarus Men: a secret organization ruled with an iron fist by the enigmatic Mr. Shine. His agents are the worst humanity has to offer and they are everywhere.

Gerald LaPlant's life changes forever the day he accidentally witnesses a murder and discovers an alien artifact in his pocket. Forced to flee, he is chased across the stars by desperate men who want what he has and are willing to stop at nothing to get it. Along the way Gerald meets a host of villains and heroes, each with hidden agendas. If Gerald has any hope of surviving, he must rely on his wits and avoiding the one thing that could get him killed more than the rest: trust.

For he has the key to the galaxy's greatest treasure. Half want him dead. Half need him alive.

It's a race against time to see which wins.

THE CHILDREN OF NEVER

A WAR PRIESTS OF ANDRAK SAGA

CHRISTIAN WARREN FREED

The war priests of Andrak have protected the world from the encroaching darkness for generations. Stewards of the Purifying Flame, the priests stand upon their castle walls each year for 100 days. Along with the best fighters, soldiers, and adventurers from across the lands, they repulse the Omegri invasions.

But their strength wanes and evil spreads.

Lizette awakens to a nightmare, for her daughter has been stolen during the night. When she goes to the Baron to petition aid, she learns that similar incidents are occurring across the duchy. Her daughter was just the beginning. Baron Einos of Fent is left with no choice but to summon the war priests.

Brother Quinlan is a haunted man. Last survivor of Castle Bendris, he now serves Andrak. Despite his flaws, the Lord General recognizes Quinlan as one of the best he has. Sending him to Fent is his best chance for finding the missing children and restoring order. Quinlan begins a quest that will tax his strength and threaten the foundations of his soul.

The Grey Wanderer stalks the lands, and where he goes, bad things follow. The dead rise and the Omegri launch a plan to stop time and overrun the world. The duchy of Fent is just the beginning.

The follow up to the L Ron Hubbard Writers of the Future award winning short: The Purifying Flame, the Children of Never is an all new novel set in a world of raw imagination.

Evil never rests and neither can we.

Pick up a sword and join the team!

Warfighter Books

Sign up for our newsletter today and follow us on social media for updates, new releases and more!

Newsletter: https://www.subscribepage.com/warfighterbooks

Amazon: https://www.amazon.com/author/christianwfreed

Facebook: https://www.facebook.com/WarfighterBooks

Twitter: https://twitter.com/ChristianWFreed

Instagram: www.instagram.com/christianwarrenfreed/

BIO

Christian W. Freed was born in Buffalo, N.Y. more years ago than he would like to remember. After spending more than 20 years in the active-duty US Army he has turned his talents to writing. Since retiring, he has gone on to publish more than 20 science fiction and fantasy novels as well as his combat memoirs from his time in Iraq and Afghanistan. His first book, Hammers in the Wind, has been the #1 free book on Kindle 4 times and he holds a fancy certificate from the L Ron Hubbard Writers of the Future Contest.

Passionate about history, he combines his knowledge of the past with modern military tactics to create an engaging, quasi-realistic world for the readers. He graduated from Campbell University with a degree in history and a Masters of Arts degree in Digital Communications from the University of North Carolina at Chapel Hill. He currently lives outside of Raleigh, N.C. and devotes his time to writing, his family, and their two Bernese Mountain Dogs. If you drive by you might just find him on the porch with a cigar in one hand and a pen in the other.